D1215259

A Reckoning in Brooklyn

A Novel

By Michael O'Keefe

ISBN: 978-1-6975-6670 (sc)

In honor and loving memory of my fellow law enforcement officers who have made the ultimate sacrifice.

Fidelis ad mortem.

Requiescat in pace

For Janet,

of course.

All that is necessary for evil to triumph is for good men to do nothing.

Edmund Burke.

When you see something evil in the world, you can either do something, or do nothing, and I already tried nothing.

Captain Steve Trevor

CHAPTER ONE

July 12, 1979
Bushwick

Butchie found the numbness washing over him perplexing. He had relished this moment for years—expecting to be elated celebrating his triumph over a hated enemy. Instead, he felt nothing—save the brief instant of exhilaration when the opportunity lay before him. Now that the deed was done, he was left with was a tired ambivalence, and a wave of nausea. He chalked-up the urge to vomit as an artifact of the rich coppery taste from all the blood—mixed with the acrid smoke from the expended gunpowder hanging in the air. A malevolent cloud, it lingered on Butchie's tongue, and in the back of his throat, invading his nostrils and staying there like a vagrant accusation. He chose to ignore the slight tremors in his hands and aching in his joints. *Surely, they weren't anything like regret.*

There were three dead men on the ground, scattered about the rear courtyard, which served as an extra dining room for the small, Italian eatery on Knickerbocker Avenue. Butchie knew all of them. Two were associates of the hated Carmine *Lilo* Gigante, the head of the Bonanno Crime Family. The third man, at Butchie's feet, was the Don himself. Butchie didn't know who killed the associates, and frankly didn't care. They were criminal scumbags who deserved every bullet—in this case shotgun blasts. But he knew who killed Lilo. He understood he would have to look that murderer in the face when he shaved every morning. He was surprised when the realization didn't seem to bother him, struggling right now to feel something…anything.

As he stood over Gigante, he could feel the residue of Lilo's fear-sweat on the fingertips of his right hand. He wiped them absently on the leg of his uniform duty trousers, considering what he had just done; killing the last living witness to a mob rub-out with his bare hands. It certainly didn't sort well with the vow he took when he was sworn in as a police officer almost a dozen years before. *To protect life and property*; but he had come to realize some lives deserved more protection than others, and some lives deserved none at all. Gigante *needed* killing. So Butchie rationalized his murder as a community service, or at least a lesser sin. Besides, he reasoned, the mob boss was already dying when he and Walton came into the courtyard. Lilo wouldn't have identified his shooters even if he had survived. So, the final squeeze was of little consequence to anyone, save Butchie's conscience, which was surprisingly untroubled.

Surveying the shot-up remains of the mobster he had just dispatched, Butchie saw Lilo had been struck twice by the shotgun; once in the lower abdomen, and a glancing blow to the right side of his face. But, he mused, glancing is a relative term with shotguns. Like hand grenades, it's hard to miss, and they do fearsome damage just the same when you do. It had torn up the right side of Lilo's face and took the eye. Butchie knew both wounds would have ultimately killed the thug, irrespective of even a herculean effort to save him.

If by some miracle Lilo made it to the hospital, he would have been brought to the Old German Hospital on Wyckoff Avenue. It was well-known in Brooklyn there were only hacks, quacks, and witchdoctors at that particular temple of medical malpractice.

So, Gigante was a dead man, with or without Butchie's help. It was not a matter of necessity, but principle which prompted his hand. He had predicted, even promised he would be the one to usher Lilo out of this world. Now he had. He wasn't sure what he expected to feel, but it hadn't been *nothing*. He had just rid the world of the vilest man he had ever encountered, in a short life chock-full of wicked men. He thought he might derive some satisfaction from the act—even an epiphany of sorts. Instead, there was only the maddening numbness.

The closest he came to an emotion was enjoying the fear in Lilo's eyes at the moment the Don recognized him. The last spasms and final futile kicks, as the helpless mobster died with Butchie's hand clamped like a vise around his throat should have elicited some sort of satisfaction. But all he felt after was a nagging sense of hopelessness, and the urge to puke. He had slain a monster, but Butchie suspected there would be more monsters to fill the void left by Lilo's murder, and they might be far worse.

Strangely, Gigante's broken eyeglasses remained propped—however askew—on his mangled head. Butchie thought the only thing missing from the picture was the little Cuban cigar Lilo always had sticking out of his sneering maw. He had looked for it, but it was nowhere to be found. He spotted it's substitute earlier when his partner for the day, Ernie Walton, returned to the courtyard from the street with an anisette cheroot sticking out of his fat face.

***

The Bushwick section of Brooklyn in the summer of 1979 was the epitome of urban decay. The once working-class Irish, German, and Italian enclave had descended into a teeming, heroin-infested slum. The Irish and the Germans had long since fled, moving to parts east. Most of the Italians were gone also. What was left were the newly arrived Puerto Ricans, and those not affluent enough to move. The neighborhood had become a crime-ridden drug supermarket. People were killing each other over ten-dollar bags of white powder.

By the time Butchie had hit puberty, the migration was in full swing. Joey *Butchie* Bucciogrosso had been raised in a railroad flat on Troutman Street. He had watched the character of the neighborhood change over the years. Unlike many of his fellow Italians, Butchie held no resentment for the Spanish influx taking place with the arrival of the Puerto Ricans. If anything, he felt they lent the community a cultural diversity it sorely needed. Other than the language, the new-comers weren't all that different from the Italians, some of whom also refused to speak English. It was no barrier anyway. Butchie's fluency in Italian soon allowed him to speak Spanish as well. A matter of saturation and familiarity; between school, home, and running the streets of Brooklyn, by the time he was thirteen, he could read, write and speak in all three languages.

With respect to changing his culture, Butchie was ready for almost *anything* different. The three generations of his parents' families—all crammed into the apartment house on Troutman Street, yammering away in Italian, complaining about the state of the neighborhood and how they missed the old country was wearing on his last nerve. He was also tired of eating tomato sauce every Sunday. Mostly though, he was exhausted with the eternal argument over whether it was *sauce* or *gravy*, waged like a holy war between his two grandmothers—one of whom was from Sicily, and the other from Naples. When he was fourteen and had the temerity to finally voice his opinion on the matter, he infuriated both *Nonnas*, and incurred a punch in the face from his father.

"Why don't we just call it *that red shit we eat every Sunday*," he asked wearily.

After the beating, Butchie was never again included in that particular discussion. They never again had it in his presence either, which suited Butchie just fine. When one of the tribe asked for someone to pass the sauce or gravy, depending upon their affiliation, one or both of his grandmothers would regard him with a wounded look, but that would be the extent of it.

Butchie made friends easily with his new neighbors. They had the same interests boys have everywhere. The Puerto Rican kids liked sports. They liked to fight, and they developed the same neighborhood pride the Italians had always had for Bushwick. Adding this to the food and music, there wasn't much about his Puerto Rican friends he didn't like. They seemed to have the work ethic and proud sense of self-reliance as the Italians, possessing the ingrained respect for family, living in the cramped multi-generational arrangements with which Butchie had grown accustomed. They attended the same church, cramming the pews at Saint Brigid's in their Sunday best. They struggled right beside their Italian classmates in school, endeavoring to overcome the challenge of English as a second language. They shopped in the same stores. They worked the same low-paying jobs, struggling to feed their families, singularly devoted to trying to provide something just a little better for their children—just like the Italians.

Butchie's natural curiosity and guileless openness to the new and unfamiliar was regarded at first with a measure of suspicion by his new neighbors. When they figured out his curiosity was genuine, and he truly wished to foster a friendship with them, the Puerto Ricans were happy to have him. If anything, Butchie got more static from his Italian friends, some of whom became former friends before long. These were the sons of the old-guard Italians who bitterly resented the ethnic change. They hated the Puerto

Ricans, because they were following the worst ethno-centric instincts of their parents.

Coincidently, heroin arrived in Bushwick around the same time as the Puerto Ricans. Because of this, many of the old *geeps* blamed them for the scourge, which was ironic. No ethnic group ever suffered more from the importation of heroin than the Puerto Rican emigres of the 50s, 60s, and 70s. They suffered bitterly because of the misfortune of arriving in New York's shrinking economy at a time when the streets were about to be saturated with dope. What began as a seemingly inexpensive chemical escape from the drudgery of their poverty, ended up destroying millions of lives. Entire generations in New York would be lost to this wasteland of addiction.

The irony wasn't lost on Butchie. He knew the biggest mouths blaming the Puerto Ricans for the drug problem belonged to the sons of the Mafiosi who were responsible and benefitting from it. They were the equivalent of shopkeepers blaming their customers for buying poison from them. This contentious environment in Bushwick, coupled with Butchie's uncertain position within it, created the opportunity which spawned his boxing career.

***

In 1964, Butchie was thirteen. Walking on Suydam Street toward Knickerbocker Avenue, he saw his friend, Armando Molina, being surrounded and hassled by four of Butchie's former Italian compatriots. They were from the crew of teen thugs who ran on Jefferson Street and Knickerbocker Avenue. All Italian, they were the sons of the *Mustache Petes* who were running the criminal business in the neighborhood for Joe Bonanno. Everyone started referring to them collectively as *The Farm Team.*

Their ascension to the ranks of the Bonanno Crime Family was just assumed. They were the kind of guys who entered every confrontation wanting to make sure you knew who they were, and who they knew. In a neighborhood where everybody knew everyone else, it was a stupid question. But it wasn't posed for gathering information. It was a tacit threat, and usually an effective one. Not this day.

"Hey, *Mousey*," Butchie called out to Massimino Basaluco. "Why don't you stop pressing on my friend? Give him a little room to breathe."

"Fuck you, Butchie!" said Carmine Donofrio.

"This is none of your business, *Spic-lover*. So, stay out of it," warned Angelo Mercante.

"My business is what I decide it is," Butchie said. "Right now, I got nothing better to do. So, let's do this."

At that, Roman Sciula, as big and menacing a fourteen-year-old as ever there was, awakened from the dream-state of muted stupidity in which he always seemed to be.

"We can take care of the *spic* when we get done with this meddling fuck here. It's time he learns who runs this street," Roman decreed.

As big as he was, his young hoodlum friends weren't inclined to argue. As the four of them advanced on Butchie, they left Armando with an avenue of escape.

"Run!" Butchie commanded.

Armando hesitated. He wanted to stay and fight. Butchie was having none of it. He knew Armando couldn't fight and would only prove a distraction and an imposition. He made himself clear on the point.

"Get the fuck out of here, Armando! I got this."

Armando finally got the hint and ran off as instructed. Big Roman Sciula menacingly approached Butchie.

"The only thing you got, Bucciogrosso, is a beating coming your way. I'll tell your mother she can find you at *Kraut Town*," Sciula said, referring to The Old German Hospital around the corner.

"I guess we'll see about that," Butchie said, sounding curious about the matter himself.

Roman started landing thunderous blows down on the sides of Butchie's head, who made no real effort to duck or counter the punches. What he did was lean into them, as if he were trying to get the punishment over with. He had learned to do this over the years catching frequent beatings at home. While it wasn't Butchie's intention, it had the effect of robbing some of the incredible impact from Sciula's brick-fisted hay-makers. It also slightly changed the point of impact. Roman expected to be connecting with the softer areas of Butchie's face. When he kept landing his fists on the very hard surface of Butchie's skull, Roman's hands started to hurt—a lot. So, each successive punch was delivered with a little less enthusiasm than the previous one. It only helped incrementally.

While Roman Sciula was hammering Butchie like a veal cutlet, the other three thugs took advantage of the distraction to move in and start landing pot-shots of their own. Butchie would receive each attack, mounting no form of defense whatsoever. He would merely back up a step or two and brace himself for the next assault. Finally, with his back against the brick of the building on Suydam Street, he had nowhere else to go. He absorbed Roman's last two punches. Reaching down as if he were trying to pick something from under the heel of his shoe, Butchie propelled himself up and forward, delivering a vicious, round-house right. The punch connected squarely with Roman's jaw, but narrowly missed the mandible nerve. It didn't put his lights out, only waffling the big boy.

Butchie continued his attack, leaping up into the arms of the stunned Roman. Instinctively, Sciula started squeezing Butchie in a bear-hug, trying to crush the air out of his lungs. With Roman's hands so occupied, Butchie reached up and grabbed him by the ears. He brought the crown of his head down three times as hard as he could on Roman's face.

The first strike shattered Sciula's nose and rendered him unconscious. The next two shots broke most of his teeth, and left his mouth looking like a bag full of bloody chiclets. Roman Sciula was out of this fight. The big loser, he was the one who would have to be collected by his mother at *Kraut Town.*

With their Goliath lying face down in the gutter, the other three goons were less than enthusiastic about getting close enough to Butchie to share Roman's fate. Their attacks lacked coordination, making their greater numbers count for little. Butchie was able to focus on each of his attackers, one at a time. This was bad news for them.

The beginning of the end started with Butchie taking two head shots from Massimino Basaluco. This allowed him to get close enough to deliver a left hook to Basaluco's ribs, in quick combination with a right cross to the jaw. The last shot found the mandible nerve like they were long lost cousins. As Massimino was hitting the floor, Angelo Mercante rushed Butchie, running into an overhand right. The contact was so pure, Butchie half expected to hear it accompanied by a carnival bell. Mercante's eyes rolled up in his head as he fell to the floor in slow motion, like a sack of falling flour.

Butchie focused on Carmine *The Mouth* Donofrio. The loudest and most obnoxious of The Farm Team, he was the guy who made all of the noise and started all of the fights. But other than being a facilitator of violence, he brought nothing to the table in the way of fighting skills. When Butchie waved his adversary on, The Mouth remembered he needed to be somewhere else. Exhausted at this point, Butchie could only watch as Donofrio ran down Knickerbocker Avenue toward Jefferson Street. Carmine was all asses and elbows as his image receded into the fading afternoon sunlight.

Butchie was surveying the damage to himself in his reflection in the window of the smoke shop there on the corner. He was bleeding from the cuts above his eyes. The skin had split where Roman had hit him. Butchie could see he was bleeding from his ears and nose as well. His mouth had become a river of blood, leaving him choking on the salty, coppery tasting effluence pooling there. Even through the buzz of the adrenaline rush he was experiencing, Butchie's body began to ache all over. His victory—unexpected and spectacular—was starting to feel pyrrhic in nature. When he saw Patrolman *Mick the Quick* Doheny approaching from across Knickerbocker Avenue, Butchie thought it started to taste like a shit sandwich.

Doheny had watched the whole thing transpire from his foot-post in front of Badlamenti's lattacini across the street. When he saw The Farm Team from Jefferson Street surround that nice Puerto Rican kid, he was about to come over and end it before Armando got hurt. But then he saw the Bucciogrosso boy come down the block and intervene. He decided to let the scene play itself out for a while.

Doheny didn't yet know what to make of Butchie. Unfailingly polite, the kid was always respectful. But, oddly for a fourteen-year-old, he wasn't ever deferential. He made eye contact with everyone and held it. His unwavering gaze had the effect of being unsettling, even to adults. It also looked like smiling was not within his skill-set. He didn't seem particularly angry or unhappy, just unimpressed and vaguely suspicious—with everyone and everything. Doheny prided himself on being able to read people. Before today, he just couldn't get a read on this kid. His primary professional concern was determining whether or not he was a good guy, or just another neighborhood tough on his way to thugdom. While the jury was still out, Doheny thought the evidence on Butchie's behalf was starting to look formidable.

Doheny came across the street and addressed Basaluco and Mercante, who were just climbing unsteadily to their feet.

"Go pick up the gorilla and drag his ass to *Kraut Town*. You jerk-offs got the beating you deserved today. Remember that the next time you want to fuck with somebody. Now disappear, scumbags."

As the vanquished punks limped away, Doheny addressed Butchie.

"How are *you* doing, Mr. Bucciogrosso?" Doheny asked, with genuine concern.

"Am I in trouble, Patrolman Doheny?"

"If you don't learn how to keep your hands up and slip a punch every once in a while, you'll be in big trouble."

"I meant with the law."

"I know what you meant, kid. On that score, you're fine. You did a lot of damage today, but those assholes deserved every bit of it. You *do* need to learn how to fight, though."

"I thought I did pretty good. It *was* four on one."

"No doubt. You knocked out three goons and chased off the loud-mouth. That's a whole month's worth of work. But you took a lot of unnecessary punishment."

"I was letting them hit me so I could set them up. What should I have done differently?"

"You need to learn how to fight more defensively."

"I don't know how to do that."

"Clearly," Doheny laughed.

"Did I do *anything* right?"

"Sure. You knocked out three scumbags. That's no easy trick. I can see you have some talent. You got great balance, and you're fearless. Those things can't be taught. Best of all, you got hammers for hands. Like nine-pound sledges, everything you hit breaks. The problem is, you think your face is an anvil. You're not supposed to let people hit you. Even if it is to set them up. There's a better way to do that."

"You sound like you know what you're talking about. *Do* you?"

"You know why they call me *Mick the Quick*?" Doheny asked. "I got that handle in the Marine Corps. It's a boxing name. Skinny as I am, I'm not knocking anyone out, but no one is laying a glove on me either. In the ring, I get on my horse and make them chase me all night long. By the end of the fight, I don't have a mark on me. The other guy looks like he got his head stuck in a beehive. So yeah, I know what I'm talking about. I run the PAL boxing program in Brooklyn. We train out of Brewster's in East New York.

I can teach you how to fight, if you want. With your punching power, there's no telling how far you can go."

Two days later, Butchie showed up at Brewster's. He took to the training, learning how to fight more defensively. But he was never as committed to it as he should have been. He had grown so accustomed to absorbing abuse, if he knew he was going to get an opening for the knockout, sometimes he would allow himself to take the punches, until he got the chance to deliver one. It was a hard habit to break, and Butchie never completely broke it.

Despite this, he had some stunning success as a boxer. He could have made a nice living fighting as a professional. At 5' 11" and 190 lbs., he had the punching power of someone a half-foot taller and fifty pounds heavier. But the circumstances of the time, and a war in Southeast Asia prevented him from pursuing that particular career.

CHAPTER TWO

1950s
Bushwick

Butchie was born the eldest of three children to Leonardo and Carolina Bucciogrosso. He was followed a year later by his sister, Rosemarie, who in turn was followed a year after by the baby, Antoinette. Unlike his sisters, who were doted on, Butchie was resented by everyone in the household, which contained three generations of his mother's and father's families. Other than his mother, who loved him intensely and protected him zealously, Butchie was treated like a stain on the family name. Carolina was by necessity hyper-vigilant in protecting her young son, such was the heat of her husband's enmity for the boy. She would often cover Butchie's body with her own, to deflect the drunken violence *Nardo* Bucciogrosso visited upon him.

In stark contrast, Butchie's sisters were worshiped and treated as Italian princesses. Thankfully, the girls looked like their mother, who was stunning in a classic Neapolitan way—with dark brown hair, smooth olive skin and deep brown eyes, which were nothing short of captivating. The girls were the object of all of Nardo's love and affection. He never uttered a cross word to either, as he spoiled them rotten. As the Bucciogrosso family bakery continued to grow and prosper, Nardo would give Carolina more and more money to adorn *his* girls with fine clothing and presents. Still, Nardo's greatest gift was the fact his gene-pool had proven recessive to Carolina's. They looked nothing like him.

Neither did Butchie, but for another reason. Conversely to the girls' fine apparel, Butchie looked as if he had been dressed out of the Saint Vincent de Paul box at the church, which in fact he had. His treatment in the house was deplorable. He was randomly beaten and spat upon by his father and his loathsome uncle, Francesco. The rest of the extended Bucciogrosso family treated him with a seething resentment. His mother's clan were less ardent in their dislike for him, but in no way showed him any regard. When not being ignored by the Zacardi clan, he was viewed with pity as an uncomfortable thing—like a boil that couldn't be lanced. While this treatment was not pleasant, at least it wasn't injurious to his health.

In this toxic environment, Butchie learned quickly, not bringing attention to himself was his best defense for avoiding the abuse. As a result, he grew up exceptionally quiet and thoughtful. He watched everything—anticipating danger everywhere. He developed a three-dimensional awareness of his surroundings, with a focus on possible avenues of escape. Increasingly as he grew, he started noting potential soft spots in the danger, which he might one day exploit. He didn't know it yet, but he was formulating a plan for when he was big enough to make the abuse stop. One day he would fight his father and uncle, but for now, he occupied himself with fleeing.

Though adored by their father, the girls were not totally exempt from discipline. In the structure of a multi-generational Italian home, where the mother by necessity worked in the family business, they spent many hours in the care of their grandmothers. The girls were properly terrified of their fury. A fierce species, there are few task-masters as stern as the Italian grandmother. When Rosemarie and Antoinette had broken their grandmother's beloved gravy tureen, used every Sunday to serve the red sauce *Nonna* Bucciogrosso made in tandem with *Nonna* Zacardi, the girls were panic stricken. Rosemarie and Antoinette had been fighting over a favorite doll when they knocked the tureen from the credenza it was proudly displayed on. It shattered in a thousand pieces. Neither of the grandmothers had discovered the loss yet. The girls ran to Butchie for guidance.

"Butchie, we broke Nonna B's gravy tureen. She's going to kill us," Rosemarie shrieked.

"How did you do that, Ro?" Butchie asked.

"We were fighting over Vincenza," Antoinette admitted.

"I don't get the fascination with that thing. You know she's not even a real doll? She's just a stuffed sock, for Christ's sake!"

"What are we going to do?" Rosemarie beseeched him.

"You two go play in your room. I'll tell Nonna I did it."

"She's going to beat you with the ladle again, Butchie," Antoinette said.

"At least this time she'll have a reason. Now get lost. I'll take care of this," Butchie told them.

After the girls had scampered off and hid in their bedroom, Butchie went upstairs to find Nonna Bucciogrosso. She was in her apartment sewing lace collars onto the girl's dresses.

"Nonna B," Butchie interrupted.

She looked up from her Singer sewing machine with surprise, quickly supplanted by a look of disdain.

"*Che cosa*?" Nonna demanded.

"I accidentally broke your gravy bowl," Butchie said. Then he braced himself.

Nonna B jumped up from the sewing machine so abruptly she knocked her chair backwards onto the floor. She ran into the kitchen to retrieve the stainless-steel soup ladle from the peg it hung from—above the stove.

Butchie dove to the ground. He covered his face and accepted the harsh blows from Nonna's ladle. She beat him about the head, neck and back repeatedly. When she tired of striking him, Nonna ordered Butchie to go to his room. He was to await his father's return home from work. Then he would absorb a second beating for the tureen he had no part in breaking. He would be left bruised, welted, and bleeding. He was nine-years-old.

Butchie spent all of his youth in that house protecting his sisters in this fashion. For their part, Rosemarie and Antoinette grew so accustomed to Butchie taking the fall for their carelessness, they viewed it as an entitlement—something which was just supposed to happen—like the lavish attention and gifts they regularly received from their father. As Butchie never complained, the girls came to expect his intervention as a birthright. Expecting it was not the same as appreciating it, however. While they didn't actively seek Butchie's punishment on their behalf, they didn't seem to mind much when it happened.

Despite their indifference, Butchie continued to protect his sisters. He would absorb their avoided penances without complaint or thanks, until he was sixteen. Then he would still protect his sisters, but he wasn't absorbing *anyone's* abuse after that.

CHAPTER THREE

1950s
Bushwick

When Butchie was thirteen, he met the beautiful Monica Badlamenti at the seventh-grade sock-hop at Saint Brigid's. He had actually noticed her a year earlier when Monica's family had moved to Bushwick from East New York. Her father, Bruno, was the owner of Badlamenti's Latticini on Suydam Street and Knickerbocker Avenue. Bruno moved his little family into their new apartment on Troutman Street, so he could be closer to them during the long workday.

When Butchie saw Monica in the schoolyard at St. Brigid's that warm September morning, he couldn't take his eyes off her. He spent that year, and half of the next, mooning over the girl. She would catch Butchie staring at her, look back and smile, but the reticent boy with the ragged clothing would just avert his gaze and move on. Monica wanted to talk to him, but there were three classes in each grade at Saint Brigid's. They were broken up randomly. Because of the vagaries of chance, they were never in the same class. She had hoped the handsome, serious boy would overcome his shyness. But, he never did.

Monica was therefore astonished when Butchie screwed up enough courage to ask her to dance at the sock-hop. *Sealed with A Kiss* had just started playing. Having watched the impossibly beautiful girl since she arrived, Butchie suppressed his bashfulness when he saw one of the other boys in his class approach her. Butchie rushed over to beat his time.

"Hi. I'm Joey Bucciogrosso. I saw you in your father's cheese shop. I like this song. Want to dance with me, Monica?"

"How do you know my name?"

"Everybody knows your name. You're the prettiest girl in Bushwick. C'mon, dance with me."

Monica blushed, which made her startling green eyes shine all the brighter. Her long, thick black hair was pulled back from her delicate neck and tied in a pink ribbonned ponytail. Butchie thought she was a vision in her white cardigan, poodle skirt and saddle shoes. His heart soared when she agreed.

"Okay. I love Bobby Vinton," Monica said, taking Butchie's hand and following him out onto the dance floor.

They danced and talked for the rest of the night. Butchie turned out to be a good dancer, which surprised them both. He preferred the slower numbers, because it gave him the chance to be near her. His shyness gone; in this intimate setting he couldn't get enough of asking her all about herself. When she would ask Butchie about himself, he would deflect the conversation back to Monica.

When she told Butchie she wanted to be a teacher when she grew up, he was surprised, but pleased. He found Monica's ambition and certainty about her future a refreshing change from his own flat, day-to-day perspective of the world. He told her she would have no trouble keeping her student's attention, as pretty as she was. He enjoyed it when she blushed again. When she asked him what he wanted to be, Butchie drew a blank. He had never considered even having a future. All of his concentration to this point in his life had been directed to merely surviving.

"I have no idea, Monica. What do you think I should do?" he asked.

"I think you can do whatever you want, Butchie. You just have to figure out what it is."

When the dance ended, Butchie walked Monica out to the front of the school where she was being picked up by her parents. Butchie was surprised, and Monica's parents aghast when she kissed him on the cheek and said goodnight.

The following Monday morning, Butchie was waiting outside Monica's door to walk her to school. He was there again every morning, and every afternoon he walked her home. This gave her father Bruno great concern. When it became clear to the burly cheese maker his beloved daughter had every intention of spending all of her free time with the baker's ragamuffin son, he was troubled. He discussed the problem with his wife. She calmed her husband, assuring him Butchie was a good boy whose intentions were honorable. She thought he was sweet, if somewhat sad. They had a rudimentary understanding of why.

Bushwick talked. No one had any secrets in this tight-knit community. Monica's parents had heard the troubling rumors about the Bucciogrossos. Bruno was hesitant, but willing to give the young man a chance. He saw how well Butchie treated his daughter, how protective he was of her, how polite and deferential. He saw how happy the boy made Monica. That clinched it for him. As stubborn as the old-world Sicilian could be, he was powerless to deny his only child anything. He would allow the relationship to continue, but he wanted to keep Butchie close, to keep an eye on him. His wife, Angelina, conceived of a mutually beneficial way for her husband to do just that.

"That awful baker does not allow his son to work in the family business. He won't even bear the boy's presence. You want to keep an eye on him? Offer him a job. You need the help. When he is not at school or with Monica, he will be with you. You can show him what it means to be a good man. And he can buy some clothes that don't look like thrift store throwaways."

Butchie jumped at the opportunity for employment, but not for the reason Bruno would have preferred. Working in the cheese shop gave Butchie the chance to be with Monica all day long. She worked with her mother after school behind the counter of the latticini. Butchie relished the hours she would spend watching him stocking shelves, making sausage, and rolling and drying the fresh mozzarella on the racks in the back of the store.

After the ladies had gone home to fix Bruno's supper, the men would talk as they finished the day's business and prepared the store for closing. A strong mentoring relationship took root. Complimenting his heroic work ethic, Bruno Badlamenti was a staunch believer in honor. He spent hours discussing the virtues of loyalty, of having a strict ethical code—inviolate for any reason. Bruno stressed the importance of family, of putting their safety and comfort above all else—and integrity. Bruno believed a man was nothing, if not true to his own convictions.

The message took, coupled as it was with Butchie's natural protective instincts. He admired the man. To this point, Bruno was the only positive male influence he had ever known. As much as he wanted to be with his daughter, Butchie also wanted to emulate Bruno, so he could better provide for Monica, and protect her against whatever the world might throw at them. At thirteen, he was already thinking about her in those terms.

Bruno was fully aware of Butchie's troubled family history, but he never discussed it with him. His sense of honor would not allow him to divulge another man's awful secrets, even to the boy they directly concerned. Even though Bruno had come to love him, Butchie would have to find out the appalling truth from someone else.

Through all of that, and the next few years, Butchie and Monica were inseparable. When Butchie began boxing, Monica would often accompany him to Brewster's to watch him train. She attended all of his fights, learning to serve as Butchie's *cut-man.* Given his fighting style, and his propensity to try and turn every fight into a punch-in-the-face contest, he was frequently cut. Mick Doheny taught Monica how to flash-freeze the cuts and stem the bleeding. Monica didn't enjoy it as much as she embraced it as another way to stay close to the boy she thought was beyond adorable. They would remain that close, until a war took Butchie away from her.

They graduated from high school in 1966. Not having the money for college, Butchie knew there would be no student deferral for him. He was sure to be drafted. Rather than let the Army or Navy take him, he enlisted in the Marine Corps—in an effort to exercise some control over his own destiny.

On the night before Butchie was to leave for Paris Island, he borrowed Mick Doheny's Buick and picked up Monica. He was determined to wring every last minute out of their time together before he had to leave her. Monica had plans of her own.

The passion between the young couple had always run hot. They had a hard time keeping their hands off each other. But they seldom had the opportunity to be alone, where they could explore their natural inclinations. Bruno was careful to limit the time Butchie could be alone with his daughter. As vigilant as he was, he couldn't be everywhere all the time. Whenever he would leave the room, or even turn his back, they would be on each other like a fever. But these opportunities were few and all too brief. They were never able to consummate their profound love or indulge their raging carnal desires.

In light of the fact Butchie was shipping out in the morning—maybe never to return—he set aside his deep respect for Bruno, for once not concerned with the old man's wishes. He wanted Monica—all of her. He wasn't putting it off for another minute. If her parents would not allow them to be alone, they would make their own opportunity. They pre-arranged for Butchie to pick her up on her corner at sundown. Butchie had a secluded spot picked out for them on a footpath in the woods in Highland Park—overlooking the reservoir. The path was just big enough for Mick's Buick to disappear into. The leaves and low hanging branches would envelope them, providing the solitary and intimate setting they had both been craving.

That afternoon, Butchie had made a few additional preparations. He had bought a single boxed orchid for Monica when they went to the prom the year before. She was moved to tears. She didn't know how he knew. The white orchid was her favorite flower. But, she didn't remember telling him. She chalked it up to his remarkable ability to pay attention to every detail about her. Butchie just thought orchids looked sexy. They smelled good and were just dripping with sensuality. What Monica thought was Butchie's attentiveness was actually just intuition and good luck. He bought Monica another one tonight, hoping to duplicate the effect. He also bought a bottle of chianti and two crystal wine glasses. Champagne was considered but didn't fit the situation. They weren't really celebrating as much as giving in to their desperation.

Butchie pulled up to the corner of Troutman Street and Knickerbocker Avenue. Monica was waiting for him, wearing a floral print sundress. Butchie immediately felt underdressed in his jeans and tee-shirt. He needn't have. She jumped into the passenger seat and slid all the way over, grabbing him by the neck with her left hand. She leaned in to kiss him wetly on the mouth, reaching down to take hold of his crotch, which became instantly hard in her hand. If the sudden bulge in his pants hadn't been so uncomfortable and painful he might have released right there in his underwear. Instead, he was extra motivated to get to the park. He made the right on Troutman and raced up to Cypress Avenue to get there as quickly as he could.

On the way to the park, Monica had freed Butchie from the painful predicament in his pants. and was stroking him as he drove. It was all he could do to concentrate on the road. Once into the park at Cypress Avenue, Butchie pulled around the left side of the reservoir until he came to the secluded footpath he had scouted the week before. He drove into the trees until the path disappeared behind them and came to a stop overlooking the man-made lake. He pushed the front seat all the way back and looked over at Monica with a rapacious hunger. She met his gaze with a ravenous look of her own. She pulled her dress above her hips to reveal she was naked underneath. Enjoying the look of astonishment on Butchie's face, she straddled him, finding each other as if by instinct. Monica shrugged the spaghetti straps off her shoulders. She wasn't wearing a bra either. Her flawless breasts were pressed against Butchie's face. She rode him furiously. Grabbing his wavy hair at the back of his head, she pulled back just far enough, so she could bring her hot wet mouth down on his. They grinded against each other, kissing deeply.

As their thrusting became frenzied, Butchie remembered the condoms Eddie had given him. Not wanting to get her in trouble, he fished them out of his pants pocket and handed them to Monica. Without pausing her gyrations, she grabbed the sleeve of prophylactics and tossed them into the back seat with the wine and flowers. She redoubled her frenzy, pounding herself down onto his hips, until they both shuddered in climax.

Monica continued to straddle him, trying to keep Butchie inside her as long as she could. He found himself overwhelmed by the intense wave of emotion washing through him. If he knew what an epiphany was, he would have called it that. Holding onto Monica, with his face buried between her breasts, all Butchie could hear was the rapid beating of her heart. Though warm, Butchie started shivering. He had known since he met Monica he loved her, but now he began to understand the awesome portent. The idea of losing her intruded on his thoughts, scaring him. He couldn't bear the possibility of having to live outside the safety and well-being her love provided. A few random tears escaped from his eyes, running down his cheeks. This emotional cataclysm was made all the more raw for him, knowing within the next few months he would be sent to the other side of the world to deal with people intent on killing him. Now that he knew beyond all doubt what he wanted, he was horrified by the prospect of someone—who he didn't even know—taking her from him—or, more accurately, taking Butchie from her.

Monica sensed his unease. She could feel his tears, hot against her heaving breasts. She stroked the back of his neck, assuring him they were alright—this moment would be theirs forever, to have again whenever they wanted. Butchie convinced her he was fine, better in fact than he had ever been. Monica took the opportunity to take care of what she thought was their most urgent business.

She leaned in to hoarsely whisper in his ear, her voice still ragged from their passion.

"Come back to me, Butchie. Promise me."

"I promise," he said.

"Promise you'll come back to me."

"I promise," he said, again.

"Promise again," she insisted.

"I promise. I love you, Monica. I know what I want now, and it won't be a life worth living without you. I'm coming back."

"That's three times you promised," she said. "God heard you. You can't let anything happen to you now. I need you with me. Besides, I think we just made a baby. Now you *have* to come home."

Monica turned out not to be pregnant, even if they did their damnedest to try. They spent the rest of the night until sunup devouring each other. The wine wasn't opened. The orchid forgotten. Butchie said he would marry her after boot camp if she was expecting. He thought it was the easiest thing he had ever promised. Monica decided to wait for him to come home from Vietnam. She thought it better to dangle their future marriage as an additional carrot to motivate him to return.

CHAPTER FOUR

June 1966
Parris Island, South Carolina

When Butchie left for Parris Island, Bushwick was already in a rapid decline. It was no secret why. Everyone knew Joe Bonanno—the self-proclaimed *man of respect*—was peddling heroin in his own neighborhood. The ensuing decay was profound and immediate. As much as Butchie would have liked to have done something about the bitter deterioration of his community, he would be otherwise occupied.

When he filed off the bus with his fellow Marine recruits, he had the advantage of having been forewarned by Mick Doheny to travel light. As a result, he showed up with the clothes on his back and an extra tee-shirt and change of underwear in his ratty canvas gym bag. He was prepared to discard everything, even his torn jeans and worn Chuck Taylors.

After the recruits had been mustered into formation, berated, cajoled and otherwise dehumanized by the three sergeants, they were left at attention in the blistering mid-day sun. Meanwhile, the drill instructors toured the lines and proffered individual attention on the young men assembled. A verbal deconstruction began. The recruits were made to intimately understand they were worthless pieces of excrement, who didn't deserve to serve in the sergeants' beloved Marine Corps. The other main thrust of this opening diatribe was a healthy questioning of the recruits' sexual proclivities.

The most animated of the sergeants was a short, stocky, piece of knotted muscle stuffed into an immaculate uniform. His drill-instructor hat, called a *Smokey,* was slung forward over his forehead, framing, but not obscuring the angriest eyes Butchie had ever seen. The Marine recruits were terrified of him. Partly for the sheer physical menace he could project out of his 5' 6" frame, but mostly because they couldn't understand a word he was saying through his thick Spanish accent. This was by the sergeant's design. In fact, he didn't have an accent—beyond the one he was affecting. He began by warning the recruits they would pay miserably if he had to repeat himself. Then he slipped into his accent to assure that he would.

Sergeant Cruz made his way around the formation, stopping to offer individual attention as he saw fit. He was twenty-five-years-old, but his countenance suggested a sagacity which defied putting an age on him. He could have been as old as fifty, or as young as twenty. Such was his aura of menace, you wanted him nowhere near you, irrespective of what age he might be.

Butchie knew Sergeant Cruz well. They had both boxed out of the same gym in East New York. This was a few years earlier, when Butchie's boxing career was just starting out, and Nelson Cruz' was just winding down. In 1964, they had separately won Gold Glove titles in the same tournament at Madison Square Garden. Butchie won the sub-novice title as a sixteen-year-old middleweight. Nelson Cruz, at the time a *former* Marine, was the best fighter in the stable at Jacky Brewster's Boxing Club. Called *the Bruise Factory* with respect by the rest of the fight community, the gym had a reputation for producing the toughest fighters in New York. Jackie Brewster wouldn't even allow you to join the gym until you could prove you were as hard as a coffin nail.

By 1964, Nelson Cruz' muscularity had outgrown his short stature. At twenty-three-years-old, he had already packed two-hundred-ten pounds of rock solid muscle onto his diminutive frame. As a three-time Gold Glove Champion, Nelson had to fight in the open division, as a super-heavyweight. All of the other fighters in the division were over six feet tall. As a result of this height disadvantage, Nelson was forced to endure a seemingly endless barrage of punches in an effort to get close enough to knock out his opponents—who were building an otherwise insurmountable lead on points.

He flattened every one of them, but it became clear his boxing career had hit its ceiling. He celebrated his championship for a week before re-enlisting in the Marines.

If Butchie had been given more to smiling, he might have smiled then. Fortunately, he did not. Another recruit made that mistake in front of Sergeant Cruz. He ended up being choked to his knees until the offending smile vanished. Technically, the drill instructors were not permitted to touch the recruits. They were only allowed to physically *adjust the position* of a recruit who needed it. There would be much position adjusting required in the coming weeks.

Sergeant Cruz and the other drill instructors then sought to prepare the recruits for Staff Sergeant Deforest, the Senior Drill Instructor. Cruz explained it to them.

"You miserable pieces of shit need to listen-up. No one gives fuck-all about how you feel, or what you think. What is on your mind is utterly meaningless, and it is our job to flush out your head-gear, so you can start thinking like a Marine. Right now, none of you pack the gear to do so. Staff Sergeant Deforest is going to issue you that gear. It's going to take some time and a lot of effort to do that. You are not going to like it. That's just too-fucking-bad for you. You are not to speak unless directed to do so, and the first and last words out of your filthy, hippy mouths *will* be Sir. If you are not sure who to salute and obey, follow this simple rule; if a rat runs out of a crack in the wall and tells you to shit, your response had better be 'Sir, how much and how high, Sir?' Do you filthy *fuck-wads* understand that?"

"Sir, yes Sir!" the platoon screamed as one.

Having prepared the recruits for the abuse to come over the ensuing weeks, the sergeants let it sink in. The uniform look of dread washing over their faces for having volunteered for the Marine Corps was amusing to Sergeant Cruz. He knew they had no idea what true fear was. They hadn't yet met the Staff Sergeant.

Staff Sergeant Melvin Deforest was 6'4" and two-hundred-twenty-five pounds of thickly muscled, Georgia malevolence. He liked nothing and no one, and he couldn't wait to tell you all about it. He had joined the Marines at seventeen, just in time to fight the Japanese at Guadalcanal. Surviving the Pacific, Melvin had no desire to return to peanut country in Georgia. So, he stayed in the Corps. He was a Buck Sergeant with the 1st Marines in 1950. He thought his arrival in Korea via Inchon was interesting. He thought his tour of the Chosin Reservoir was somewhat less compelling. He did not appreciate having to rescue the disintegrating US Army from the Chinese, nor did he appreciate having to leave the Chinese border without having pissed in the Yalu River. But mostly, he resented having to walk out of Korea with three bullet holes in him, while nearly freezing to death. Still, he survived and was a proud member of *The Chosin Few*. He would have the opportunity to regale these recruits with stories from that time to illustrate what a genuine US Marine was.

Sergeant Deforest would exploit the examples of the valor he witnessed in war to help make Marines out of what he considered sub-standard wads of civilian dough. He was motivated by more than duty. Deforest was due to be promoted to Gunnery Sergeant. When he was, he knew he was headed back to Vietnam. He wanted to make sure the Marines he would lead there would be worth leading.

To do this, he knew he would have to break them down first. In this way, he could rebuild them from the ground up, until their first and every impulse thereafter was to follow orders and make war. Deforest had spent the last thirty minutes studying the personnel sheets of the recruits he was about to intimidate. He now had a good idea of everyone's name and place of birth. But intimidation was not a strong enough word for the terror he would instill in them.

Melvin Deforest had developed an entire script of abuse centering on this one piece of information. Where you came from and what was fundamentally wrong with people from that particular location was as good a place to start as any. He would begin his probe of the already tenderized recruits with that.

Deforest approached the first private. He was from Nebraska, and until now, proud of it. Deforest stood glaring at him—nose to nose.

"Where are you from, maggot?"

"Sir, Omaha, Sir!"

"I thought only steers and queers came from Nebraska, and I
don't see any fucking horns, now. So I guess we know what's what."

Deforest walked down the line, skipping recruits at random. He would stop at a recruit as he saw fit. The Staff Sergeant next confronted a tall private from New Orleans.

"What's your story, Treetop? Did they hang you from a door to stretch you? I didn't know they stacked shit that high."

The private from Pensacola was next on Deforest's hit list.

"What in God's name is wrong with your face, Mary? Did it get like that from sucking dick?"

"Sir, no Sir!"

"Bullshit! I know a cock-sucker when I see one, and you are a natural cock-sucker of herculean proportions. In fact, you suck dicks all day. So many, that when you do, a light goes off on your forehead that says *cockamatic*. From now on you will be known as *Private Fellatio*."

Sergeant Deforest loved nicknames, and he loved irony. The shortest recruit—barely five feet tall—became *Private Chamberlain*. The tallest; *Private Tinkerbell*. The skinny, slight recruit was *Sampson*, and the great big, muscular football player *Olive Oyl*. The recruit with the darkest complexion was *Private Casper*. The recruit from Wisconsin—who was so fair and pale, he might have been carved out of cream cheese—naturally became *Private Soul Brother*. And so it went, until Sergeant Deforest got to Butchie.

Deforest hated nothing so much as he hated New York. As he approached Butchie, the sergeant was almost giddy with anticipation.

"Where are you from, grease-ball?"

"Sir, New York, Sir," Butchie screamed in response.

"Holy-fucking Christ on a cactus!" Deforest began. "Who the fuck snuck a communist, Jew, cock-sucker into my platoon? Why are you here, commie? Do you want to steal my money or sell me out to my enemies? Did Nikita-fucking-Khrushchev send you to infiltrate my Marine Corps? I bet he did. I'll bet you're wearing faggoty pink underwear. Aren't you, Comrade?"

Deforest went on like that for a minute or so. He liked to pretend New York consisted exclusively of Jews. But he never did this when the recruit was actually Jewish. His goal was to get a negative reaction. Most of the non-Jewish recruits became combative when accused of being one. Once he got them in a defensive posture, Deforest went to work on them for being prejudiced and anti-Semitic. Deforest informed his recruits there was no bigotry of any kind in his Marine Corps. Here, everyone would be treated like shit—equally. He was surprised at the impassive posture of the recruit in front of him. Butchie's lack of reaction to being accused of being Jewish told Deforest he was either uncommonly self-confident or had not one iota of anti-Semitism. This was rare. He needed to find a weak spot. So he kept probing.

After asking Butchie his name, Deforest ran off with that.

"Are you a pizza-maker, or in the Mafia, scumbag?"

Something in all of that got a twitch out of Butchie. Deforest wasn't sure if he was bothered by being called a pizza-chef, a Mafiosi or a scumbag. So he narrowed it down. When he told Butchie he made pizza which tasted like his own sister's asshole, he got nothing. When Deforest called him a scumbag again, he was likewise disappointed. But when he asked Butchie if he was a pimp, or a hit man, the tension in Butchie's face told Deforest all he needed to know. It was time for him to abuse a different recruit, but he knew what subject he would address the next time he went to work on Butchie.

The next day during drills, Staff Sergeant Deforest got his opportunity. Butchie was marginally out of position. This gave Deforest the chance to *adjust* him. A few opened-handed smashes to the head, and Sergeant Deforest had Butchie's undivided attention.

"Are you incapable of following direction, or are you just obstinately stupid, you miserable guinea gangster?"

Butchie just glared at Deforest. The whole countenance of his face changed as he communicated his fury with that alone. It became a confrontation when Butchie was ordered to respond.

"You will answer me, scumbag. Are you in the Mafia or not?"

"Sir, no Sir!" he screamed.

It went down-hill from there.

"Bullshit!" Deforest yelled at him.

"Sir, don't call me that again, Sir," Butchie said, seeming to burn holes into the face of Deforest with his eyes.

"Don't call me that again or what, you shit-faced, maggot, criminal, cock-sucker?" Deforest demanded as he pressed into Butchie's space, standing nose-to-nose with him. By now the three other drill instructors had come over, anticipating trouble.

"Call me Mafia again and I'll rip your fucking throat out," Butchie whispered into the astonished face of Staff Sergeant Deforest.

This precipitated a four sergeant, five-minute, enthusiastic position adjustment. While it hurt like hell, Butchie took the beating like he had been taking beatings all his life. It didn't mean anything, and he would tolerate it on end, before he would ever tolerate being called the one thing he hated more than anything in the world. The sergeants got tired of beating him before Butchie got tired of being beaten. Other than grunts from having the wind knocked out of him, he didn't make a sound. Finally, Deforest ordered Sergeant Cruz to escort Butchie back to the barracks, where he would be confined until he figured out what to do with his insubordinate recruit.

Sergeant Cruz marched Butchie back to the barracks. He ordered him to clean himself up and change, telling him he was to remain at his bunk until further notice. Then Nelson Cruz briefly stopped being Sergeant Cruz.

"Butchie, what the fuck are you doing? You can't talk to the Senior Drill instructor like that."

"Yeah? Well nobody gets to call me Mafia. And you fucking well know why. I don't care what he does to me, Nelson, but if he calls me that again, I'm killing him."

"He's got to break you, Butchie. That's his job. Just let him do it." Nelson implored him.

"He's not breaking me like that," Butchie said.

"I know, Butchie. As it is, you're going to have to go to Motivation Platoon. They're gonna fuck with you hard there."

"As long as they don't call me Mafia, I'll take whatever they wanna do to me."

"I'm not supposed to, little brother," Nelson said, sighing. "But I'll see what I can do for you."

Later that night, Staff Sergeant Deforest called the other drill instructors to a meeting. They were to help Deforest decide what to do about Private Bucciogrosso. The consensus they arrived at was that Butchie would attend the punitive Motivation Platoon for a week. It was hoped he would return sufficiently softened to be carved into the type of Marine Deforest had been molding for years now. After the sergeants were dismissed, Sergeant Cruz asked to speak with the Senior Drill Instructor.

"Staff Sergeant Deforest, I know Private Bucciogrosso. I've known him since he was a kid. The cop and Marine who rescued me from the streets is the same one who rescued him."

"I thought you were a little unenthusiastic when we were tightening him up," Deforest said. "You got a soft spot for the boy?"

"To be honest, Sarge, I admire him. I know you have to break him. But on the subject of being in the Mafia, you *never* will. He will kill you and face a firing squad with a smile on his face. If you send him to Leavenworth, he'll do forty years standing on his head. He'll obey any order you want to give him, but on that one thing, he will *never* break. When I tell you his story, you'll understand why.

CHAPTER FIVE

July 1966
Parris Island

After six days, Staff Sergeant Deforest went over to see his counterpart at the Motivation Platoon. Staff Sergeant Robert Mayhew was happy to receive his friend. They had served together in Korea. After catching up, they got down to the business of Private Bucciogrosso. After hearing out Sergeant Cruz, Deforest elected not to mention the Mafia thing when he sent Butchie over for tenderizing. Not knowing about it, Sergeant Mayhew and his charges never found Butchie's sensitivity. The Mafia thing never came up. They thought he had a problem obeying orders. They addressed that.

"I don't know what your issues are with that kid, Melvyn, but he has been nothing but compliant over here. And we gave him a hard time. We busted him up, and worked him till his body broke. We deprived him of food and water. We wouldn't let him sleep. We worked him like a dog. Even when his whole body cramped up, he tried to work through it."

"We might have just had a misunderstanding."

"Misunderstanding? You don't have those, Melvyn. What are you not telling me?"

"You're going to make me say it, aren't you?"

Mayhew was very pleased, nodding his head enthusiastically.

"I might have been mistaken about Private Bucciogrosso," Deforest allowed.

"Do you mean to say you were wrong?"

"Yes."

"I need to hear those words."

"Fuck you, Robert. I'm not playing this game anymore. Just tell me: in your opinion, is the private fit to return to my platoon?"

"I don't usually say this, but that kid was born to be a Marine. He's the hardest little motherfucker I've ever seen."

"If you say so, Bob, then that's good enough for me. Rest him today. Get him fed and watered and send him back to me at 0500 hours tomorrow."

***

When Butchie returned to his platoon, Staff Sergeant Deforest immediately started paying close attention to him. He rode him hard. He started calling Butchie *Private Greaseball*, but he never again insinuated an affiliation with the Mafia. By the time the abbreviated boot camp ended, Butchie left with the highest fitness rating in his platoon. He and the other Marines would ship out to the Republic of Vietnam, where they would do their Advanced Infantry Training in the field.

By then Butchie had found out from Monica she wasn't pregnant. He wanted to marry her anyway. When she came down to Camp Lejeune with her mother, to attend the boot camp graduation, she reminded Butchie of his promise.

"When you come home to me in one piece, I will marry the hell out of you."

CHAPTER SIX

September 1967
Republic of Vietnam

By September of 1967, Butchie found himself with the 5th Marine Division. They were assigned to the Khe Sanh combat base, running patrols into the A Shau Valley. The valley was a key objective for both sides. The North Vietnamese used this narrow corridor as a supply line. Various branches of the Ho Chi Minh trail ran through it. Butchie got his combat training hunting the North Vietnamese Army and the Viet Cong in the surrounding hills and rice paddies.

He saw plenty of action, but they were of the slash and burn, small unit variety. With the exception of patrolling through some hamlets and villages, the Marines encountered nothing in the way of urban combat. There were no set-piece battles—just skirmishes. Those were dangerous enough.

Khe Sanh was considered a meat grinder. The casualties were many. Butchie was able to polish his instincts for spotting trouble. While these were sharp for all of his life, the A Shau Valley honed them to a razor's edge.

In January of 1968, the Marines were air-lifted to the Phu Bai Air Base outside of Hue. They felt like they had drawn a reprieve and been granted *R and R*. Through most of the month, it appeared they had. While performing patrols in the hills around the base, they encountered little more than sniper fire. They never actually saw their adversaries. There were a lot of rumors flying around the base with regard to a planned NVA offensive. With the Tet holiday approaching, it was assumed if the enemy were going to launch something, it would be before or after the customary week of Tet observance. The most important Vietnamese holiday, Tet was a celebration of the Vietnamese lunar New Year. It was so spiritually important to both sides, when the NVA hadn't yet attacked by the Eve of the ceasefire on January 30th, Butchie and his platoon thought they had the week off—until the morning of January 31st.

CHAPTER SEVEN

January 31, 1968
Hue, Vietnam

Overnight, the NVA and VC launched an overall offensive across the country. They had taken the Citadel in Hue and were trying to consolidate their forces to take the rest of the city. The North Vietnamese expected a ground swell of popular support from the residents of the city. When this never materialized, the NVA and VC were too undermanned to hold the areas of the city they had already taken. They were forced to abandon their gains for the push into the citadel.

The Marines were ordered to head north on Highway 1. They were tasked first to relieve the exposed MACV (Military Assistance Command Vietnam) compound just south of Hue. They encountered light resistance all the way up Highway 1. The enemy, visible in the distance, did not seem particularly anxious to engage the Marines. They merely peppered the convoy with harassing fire. The NVA seemed more intent on making their way north toward the center of the city. Butchie could see them as they streamed there on their alternate, parallel routes.

Thus far, since arriving in Vietnam, Butchie had found himself oddly frustrated by his limited contact with the enemy. Although frequently engaged in small arms skirmishes and brief fire-fights in the hills around Khe Sanh, he had seldom seen the enemy in large numbers, and they never attacked his platoon en masse. The numbers and aggressive posture of the NVA opposite the Marines this day gave Butchie the unmistakable impression that would no longer be true. The tight ball of trepidation screwing up in his guts now made him wonder what the hell he had been thinking.

Rather than frustrated, Butchie realized how grateful he should have been. The only benefit to all the anxiety gripping him was the hyper-alertness the adrenaline surge provided. Butchie had no idea how he would finally feel when the enemy attacked, but he was sure it would be hair raising. He wasn't the only one.

"Why aren't they attacking us?" Ernie Commiskey asked.

"It looks like they have somewhere else they need to be," Butchie said. "I don't think they want to stop our progress as much as keep us off their flanks while they get where they're going."

"I wish they'd stop taking potshots at us already."

"Yeah, me too, Ernie. Some of those rounds are getting danger-close. They're either going to pick the spot from where they want to attack, or they'll choose the ground they want to defend. Either way, it's gonna suck for us."

The Marines reached the MACV compound. After clearing light resistance from the surrounding plains and the hills to the north, a company of Marines were left behind to set up a defensive perimeter and clear a deck for a helicopter landing-zone. The rest of the Marines, Butchie among them, continued north. Their next objective was to relieve the embattled 1st ARVN (Army Republic Vietnam) Division Command Post, inside the Citadel in Hue City.

Butchie's platoon got to the place on Highway 1 where it crossed the Perfume River. To get over the river, they would have to cross the Nguyen Hoang Bridge. The bridge was eerily quiet. This was comforting to no one. In Vietnam, the Marines had learned to dread the silences. They had come to understand the only time it was quiet were in the seconds before all hell broke loose.

"Do you hear that?" Butchie asked Commiskey.

"I don't hear anything. It's dead silent."

"Exactly. Keep your shit wired tight, Ernie. I think Uncle Ho has got some bad intentions for us."

While the Marines had three tanks, several Armored Personnel Carriers, and a few trucks, these had to proceed slowly, in single file across the bridge. There was an ARVN convoy abandoned and shot up—scattered across the roadway. The Marines would have to advance on foot. Butchie's squad was in the lead. The bridge was over 400 meters long. They couldn't see the other side until they had crested the center. Once they had, Butchie had to squint to see the other side through the diaphanous haze of cordite and lingering gun smoke. He could taste the peculiar mix of petroleum and what smelled like burnt hair. He understood this odor was exclusive to rocket propelled grenades. The recognition ratcheted up his pucker-factor exponentially.

As if on cue, the Marines started taking fire from the buildings on the other side.

They continued their advance on foot, using the abandoned ARVN vehicles as cover. They were able to return fire, temporarily silencing the snipers in the buildings.

They had reached the final ARVN vehicle, a disabled and abandoned M24 Chaffee light battle tank. The left tread had been blown off. The top hatch was open and there was an M60 machine gun mounted on it. There didn't seem to be any more resistance. Private Jesus Mendez, the point man, advanced out into the open, near the north end of the bridge. As he did, the NVA hiding in the buildings opened up on the exposed Marine.

Mendez was shot twice through the legs and spun to the ground. As he fell, Butchie could feel his own rectum snap shut, and a cold wash of dread shoot through his core. Even as cautious as he wanted to be, he couldn't leave Mendez unprotected in the open like that. He knew the NVA would cut him to shreds out there.

"Get rounds on those windows!" Butchie directed his squad mates. "I'm going to get Jesus."

The rest of the squad moved up quickly and provided covering fire, while Butchie dashed out to carry Mendez behind the safety of the tank. He hoisted the private up and over his shoulder, lugging Mendez back with him. As he got to the corner of the Chaffee, an NVA soldier popped up at one of the windows in the buildings behind him and fired a rocket propelled grenade.

The shot was short, missing him. It hit the pavement a dozen feet behind Butchie, but with grenades, a miss isn't necessarily a miss. The torn-up roadway and shrapnel from the RPG tore into the rear of Butchie's right leg and buttocks.

"You miserable cocksuckers! Not in the ass! Anywhere but in the ass!" Butchie railed.

When he got Mendez to safety behind the tank, Jesus was taken by his squad mates to the rear to be evacuated. Butchie's squad sergeant checked his wounds. He called up a corpsman, who examined them and thought they were superficial. Sergeant Cochrane gave Butchie the choice to be evacuated.

"Do you want to head back to MACV with Mendez?"

"No fucking way, Sarge. I'm in this fight. Just have Buchwald patch me up."

"I'm not going to argue with you, Butchie. I need every swinging dick I can get for this op."

Corpsman Buchwald set about cleaning the wounds as best he could. They were bleeding, but not very deep. There was no arterial damage the corpsman could see. After brushing away any debris on the surface of the wounds, Buchwald applied Sulfur powder as a disinfectant and coagulant, and a pressure bandage.

"He's good to go," the corpsman declared.

The NVA grenadier in the window kept popping up and firing his RPG. He had adjusted his aim and was causing fearsome casualties on the Marines advancing. The sound of wounded and wailing men mixed with the intermittent explosions of the grenades, and the incessant pops and cracks from the various small arms being fired. Butchie identified this as the sound of utter chaos. He had to choke down the urge to vomit. The nausea was accompanied by the adrenaline thrumming through his head. He intuitively understood these were just bi-products of his terror. Once he realized he would likely be killed—and accepted it—a strange serenity came over him. He just wanted to get some pay-back before the inevitability of getting shot occurred. Rather than afraid, it made him angry. He used this anger to motivate himself to act decisively—with malice toward his enemy.

None of the tanks or vehicles had advanced far enough to put their big guns into play. No amount of suppression fire was keeping the NVA grenadier from punching holes in the Marine ranks. Their precarious situation was compounded by the fact they were forbidden to use artillery and were denied any air support. The commanders withheld these very basic and important tools for fear the Marines would destroy the ancient and sacred buildings of Hue. So, instead they were pinned down, in harm's way.

Seeing the quandary, Butchie took matters into his own hands. He climbed up the back of the Chaffee and manned the *sixty*. It was loaded and ready to fire. Butchie waited for the grenadier to pop his head up again. When he caught him running from one window to the next on the third floor, Butchie let loose with the machine gun. He knew he had hit his target, but he kept raking the third floor in case he hadn't. He watched with satisfaction as every fifth round—incendiary tracer rounds—entered the windows in a show of flame and spark and obliterated everything behind them. An instant later, a series of secondary explosions collapsed the third floor. As the third and fourth floors descended into the remaining building, the whole building imploded into a burning mass of wreckage.

"Holy shit!" Butchie said, gaping in wonder as the building collapsed in on itself.

Rising back up as a plume of smoke, dust, and rubble, Butchie could taste the awful residue of exploded ordinance, brick dust, and burnt flesh. He realized he had hit the extra grenade ammunition with one of the tracers. It was a million to one shot, but he wasn't looking any gift horses in the mouth.

"Did you see that building disappear?" Butchie asked Ernie.

"It looked like the Earth swallowed it whole," Ernie marveled.

The ensuing respite gave the Marines the opportunity to clear the bridge and bring up their heavy tanks. While the wounded and dead were being evacuated to the rear, the tanks opened up with their main guns. They reduced the buildings overlooking the bridge to rubble. Butchie was again offered the opportunity to head to the rear with the casualties. He declined, insisting he was functional.

"The bleeding has already stopped. It hurts like hell, but all that's doing is pissing me off. I'm not leaving until I shove a boot up old *Uncle Ho's* ass."

The tanks and a squad of Marines were left to hold the bridge. The rest of the infantry and the APCs continued up Highway 1. They were now in sight of the south gate into the walled city. The 1st Army Republic of Vietnam Command Post was just a half click from there.

As the Marines stepped out from the bridgehead, they were immediately taken under fire from a bunker under the demolished buildings on the earthen berm above the highway and river. They were pinned down again.

The tanks were in no position to take the bunker under fire. It was too well enfiladed. From cover, Butchie scoped the situation out. He thought the bunker was vulnerable if attacked from behind. He believed he could get there by approaching through the building ruins above it. He bounced his idea off Sergeant Cochrane.

"If I go back and get that *sixty* from the Chaffee, I can roll up on the bunker without being seen. I'll take the fuckers out before they know what hit 'em."

"Are you sure, Butchie? That's a .51 caliber in there. They shoot down air planes with those."

"What choice do we have? The *pogues* in the rear won't give us any air support. If I don't do this, we'll be pinned down here all day. Besides, I'm gonna be flying lower than a plane. Let me try this."

"Okay, Lance Corporal. What else do you need?"

"Gimme Commiskey. I need the big donkey to carry ammo, and I'll take a grenade launcher, too."

They went back to the disabled tank. Butchie unhooked the *sixty* from the mount. Ernie Commiskey went into the tank and came out with two boxes of ammunition. He removed the belts and draped them over his shoulders and around his waist. Sergeant Cochrane gave Butchie an M79 grenade launcher, and both Maines two full grenade bags—including incendiary rounds. They slung all of this gear over their shoulders and headed out to sneak up on the bunker.

Butchie and Ernie snuck up into the high ground behind the screen of the tanks. They made their way north through the rubble of the buildings, until they were directly behind and above the machine gun bunker. Butchie could look into the rear of it

He signaled to Ernie with a raised fist, indicating for him to halt. He crept back to whisper to him.

"I see at least three people in there, but there are probably more. Plus, it looks like they got a fuck-ton of gear."

"What do you want to do?"

"Grab some cover. I'm gonna creep up and unlimber the *sixty*. That bunker's gotta go."

Butchie crabbed forward until he got within fifteen feet. Then he propped the *sixty* up on its bipod. When he opened up on the bunker, he heard the wails of panic from the NVA inside. A split-second later, the whole bunker exploded into the sky. It rained down in a torrent of earth, timber and human viscera. Butchie realized he had ignited another stash of grenades. Evidently, this was not just a machine gun bunker. They had at least one RPG in there.

"Well, that was quick," Ernie said, when he crawled up beside his squad mate.

"The tracer rounds must be as hot as a motherfucker, cause the grenades are going right up. I am *really* starting to like this *sixty*!"

Butchie spent too long admiring his work. A searing pain erupted in his left shoulder, along with a shower of blood he scarcely believed was his own. Butchie didn't see the NVA soldier who crawled out of the back of the next bunker until he had shot him, above his heart.

"Ernie, get in the fucking crater, now!" Butchie yelled, before blowing away the NVA with his *sixty*.

They scrambled down into the bomb depression which had just been a bunker. Ernie examined Butchie's wound. It looked bad. Butchie said it hurt like hell, but it wasn't bleeding much. He was already talking about taking out the next bunker. Ernie applied more sulfur powder and another pressure bandage around his shoulder.

"This is a whole bunker complex," Butchie informed Ernie. "I can see the next two. They have no angle to shoot at us from the front. So, we're safe here. It's time for the grenade launcher."

Using the M79 to level each successive emplacement, Butchie and Ernie leapfrogged from one destroyed bunker to the next—until there were none. There turned out to be a total of five. After they were sure they had cleared the whole complex, they waved the rest of the Marines up. Sergeant Cochrane saw the bloody pressure bandage around Butchie's shoulder.

"Are you a fucking bullet magnet, Bucciogrosso? I'm having you *dusted off* now," Cochrane said, forgetting for a moment they had no helicopters.

"No, Sarge. This is nothing. It was a through-and-through. It's not even bleeding anymore," Butchie protested, raising his left arm above his shoulder.

"Alright, Butchie, but no more heroics. Stay behind cover, and for fuck's sake, stop volunteering to do shit."

When Sergeant Cochrane turned to walk off, Butchie's eyes rolled up in his head, and he faceplanted at Ernie Commiskey's feet. He picked Butchie up before Cochrane became aware of just how bad off his Marine was.

"You okay, Butchie?" Ernie said, propping him up.

"That hurt so fucking much!" he admitted.

"Then you probably shouldn't lift your arm like that. It could get dangerous."

The two of them cackled uncontrollably at this, the sublime madness of their situation occurring to them.

The Marines headed out again. The column moved north until they were facing the south gate of the Citadel. Its walls were intimidating, as was the giant ornate brass gate. When Butchie looked up at the top of the Citadel, what he saw there gave him the creeps. A giant NLF (National Liberation Front) flag, with its venomous yellow star, taunted the Marines from within its dual fields of soulless crimson and wan blue. It flew from the enormous flag pole atop the building. Butchie had never seen one, other than in pictures. He found the stark reality of the enemy's colors chilling.

The point man in the Marine formation, Corporal Earl Jennings, was a good old boy from the hills of western Kentucky. He had spent his entire life before the Marine Corps hunting and trapping in those wooded hills. He was an adept tracker. He bragged if he had a rifle and a half hour, he had dinner. He was also an excellent point man. Unfortunately, he knew Earl was just as gifted at finding trouble, and never failed to do so. Butchie was on edge—more so than he already was. The wounds in his back and leg were throbbing by now, and the bullet through his left shoulder was causing a pain worse than excruciating.

The Marines were fifty meters from the gate when the unseen NVA soldiers inside opened up on them. Jennings was shot twice through the chest, and tumbled down in the road. Butchie found cover behind a tree by the side of the street. He was more than twenty feet from Jennings. Earl was still being fired upon by the NVA. When he was shot in the foot and cried out in agony, Butchie left the protection of his tree. He dashed out into the road, and grabbed the collar of Jennings' flak vest. He started to frantically drag him backwards toward cover.

"Hold on, Earl," Butchie told him. "I'll get you safe."

Just then, the NVA opened up on Butchie, shooting him through the stomach twice. He fell to the ground, but never let go of Jennings. He crabbed backwards, hopping on his wounded ass, dragging Jennings until they were behind the safety of the tree. The two Marines were seriously wounded, and lay there bleeding out on each other.

"Am I gonna die?" Jennings asked Butchie.

"Not today, Earl. I'm gonna patch you up," he said, as he applied a tourniquet around Jennings' lower leg, to stanch the blood spurting out of his boot. When he had it in place, he applied sulfur powder and a pressure bandage around Earl's abdomen. After being sure he had stopped Jennings' bleeding, Butchie took a brief look at his own gut-wounds.

"Oh, fuck," he moaned, before passing out in the growing puddle of his own blood pooling beneath him.

Meanwhile, the rest of the lead squad was getting cut to pieces.

The captain directed a machine gun team up to the roof of the pharmacy on the right side of the road. From up there, they had a better vantage to duel the soldiers inside the gate. They suppressed the NVA fire enough to allow the APCs to roll up and screen the Marines, who tended to the wounded and the dead, loading everyone into the transports for evacuation.

The Captain already decided they were aborting the mission. They were going to need more Marines and a different approach to take the citadel back.

Butchie and the other wounded were rushed back to the MACV compound. By now the landing zone for the helicopters had been set up and was in use. He was not expected to survive the flight, but they dusted him off anyway.

CHAPTER EIGHT

February 1968
USS Forrestal, Gulf of Tonkin

Butchie ended up in the hospital aboard the aircraft carrier USS Forrestal. The surgeons had already given up on him. His gurney was moved to the KIA section.

The chaplain came by, checking Butchie's dog-tags for his religion. When he saw RC listed on the tags, the young priest began administering the last rites of *Extreme Unction.* When he had completed the prayers, the padre covered Butchie's face with the sheet.

"Get that fucking sheet off my face," Butchie growled.

The priest almost fainted, but he complied with Butchie's demand. He also went and got an orderly to move Butchie from the queue of KIAs to an area where he would receive further monitoring and treatment.

Butchie was made of tougher stuff than the surgeons realized. He had also made a promise to someone they knew nothing about. The Navy surgeon came by to examine him and marvel at his tenacity. He didn't think his patient would be alive at this point. Imagine his surprise when he found Butchie alert and able to speak.

"How are you feeling, Sergeant Bucciogrosso?"

"Lance Corporal," Butchie corrected him.

"No. You're a sergeant. They promoted you twice since you've been here. They also awarded you a Purple Heart, posthumously. We had to let them know you weren't dead yet. Frankly, I'm astonished you aren't."

"I was that bad?"

"When you got here, you were almost tapped out. You were white as a ghost and had almost no blood left. You got lucky in triage. The nurse there was an old war horse. When the newer girls tried to cut your clothes off and clean your wounds, Lieutenant Dannifer stopped them. The filth and the pressure bandages were all that was holding you together. You would have bled out if they had taken it off."

"Wow. If you get a chance, give Lieutenant Dannifer a kiss for me."

"Not a chance, Sergeant. She's got a face that could stop an eight-day clock. Great trauma nurse, though."

"What's your name, Doc?"

"I'm actually a Captain. Kevin Spellman. Mind if I ask you a few questions, Sergeant?"

"Sure, Cap. But call me Butchie. Everyone does."

"Okay, Butchie. I've been doing this a long time. This is my second war. You might say at this point that meatball-surgery is my thing. So, I've seen a lot. People in your condition don't usually survive. It's not necessarily the wounds, although those were bad enough. When people lose that much blood, what ebbs out with it is their will to keep going. The mind tells the body to give in to it—to just let go. And so, they do. The pain stops. We put them in a box with a flag on it, and another hole gets filled at Arlington. But you didn't give in. That tells me you have something very dear—very important to make you want to keep living, when dying would be the easier thing. What is it, Butchie? What do you need so badly to live for?"

"There's a girl," Butchie said.

"Of course, there is," said the captain, smiling wistfully. "Behind every miracle, every great hero's journey, somewhere there is always a girl. Well, this one saved your life. What's her name?"

"Monica."

"She must be very special."

"She's my everything, Cap," Butchie admitted.

Butchie had vowed to Monica he would return to her from Vietnam—in one piece. His continued survival despite his grievous wounds was predicated on sheer force of will, as much as it was by any medical miracle—as Captain Spellman confirmed. Despite his grave injuries, Butchie continued to improve. He was flown to the naval hospital in Japan, where he recuperated until he was well enough to be moved to Walter Reed in Washington DC.

By January of 1969, Butchie completed his rehab simultaneously with his enlistment. He was awarded—not posthumously—the Navy Cross for Valor and a Purple Heart with two oak leaf clusters for his gallantry at the Battle of Hue. Private Mendez and Corporal Jennings thought it should have been a Medal of Honor. Both Marines knew they only survived because of Butchie.

He returned home to Brooklyn and continued to get his strength back. He was at Brewster's on a daily basis, running, training with weights, and boxing, until his body was back in the shape it had been before the NVA decided to use him for a target. Just in time, too—Butchie entered the Police Academy in July.

CHAPTER NINE

July 1969
Bushwick

Honorably discharged from the Marines, and now fully healed, Butchie entered the Police Academy. While he was away, the Bucciogrosso family managed to escape to Madison Street in Ridgewood, but Butchie's heart never left the old neighborhood.

His father and his uncle owned Bucciogrosso's Italian Bakery. In the time Butchie was gone, a new landlord had managed to take over the building. Santino Indelicato not only jacked up the rent, he charged the Bucciogrossos a weekly "protection fee." If this fee was not paid promptly, windows were broken, equipment stolen, or mysteriously burst into flame. Once, their delivery truck got hijacked and held for ransom. Of course, by the time the payment could be made, the bread had gone stale and had to be thrown out. So in addition, the brothers lost a day's proceeds.

Though the brothers Bucciogrosso didn't want to pay, they really had no choice. They had already demonstrated a profound unwillingness to stand up to the Mafia, and Indelicato, or *Fat Sam* as everybody called him, was connected. If they wanted to do business in Brooklyn, Fat Sam was going to have to be paid. The money was exorbitant, but it was preferable to what his father had to pay the last Mafioso landlord.

By the time Butchie heard about the new arrangement, he was already a cop in the 83rd Precinct for two years. His impulse was to go over to the clubhouse on Suydam Street to beat the fat gangster to death with his own espresso machine. He was only dissuaded from doing so by his mother's pleading.

Butchie had long regarded the neighborhood Mafiosi with contempt. He saw the cowards they had made of his father and uncle, afraid even to defend that which should have been more precious than life itself. He hated the two of them on a more nuanced level than he hated the gangsters. But it was a toss-up over who he hated more. Butchie saw the mob as parasites, preying upon the innocent and working poor of Bushwick. His father and uncle were merely craven men—without honor. What they had done was inexcusable, but the damage was reserved to themselves and their family.

Butchie understood the Mafiosi preyed upon everyone. He didn't buy into the Sicilian myth that the bent-noses were somehow protectors of the neighborhood. The evidence to the contrary was all around him, from the junkies nodding out on the corners, or dying in the filthy hallways, to the stripped cars seeming to multiply on the curbsides. Buildings had been abandoned, now used as shooting galleries by the junkies, who ventured out only to get *fixed*, or steal something they could sell. Butchie fully appreciated that rather than protectors, the mob were more like locusts, stripping the land bare, sparing nothing.

If that weren't enough motivation for Butchie to hate them, there was the matter of his would-be father-in-law. While Butchie was overseas, Bruno Badlamenti, the beloved owner of the Latticini on the corner of Suydam Street and Knickerbocker Avenue, was one of those hard-headed Sicilians who wouldn't pay. He was adamant. He declared he had left Castellamare del Golfo to rid himself of these swine. He wasn't about to pay them for the right to do business in Brooklyn. The threat of violence only bought a savage beating from the burly cheese maker.

A week later, while walking home from work, Bruno Badlamenti was surrounded by three men in Knickerbocker Park. When they were done shooting, what was left was hardly recognizable as a man. Badlamenti died ventilated on the crushed clam shells of the bocce ball courts. Even though the murderers had made no attempt to obscure their identities, and the bocce courts were filled with the friends and former customers of the victim, his murder went unsolved.

While no one would talk to the police about what had happened, the story was well-circulated in the neighborhood. This was as intended. A clear message was sent. Payment to the Mob was not negotiable, and the penalty for not paying was severe.

Bruno's widow was forced to sell the building at a deep discount to Fat Sam. She and her daughter, Monica, moved into a smaller apartment on Hart Street. This was where Butchie found them when he returned from Vietnam.

The young couple rekindled what they understood was inevitable. They had been drawn to each other since the 7th grade, the first time Butchie found the courage to ask Monica to dance. Butchie was hooked. So was Monica. She made him promise to come back from Vietnam in one piece. Because he didn't know how to deny her anything, he swore he would. She was furious at him for getting shot. She got over it when he told her he survived his wounds only because he needed to see her again. She took him at his word, and the two again were inseparable. Monica made him promise to let things lie with Indelicato, but he would only go so far as to promise he would do so for the time being.

The wreckage Bushwick had been left in by the Bonannos sickened Butchie. He was determined to do something about it. His disdain for the Mafia was nothing if not consistent. When he first graduated from the police academy, he was assigned to the 83rd Precinct. He quickly became an enormous pain in the ass to the Mafiosi. The mobsters first tried to buy him off, but he wouldn't be bought. When they tried to appeal to their common Italian ancestry, they discovered this only achieved further acrimony from the already angry cop. When they finally resorted to their favored tactic—intimidation—it went very badly for the goons who tried it. The three of them ended up under arrest after Butchie took their gun away and rearranged their faces with it.

Butchie became known as the Italian cop who hated Italians. It became abundantly clear there was no percentage whatsoever in trying to mess with him. Irrespective of the mobsters' belief about Butchie's feelings regarding his heritage, the opposite was true. Butchie loved and respected the poor Italians of Bushwick, who were toiling at the brink of poverty—trying to eke out an honest living. He hated the mobsters who made their livelihoods by sucking the blood from them.

He saw things in Bushwick go from bad to worse despite his best efforts. Joe Bonanno had already been forced into exile. The new boss, Phillip *Rusty* Rastelli was no better, focusing even more of the Bonannos' interests in narcotics. In 1974, Rastelli was sent to prison. Carmine *Lilo* Gigante became the acting boss. Under him, the bottom fell out.

Gigante concerned himself almost exclusively with the importation and sale of heroin. In order to secure loyalty and a greater share of the proceeds from the drug business, Gigante created his own Pretorian guard within the Bonanno crime family. Lilo imported Sicilians who were already well-versed in illicit drug smuggling and distribution to join him in New York. Gigante set up a vast narcotics empire which excluded the bosses of the other four crime families. The traditional Italian-American members of his own family were also excluded from the drug bounty. Gigante only trusted his Sicilians, who were referred to derisively as *Zips* by the other mobsters. The fact they were vicious psychopathic killers only further insulated their boss.

Because they had been cut out of the lucrative narcotics operation, the non-Sicilian-born Bonannos were forced to become even more predatory toward the businesses and residents of Bushwick. The honest working people in the neighborhood found themselves getting picked clean.

It was during this time Fat Sam started to put an even heavier hand on the Bucciogrosso Bakery. Butchie became aware of the problem accidentally. He overheard his uncle complaining bitterly in Italian to a neighbor about the deteriorating situation. Evidently, Uncle Francesco forgot his nephew was fluent in Italian. The rest of the information Butchie had to drag out of his father.

"What do you care for? It's none of your business," his father told him.

"I wish it weren't, Nardo," Butchie told him. He had stopped calling him Papa when Butchie found out he wasn't really his father. "But like it or not, the name on your awning is mine. I'm not going to let you disgrace it any further. You will respect my wishes. Or, I'll gut you worse than Fat Sam ever dreamed. I don't need you. I am already taking care of Mama. You exist only by my grace and discretion. So don't fuck with me on this."

Leonardo Bucciogrosso and his brother Francesco were cowards. They would not defy Butchie. They had come to fear him more than the Mafiosi they had been laying down to for years.

Butchie's mother again begged him to leave well enough alone.

"I love you, Mama," Butchie told her. "But I've taken all the shit I intend to from these bloodsuckers. It ends today. The Bucciogrossos have paid their last dollar to the Bonannos."

"But they're killers," Butchie's mother reminded him.

"So am I, Mama, and I'm better at it than they are."

"Please don't do this," she pleaded.

"I'm sorry," Butchie said. "But this has to happen. I owe them this. I will kill every last gangster in Brooklyn if I have to. You've paid too much already. Our servitude to these vultures is over. This is getting done."

CHAPTER TEN

July 1964
East New York

Butchie would ultimately discover the source of his father's enmity towards him when he was fifteen. His father and his uncle had treated him like a punching bag since he was old enough to walk. What he couldn't understand was why. His father was a gentle doting and protective parent to his younger sisters. But Butchie had never been shown even the slightest kindness by him, or for that matter, whole Bucciogrosso side of the family. He seemed to be regarded by the lot of them with absolute disdain.

His mother's side were only incrementally better. They clearly meant him no harm, but they treated him with a distance. They looked on him as if he was something unfortunate. Only his mother showed him any kind of love or affection. But even her tenderness was tinged with an unspecified sadness. They were each other's only allies in that house.

When Butchie was small, his mother would protect him from his father's wrath, absorbing beatings to prevent the angry Nardo from getting at the child. By the time Butchie was six years old, he started intervening when his father would start beating his mother. Then Butchie would have to be pummeled by both his father and uncle, who always seemed to be around when bad things were happening.

Butchie learned to absorb the punishment without complaint. As he got older, he realized his father and uncle couldn't fight very well. Other than viciousness, they didn't bring much game to the fight. They weren't quick enough for Butchie not to receive their punches on his own terms. He started moving into the blows, which weren't very hard anyway. They still did damage. They were grown men striking a child, after all. By the time Butchie was fourteen and started training with Mick Doheny, he got the idea if he were to fight back, he could whip the both of them. Of course, he wouldn't. Butchie believed disrespecting one's father was just wrong—no matter the circumstances. He also knew doing so would not improve his mother's situation one iota.

When Butchie showed up at Brewster's with a black eye and a bruised cheek, Mick Doheny noticed. He knew Butchie hadn't been in a fight in the neighborhood. He would have heard about it. Patrolman Doheny knew everyone in Bushwick—and all of their business. He wasn't a busybody, just a good cop, and everybody talked to Mick Doheny. They told him everything. Some of it made his skin crawl. What he already knew about Butchie broke his heart. There were times he wished he didn't know it. But he did, and he was too good a cop, and too good a friend to run from it now.

"What's with the bruises, Spartacus?" he asked.

"I fell."

"I'm calling bullshit, Butchie. You have better balance than any fighter I've ever seen. You don't fall down. You're practically immune to gravity. So, what gives?"

"My father and my uncle tuned me up last night. But it's no big deal."

"Yeah, it's a big deal, Butchie. You're just a kid. You're not supposed to be treated like that—by anyone. Why did they get after you?"

"They get drunk on their own *grappa*. Then they get nasty, starting in on my mother. They call her a *butana*. Then the slapping starts. I have to jump in, Mick. I can't let them do that to her."

"There's a lot going on there you don't know about. They resent you both for the same reasons. The two of you are a constant reminder of their own cowardice and shame."

"What are you talking about, Mick?"

"Did you ever notice how differently you're treated in that house? Are your sisters treated the same way?"

"No, it's different for me."

"How about in the street? How does the neighborhood treat you?"

"People have been snickering at me behind my back my whole life. They whisper *Bastardo*, like I can't hear it. I don't understand it, so I learned to tune it out. What the hell is wrong with me, Mick?"

"Oh, Butchie, not a thing. People are just fucking cruel. I don't know if it will help, but you deserve to know why this is happening."

Mick Doheny went on to patiently relate Butchie's true family history. Butchie was in turn fascinated and horrified, but he wouldn't let Doheny stop telling it until he was out with all of it.

His mother, Carolina Zacardi, was just sixteen when she was promised to Leonardo Bucciogrosso by her father. The Sicilian émigré and his brother were already accomplished bakers. Carolina's father produced the cash for the down payment for their bakery and co-signed the loan in exchange for the little baker agreeing to marry her. This was her dowry. Their union was a business transaction.

Nardo put Carolina to work in the bakery, while he and his brother built their business. The couple—if you could call them that—were to be married in June. They got along well enough. If well enough meant being civil to one another. They were a mismatched pair to begin with. Nardo was homely, short, and thick. Balding at twenty-five, he had blunt features, made rougher by his stern, surly personality. By comparison, Carolina was a breath of fresh air. She was astonishingly beautiful, with fine Neapolitan features. Her green eyes always seemed to be smiling. If she found her unattractive fiancé difficult, she bore him without complaint.

There has always been Mafia in Bushwick. Before Fat Sam Indelicato, there was Salvatore *Sallie Gorgeous* Ruttigliano. He was the Capo in Bushwick in late 1948. The brothers Bucciogrosso had avoided paying protection to Ruttigliano's underlings. He dropped into the bakery to straighten the matter out himself. He informed Nardo the last three months were due. He expected that money, and the fee for this month as well. He told the bakers he wasn't leaving until he got it.

Sallie Gorgeous was exactly that. Six feet tall and fit, he wore thousand-dollar suits when a suit of clothes could be had for thirty-nine bucks. Granted, they came off the back of a truck, but they were no less impressive. Sallie had the sharp Sicilian features of a Mediterranean prince, with a thick head of black shiny hair—which he wore in a pompadour—the style of the day. With the flashy diamond rings and gold watch, he was movie star beautiful. The only hint of the danger inside of him were his eyes. They had an unhinged vacant quality. He appeared as if he was perpetually looking for trouble and was ready to make it himself if he couldn't find any. Those eyes were upsetting Carolina now. So she kept her head down. This only intrigued Sallie Gorgeous all the more.

"It's a hundred a month, Nardo. That's four hundred. Pay me—now," Sallie demanded.

Nardo went to the cash register and emptied it. The take totaled one hundred dollars. He gave it to the gabgster.

"Here's a hundred dollars. It's all I have."

"That takes care of this month. Three hundred more squares us."

"I can't pay you what I don't have."

"Oh! A negotiation, I love to negotiate. Let me start," Sallie said, as he pulled the .45 out from under his suit jacket. "You're gonna pay me three hundred dollars. Or, I'm going to shoot you in both elbows. Let's see how much dough you can knead with both of your arms casted in plaster. Or, I might be convinced to accept another form of payment," Sallie said, eyeing Carolina.

"Please, not that." Nardo pleaded.

"So you want it in the elbows?"

Nardo stood mute for a moment. He seemed troubled, but in the end, not troubled enough. When his brother came over to tell him to let Sallie have what he wanted, it cinched it for him.

"Take the girl," he said, gesturing toward the back of the bakery, where the mixers, ovens and pallets of flour were.

Sal grabbed Carolina by the arm and dragged her into the back. He took her against her will on the sacks of flour, delighting in her screams of pain and protest. When he was done, he threw a towel at her, calling her a whore, and telling her to clean herself up. Then he went out to confront Nardo again.

"When I send my guys around, you fucking pay them. Or, I'll turn that *butana* out in the street to give two-dollar blow jobs to every truck driver in New York. *Capisce*?"

Nardo nodded. The shame was just beginning to wash over him. It would be his forever.

Within a few months, Carolina was showing. It was no secret whose child was growing inside of her. Nardo punished her for it, but he still married her. He had to if he wanted to keep the bakery. Everyone in

Bushwick knew the story. Those who didn't soon heard about it from Sallie Gorgeous, who relished in telling it.

The following year, Sallie Gorgeous was arrested for three mob hits in the Bronx. He was convicted and sent to prison for a twenty-five to life sentence. He was still there when Mickey related the story of his true paternity to Butchie.

"That's why Nardo hates you, Butchie. You look just like Sallie Ruttigliano. Except for your eyes, those you got from your mother, and they're kind. Ruttigliano doesn't have a kind bone in his body. You are a symbol and a daily reminder of Nardo's weakness. His brother hates you because he's a fucking asshole. You don't have to take shit from those scumbags anymore. Say the word and I will straighten them out," Mickey offered.

"If you don't mind, Mick, I'd like to square this deal myself," Butchie said.

***

He waited until the brothers got drunk and nasty again. When they started insulting his mother, Butchie stood up to them.

"Call her a *butana* again and I'll bite your windpipe shut, you fucking coward," Butchie said, shoving his father.

Nardo rushed at Butchie and got knocked out cold for his trouble. After dropping the old man, Butchie ran around the table to get at his uncle, who was trying to get away. After seeing his brother felled like a dead tree by one vicious right hand from his nephew, he decided he wanted no further part of this fight. Butchie snatched him by the scruff of his fat neck and the seat of his pants. He dragged him over to the open kitchen window, and hung him out face first.

"You don't come up here anymore, Frankie. If I catch you in this apartment again, you're going right out the fucking window."

Butchie let Francesco plead for his life for a minute. Not wanting to be dropped three stories to his death, Francesco begged with a purpose. When he agreed to leave the apartment and never come back, Butchie led him to the door by his ear, before slamming it in his face.

When Nardo came to, Butchie explained their new living arrangement. He would never again call him Papa—not in front of anyone, not for any reason. If Nardo so much as laid an angry hand on his mother again, Butchie assured him he wouldn't live long enough to regret it. If he even spoke disrespectfully to her, Butchie promised he would drag his fat ass out onto Knickerbocker Avenue, where he would beat him like the cur he was. After Nardo said he understood, Butchie back handed him across the face—twice.

"The first one was a lesson. The second one was so you don't forget it. Now, get the fuck out of my sight."

CHAPTER ELEVEN

January 1971
Bushwick

When Butchie got to Fat Sam's clubhouse, in the former storefront of Bruno Badlamenti's latticini, he was prevented from entering by two of Sam's goons.

"This is private property, *copper*. You don't get to come in here," Donato Trinchera spat. He was the larger of Fat Sam's bodyguards.

"I need a word with your boss," Butchie told him.

"He's not seeing visitors," Vito Meloro, the other bodyguard jumped in, poking him in the chest. "Least of all, Italian cops who hate their own."

Butchie looked down at the gangster's fingers in his chest. He grinned at the thug. Meloro had only the briefest moment to appreciate the derangement behind that smile before all hell broke loose.

Meloro hit the ground with a thud after Butchie shattered his jaw with his lead sap. Trinchera took two shots to knock out, but his jaw was just as broken. He leaned over the two goons to admire his work and ensure they didn't require any more of his tender administration. Satisfied, he stepped over the fallen thugs and entered the clubhouse.

He spied Fat Sam at the card table in front of the espresso bar. He was playing pinochle with a group of the older Italian men from the neighborhood. Also in the group was Father Alphonso Spinatro, one of the parish priests from St. Brigid's. He said the Italian mass on Sunday mornings which Butchie's parents attended.

"Hi, Father," Butchie greeted the priest as he advanced on the card table. Fat Sam looked up, confused.

"How the fuck did you get in here?" the gangster demanded.

"I let myself in," Butchie informed him as he overturned the card table, scattering cards, money, the players and their espresso cups in every direction.

He grabbed Fat Sam by the throat and lifted him out of his chair and drove him to the floor. Standing over him, Butchie took out his five shot off-duty revolver and shoved it into his mouth. Fat Sam looked into Butchie's impassive, dead eyes and instantly comprehended the very great peril he was in. Indelicato's face became a mask of terror.

"Listen carefully," Butchie cautioned him. "Because you only get to hear this once. The Bucciogrossos are now exempt from paying you for protection. If you set one foot in the bakery, if you come near any member of my family, I will end you. If anything should happen—a broken window for instance, or an electrical fire, even an act of God—I'm coming to talk to you about it. But trust me on this, if I come back here, my face will be the last thing you ever see in this life. *Capisce*?"

Butchie took the gun out of Sam's mouth to let him answer.

"I'm not going to fuck with you, Butchie. But when Lilo hears what you did today, he's not going to like it. He'll have something to say about it."

"That's why he's next on my list of phony-baloney tough guys who get a visit. I'll discuss it with him when I see him."

Butchie put his gun away and got off the frightened gangster. He made a point of *not* helping Fat Sam off the floor, slapping his hand away when he reached up for assistance.

"One other thing," Butchie told him before he left. "You will *not* come to the bakery for the rent. You want it, you get it from me. But you're going to have to come to the precinct for it."

As Butchie stepped over Trinchera and Meloro, still laying in the doorway, he knew Fat Sam would never come within a block of the ancient precinct-house on DeKalb Avenue. The bakery was now rent free, as well as unencumbered by the fictitious protection fee. Now Butchie just had to make Carmine Gigante understand the new rules.

Before heading down to the Magic Lantern Bar on Bath Avenue in Bensonhurst, from where Lilo Gigante was known to hold court and run the Bonanno's business, Butchie called his partner to let him know where he was going, and why—just in case he didn't come back.

Eamon *Fast Eddie* Curran had been a boxer in his native Belfast. He got the nickname because of his lightning-fast hands, and propensity for quick knockouts. Butchie had volunteered to work with Curran for the very reason every other cop in the command refused to. Curran was assiduously honest, and would have nothing to do with the payoffs from the mobsters which were a common practice in the NYPD at the time. This rectitude cast suspicion on him from the other cops, who routinely took money to look the other way. Butchie heard about it, and asked Curran directly why he wouldn't take the money.

"I come *tree tousand* miles to enforce the law in Brooklyn, Boyo. *Dat's* exactly what I intend to do," Eddie told him, in his thick Irish brogue.

Butchie had noticed Curran's brogue was as much for effect as it was ingrained in his manner of speech. He seemed to get more Irish when he wanted to drive home his point. Evidently, he wanted to be sure he was understood on *this* particular subject.

"It's just a little gambling and whores," Butchie challenged. "What's the harm?"

"There's a plague over *dis* land, Boyo, and it's called *La Cosa Nostra*. If you don't *tink* every dollar of bribe money isn't geared to further *dat* very *ting*, then you're a *shite* and an *ijit*. They are enslaving and killing the people of *dis* neighborhood as surely as if they were to put them in shackles. And every cop who takes their money is complicit. It's no different than Judas and his *tirty* pieces of silver. But *ye* already know that, Giuseppe. *You* don't drink from the poisoned trough either. So, what do *ye* say ye stop pulling *me* wire and get to the *fookin* point?"

"I wanna work with you, Eddie," Butchie said. "You do the right thing for the right reasons. I won't take their money either. I want to hurt them. I want to drive them out of Bushwick."

"I don't *tink* we are enough to be rid of *dem*. Sure, we'll get no other help. We can make their lives miserable though. So, if *yer'* willing, Boyo, then I'm in."

Much to the chagrin of the mobsters, miserable and more is exactly what the two cops made them. Together they became an ever-present nuisance to the gamblers, pimps and drug peddlers. Early on, several of their more entrenched and corrupt fellow officers tried to intervene on the gangsters' behalf. After the first few were beaten bloody in the locker room, they stopped asking. Everyone finally realized these two cops would never relent. They would just have to be avoided. The most obvious solution was out of the question. The mob knew that killing two uniform police officers would bring down such swift and absolute retribution, La Cosa Nostra would cease to exist.

When Butchie told Eddie what he intended to do, Curran had only one question.

"Are we taking my car, or yours?"

CHAPTER TWELVE

July 1964
Belfast

Eddie Curran had not always been known as *Fast Eddie*. As a sixteen-year-old amateur boxer with great promise in his native Northern Ireland, Eddie was originally known as *Pretty Boy Curran*. Tall for a middleweight, Curran was 165 pounds of lean, wiry muscle. With a fine bone structure, featuring high cheekbones and a strong cleft chin, he couldn't help being handsome. His tousled blond hair—thick and wavy on top—framed his face and exposed his muscular neck, as he kept it short on the sides and back. But it was the warm, inviting blue eyes, and the perfect, perpetual smile which inspired women to literally swoon. It's hard not to like someone who seems so genuinely happy. Hard, but not impossible.

Danny Boy Hatton did not like Eddie Curran. He had watched with dismay as Curran took apart every Protestant fighter in Belfast. Hatton boiled inside when he heard the women—Catholic and Protestant alike—cooing over Eddie's movie star good looks. Dan didn't like that at all. He also didn't like Eddie's long dead Republican father. He didn't like his mother—re-married to the Provo Commander for this district. He hated that Provo Commander, Martin Boland, so much he wanted to kill him. He was only prevented from doing so by Special Branch Head Constable Terrance Chichester, who told Dan, Martin Boland was not to be touched.

Hatton also didn't like the rest of the uppity papists, clamoring to take the hard-earned benefits from the loyalists in Belfast, who he believed rightfully deserved them.

Dan Hatton was a loyal subject of the Queen, a member of the Orange Order, and a Major in the Ulster Special Constabulary. This was the civilian auxiliary of the official RUC. While the Specials were given tacit powers to help keep the peace, they were not authorized to detain, arrest or otherwise interfere with the citizenry.

They kept half of that promise. They left the Protestant people of Belfast alone. However, the Catholic portion of Northern Ireland discovered the Specials to be an ever-present, hyper-violent organ of the Royal Ulster Constabulary—doing things the RUC would have liked to but couldn't. Things like indiscriminate beatings, kidnappings, and murder were their own special purview. The RUC had to be more discreet. They were after all, the police. They had taken an oath to protect *all* of the people. They were decidedly less enthusiastic when it came to protecting Catholics. But, they left the outright abuse to their auxiliary, who had taken an oath only to protect and promote the Protestant ascendancy in Northern Ireland.

Dan Hatton was a thirty-year-old shipbuilder who worked at the Harland and Wolff Shipping yards. He had ascended to a lower management position as a crew chief. His responsibilities consisted of the hiring of crews to work on a daily basis. It was fortunate there were other crew chiefs working at Harland and Wolff. Or a Catholic never could have been hired. Dan took it a step further. He wouldn't hire a man unless he held a membership card in the Orange Order—the secret society dedicated to the Protestant ascendancy and keeping at bay the Catholic majority. It went without saying, Catholics need not apply.

Hatton was particularly incensed at the Catholics in Belfast since his wife left him. Through three years of marriage, he was seldom home. Between working at the shipyard, going to secret meetings of the Orange Order, and patrolling nightly with his squad from the Specials, his wife Ciara rarely saw her husband. She developed a brooding resentment because of it. On the rare occasions when he would be home for supper, Ciara grew tired of hearing her husband rail against "the bastard papists" ruining the country. When finally, she disagreed with him, suggesting he was somehow afraid of them, he beat her so severely she had to be hospitalized. She left the hospital when

Dan Hatton conveniently was at work. She returned home only long enough to pack a suitcase and leave forever.

She ended up in the Bronx, working as a live-in nanny in Riverdale. Dan never thought to look in America, so he never found her. Truth be told, with his anti-Catholic tripartite of self-appointed duties; shunning the Catholics at the shipyards, plotting against them with the Orange Order, and outright abusing them with the Specials, he was too busy to mount much of a search. Being a stupid man, he let his mind run wild with Catholic conspiracy. While there was no evidence to suggest as much, Hatton imagined his wife had left him for a Catholic, and was laughing at him from the other side of the Shankill Road. With this toxin effecting an already poisoned mind, Hatton began taking particular exception to couples failing to respect this segregation Hatton believed was his God-given mission to enforce. He would have no mercy for a Catholic man found in the company of a Protestant woman, nor vice versa.

Eddie was escorting Caitlin McGurk home from the City Central Boxing Gym. The gym, on the protestant side of the Shankill Road, was owned by her father. Eddie's trainer, Brian *Bounce* McGurk was a Protestant. McGurk was also a reluctant member of the Orange Order. Being so was an absolute requirement for a merchant in Belfast. Bounce would have preferred to remain neutral. In most issues, he did. His stable of fighters were evenly divided between Catholics and *Prods*. He didn't discriminate. But, as a business owner, he was forced to declare a side. There really was no choice which side he had to pick. Not if he wished to stay in business. If he didn't join the Orange Oder, the B Specials would have burnt his gym to the ground. He knew Danny Boy Hatton was a bigot, but not really being an insider, Bounce had no idea how dangerous he truly was.

He never anticipated Hatton would be there to shatter his life to pieces the night he asked Eddie Curran to see his daughter home safe from the gym. Bounce trusted Eddie explicitly. He knew he would protect his daughter with his life if need be. So he had little worries about the three block walk. Eddie and Caitlin were two blocks into the Protestant side of the Shankill when they saw Dan Hatton and his Specials come out of the RUC Barracks up the road.

The two were just friends. Caitlin was fourteen. She had a healthy crush on the handsome young boxer. Only sixteen himself, Eddie was awkward around girls, despite the inordinate attention women paid him. He liked

Caitlin, but propriety and the deep respect Eddie held for her and her father would not permit him to overstep his bounds. He would keep his feelings for her to himself but remain exceedingly protective. They could hide their feelings for each other all they wanted. They weren't fooling Dan Hatton.

The two of them were laughing and joking as they walked up the Shankill Road. They didn't concern themselves with the approaching squad of Specials, oblivious of them until they had blocked the young couple's path, and surrounded them.

"Good evening, Constables. May I be of some assistance?" Eddie asked politely, as he put his arm protectively around Caitlin's shoulders.

This was exactly the worst thing he could do in front of Major Hatton.

"Take your filthy, papist mitts off the girl, Provo," Hatton growled at Eddie.

Eddie complied only as far as removing his arm from around her shoulder, but he instinctively moved a step closer, and gently put his hand on her elbow.

"I *tink ye'* have me mistaken for some other *feller*," Eddie said. "I am Catholic, but I'm certainly no papist. I wouldn't know the Pope if he fell on me. Sure, I wouldn't go to church at all, but for *me* Ma. She insists, you know. And I am no Provo. The IRA are a tinker's promise, offering deliverance to the willfully naïve. They're *nuthin* but gangsters with political slogans. No reasonable person would have fuck-all to do with them. And I am *nuthin* if not reasonable."

Eddie said all this with the practiced, humble, and disarming smile he had been charming everyone with since he was a young boy. It had been serving him so well for so long, he had every expectation it would work with Dan Hatton.

Eddie's expectations were shattered simultaneously with his nose. He never saw the butt-stroke coming. The second stroke of Hatton's Enfield rifle hit Eddie square in the left cheekbone, breaking it. The return stroke landed flush on the right side of Eddie's jaw, shattering that as well, and casting his broken teeth into the street. His face was now a mass of chewed meat, gushing blood. Eddie finally hit the floor. A handful of the Specials then exuberantly applied their brogans to his prone and writhing body—until finally he stopped moving. They thought he was dead.

At this point he would have considered death a mercy. Instead, he found himself broken, but fully conscious—incapable of even making a sound. All he could do was watch, unable to intervene for what happened next. Seemingly paralyzed, he was denied even the slightest mercy of being able to look away.

Caitlin was wailing in horror. She was consumed by fear and disbelief. She had never witnessed such brutality. Even accustomed to violence as she was—being raised in a boxing gym in the heart of inner-city Belfast—she could not have been prepared for the outright hatred emanating from the Specials in general, and their leader, Major Dan Hatton in particular. In a world of viciousness and barbarity, Dan Hatton was without peer in his mastery of those things.

"Shut your *fookin*, filthy cake-hole, you miserable race-traitor cunt!" Hatton said, delivering a vicious backhand across Caitlin's face.

It drove her to her knees. Hatton lifted her up by her strawberry blonde hair and dragged her roughly over to the hood of the car parked at the curb. He bent her over the hood and held her face down by her hair. Though terrified, her eyes met Eddie's. They shared that one brief moment of confusion, each more scared for the other.

"You've been giving *yer* little honey-pot to that papist boyfriend of *yers'*. It's now as polluted as a sewer. Who else have *ye* been fucking? The Monsignor? The Archbishop? And every other mongrel who brings his tongue to the rail, no doubt. It's going to take some doing, but I'm going to fuck the Catholic right out of *ye*."

Caitlin was so terrified, she started hyperventilating—not that she would have been able to form words anyway. So, she was unable to protest. She wouldn't have been able to tell Hatton she was a virgin, even if she had wanted to. All of her fear and concern was for Eddie, who Caitlin thought was either dead, or about to die. She was unconcerned for her own safety—let alone her virtue—and blamed herself for Eddie being murdered. Which seemed to her to be the case. Her concentration was fractured like that. But still, her gaze was focused on Eddie's fallen form. Until Hatton cut away her bell-bottomed jumper and underwear with a trench knife, pulling them away from her body. When he violently shoved his oaken truncheon up, and into her, all of her concentration was focused laser-like on the unbearable searing pain she was suddenly experiencing.

Mercifully, Caitlin lost consciousness, the body being able to endure only so much. The last thing she saw before passing out was the perfect look of agony fixed on the face of Eddie Curran. She did not hear Hatton's surprised laugh when he discovered he had broken her hymen. She was unaware as he continued to brutalize her with that awful stick—shoving it anywhere he thought he could do her harm. She was spared the indignity of hearing the other Specials argue, and jockey for position to violate her next. They did violate her, taking turns raping her already fractured body. When Hatton had grown tired and unsatisfied with the damage he was inflicting by inserting his truncheon into her, he began beating her with it. While his charges continued to rape and sodomize her, Hatton used his bloody stick to turn her head and body into a roiling sea of bruising.

Caitlin was aware of none of it. She would only come to understand the totality of the horror she had been subjected to when she came out of the coma several days after. But Eddie heard it all. He heard Hatton's threats. He heard Caitlin gasp, and then scream when Hatton first violated her. Eddie heard her go silent, while the pack of animals cackled and grunted and continued to tear at her. He endured the sounds of the Specials laughing and backslapping each other as Hatton and his troops stepped over Eddie and Caitlin and left them for dead.

Eddie laid there silently weeping, praying God would let him die. He regarded himself with absolute repugnance for failing to protect Caitlin. He admitted to himself for the first time he loved her, and hated himself for witnessing her destruction—doing nothing to prevent it. That he had been maimed and incapacitated by the same brutal mob was of no consolation. He would never forgive himself. But, as he lay in the pool of blood and desolation, he vowed if he lived, he would have vengeance. Not for himself—he didn't care what they did to him. But they would pay for hurting Kaitlyn.

CHAPTER THIRTEEN

July 1964
Belfast

Eddie and Caitlin did not die. Someone had called an ambulance. There were witnesses. They had watched Hatton and his squad beat Eddie half to death, and gang-rape and brutalize Caitlin. They knew who the perpetrators were. Everybody knew who the dreaded B-Specials were. The witnesses even tried to tell the RUC Special Branch detectives what they had seen. But when they were assured they were mistaken, and if they valued their lives even a little, they would refrain from telling people what they thought they saw, they came to their senses and didn't see anything after all.

There was still the matter of Caitlin and Eddie. They knew what happened to them, and who was responsible. They were prepared to share it with the Special Branch. Hatton hadn't intended to leave them alive. Because of that mistake, he resolved he was going to have to kill them all over again.

Head Constable Terrance Chichester was the senior detective in the Special Branch of the RUC. For many years, his primary responsibility was to keep the Catholic majority of Ulster in their place. Mandated to protect the Protestant ascendancy, he used the Ulster Special Constabulary as his secret weapon to instill fear in the hearts of the hated Catholics. The Specials were the iron fist. Chichester was the velvet glove. The result was the same. The Catholics remained fearful and hammered into compliance.

In recent years, Chichester's job had become complicated. With the creation of the Northern Ireland Civil Rights Association, the Catholics now had a unified voice of reason, which had the temerity to insist they somehow deserved equal treatment. They started making what Chichester and the sitting power in Ulster considered to be unreasonable demands. They were looking for basic human rights and dignity—like the vote, and fairness and equality in housing and employment. With a high profile and access to the media, Chichester was finding it increasingly difficult to continue to indiscriminately beat them down.

That's where the Specials were useful, but it was not without its problems. Chichester knew they were savages given to random violence. He had no problem with the use of violence. He just wanted it applied for an effective purpose.

The other problem with the Specials, Chichester knew, was their imbecilic sense of entitlement. They didn't care what they did, or in front of whom they did it. This included murders, rapes, kidnappings and whatever else the Orange idiots felt like doing to slake their bloody thirst. Chichester knew if one of the bleeding-heart media outlets like the BBC decided to start following the Specials around with a camera, the Ministry of Justice would run out of rope before they got finished hanging everyone who deserved it.

In conjunction with the civil rights movement, Chichester had to deal with the re-emergence of the Provisional Irish Republican Army. At this point they were little more than a nuisance, engaging in commercial robberies and the destruction of Protestant-owned businesses and property. Chichester knew with the civil rights movement gaining attention, it wouldn't be long before the Irish-American public started throwing money at the *Provos*. The Americans loved giving their money to the underdog, no matter how stupid and ridiculous they might be. Once the money started rolling in, Chichester knew it wouldn't be long before they weaponized themselves. Bombings and assassinations were sure to follow.

With that in mind, Chichester busied himself with identifying the Provo Commander for the Ulster area. Then he introduced an undercover operative to Martin Boland with weapons to sell in exchange for blowing up the House of Parliament at Stormont Castle. The bait was too juicy, and Boland jumped at it.

Grabbed in secret, Boland rolled on himself and his compatriots in record time. When he was offered the opportunity to remain in place, as Chichester's secret informer, he immediately accepted. But, first he had to admit his criminal past on behalf of the Provos. When he told his story, the level of treachery, the things he had already done, was chilling even to the blood of a committed sociopath like Terrance Chichester.

Chichester would use Boland to great effect, but he was increasingly wary of him. He started to feel, despite having a window into the plans of the Provos, working an asset like Boland was a bit like holding onto a tiger by the ears. You didn't want to do it, but you didn't dare let go.

This conniving, duplicitous, and morally corrupt man was the same Head Constable of the RUC assigned to go see Brian Bounce McGurk. Bounce thought the constable was there to help. Chichester was. He was going to help himself, and this boxing coach and his broken daughter could be damned in the process, for all Chichester cared.

"What does your daughter remember, Mr. McGurk?"

"She remembers everything—right up to the time she passed out. But the Curran boy saw and heard all of it. They'll tell you. It was Danny Boy Hatton and those animals of his."

"If your daughter passed out during the attack, it's impossible to say what happened to her, and the boy's jaw is wired shut. He won't be talking to anyone for a while."

"Are *ye* outta *yer fookin* mind, Constable? My little girl is lying in hospital ripped to shreds. She may yet die—Hatton tore her insides up so bad. She's feverish and delirious. They think she has an infection. She spends half the day weeping, and that's only when she's not screaming. You can't be contemplating letting that animal get away with this?"

"How am I to make a case with a delirious girl, and a boy beaten silly and mute as witnesses? No prosecutor would touch such a case."

"You're going to cover this up," Bounce realized. "Then, just get the *fook* out of here, Chichester. I've no need of *ye*. I'll kill the stick swinging bastard *meself*!"

"And I'll see you hang for it," Chichester told him calmly. "You don't want to hear this, McGurk, but Major Hatton is all that stands between us and being overrun by those papist animals. He protects our way of life. While those diseased vermin are breeding like rabbits, Hatton is keeping them where they belong; behind that sodding fence. He is useful to me. You and your slut daughter are not. So, he will not be prosecuted, and he will not be touched. Do I make myself clear?"

"You bloody bastard!"

"Yes, I suppose I am. But unlike you and your family, I provide an essential service. I keep the barbarians at the gate. Does Belfast really need a boxing gym? For that matter, does it need a boxing coach? I don't think you want me considering those questions for too long. And your righteous indignation will do you no good whatsoever while you're beating out the flames on your children's backs."

McGurk was beginning to understand the difference between being a reluctant member of the Orange Order—as he was—and being a committed zealot with an insatiable appetite for mayhem—as Dan Hatton most certainly was. The fact of the matter, pointed out in excruciating detail by Constable Chichester, was Bounce McGurk had nowhere to turn. Dan Hatton was at the very top of the Protestant food chain. Brian McGurk and his family were the meat. Chichester assured him if they didn't behave, they would be eaten.

"You're going to have to explain the ways of the world to your daughter. Make her understand. Your family's lives depend on it. Then you're going to have to sit on that fighter of yours. I'll be having a word with him when those wires come off his jaw. But if he somehow manages to communicate something else between now and then, I won't be the one coming to see him. Then he gets Danny Boy Hatton, in all of his rage and glory. I think we both know how that ends."

McGurk did explain the situation to his daughter. He told her they had no other choice but to forget about the event and move on. She understood perfectly. Caitlin, still believing Eddie Curran was dead, turned her face forlornly away from her father and began to quietly weep.

Brian McGurk never mentioned Eddie had survived. He didn't realize his daughter's attachment to the boy. It might have helped if she knew. But, perhaps nothing would have helped. Her fever spiked that night. The infection running rampant in her torn and shattered insides caused her to start bleeding internally again. The fevered seizures took their toll. She died alone and in agony, never knowing the only boy she had ever loved was lying on a gurney down the hall, desperately in love with her.

After burying his daughter, Brian McGurk went in to see Eddie Curran. He broke the news about Caitlin, but Eddie already knew. Because he couldn't speak, the nurses thought he was deaf as well. They showed absolutely no restraint with respect to their conversations on the ward. By this time, Eddie was healing. He was able to talk after a fashion, around his wired jaw.

Brian McGurk had a hard time looking at the disfigured face of his fighter. Eddie's once exquisite bone structure had been marred forever by the rifle butt of Dan Hatton. Until a week ago, he had been known as *Pretty Boy* Curran. No one would ever be tempted to call him that again. Because of his extraordinary hand speed, in deference, they would call him *Fast Eddie*. Behind his back, they would call him *Hatchet Face*. But this was in the future, and a continent away. Right now, they both had things which needed saying. When they were done, Brian would have preferred not to have heard Eddie's point of view. It would leave him thoroughly ashamed of himself.

"The last thing Caitlin would want us to do is to sacrifice ourselves for a fight we can't hope to win," McGurk said.

"Is *dat* what *ye* believe, Brian? Or are *ye* so in love with the idea of being *the* Protestant boxing coach in Belfast, *ye'd* forsake *yer* own daughter?"

"All I have left is the gym, Eddie. What would you have me do?"

"*Ye* could have the balls *ye* were born with, for starters."

"I can't do that. This is a war I can't win, and the cost of losing is too dear. I'm not young. I can't start over."

"You are the worst kind of coward, Brian. *Ye* have literally lost *everything*, and *ye're* unwilling to confront the evil and the injustice which took it from *ye*."

"You're just a boy. What do you know about anything?"

"I know *dat* all *ye* care about is *dat* box of bricks with a ring in it. *Ye've* turned *yer* back on the murder and rape of *yer* own family, just so *ye* could keep it. Why? Because it has *yer* name on it? Good. They can bury *ye* in it. It isn't worth the brick and mortar that built it. I'll never set foot in there again. I'm going to stay on the Catholic side of Belfast from now on. I'll fight for the Republican Club up on the Crumlin Road, until I've crippled every one of *yer* fighters. I'll leave *ye* with nothing, because it's what *ye* deserve."

"I have a wife and another daughter I have to protect. What would you do, if you were me?"

"Send them away, Bounce. *Ye* can't protect them, and *ye* won't when the time comes anyway. It's going to get dark around here. *Ye* don't have the minerals for what comes next."

"What are you thinking about, Eddie?"

"I'm well past the point of *tinking*. When I heal, Belfast will find itself knee deep in blood. To start with, I'm going to burn *yer* gym to the *fookin* ground. *Ye* think *ye* traded *yer* daughter's life for it. But, *dat's* not a fair trade. I'm won't let you keep it. When it's gone, I'm going to murder every last one of those savages who hurt Caitlin. I couldn't save her life, but I *will* avenge her."

CHAPTER FOURTEEN

September 1964
Belfast

When Eddie Curran got home from the hospital later in August, he was discomforted by many things. Not the least of which was his own reflection staring back at him from the mirror. The wires had come off, and the bones were mending. But the surgeons had given him fair warning. His appearance would never approximate its former self. They never mentioned plastic surgery. They knew without asking the medical treatment required to fix his face beyond functionality was not an option for a 17- year-old amateur fighter, living in a tenement in the Catholic ghetto of Belfast. Eddie understood the wad of featureless dough staring back at him, with the mouth full of broken stumps which once were perfect teeth, would be permanent companions. The only remnant left of his once fair countenance was his movie star blond hair, and the piercing blue eyes. These had already begun to feel like an anachronism to him.

Beyond the disappointment of his shattered face, Eddie was suffering far worse from an inner torment. He had been carrying the weight of Caitlin's death like a millstone. He knew he needed to remain patient until he was fit enough, but patience was not his strong suit. He had a plan and he wanted to act upon it. He thought avenging Caitlin would somehow ameliorate his anger and assuage his guilt for letting it happen. He understood Caitlin's death was at the hands of others, but the responsibility for her safety was his. His failure to protect her would weigh on him for the rest of his life.

While all of this was pressing down on Eddie, he had the added distraction of having to listen to his stepfather. Eddie had never liked the man. Not since he muscled his way into his and his mother's lives after the murder of his father. Martin Boland moved in when Eddie was six years old. The bad vibes were immediate and constant.

Martin Boland worked for a trucking firm in Castlereagh. In short order, he came to manage it. This was useful for his true calling. Martin Boland was the Area Commander of the nascent Provisional IRA in Belfast. The trucking business gave Martin the cover to smuggle all manner of things throughout the six counties of the north. Things like secret plans, weaponry and explosives could now be put into willing hands. Increasingly, the primary cargo moving in Boland's trucks was heroin. Despite his other stated affiliations, Martin Boland was a drug dealer.

With his work down at the port, and a natural criminal acumen, Boland came in contact with a good number of ships arriving from Turkey and Italy. Many of the merchant shipmen were entrepreneurs in their own right. Living in a poor ghetto, Boland understood the demand of heroin. With his transportation network already set, he just had to solidify his distribution. The Provos were a ready-made and organized apparatus. All he had to do was convince the other area commanders the foray into narcotics was a necessary evil to raise the funds required to carry on the struggle. The other zealots blindly jumped at the chance to participate. In truth, very little of the proceeds ever made it into the coffers of the IRA. This was Boland's thing, and he was keeping the lion's share for himself.

Eddie remembered only vaguely the time before his father's murder. In the year or so before, he remembered Boland being a constant presence at the house. Eddie's father was a committed Republican, and a stout supporter for Catholic civil rights. His father saw the forming Provos as a possible vehicle to achieve equality. Michael Curran was a trained accountant and a born manager, but he could see the IRA needed much in the way of organization. Most frequently Curran knew, the left hand didn't know what the right hand was doing. This he hoped to change. He joined the Provos with the intention of helping them better consolidate their efforts at fund raising and management of their everyday affairs. He was recruited by Martin Boland for that express purpose, or so he was led to believe.

Michael began by setting up books for the various revenue streams coming in. In addition, he instituted a system of accounting for their dispersals of funds, which seemed to be all out of kilter with the reported revenue. A full ninety percent of income was being reported as spent on weapons and other material. However, less than ten percent of that expenditure could be justified by receipts or other documentation.

Boland convinced Michael he needed his help to rectify this. In truth, he needed a skilled accountant to help him organize and hide his growing profits from the narco trade he had spider-webbed all over the north. Boland's mistake was in imagining a man like Michael Curran would ever willingly participate in such an undertaking.

Eddie remembered a bitter argument between his father and Martin Boland. They came to blows before his father physically ejected Boland from the house. This was two days before his father had been found shot and beaten to death. Whoever committed the murder dumped Michael Curran unceremoniously on the Catholic side of the Shankill Road.

Boland made a big production of lionizing Curran as a martyr to the cause. The Provos buried him in uniform with full military honors. Boland worked the story hard. He convinced everyone the murder was done at the behest of the Orange Order, and by the hands of the RUC. But the bullets dug out of Michael Curran's body at the autopsy were American made, not the British ordnance it would have been if the RUC, or even the B-Specials had been involved.

Eddie's mother was just twenty-two. She had no other family, and no means of support. Having a thing for the pretty Meg Curran already, Boland used her financial need as the leverage to insinuate himself into the family. They married a year later. Eddie thought the whole arrangement was just wrong. It felt like an invasion. As he grew older, he accepted his enmity for Martin Boland might just be the resentment of a boy who missed his father. He knew it wasn't Martin's fault he wasn't Michael Curran. But try as he might, he could never cotton to the man. He sensed a profound aura of falseness about him.

Presently, Martin Boland was annoying Eddie with a constant recruitment pitch, imploring him to take his place within the struggle. When enticement failed, he tried guilt.

"Your father was murdered by these swine. He gave his life for the cause, so you could have something better. Will *ye* do nothing? Will *ye* turn your back on your *da'*?"

"Ah, *fook* off, Boland. I've no interest in your bloody gang of misfits. What are *ye* gonna do for me, knock over a few bakeries, and sing songs about me in the pubs?"

Since the attack, Boland was anxious to recruit Eddie. Now he saw another opportunity arise. Head Constable Terrance Chichester was looking to speak to the boy. Boland knew this was only to make sure Eddie wouldn't be rocking the boat about the murder of the McGurk girl. If he could convince Eddie that Chichester meant him harm—he had something to do with the murder of Caitlin—Boland thought he might be able to direct the young man's anger for his own purposes.

As Chichester's informant, Martin Boland enjoyed his protection. Recently, the constable had gotten an inkling about the narcotics scheme. Chichester had no idea of the vastness of the operation, or the incredible revenue stream it generated, but Boland knew he would tip to it eventually. Then he knew Chichester would insist on a piece. It wouldn't be a small piece.

Boland was hoping he could remove Chichester from the equation, and sacrifice Michael Curran's bastard to do it. He never liked the boy anyway. With his diffident attitude and accusing eyes, Boland would be glad to be rid of him. People with a conscience were so inconvenient to sociopathic criminals without one.

"When are you going to see Chichester?" Boland asked.

"The day after tomorrow," Eddie said.

"Do you know what he wants?"

"Yeah. That coward, Bounce told me. He wants me to agree to forget all about what happened to Caitlin."

"What are you going to tell him?"

"*Dat* I didn't see a *fookin ting*. But there won't be any forgetting. He's on the list."

"You've got a list. That's good. We may be able to help each other."

"How do *ye* figure?" Eddie asked him.

Martin went into his study and came out with a flat packet of gray, clay-like material wrapped in cellophane. He had a watch face with tiny electric spring-loaded tines sticking out of the back. These were wired to red and black objects with copper prongs sticking out of one end. He showed Eddie how to assemble the items. Then he told him what they were.

The clay-like substance was gelignite, enough to take down an entire floor of an RUC barracks. The red and black prongs were detonators. They would be inserted into the plastique and wired into the back of the watch. Once the tines on the back of the watch face were pressed into the plastique, the whole thing went active. The watch was set as a two-hour timer. After the time elapsed, the circuit would close, sending a small electrical charge, detonating the explosives.

"When *ye* get to his office and he's not looking, place the packet at your feet. Gently step down on the watch face and slide it under Chichester's desk. Then wrap up the interview, because you've only got two hours, unless *ye* want to be just so many blood spots on the rubble."

"How am I supposed to sneak a bomb into a police barracks?" Eddie asked.

"Chichester doesn't know how injured *ye* are. We're going to put your left arm in a cast. We'll carve out the inside and insert the package into the void. Put the arm in a sling, and no one will ever see it. We'll wrap the package in gauze. The whole thing will be tucked neatly against your body."

"*Dat* was some fast planning, Martin. *Ye* had the bomb, and a plan to deliver it, just like *dat*! Why don't *ye* stop pulling *me* wire, and tell me why *ye* want Chichester dead?"

"He's the senior detective in the Special Branch—in charge of every IRA investigation in Belfast. He also runs those B-Specials as his personal murder squad. He is a dangerous nuisance, and threatens the very existence of Catholic Belfast."

"And yet, he never touches *you*. Everyone knows *yer* the Belfast IRA commander. Why does the senior detective in charge of investigating the IRA pay *ye* no mind? Peculiar, don't *ye* think?"

Boland glared at Eddie, but he did not answer the question.

"Do *ye* want to take care of this *fook* or not?" Boland demanded.

"Set the packet up. I'll kill him, but it won't be for you."

"I don't care who it's for. Just so long as it's done."

CHAPTER FIFTEEN

August 1964
Belfast

The day after next, Eddie let Boland and one of his trained monkeys from the IRA set the cast on his left arm. After it hardened, they cut a rectangular space into the inside, and secreted the bomb. He put the arm in a sling and headed out to his appointment with Head Constable Chichester. On his way, Eddie had the most intense premonition of doom. He had never trusted Martin Boland. Now every instinct in his body was telling him Boland was setting him up. He knew Boland wanted Chichester dead. He wasn't sure why, but he sensed the motive was genuine. So Eddie knew instinctively the bomb would work. The only question in his mind was, would the timer?

Two blocks from the barracks, Eddie stopped in front of a house with a planter in front of it. He pried the watch face off of the bomb and disconnected the detonators. Eddie inserted the spring prongs into the soil of the planter. The second hand began moving. Eddie watched it tick around the watch. At one minute he heard a click, and the faint sound of an electrical charge. The watch stopped moving. The circuit had closed. Eddie left the watch there in the dirt and laughed at the infinite treachery of Martin Boland.

When Eddie got to the RUC barracks he was recognized by every constable there. They knew him as the Catholic fighter who watched his girlfriend get raped and murdered. He was treated to almost universal derision. There were one or two constables who looked on him with pity. Eddie noticed and smiled at them, flashing his broken teeth. He knew they wouldn't be wasting their empathy after that. He was directed upstairs to Chichester's office. No one gave his arm a second glance.

When Eddie got to Chichester's office, he was ushered in by the Head Constable and shown to a seat in front of his desk. Chichester offered him tea. He turned his back to prepare it from the tea service on the shelf behind him. Eddie looked down at his feet and the bottom of the constable's desk. Chichester would never know how close he came to being blown to smithereens this day. Eddie thought perhaps he might tell him before he killed him. Perhaps not.

"It's a terrible thing that happened to you and Miss McGurk. How are you feeling?" Chichester asked.

"Like an ugly *ting*, weak, pathetic, less than a person. Powerless, I guess you could say."

"I meant physically," Chichester said, through narrowing eyes.

"Well then; I'm healing. But *ye* don't care about *dat*. Why don't *ye* just ask me what *ye* want to know?"

"What did you see and hear the night you were attacked?" Chichester asked directly.

"If hypothetically I was to say *dat* I saw Dan Hatton bash *me* face in with a rifle, and *den* watched as he and his goons raped and brutalized Caitlin McGurk—what would happen *den*?" Eddie asked.

Chichester glared at Eddie for a moment. Then he smiled acidly.

"In that case, I would bring your sworn testimony to the Royal Prosecutor to prepare an arrest warrant for Hatton—if that's what you saw. Then it would just be a matter of whether I get to Hatton before he gets to you."

"I'm sure *ye* would break *yer* back trying to win *dat* race," Eddie laughed bitterly. "While I would love to help *ye* with the warrant for Hatton, I'll have to decline. It was dark. I didn't see who confronted us. I have no idea who bashed *me* mug in. I don't know what happened to Caitlin. I was unconscious. I didn't see or hear a *fookin ting*. The next *ting* I remember is waking up in hospital with *me* face wired together."

"In that event, Mr. Curran, without any witnesses to the crime, I will be forced to close the case," Chichester said. Then he smiled that acid smile again. "If you should change your mind, if you decide you did see something, please don't. In that eventuality, I'm quite sure you wouldn't survive the next beating."

"Ah, *dere* it is; the threat. For the record, I am thoroughly and properly scared to death. There'll be no change of mind. But, may I ask *ye* a question, Constable?"

Chichester nodded.

"Why does *me* stepfather want me to kill *ye*?"

"I beg your pardon?" Chichester stammered.

"Oh yeah. He even had a device he wanted me to deliver today—plastic explosives, detonators, and a watch face for a timer. He showed me the whole *ting*, right before I told him no."

Chichester considered this information. He sensed Martin Boland had become a little too independent lately. He had already decided he was going to have to rid himself of the nuisance eventually. Now evidently was the time. He regarded the extraordinarily angry young man in front of him. Chichester thought he could use Eddie's anger to achieve his own purposes.

The constable got up from his desk and removed two folders from a file cabinet behind him. Then he sat down. He removed a reel-to-reel tape player from the drawer in his desk. Eddie recognized a photo of his father on the top file cover. It was a crime scene photo from when he had been murdered. He didn't look too fit in the photos.

"Let me tell you about Martin Boland," the Constable began. "Two years after your father was murdered, I nabbed Martin Boland in a sting. He couldn't *grass* on his mates fast enough. He wanted to give up everybody. When I offered to leave him in place as my secret informant, he leapt at the chance. But before we can register an informant accused of a crime, he has to divulge all of his criminal past. We hold that as leverage against him if he tries to renege on the deal. I'm going to play for you a portion of his debriefing tape. You can decide after where your loyalties lie."

Chichester opened the bottom file. Eddie clearly saw the police arrest photo of Martin Boland attached to it. Chichester removed a tape on a spool from the folder. He cued the tape up and advanced it to a particular place. Then he pressed the play button. Eddie instantly recognized the voice of his stepfather. He listened intently.

I recruited an accountant to help me run the business end of the Provos. He was good with the books and seemed committed. Turns out he wasn't. We live in Belfast for fook's sake. Where does all this principle come from?

He threatened to turn informer. I wanted to clip him right then, but I was having a morale problem in me area. Me numbers were dwindling. I figured I could kill two birds with one stone. So meself and three of me soldiers grabbed Michael Curran right from the front of his house. We took him down to the truck depot where we beat him properly and shot him dead. After dark, we dumped him in the street on the Shankill Road.

It didn't take much to get people to believe the RUC did it. I buried him as a martyr to the cause with full military honors. Before long I had more conscripts than I knew what to do with. I ended up marrying his widow. She's a daffy cunt, but she's fit. After a while the three mugs I used for the job started making noises. They thought they deserved some special consideration for keeping the hit confidential. It occurred to me that if I wanted to keep a secret, I would have to be the only one left alive who knew about it. Since I ran the truck depot and conducted most of me IRA business out of it, it was nothing for me to order them to meet me there.

So, one at a time, I did. They had no idea what was coming until I shot them in the face. Then it was just a matter of waiting until dark before I tossed them out. In six days, I had three more martyrs. It looked like it was raining dead Provos on the Shankill Road. I actually started turning volunteers away. Everyone wanted to join. I was a one-man murder wave, and I blamed it all on the RUC.

Chichester turned off the tape. He regarded Eddie for a moment, trying to gauge his reaction. It was difficult. With the terrible damage to his face, Eddie's expression was an emotionless mask, but his eyes were burning like hot coals. Chichester took three photos out of the homicide file and gave them to Eddie to look at.

"Those were the bullets taken out of your father. They are .30 caliber rifle rounds. We tested them. Nothing available in the UK arsenal could have fired them. But the American M2 carbine could. Now, the only people firing American ammunition through American rifles in Belfast at that time were the Provos. We fished the same ammunition out of the other three idiots who had the bad judgment to try and shake down Martin Boland. That's who your stepfather is, Eddie. I suppose he wants me dead because I know all of that. Now you know it, too. Whatever are you going to do with information like that?"

Eddie stared impassively through the constable. He didn't let on a thing, but the constable could feel the seething fury emanating from him. It was all he would get. Chichester dismissed Curran and sent him home. Eddie's kill list had gotten one name longer.

CHAPTER SIXTEEN

August 1964
Belfast

When Martin Boland got home that night, he encountered Eddie drinking a glass of water in the kitchen. Boland looked like he had seen a ghost.

"What the fook are *ye* doing here?" he demanded.

This confirmed for Eddie that Boland fully expected him to have been blown to smithereens along with Terrance Chichester. The one-minute timer was no mistake.

"I live here, *ye* dumb *fook*! My question is, why didn't your bomb go off? I risked *me* life to deliver it. The least *ye* can do is give me a workable device, *ye fookin* amateur!"

"You delivered the bomb?"

"Yeah, I told *ye* that."

"*Ye* primed the timer by pressing it into the plastique?"

"Yeah. I did everything *ye* told me to," Eddie said, showing Boland the empty rectangle in his cast where the bomb used to be. "Now cut this *fookin ting* off *me* arm."

The hollow in the cast was empty because Eddie had stopped off on his way home from the RUC barracks at his friend Billy Connolly's mechanic shop on the Crumlin Road. He asked Billy if he could keep something for a while at the shop. Billy gave him a padlock with a key and told Eddie he could use one of the lockers in the bathroom. He didn't ask what it was. In Northern Ireland, young men learned early on that not knowing other peoples' business was easier than having to answer for it later. After Eddie had deposited the plastique and detonators in the locker, he came out to ask his friend some mechanical advice.

"Martin is having trouble starting his Edsel. It's a new part—along with the alternator—so I'm thinking it's the ignition switch. Is there a way to test the starter with another source of power, like a battery for instance?"

"Sure, Eddie. *Ye* can see on the starter where the line from the ignition is mounted. *Ye* just connect your leads from a battery on those positive and negative screws. The engine should turn right over if the starter is good."

"How much current would I need?"

"Not much. The ignition switch is only ten amps. That's more than enough."

"Is it a constant current, or just an electrical charge when the switch is turned?"

"Just when the ignition switch is turned. That closes the circuit. It's an intermittent pulse until *ye* turn it off."

"*Tanks*, Billy. I'll be by in a day or two to pick up *me tings*."

"Take a key. If I'm not around, *ye* can let yourself in. Just lock up on your way out."

"Ye'd do that for me, Billy?"

"You're a good lad, Eddie. You've had a terrible run of luck. I don't know what else I *can* do for *ye*. Giving *ye* a key to my shop is the least of it."

The next evening after closing, Eddie returned to the shop and collected his things. While there, he helped himself to two fistfuls of ball bearings Connolly had in a pan of motor oil, with which he was cleaning his tools. After rinsing, drying and bagging up the bearings, Eddie returned home. There, he cut the brick of plastique into three even pieces. Sneaking into Martin Boland's study, he picked the lock on the closet door. Seeing two additional packages of plastique and a box of detonators on the shelf in there, he took them. Noticing the large floor safe, he was pleased to see it had external hinges. Eddie locked up everything in the study on his way out. Returning to his room, he secreted the stolen plastique, detonators and ball bearings beneath the floorboards in his closet.

Eddie changed his clothes. Putting on a black sweatsuit with a hood, and black boxing shoes, he taped his hands. Boxers have always taped their hands. This time though, Eddie taped two four-inch lengths of ¾ inch iron rebar into his palms. Covering these with black leather gloves with the fingers cut off, Eddie took a leisurely run up the Shankill Road, deep into the Protestant side of Belfast—to the home of Danny Boy Hatton.

When they found Hatton the next day, he was slumped dead over the arm of his sofa. Fully clothed, his torn and bloody rear end was sticking up towards the sky. His face had been beaten to an unrecognizable pulp. Every bone had been shattered to paste. But it wasn't what had killed him. The intruder had fired Hatton's own twelve-gauge shotgun, right up his own rectum. He died slowly, and in agony, as he bled out from his shattered insides.

The following night, Eddie was on the sidewalk across the street and up the block from the RUC barracks on the Shankill Road. It was exactly the same time, on the same day of the week, that he and Caitlin had been attacked by Hatton and his goon-squad a month before. Leaderless, Eddie had bet the Specials would still go out on patrol. Vicious pricks that they were—with Hatton or not—Eddie figured they wouldn't let a night pass without trying to ruin someone else's life.

Across the street from where he was hiding between two parked cars, there was a streetlight. On the pole, approximately five feet from the ground, there was affixed a third of a brick of plastique. It had been shaped around the pole so it would explode out toward the sidewalk in a convex pattern. Wedged into the plastique were the two fistfuls of ball bearings. Stuck into the back of this makeshift bomb were the two detonators—with wires connected to them—stretching across the street to where Eddie was kneeling over a ten-amp battery with its positive and negative diodes exposed.

Hatton's squad of Specials came out of the RUC barracks on schedule. Having discovered the fact of their major's murder that morning, Eddie thought they looked like they were spoiling for some payback. Angry and serious, they walked with a determined purpose. While they had no real idea of who was responsible for the crime, Eddie thought they nonetheless were committed to punishing some Catholics for it. They made the left and headed down the sidewalk toward the Catholic section.

When they got adjacent to the light pole, Eddie yelled out "Oy!" to get their attention. He wanted to be sure in the few seconds they had left to live that they understood it was Eddie Curran who was the one who blew their heads clean off. When he saw the look of recognition on their faces, Eddie touched his wires to the battery diodes.

The ensuing pandemonium occurred in the dark. The exploding plastique had sheared the light pole in half. As the top end crashed to the ground, the street was cast in darkness. Eddie casually strolled back to the Catholic ghetto unnoticed.

Several hours later, after closing time, the City Central Boxing Gym abruptly disintegrated into a flaming cascade of flying brick and mortar dust. It was first believed the boiler exploded—and it had—along with everything else. But the overwhelming odor emanating from the rubble had a harsh chemical smell to it. One of the RUC men there to investigate the explosion had been an ordinance man in the British Army. He immediately identified the smell as exploded plastique.

When the RUC later found the wires stretching out of the rubble and across the street, where they were connected to a ten-amp battery, they just assumed Bounce McGurk had run afoul of the IRA.

McGurk knew who made his beloved gym disappear, and it wasn't the IRA. The bomber had told him weeks before he was going to take it from him. He didn't share what he knew with the constables. Old or not, McGurk was starting over. He understood he deserved to be punished after forsaking his daughter. He was forced to concede; this punishment was altogether just.

At 5:00 A.M. the following morning, Martin Boland got into his beloved 1960 Ford Edsel. He bought the car because of its spaciousness. Once he had turned the ignition, the starter kicked the engine right over. The two wires leading from the starter were connected to the third of a brick of plastique wedged into the underside of the car—just under the driver's seat. When the electric charge reached the detonators, Eddie knew what was left of Martin Boland would have to be collected with a spatula. It turned out he didn't need all that spaciousness. In his present state, Boland would have fit in the ashtray.

At 7:00 A.M. the same morning, Head Constable Terrence Chichester was in a buoyant mood as he got into his department-issued, unmarked Wolseley. He had gotten the call about the demise of his renegade informant approximately an hour before. Chichester thought this was going to be a very good day indeed. Until he turned the ignition key and heard an extra click. The extra click caused the constable to briefly experience a feeling of vague uneasiness, but only for a second. A second after, he ceased to exist in solid form.

Later that day, Eddie Curran was inside the closet in Martin Boland's study. He had used a small amount of the remaining plastique to fashion shaped charges around the exterior hinges of Boland's safe. Setting up the detonators, Eddie ran the wires out of the closet, and away from the line of the blast. Touching those wires to a ten-amp battery, there was a satisfying *crumph* as the explosive ignited. If he had been a Marine, Eddie would have thought to yell "Fire in the hole!" When he went into the closet to investigate the safe, the door was hanging off, the contents inside undisturbed. What he found in there was a little over a million British pounds. He took ten thousand of them for himself. He left the remainder on the kitchen table, along with a note, which said simply, "Bye, Mum."

Eddie grabbed his passport and packed an overnight bag. He got in a cab to Aldergrove Airport. There he caught a flight to Heathrow in London, where he made his connecting flight to the newly renamed John F. Kennedy International Airport. Eddie was meeting a policeman in New York he had befriended a year before, when he was part of a Northern Irish delegation of boxers who travelled to New York to compete against the NYPD boxing team. Mick *The Quick* Doheny would be waiting for Eddie Curran at JFK.

CHAPTER SEVENTEEN

January 1969
Bushwick

Butchie and Eddie got to the Magic Lantern in Eddie's beat up Dodge Dart. At the trunk, they armed themselves with cut-down shotguns. Over those, they wore knee-length trench-coats with the pockets cut out. They entered the bar with their fingers already on the triggers beneath their coats. Butchie spotted Lilo in the back of the bar reading a racing form. He walked directly over to him. Meanwhile, Eddie spied the two Sicilian henchmen who were Lilo's bodyguards ensconced at the front of the bar. He brought his shotgun up and cautioned them.

"Right about now would be a good time to stay perfectly still, unless *ye* want me to make it a permanent *fookin* condition," Eddie said.

The two zips held their hands up in compliance.

Butchie walked right up to Lilo's booth and slid into the bench across from him. Gigante looked up and registered recognition. But Lilo was confused. He knew who Butchie was. He just didn't know why he was here. He was particularly curious as to why the angry cop had a shotgun pointed at his groin from across the table.

"Do you know who I am?" Butchie asked.

"Of course, I do," Lilo said. "You're the Italian cop in the 83rd who hates Italians. You work with that Irish lunatic who has my bodyguards playing Simon says right now at the front of the bar."

"Close, but not exactly," Butchie corrected him. "What I hate are you Mafia scumbags preying on the innocent people in the neighborhood. You're like carrion picking at the flesh of a dying animal. But I'm not here on behalf of them. You've got them so scared shitless; they wouldn't let me help them anyway. I can't save everybody. I'm here for one family only—my own."

"How does this concern me?" Lilo asked.

"This morning I straightened out one of your *Capos*. I had to put his bodyguards in the hospital to get in to see him. I explained some new rules to him. I also treated him somewhat less cordially than he is accustomed to. I wanted you to hear about it from me. I'm not apologizing. I just want you aware of the new rules. Your life depends on you and your people adhering to them."

"Does it?" Lilo said, smiling. "So, what's this new arrangement?"

"The Bucciogrossos are no longer to be touched. We are not paying you vermin—for anything. If any of his goons or yours' should come to the bakery—if so much as a window gets broken, or a truck gets vandalized—I will wipe you out from the bottom to the top. I want you to understand; this is *your* problem now. You need to make it an edict. Because if it's not upheld, you'll be the one to pay for it."

"What's my end in all of this?"

"You get to live."

"Nothing else for my trouble?"

"Not one other fucking thing," Butchie said. "Eddie and I are going to enforce the law—no special dispensations. If your goons want to avoid our attention, they need to stop doing stupid shit when we're working."

"I gotta hand it to you, Bucciogrosso. You got some set of balls on you."

"It's not balls, Lilo. I'm mad dog, batshit crazy, and I don't give a fuck anymore. I'm not afraid of jail, and I don't care if I live or die. That's bad news for you. Because if you cross me on this, your survivability drops to zero. Now, you need to sound off that we have an agreement, or should I just make a modern-art masterpiece out of your guts on the wall behind you?"

Lilo considered his options briefly. In the end, his business acumen and instincts reasoned that giving a pass to a bakeshop was an indignity which was not so hard to swallow. Lilo understood his bread and butter was the narcotics trade. He knew Butchie and Eddie were still just uniform cops. The damage they could do with respect to the heroin racket was minimal. But Gigante needed the last word.

"We have a deal," he said. "But you and that insane Irishman better behave. If either of you gets jammed up, the minute you're not cops anymore, I'll make grease spots in the street out of the both of you."

"Thanks for the heads up, Lilo. But I have faith in you. I got a funny feeling when you go down for the dirt nap, I'm gonna be there to tuck you in. It will be my pleasure to send you straight to hell."

Butchie and Eddie left the Magic Lantern, having the agreement they came for. They went back to Bushwick to continue to treat the Bonannos with the same contempt they always had. None of the forewarned gangsters had the temerity to defy Carmine Gigante. The Bucciogrossos were left alone. Just as Butchie had predicted, Fat Sam wanted no part of the rent—if he had to go to the precinct to get it. So the bakery had one less operating expense. An uneasy peace existed between the partners and the crime family destroying Bushwick. They would have liked to do more, but as uniform cops, they weren't in a position to cut off the heads of the hydra that was the narcotics trade.

The urban decay that came with the drugs also brought a surfeit of violent crime. Butchie and Eddie had plenty of work. They racked up an impressive record of arrests, for things like burglaries, robberies and guns. They were still regarded with suspicion by their colleagues for their refusal to take money, but when it became clear they were not on a crusade to overturn the apple cart, they were given a wide berth, and left alone.

CHAPTER EIGHTEEN

August 1964
New York

When Eddie Curran landed at JFK, Mick Doheny was waiting for him at the gate. Mick recognized Eddie from all the way down the jetway. Those piercing blue eyes, topped by that unruly mop of blond hair were unmistakable. But as Eddie drew closer, Mick thought there was something wrong with his *own* eyes. Eddie's face seemed like it was out of focus, until they were directly in front of each other. Then Mick saw the fearsome destruction. When Eddie had called to say he had to leave Belfast, Mick didn't ask why. He just wanted Eddie's flight information, so he could meet him at the gate.

After embracing his battered friend, Mickey took a long and agonizing look at Eddie's face. The broken teeth were the giveaway. The veteran cop recognized the difference between a beating and an automobile accident. Nothing else that wouldn't have killed Eddie could have been responsible for this much damage. But unlike car accidents, all of the injury was to his face, Mickey understood without asking—his young friend had suffered a horrendous beating.

"Who did this to you?" Mickey asked.

"Oh this? It's nothing," Eddie said dismissively.

"Who did this to you?" Mickey asked more insistently.

"No one *dat* draws breath on this earth presently," Eddie allowed. "I'll tell *ye* all about it later. Right now, I'm God-awful hungry, and I need to bathe."

"Fair enough, Eddie. But tell me now; do I need to get you a lawyer?"

"There's no one left alive who would know to look for me. I'm a ghost."

When Mickey got Eddie home to his neat Dutch Colonial in Glendale, his wife Bunny was waiting expectantly for their arrival. She had met Eddie with her husband during the boxing exhibition at the Garden. She was immediately taken with the handsome, shy boxer. He was unfailingly polite and deferential. When he looked at her with those earnest blue eyes, Bunny felt like her heart had been caught in a vise. Eddie looked like a younger, blond version of her husband. She felt like she was staring into the face of the son she and Mickey had never been able to have.

When Eddie came into the kitchen, Bunny saw his shattered face and started crying. She hugged Eddie and rocked there with him in her arms—aching for him. It was killing Eddie to see her suffer like this. He whispered in her ear.

"Please stop crying, Bunny. It doesn't hurt anymore. It's still me under here. I will get better. But if *ye* don't stop crying, I'm going to start. Don't make me do that. I don't know if I have any tears left."

Bunny struggled to compose herself. She made sure Eddie had what he needed for the bath, and a change of clothes. She thought it was fortunate he and Mickey were approximately the same size. Eddie was substantially thicker through the chest than Mickey, but Eddie didn't seem to mind the tight fit of his tee shirt. While he was in the bath, Bunny and Mickey puzzled over what to feed him. Eddie's broken teeth presented a quandary. They weren't sure what he could eat. To be on the safe side, Bunny decided to whip up a stack of pancakes and bacon. She thought he could handle that much.

When Eddie came out of the bath, he sat down and devoured the repast. He had no trouble with the bacon. He told Mick and Bunny the Specials had been kind enough to leave him a few molars top and bottom on the one side of his mouth. It saved him the indignity of having to gum his food.

Eddie told them all about the horror he had been living for the past three months. When he told them about Caitlin, Bunny started crying again. This caused Eddie to focus on his own pain. The crippling sense of loss, the guilt he carried for failing to save her, all washed over him at once. He finally broke down and wept bitterly. Bunny and Mickey enclosed Eddie in their arms and held the boy, until he was all cried out.

When this storm of grief subsided temporarily, Eddie told them the rest. He left nothing out. He described the swath of murder and destruction he unleashed on everyone culpable for Caitlin—and everyone responsible for covering it up. He said the only reason he hadn't rigged the explosives to go off when Bounce opened the gym in the morning was because he wanted him alive. He wanted to be sure Brian McGurk had to live with his shame and guilt.

"Did it make you feel any better?" Bunny asked.

"No, not even a little."

"How did you feel after killing those people?" Mickey asked.

"I felt nothing."

"Do you regret it now?" Bunny asked.

"No. It's what had to be done. I was the only one willing to do it. If I hadn't, how many more Caitlin McGurks would they have destroyed? And how many times would that bastard Chichester cover it up for them? As far as Martin Boland is concerned; he was an abomination who should never have been born. There's no telling how many may live, now *dat* he's dead. I took no pleasure in it, but I don't regret it."

After the meal and the cataclysm disguised as a conversation, Eddie was exhausted. Bunny had set up one of the three guest bedrooms for him. They had bought this house when they were first married and thought Bunny was pregnant. The false pregnancy turned out to be cervical cancer. The ensuing hysterectomy made it impossible for her and Mickey to ever have children of their own. They had tried to adopt, but the only venue for doing so in the 1950s and early 60s was through the Catholic Church.

Both of them were devout Catholics, attending mass every Sunday at Sacred Heart. It shouldn't have been a problem. But Barbara *Bunny* Doheny's maiden name was Myersohn. She had been born Jewish. When her family disowned her for announcing she was marrying the Irish policeman they so disapproved of, she discarded them and their religion, converting to Catholicism. Mickey told her it wasn't necessary. He would marry her at the courthouse.

"No, Mickey. God let us find each other. We're getting married in *His* house, under *His* care and protection. Besides, at the synagogue they never let the girls learn Hebrew. It'll be nice to be able to understand what everyone is saying."

"Uh, Bunny," Mick said laughing. "You don't by any chance know Latin, do you?"

"No. Why?"

"Then you're not gonna understand fuck-all what they're saying in church either," Mickey said.

Bunny did learn Latin. It was a condition of her conversion. She would afterwards follow along in church with every word the priest said. It turned out she knew far more Latin than her husband, who only knew enough to fake it. After 1962, it wasn't an issue anymore. Vatican II turned the altar around and converted the mass to English. In whatever language the mass was said, the Dohenys were there at Sacred Heart every Sunday to hear it.

Shortly after Bunny had her hysterectomy, the Dohenys filed their application to adopt with the New York Foundling Hospital. This was the organ of the Archdiocese responsible for placing unwanted Catholic children with childless Catholic families. Their application stalled at the very same place, every time. When the documents were reviewed by the priests at the Archbishop's office, Bunny's maiden name stuck out like a sore thumb. The completed conversion was no help at all.

The anti-Semitism ingrained in the Catholic clergy at the time would never allow them to regard Bunny as a true Catholic. Ironic, Mickey thought, inasmuch as Jesus Christ himself was a converted Jew. The Church wasn't impressed with this argument either, and they made no effort whatsoever to disguise it. Their application was declined on that basis every time. The Dohenys made a nuisance of themselves by re-applying for eight years. They hoped to wear the church down, but they could never bring down the wall of suspicion and prejudice.

Finally, they gave up. Mickey wanted to renounce his religion and turn his back on the church. Bunny wouldn't hear of it.

"We still have so much to be grateful for. It's not about the priests wearing the vestments. They're just men. They can deny us a child, but they can't define us. We're good people, Mickey. And we need God in our lives."

Mickey relented, but he made certain to stay out of arms reach of the priests and the Monsignor. His impulse was to bash their hypocritical teeth down their throats. He didn't think he could trust himself not to do it if he got close enough. To be on the safe side, he resigned from the Holy Name Society and the Knights of Columbus.

The Dohenys ended up doing more parenting over the next few years than most people blessed with their own children *ever* did. The year they took Eddie in, Bunny met a fifteen-year-old Puerto Rican boy in the emergency room at Jamaica Hospital in East New York.

Bunny was a nurse. She had been working at Jamaica Hospital since 1950. It's where she met her husband. Mickey had been brought there by his partner after he had been grazed in a shootout with a stick-up team. Mickey had killed them both, but he suffered a nice crease across his rib cage. He joked if he hadn't been as thin as he was, it would have been more than a graze.

When Mickey met Bunny in the emergency room, he thought she was so beautiful he fell all over himself trying to talk to her. Ordinarily, the handsome cop and war veteran was a smooth operator when it came to women, but he had never been knocked out of his socks before. Bunny did that for him, and then some. Despite the marbles in his mouth, Bunny thought Mickey was adorable, and charming, too. She readily agreed to let the handsome policeman take her to dinner. Neither could pinpoint the moment they fell in love. Mickey thought it was the second he saw her. Bunny thought it occurred a little after. Either way, they were inseparable from the first day.

Nelson Cruz had been stabbed in a gang fight. He was scared, filthy and hungry. Bunny's heart was breaking just at the sight of the poor wretched soul.

"How did your parents let you get in this state?" Bunny asked.

"I haven't seen my family since I got sent to juvey two years ago," Nelson admitted.

"Where do you stay?"

"I've been living in the street mostly. Occasionally—when it's cold or raining—I break into a building and sleep next to the furnace."

"Isn't there *anyone* to take care of you? You're just a boy."

"I have *mis hermanos*," Nelson said, defensively.

"Your brothers?" Bunny scoffed. "You mean your fellow gang members. Where were they after you got stabbed? They ran away, didn't they?"

"Yeah."

"They don't sound like brothers to me. What gang are you in?"

"The Jolly Jokers," Nelson said.

"Do you like being in the gang? What is it doing for you, Nelson?"

"Not very much. To be honest, I'm sick of living this way, but I don't see I have a choice. I've got to eat. With them, at least I can steal enough to feed myself."

"If you had a choice—a place to live and real healthy food to eat every day—would you give up the gang life and go back to school?"

"Who would do that for me? My family moved back to Puerto Rico when I was in jail. They didn't even write to tell me about it. They were just gone, not even leaving a forwarding address. Nobody wants me. It doesn't matter anyway. Winter is coming. I don't think I'm gonna survive this one."

Hearing Nelson's tale of woe, Bunny was determined to rescue him from his fate. To do so, she would need to get Mickey's blessing. She knew he couldn't refuse her, but she had to ask. If for no other reason than to give him the opportunity to maintain the illusion he was in charge of the decision making. Bunny managed to get in touch with Mickey through the precinct. She asked him to come to the hospital after he finished his day-tour. When Mickey got there, Bunny told him the story of Nelson Cruz. Not pulling any punches or trying to soft-sell him, she just asked.

"Can we take him in, Mickey?"

"Do you even know anything about this kid, Bunny?"

"I know if we don't help him, he has no chance whatsoever."

"This kid is a tough piece of work. That gang the Jolly Jokers are a pack of feral animals. All they want to do is steal and fight. I don't know if Nelson is much of a thief, but he is the best fighter in a whole gang of fighters. He might not be salvageable."

"Oh bullshit, Mickey! You're already thinking about what you can do with him when you get him into Brewster's to train with Eddie and your other fighters."

"Okay, ya got me," Mickey laughed. "The kid could be a champion if he worked at it. I'll tell you what, baby. If he convinces me he'll give up this crap, he can come home with us."

Nelson convinced him he wanted out of the gang life. After being released from the hospital, he moved into the Doheny house. He and Eddie had separate rooms, but they were treated like brothers. When they started training together at Brewster's, they came to regard each other as such.

Even even brothers have different needs. So did Nelson and Eddie. Nelson had to get back in school. He was enrolled at Franklin K Lane. With the help of Bunny, Mickey, and even Eddie, he was able to get on track to graduate with his class. Eddie meanwhile, had other problems. He had to pursue his US citizenship. Mickey was able to pull some strings to expedite things. Enlisting in the Marines would speed things up further. But first he needed to take care of some medical issues.

Mickey had the dental work covered. A few years ago, he had caught an orthodontist from Irving Avenue selling prescriptions for pain killers. Mickey made a deal with him. He would squash the charge under two conditions; he had to stop doing it, and he had to accept some pro bono referrals from the neighborhood from time to time. The orthodontist, confronted with losing his license, readily agreed. Mickey had sent a half-dozen kids from the neighborhood who couldn't afford braces to him. Now he sent Eddie. After several weeks of intensive cosmetic dentistry, Eddie's brilliant smile was back.

Bunny had the plastic surgery taken care of. The resident head of plastic surgery at Jamaica Hospital agreed to see Eddie as a favor to her. He was able to reshape Eddie's jaw and chin, until it approximated its former shape. It wasn't perfect, but it was an improvement. Then he rebuilt and reshaped Eddie's nose with the use of a prosthetic. This too was only an improvement. Eddie looked better, but he was still called *Hatchet Face* behind his back.

When Nelson graduated from high school, and Eddie had healed from his surgeries, the two erstwhile brothers enlisted in the Marine Corps together. Both of them ended up assigned to different platoons with the 7th Marines. They saw action together in Vietnam in 1966. In their year in combat, they acquitted themselves with honor.

After their enlistment ended, they returned to the Dohenys. Eddie had earned his citizenship and was hired by the NYPD. Unfortunately, Nelson had an extensive juvenile arrest record. This, coupled with his Puerto Rican heritage would work to disqualify him for the job. You could be Puerto Rican and still be a cop, but the bosses at the time were looking for any reason to exclude Latino candidates. Such was the clannish prejudice of the job during this era.

The arrest record made it easy. The fact Nelson was two inches shorter than the minimum height requirement for the NYPD at the time, also worked against him. It seemed a little unfair to Nelson that he was considered tall enough to carry a rifle for the Marines in Vietnam, but not tall enough to carry a .38 on the streets of New York. He found work with a moving company and pursued his boxing career. In the end, he wasn't tall enough for that either. So, he went back in the Marine Corps.

CHAPTER NINETEEN

October 1965
Glendale

Later that year, after Eddie and Nelson already established themselves as brothers, ensconced in the extra bedrooms of the Doheny house, the third bedroom was more or less permanently occupied by Butchie.

After confronting Nardo, and satisfying himself his mother would be respected, Butchie decamped to the Dohenys'—welcomed with open arms by Mickey and Bunny. He would be embraced by his new brothers as well, but first they felt the need to impress upon Butchie some rules they regarded as inviolate.

Eddie and Nelson had already carved out a niche for themselves. As Mickey had suggested, they regarded each other as brothers. Out of respect, they would never defy their boxing coach and erstwhile savior. But it was out of sheer adoration for Bunny, whom they had come to call "Mom," that they laid aside all hesitation and embraced each other as such. This was the environment into which Butchie arrived. When he took the third bedroom at the Doheny's, his new brothers explained the rules. Rule number one; Bunny was to be regarded as *she who must be obeyed.*

"*Yer* used to doing what Mickey tells *ye* to from the gym. Just keep doing *dat*. But Bunny is a different story," Eddie pointed out. "She is the kindest, most loving person *ye* will ever know. All she will ever ask of *ye* is that *ye* do what's best for *yerself.* Our wellbeing is all she cares about. *Dat* kind of unconditional love cannot be disappointed. You will do whatever *ye* must to make her happy—no exceptions."

Butchie was already crazy about Bunny. He sensed how extraordinary she was. He was anxious to please her in any way he could. After observing the dynamic between Mickey and Bunny, he understood how happy she made Mick. His whole countenance changed for the better whenever Bunny was in the room. Seeing how right they were for each other, Butchie was saddened. It was the kind of love and happiness he wished for his mother to know. Because she never would was disappointing in the extreme. So, the idea of letting Bunny down was already an untenable impossibility to Butchie. Still, Nelson felt the need to stress the point.

"Just so we understand each other, Butchie, if you make Bunny unhappy in any way, we'll kill you."

One of the things that made Bunny *very* happy was when the boys would join her and Mickey for the 11 o'clock Mass on Sundays at Sacred Heart. After which, the Doheny clan would repair to Donavan's Pub in Woodside for brunch. For the past six Sundays, Eddie had begun to act peculiarly.

The first time Eddie saw Bernadette Regan, you would have thought he had been struck mute. This was out of character for the young Irishman, who was known to be a bit of a raconteur. Since the fearful beating in Belfast, and the rearrangement of his once splendid facial features, he had learned to compensate by being gregarious. A natural storyteller, Eddie's easy manner, his dry understated Irish wit, and his now crooked but pleasant grin, captivated everyone he spoke to. In fact, he would more often than not commandeer the room. But not today. And not for the last six Sundays. Bernadette Regan ran this room, and Eddie was spellbound.

Bernadette waitressed every weekend at Donovan's. During the week, she was a live-in nanny for a well-to-do family on the upper eastside. She enjoyed the waitressing as much for the extra money as she did as a social outlet. Emigrating from Armagh, the northernmost county in the Irish Republic when she was eighteen, she immediately recognized Eddie's Belfast accent. After his voice, she was captivated by the roughhewn Irishman's piercing blue eyes. He seemed intelligent to Bernadette, until she got near. Then Eddie's conversation skills got all gummed up. Despite that, she noticed he couldn't take those blue eyes off of her.

She made a point of fawning over Eddie, seeing his coffee was topped off and he had everything he needed. But he would just smile and nod awkwardly. Bernadette found it maddening. She thought he was beautiful. She sensed a gentle kindness in Eddie. Where most everyone else saw a hatchet face, Bernadette saw something altogether different and wonderful, but she couldn't get the big galoot to speak with her. It shouldn't have been an issue. Bernadette looked like Grace Kelly with her auburn hair. Stunningly beautiful, her violet eyes brightened and enlivened every room she walked into. Eddie on the other hand, was an easy conversationalist. Shy in nature around women, he still had a deferential and charming manner. But, around Bernadette, he was a mess.

Bunny was the first to notice. She knew Eddie was smitten. His behavior around Bernadette was not dissimilar to Mickey's, the first time they met. She had been encouraging Eddie to speak to her, but he just shook his head, saying "Ah, no. Not right now."

After six weeks of trying to get Eddie's attention without success, Bernadette finally took matters into her own hands. She had taken the measure of the odd conglomeration she had come to regard as her friends. She liked the Dohenys very much. She understood Bunny was the soul and center of this clan. So Bernadette asked her.

"The handsome feller down the end of the table, with the blue eyes and blond hair; was he kicked in the head by a horse, or does he not know the language?"

Everyone but Eddie had a good laugh at that. He turned bright crimson. But it had the intended effect.

"I speak the language fine, Bernadette," he said.

"Oh, so you know my name. At least you've been paying attention. Do you not want to speak with me?"

"I didn't *tink ye'd* want me to," Eddie admitted.

"Well, you're not very keen, Eddie Curran."

"How do you know *my* name?"

"Bunny introduces us every week, you dolt. Now, I'm going over to the hostess station for a bit. You should come over and talk to me."

When Bernadette left, that's exactly what Eddie did. Freed finally of his insecurity, Eddie chatted her up. She surmised from his accent he was from Belfast. She told him she was from just over the border in Armagh.

"Perhaps we've met before," Bernadette suggested.

"I know we haven't," Eddie assured her. "*You* I would have remembered."

Bernadette smiled, very pleased at Eddie's turnabout.

"I look forward to speaking with *ye* again, Bernadette," Eddie said smiling warmly, before returning to his seat.

Later, back at the table, Bernadette came over to refill Eddie's coffee. She leaned in and whispered conspiratorially.

"If this day doesn't end with you asking for my phone number, I'm going to spill hot coffee in your lap."

"*Dat* won't be necessary," Eddie chuckled.

He handed Bernadette a paper napkin with writing on it.

"That's *me* phone number. If *ye* ever wanted to see me, or talk to me, just call. I can be by in minutes."

Eddie Curran ceased to be Hatchet Face. Moving forward, he was one of two. Whether Eddie and Bernadette, or Bernadette and Eddie, you had to say them together. They both knew they belonged that way and would remain so. Soon after, Bernadette decided she didn't need the extra money for waitressing on Sundays. She was by Eddie's side at Sunday mass, and had a permanent and reserved seat at the table for brunch.

Butchie brought Monica into the fold. Nelson became engaged to Irma Heriberto, the daughter of the shoe repair man on Knickerbocker Avenue. She became a constant presence as well. The eight of them were the centerpiece of the Sunday afternoon dining room at Donovan's. Mickey Doheny proudly oversaw his growing family from the head of the table. But seated at his right hand, in a position of no less prestige, was the benign and loving matriarch. Bunny was the true and undisputed spiritual center of this family. They all wordlessly recognized it and were proud to be referred to as *The Doheny Clan*.

CHAPTER TWENTY

July 12, 1979
Bushwick

Butchie had always thought Ernie *The Whale* Walton was an asshole. Now he was dead certain. The most ignorant, whining, fat, and obnoxious human being he had ever had to endure, Butchie had been forced to listen to him since their tour began at 0800 hours. Since roll call, Walton had been ranting about the neighborhood, the people in it, and the inferiority of the largely Italian community. It was now 1430 hours, and Butchie had heard enough. He was about to tell the insufferable jerk where to stick his opinions when the radio diverted his attention. The 911 dispatcher was assigning them a *shots fired* job. Butchie would have to wait a while to straighten out The Whale.

A few weeks earlier, Eddie Curran, had broken his hand on the head of a robbery suspect who stupidly tried to fight his way out of an arrest. While it went very badly for the suspect, the broken hand ensured Curran would be home healing for the next six weeks. Butchie's squad sergeant temporarily assigned him to work with Ernie Walton, whose own partner was on vacation.

Butchie wasn't happy about it. He knew Walton was a crude, ignorant slob with few friends. His integrity was also a problem. Butchie laid down some ground rules before the two set out on their first tour together.

"Walton, I don't care what you used to do with your old partner. It's none of my goddamned business. But if you try and take money while you're working with me, I'll rip your arm off and beat you to death with it."

Ernie Walton didn't care for being spoken to like that, but he was still smarting from the beating Butchie gave him in the locker room the year before. He would not be accepting any pay-offs while working with Butchie. While Butchie could prevent the slovenly cop from thieving in his presence, he had no control over the ignorance which kept spilling out of his mouth.

The other issue with Walton was the smelly anisette cheroot perpetually clamped between his teeth. Butchie found the smell of the smoke from those cheap cigars nauseating. He was about to tell him to lose it, when he made the mistake of getting close enough to Walton to smell his rancid body odor. He quickly decided the cigar was the less disgusting option.

"These *dagos* never heard the expression you don't shit where you eat? Look what they've done to their own neighborhood," the Whale observed. "It's disgraceful. They are dirty, dirty people. I don't know how they can live like this. They're your *paisanos*, Butchie. Can you explain it?"

Butchie just glared at him. He was debating whether or not to punch him in the face when the radio squawked.

"Shots fired inside 205 Knickerbocker Avenue, Joe and Mary's Italian Restaurant. One call, no call-back," central reported.

"Eight-three George," Butchie acknowledged. "Responding, will advise."

The reduced manning in the department left the sector with no available back-up. This was getting to be an all too common occurrence. Butchie was less concerned about handling dangerous jobs without back-up than was Walton. He had absolute confidence in his own ability to fight or shoot his way out of any situation—so he wasn't backing down from anyone. It would just be the two of them. If the shit hit the fan, he thought, Walton would just have to suck it up and carry his own considerable weight.

A moment later, the cops arrived in front of the restaurant. Butchie knew this place well. The owner, Joseph Tacopino was a connected guy with the Bonannos. He had once been a customer of the Bucciogrosso Bakery, but Butchie had forbidden his father and uncle from doing business with the Mob after brokering the un-easy truce he made with Gigante. Many of the cops in the 83rd precinct still ate there. Butchie and Eddie Curran wouldn't set foot in the place, unless it was to lock someone up. They weren't taking free meals from mobsters any more than they would take their money.

Butchie entered the restaurant and recognized the hysterical young woman pointing toward the courtyard in the rear. She was Joe Tacopino daughter, Cecile. Butchie drew his revolver and came out into the courtyard dining area. It was eerily quiet. In the rear of the courtyard, Butchie saw three men laying in puddles of their own blood and gore, around a banquet table with a flowered vinyl tablecloth. There was a plate of pastries still on it, undisturbed. On the right, Butchie recognized Carmine Lilo Gigante. His chest and face were peppered with wounds from a shotgun blast. His right eye had been shot out completely. Butchie thought he looked as dead as Julius Caesar.

He felt a momentary wave of elation at the sight of the dead gangster, until he was overtaken with regret for not having been the engineer of it. Walton came lumbering up behind him.

"What have you *guineas* done now?" Walton asked Butchie.

Butchie was considering kicking the Whale in the groin, when he remembered he didn't respect the imbecile enough to make his opinion worthy of a response.

"Is that Gigante?" Walton asked as he came around the table. "He don't look right without his cigar."

"You're right. He seems unnatural without it," Butchie agreed.

With that, Butchie snatched the cheroot right out of Walton's mouth. He knelt over the prone body of Gigante and roughly jammed the smelly cigar between his teeth. Butchie knew this was a far cry from the Cuban cigars Lilo had been famous for smoking, but it would have to do. As Butchie was admiring the indignity, Gigante's good eye opened. He looked with recognition and fear into Butchie's face. Rather than reacting with surprise, Butchie quickly pivoted and tossed the police radio to his partner.

"The radio is dead in here, Walton. I can't get a signal. Why don't you go out front and put over a *no further*? There's nobody left alive. We don't need any of our people getting hurt trying to race here."

"Uh, okay," Walton said as he turned around and left the courtyard.

When he was sure Walton had gone, Butchie knelt again and looked into Lilo's one dying eye. The terror conveyed by that face washed over Butchie like a warm bath. He found the sensation exquisite. He would have liked to bask in it for a while longer if he could have, but time wouldn't allow it. Butchie got down to his intended business.

"Do you remember when I told you I would be the one to usher you into hell, Lilo? Well, here we are, at Satan's gate," he said, smiling serenely.

When Butchie closed his hand around the dying gangster's throat, cutting off his air supply, it didn't take long for the wounded Gigante to kick his feet helplessly before shuddering one last time.

By the time Walton came back into the courtyard, Butchie was standing away from the carnage, speaking to Cecile. She had calmed down enough to tell Butchie her brother was wounded and hiding in the closet next to the kitchen. When the first ambulance arrived, Butchie directed them to Joey Tacopino. His father, Lilo, and Lilo's cousin Gaspar Collasanto were already dead. An army of cops and supervisors showed up to the scene. They were followed by an army of detectives.

Being the first officers on the scene, Butchie and Walton had to stick around. Butchie regretted taking the Whale's cigar. Now he had nothing to camouflage Walton's native awfulness. He would have to endure it for this day only. Butchie had already decided he was never working with Ernie Walton again. He would tell the ignorant, bigoted and filthy cop all about it. But that was a conversation for later.

CHAPTER TWENTY-ONE

August 1979
Bushwick

After the assassination of Carmine Gigante, and Eddie had returned from his injury, he and Butchie occupied themselves with trying to find out who held the reigns of nefarious power in Lilo's absence. Someone was in charge. That much was apparent. Whatever the criminal order in this universe was, it had gone on unperturbed by the death of the head of the hydra. A new head had grown in its place. Butchie and Eddie needed to know who he was. They went looking for Roman Sciula.

Butchie and Eddie had developed a begrudgingly respectful relationship with the very scary hoodlum. They had won his respect when they prevented him from beating his erstwhile friend, Carmine the Mouth Donofrio to death.

Roman had the misfortune of returning to his apartment on Jefferson Street to discover his fiancé in bed with his supposed best friend. Donofrio escaped out the window and down the fire escape, leaving Ernesta La Pergola to absorb her enraged fiancé's wrath on her own. Roman left her battered and bleeding before heading out with a three-foot length of rebar in search of The Mouth. As badly as Roman had beaten Ernesta up, he clearly hadn't meant to kill her. He could have done so with one punch. Donofrio would be another matter, Roman vowed. His death would be intentional.

When Butchie and Eddie responded to the *calls for help* job on Jefferson Street, Ernesta was waiting for them at the door. She told the cops what Roman had done to her, and why. Then she informed them she didn't want Roman arrested. They already knew as much. No one ever wanted anybody arrested in Bushwick. The cops were only called because the citizens' self-inflicted mayhem had propelled their lives into unmanageable and dangerous anarchy. The police were called to serve merely as referees—to prevent people from being *unnecessarily* murdered. That's what Ernesta was looking for now; someone to save her lover, Carmine, from her fiancé, Roman. The story of this affair was already well known. To everyone's dismay, now Roman Sciula knew it.

"Don't let that animal hurt my Carmine," Ernesta shrieked.

"*Yer* fiancé; is *dat* the animal *ye* mean?" Eddie asked.

"He's got an iron stick, and he's going to break Carmine's head with it. You've got to stop him!"

"We'll do that, Ernesta. But you should understand the hornet's nest you've kicked over here," Butchie explained. "These guys are *La Cosa Nostra*. By laying down with you, Carmine has violated a cardinal rule. In *the life*, the penalty for sleeping with another *made-guy's* woman is death. If not Roman, somebody is going to kill Carmine. If you're with him when they catch up to him, they'll kill you, too."

When this reality washed over her, Ernesta went into a panic.

"I want to go into witness protection!" she blurted.

"And I want to take *me* daughters to Disney World," Eddie informed her. "But I don't have the money for Mickey Mouse, and *ye* don't qualify as a witness to anything but yer own treachery."

"What am I supposed to do?"

"Pack a bag," Butchie advised. "If you and Carmine run, you might buy some time. But that's all you'll do. Eventually, they'll find the two of you."

"What if I run on my own? Will they look for me if I'm not with Carmine?"

Butchie and Eddie regarded Ernesta's question with silent disdain, but no real sense of astonishment. It was Eddie who answered her.

"I don't speak much Italian, Ernesta, but it seems to me the word *dat* keeps insisting upon itself is *butana*."

Butchie and Eddie caught up with Roman Sciula on Suydam Street, by Knickerbocker Park. He was carrying the length of rebar and had a determined, demented and altogether murderous look on his face. On closer inspection, Butchie could see the dried tears from where they had been streaming down his cheeks. He didn't think it was possible, but Roman had somehow become a sympathetic figure. Butchie stopped him on the sidewalk.

"Talk to me for a minute, Roman," Butchie requested.

"I got no time, Butchie. I got something to do."

"We know. We just came from Ernesta. She told us all about it."

"Then you already know what I gotta do," Roman said.

"The whole neighborhood knows," Butchie said. "But you don't have to do it now. In fact, it's the worst thing you could do."

Roman stopped abruptly.

"So, what do *you* think I should I do, and why do you suddenly give a shit about me?" he asked.

"First, Roman, take a deep breath," Eddie suggested. "Then *tink* about what happens if *ye* cave that *fook's* head in—in broad daylight no less. They'll bury *ye* under the jail."

"Is Carmine Donofrio worth sacrificing your own life, just to prove a point?" Butchie asked. "Your street cred won't suffer by waiting a day or two. They know what they did, and they knew the price when they did it. They chose this life. They can reap what they sowed. But why not let them dangle a bit? They won't sleep a wink—worrying about where and when they get it. Then you can do what you have to do on your own terms."

"You said yourself the whole neighborhood knows what went down today. How am I supposed to save face?"

"The best strategy right now would be to let us arrest *ye* for tightening up Ernesta," Eddie suggested. "*Ye* know she won't press charges. *Ye'll* be released later tonight from the precinct. What happens to them in the future, I imagine will be none of our business."

Roman thought about it for a moment before agreeing it was in his best interests.

"I just need one favor, Roman," Butchie told him. "Lose the rebar. Ye're making us look bad for not shooting you."

"Okay, Butchie," Roman laughed, throwing the length of rebar to the curb and allowing Eddie to handcuff him.

Later that night at the precinct, Butchie and Eddie got the opportunity to talk to Roman alone in an interview room.

"Why did you guys look out for me today? I thought we were on different sides," Roman said.

"We are," Butchie admitted. "But only when you're doing the wrong things. I don't believe you're really a bad guy. I view you as more a victim of your environment and circumstances."

"We're from the same place, Butchie. You grew up around the block from me," Roman reminded him.

"Yeah, but no one in my family was La Cosa Nostra. No one in your family wasn't. You didn't have any choice but to go into the life."

"So why did you have choices? I coulda' done something else."

"What, for instance?" Eddie had to ask.

"I guess you're right," Roman admitted.

"I don't mean to offend you when I say you're not a smart man," Butchie began. "Your choices were never your own. You were born to bad people. When you turned out to be big, strong, loyal and stupid, there was no way those scumbags weren't going to use you as a weapon. You are a perfect hammer, and you're not bright enough to ask the right questions. Make no mistake, Roman. You are being exploited. The minute someone has to be sacrificed, they're going to serve you up on a silver platter. Like the head of John the Baptist, they'll give you as a gift to protect themselves."

"It ain't quite like that, Butchie."

"Isn't it, though?" Eddie asked. "Have they ever trusted *ye* with anything more complicated than hurting someone? Have they ever even trusted *ye* with why you were hurting them? Do they let *ye* handle the money? Do they let *ye* touch the dope? How many times have *ye* been passed over for promotion? They don't trust *ye*, lad. That makes *ye* expendable, and it makes *ye* vulnerable."

Roman silently brooded. He was following the reasoning, and was coming to the realization Eddie and Butchie were correct. But he lacked the imagination to see a way out of it.

"I suppose it's what I deserve," Roman concluded.

"Being caught between a rock and a hard place is not the same thing as deserving to be there," Eddie told him. "*Ye've* never done a bad *ting dat* wasn't at the behest of someone else. Perhaps *ye'd* behave differently if given the chance."

"Who's going to give me that kind of chance?" Roman scoffed.

"We can help you, Roman," Butchie said. "But you're going to have to come over to our side for us to do it."

"I can't testify," Roman said.

"We don't need that," Butchie told him. "We just need some background from time to time. You won't have to testify. You just give us the big picture. There's going to be a lot of changes in Bushwick. We need some insight into who is in charge of what. We don't want to waste our time fucking with someone if they're not the ones pushing the buttons."

"So how am I supposed to talk to you in the street without looking like a snitch?" Roman asked.

Eddie provided Roman with the perfect cover. He was to always have in his possession a few betting slips for the horses or the number. That way, whenever Butchie and Eddie wanted to ask him something, they could pretend to arrest him for suspicion of gambling. After their conversation, they would cut Roman loose from the precinct with a bogus summons he could throw away when he got home.

This was the arrangement they had in place when Lilo got himself whacked at Joe and Mary's, which was coincidentally two weeks after Carmine Donofrio and Ernesta La Pergola were found shot in the face in Donofrio's purple Buick Riviera. As the car was parked at the time in front of DePhillipi's Trucking Garage on Mount Olivet Crescent in Maspeth, Queens, as Eddie had predicted, it truly was none of Butchie and Eddie's business.

Shortly after Eddie had returned to work from his broken hand, the commanding officer of the precinct had decided Butchie and Eddie were logging so many gun and robbery arrests in uniform, he might as well put them in plain clothes, so they could focus exclusively on those things—without being bothered by having to chase the radio. He created a job for them and called it an *Anti-Crime Unit*. This gave them the time and the autonomy to do pretty much whatever they wanted. Increasingly, they wanted to mess with the Mafia.

On this day, Butchie and Eddie found Roman hanging outside the coffee shop on Willoughby and Knickerbocker Avenues. *La Copa Azzurro* featured a younger crowd than *Il Prima Bono*, the bosses' favored hangout on Wyckoff Avenue. Roman preferred the younger crowd because they were less inclined to make fun of him and call him *stunad* behind his back. He had grown weary of the slight treatment of his superiors. Besides, he knew the old, fat mobsters knew where to find him if they needed someone dealt with. He didn't need to stay underfoot to absorb their abuse.

When Butchie and Eddie showed up on the corner and hopped out of the Anti-Crime car, Roman made a sour face and feigned annoyance as they pushed him against the wall and found the betting slips in his right pocket. Then he was handcuffed and put in the car for the short ride to the precinct. But they didn't stop on Wilson Avenue. They continued east, and into the Cemetery of the Evergreens.

Once deep inside, everyone got out of the car and Roman's handcuffs were removed. Eddie handed Roman a bottle of sparkling water and apologized about the cuffs.

"That's okay, Eddie. What do you guys want?"

"Gigante got smoked a month ago," Butchie reminded him. "The heroin business hasn't even hiccupped in his absence. The same faces are dealing the same stamps, on the same corners. This was a smooth transition—too smooth. We want to know who's in charge now."

"I only know what I overhear," Roman said. "But rumor has it an old-guard tough-guy engineered the takeover from prison. He built a coalition between the Zips and the local hoods, promising the Zips more of the dope and a piece of the traditional rackets to turn on Lilo. Everybody is getting paid now. Everybody is happy."

"How is he doing this from the can?" Butchie asked.

"Supposedly, he's some kind of avenging angel of death. Everybody is afraid of this fucking guy. He's been running things inside up there since the fifties, building some kind of criminal empire for himself. He went away on three bodies. He's up for parole next month. The fix is supposed to be in. Now he wants everything. The mustache Petes are planning some grand coronation for him."

"Does he have a name?" Butchie asked grimly, already suspecting the worst.

"I just heard his nickname. He's supposed to be a real scary guy."

At this point Butchie had lost his patience. He was about to lose his composure. Eddie had his head in his hands. He had been dreading the return of this particular monster since he first heard the story of him. He knew he would be back to torment his partner, but he hadn't expected it to be so soon—or so sudden. Now, Eddie felt his malevolent presence looming.

"What's his fucking name, Roman?" Butchie snapped.

"They call him Sallie Gorgeous."

CHAPTER TWENTY-TWO

1950s
Bushwick

Roman Sciula had the misfortune of being born to perhaps two of the more feeble-minded people ever to live in Brooklyn. Italian emigres from Sicily, Alphonso and Camille Sciula arrived in America in 1949—witless, and soon enough penniless. With neither an education nor an employable skill, they moved into the basement of their cousin's building in the Italian ghetto in Bushwick. This cousin, along with being a slum-lord, was a loan shark for the Bonanno crime family.

Alphonso's father had been the village shoemaker in Castellamare del Golfo in Sicily. The business had been in the family's hands for hundreds of years. Alessandro Sciula grew rich by shoeing the feet of the minor royalty and landed gentry of Sicily. He grew extraordinarily wealthy with the rise in prominence of the Sicilian Mafia at the turn of the twentieth century. The criminal elite insisted on the finest footwear. Alessandro Sciula became the pre-eminent shoemaker in all of Italy.

This affluence allowed the decent and honorable Alessandro to offer discounted and free shoes to the many poor people of the village. His natural sense of compassion and benevolence allowed the fishermen and lesser employed citizens of the village to keep themselves and their children shod.

He taught the craft of cobbling to his children, and employed nine of his ten offspring as assistant cobblers.

The tenth child was Alphonso. Known throughout the village as *Alphonso the dullard*, he was too inept to be trusted with the delicate art of making and repairing shoes. He was nonetheless employed by his father—given menial labor and delivery duties. As big and strong as a plow horse, he was well suited for this work. He could take simple directions, could hoist and carry the large heavy bundles of tanned leather two at a time. The deliveries were all within the village, which was small enough even Alphonso couldn't lose his way.

It should have been an easy existence. Somehow, he managed to screw it up. When he fell in love with his equally dull-witted first cousin Camille, he was warned this type of scandalous behavior would not be tolerated. When he disregarded his father's edict and got Camille pregnant, the two of them were banished. Alessandro had the pair married in secret. He put 625,000 lire—roughly 1000 American dollars into his son's hand and sent the young couple to live in Brooklyn under the care of their second cousin.

Though related, Enrico Agrippa was considered by all to be a slimy sort of fellow. He took in the Sciula's out of no real sense of family obligation. He soon separated his cousin from his 1,000 dollars. He also pocketed the money Alessandro sent every month on their behalf. He would have allowed the couple and their unborn child to starve in his basement if left to his own devices. He was only prevented from doing so because it would have been a bad business decision. If they were dead, Allessandro would stop sending money for them. Enrico ultimately found a use for his cousin.

Alphonso would accompany Enrico on his collections for both the rents and the loan payments. He was initially supposed to be an object of intimidation. Large and frightening, he was effective in this capacity. Standing behind the little Enrico, who by himself struck fear into the heart of no one, Alphonso would loom—an enormous malevolent presence. Almost nobody wanted to find out what the huge man was capable of, so they paid on time. Almost nobody; some people can't appreciate their reality until it grabs them by the throat.

Balsamo Silla was three months behind in his rent and shylock payments. An inveterate gambler, he continued to slide further and further into Enrico's debt. When Enrico threatened to sic Alphonso on him if he failed to make payment, Balsamo gambled Alphonso was merely a large and frightening scarecrow.

Along with being intellectually challenged, Alphonso was inarticulate and unfamiliar with the English language, particularly its idioms, but he was by no means a scarecrow. So when Enrico directed him to *brace* Balsamo, Alphonso thought he wanted him to *break* him. He grabbed the stunned Silla by his groin and throat. The abruptness surprised Enrico. Alphonso then hoisted Balsamo high above his head, flipped him over onto his back, and brought him down forcefully over his gargantuan knee. The snapping of the hapless Balsamo's spine sounded like a gunshot. Enrico was aghast.

Silla lay motionless on the hallway floor, moaning in agony. Enrico became panic-stricken.

"Shut him up!" he demanded.

Alphonso reached down and crushed Balsamo's throat in his big right hand, immediately silencing the suffering man. The larynx, along with Balsamo's windpipe were destroyed. They watched as the silent Balsamo struggled for air that would never come. He slowly suffocated. Enrico ordered Alphonso to drag Balsamo to the basement. He grabbed the lifeless body by the belt, carrying him down the four flights of stairs and into the basement as easily as he used to carry his father's bundles of tanned skins.

Once in the earthen basement, Enrico had Alphonso dig a shallow grave for the body. He hoped Silla would be buried there and forgotten. This was wishful thinking. He should have realized when the landlord and neighborhood shylock comes collecting, every eye is at every door. Consequently, the legend of Alphonso Sciula was carried and spread on the wagging tongues of the very many witnesses who observed the super-human feat of destruction.

As Silla lived alone, and had no friends or family to miss him, the police never found out. In truth, they wouldn't have been interested anyway. During this time in New York, the police weren't interested in anything that didn't come with an envelope of bribe money. No one would miss Balsamo Silla, or even note his passing. When Joe Bonanno heard about the otherworldly strength of the silent Sicilian belonging to Enrico Agrippa, he decided he had to have him for himself. Bonanno ordered Agrippa to bring his giant to his office in the rear of the tailor shop on Willoughby Avenue. There he dismissed Agrippa and hired Alphonso as his personal bodyguard. Bonanno brought Alphonso up front to be outfitted with several custom suits by his personal tailor. He was given an advance on his new, greatly improved salary, sent home with his suits and instructed to report for work the next morning in the rear of the tailor shop.

The timing was perfect for Alphonso. His son Roman had arrived the month before. The three of them were able to move out of the basement and into a comfortable two-bedroom apartment on Jefferson Street, and out of the clutches his cousin. By now, Alphonso's father had discovered Enrico had been stealing the money he had been sending to support his son and niece. He contacted his son via telegram, directing him to get the money back from Enrico.

When Alphonso demanded payment from Enrico, he first refused. Alphonso punched him in his left shoulder, shattering the bones to pieces. After Alphonso assured him his head was next, the little man promptly became compliant. He directed Alphonso to lift the mattress of his bed. He helped himself to two huge fistfuls of the cash piled there. He informed Enrico his debt was paid, leaving him to drag his irreparably broken shoulder to the hospital.

Alphonso enjoyed working for the big boss, but he wasn't doing as well as he thought he was. Joe Bonanno was growing frustrated with his behemoth of a bodyguard. In his defense, Alphonso was loyal. He would explicitly obey every order given to him, but he never did anything without first being told. This included ordinary, everyday tasks, like bringing the boss the newspapers and his coffee, or opening doors and searching visitors for weapons. He decided he would have to find another use for the man he started referring to as *the big stunad.*

The opportunity soon presented itself. One of Bonanno's *caporegime*s got himself into a jam. The big earner had a nasty compulsion for abusing women. This only became problematic when he raped and murdered the niece of a prominent politician. The police were cracking down on the Bonanno rackets to put pressure on them to give up the killer. The pimp, extortionist and contract killer responsible was far too valuable to Joe Bonanno to be sacrificed. So, Bonanno called his *very* expendable bodyguard in for a conference.

Alphonso was told if he took the rap for this crime, he would be promoted to *Soldato* when he emerged from prison. In addition, the boss promised his family would be well cared for while he did his time upstate. Being naïve, he saw what he thought was a golden opportunity to guarantee the well-being of his family, Alphonso readily agreed.

This was 1951. The death penalty was in full effect in New York at the time. The rape and murder of the niece of a State Senator was an express ticket for a ride in "Old Sparky." A year later, Alphonso Sciula had two thousand volts shot through his body. When this didn't kill the enormous man, the State gave him another shot. That did the trick, ending the poor sap's life once and for all.

The caporegime who Alphonso took the rap for only enjoyed an extra year of freedom. The reprobate pimp and murderer, Salvatore Ruttigliano, would be tripped up in the Bronx during a triple homicide—hits paid for by the Lucchese crime family. The victims were all mobsters, and killers in their own right. This was the only reason Sallie Gorgeous didn't follow Alphonso into the electric chair.

Meanwhile, Joe Bonanno, the self-proclaimed *oumo di rispetto*, reneged on his promise to Alphonso. He never gave his wife and young son a dime. They were forced to subsist on the money Camille's uncle—Roman's grandfather—sent them every month. The Sciula family never saw a penny from the Bonanno's until Roman had come of age and went to work for Carmine Gigante, becoming the favorite hammer of the crime family from Bushwick. Though considered the least promising of the local toughs known as the Farm Team, because of his size and strength, and seeming lack of morality, he was unquestionably the most useful. But he was shown no more respect than his poor dead father.

Unlike his parents, Roman Sciula was not a dullard. He was actually quite intelligent, though painfully shy and quiet. He had the misfortune of having a mother who had no education, and subsequently, placed no value in it. When Roman evinced a desire to stay home from school to avoid the taunts of his cruel classmates, his mother let him. Thus, his formal education ended in the third grade.

Roman had already learned to read, and he did a lot of it. Other than buying him newspapers and books, the only thing his mother provided approximating an education at all were the many stories she told him about his magnificent, noble grandfather; the man who made certain that all the children of Castellamare del Golfo had shoes on their feet—whether they could afford them or not. Though he never met the man, Roman aspired to one day be as honorable.

CHAPTER TWENTY-THREE

August 14, 1979
Bushwick

Eddie and Butchie were cruising the north end of the precinct looking for a gun, or someone suspicious to *toss*. They weren't responsible for the runs coming over the radio, but they monitored them just the same—in case one of their fellow cops needed help. Butchie heard the gruff voice of Lieutenant Russel Ederle come over the air.

"Eight three-desk to Central, K."

"Go, eight three-desk," Central acknowledged.

"Have eight-three Anti-Crime 10-02, forthwith," he ordered.

"Eight-three Crime, 10-04," Butchie responded.

The veteran cops understood a directive to return to the command immediately seldom had good news at the end of the trip. Their fear was there was an emergency at one of their homes. Eddie didn't dilly-dally turning the car around and heading with speed back to the stationhouse. He went lights and sirens down Wilson Avenue, pulling up on the sidewalk directly in front of the precinct door on DeKalb and Wilson.

They rushed inside, stopping in front of the desk. Despite not being in uniform, they saluted the former World War II Marine who was the desk officer. Lieutenant Ederle returned their salutes.

"What's the rumpus, Lou?" Eddie asked.

Ederle could see his officers were agitated. He quickly put them at ease.

"Relax, boys. Everything is fine."

Ederle waved his cops over to the corner of the desk, so he could speak with them privately.

"Butchie, you got a sister named Rosemarie?"

"Yeah, boss. What's up?"

"She called looking to talk to you—really demanding it. I think she's got a problem she wants you to handle for her. I asked her if there was anything I could do for her. She told me I could get my thumb out of my ass and find you. She told me if I had been doing my job in the first place, she wouldn't need to be bothering her 'asshole brother'. She sounded upset. That's why I gave you the 10-02. I don't mean to offend you, Butchie, but she sounds like a real cunt."

"That's because she is a cunt, Lou. She thinks you, me and every other swinging dick on this planet were put here to be of service to her. I'm sorry you had to deal with that."

"That's a relief," the lou said. "I thought it was me. I was afraid I was just getting cranky in my old age."

"Getting cranky? I'm sure *ye've* been there for quite a while, Lieutenant," Eddie chimed in.

"Who the fuck asked you, ya donkey wise-ass?" the lieutenant barked, then chuckled.

Because of the shared Marine Corps connection, unquestionable integrity, and dedication to doing the job, Eddie and Butchie were the lieutenant's two favorite cops. They were the only cops he permitted to joke with him like that. In fact, when the lieutenant was home, gathered around family, and had enough to drink to loosen his tongue, he would tell stories about his cops. The stories he told more often than not were about Butchie and Eddie.

"I'll give my sister a call. Thanks for the heads-up, Lou."

"No problem, Butchie. If there's anything else you need, just call the desk. I'll see you have it."

***

Rosemarie and Antoinette Bucciogrosso had been spoiled rotten by their father. Their sense of entitlement extended far beyond their childhood. They had never been made to take responsibility for anything. So, they never did. When Rosemarie was fourteen she found a perfect weakling to be her boyfriend. She latched onto the puny, but affluent Carmelo Casabello. Only sixteen himself, Carmelo was the only son of the local real estate broker. He was as spoiled as Rosemarie, but in a different way. A mama's boy, he never had to do anything or even make a decision that wasn't taken care of for him by his beloved mama.

Maria Casabello died of a heart attack when Carmelo was just twelve. The portly Maria was one hundred pounds overweight. She had been trying to indulge her husband and son with enormous, lavish servings of pasta, meat and pastry for years. But the Casabello men were slight, and tended to eat sparingly. Not being one to waste food, Maria usually took care of the leftovers herself. By the time of her heart attack, the blood in her arteries was so rich in cholesterol, it was more solid than liquid.

Carmelo had been subconsciously looking for a woman to replace his mother when Rosemarie found him. He was more than happy to allow the needy and manipulative Rosemarie to take over every aspect of his life. When Carmelo mentioned to Rosemarie he would be going away to college in a few years, Rosemarie was determined not to let that happen. She became pregnant because she wasn't releasing her talons from the wealthy and indulgent Carmelo. She exposed the pregnancy first to her parents. Nardo, rather than becoming angry, consoled the girl and threatened to kill Carmelo for taking advantage of her.

"No, Papa! I love him. Don't hurt my Carmelo. He'll take care of me and the baby. Just give him a chance."

So, Nardo went to see Bruno Casabello the next day. The real estate broker had been living in a trance-like stupor since the death of his wife. Functional enough only to run his business, he cared little about anything else. When Nardo demanded Carmelo marry his daughter, move in with the family, and go to work in the bakery to support his daughter and her child, Bruno was incapable of protest. He gave his consent, as well as a ten-thousand-dollar payoff to Nardo, so he wouldn't have his son arrested for having sex with the fourteen-year-old Rosemarie.

The Bucciogrossos welcomed the first of their fourth generation into the crowded house on Troutman Street. A year later, they decamped to

Ridgewood, moving all but the bakery on Central Avenue to the new house on Madison Street. By this time Carolina had given up all efforts to be involved with her disagreeable daughters. In the past when she had tried to force some responsibility on them, Nardo and his awful family cowed her into submission. The spoiling of the girls continued unabated.

Antoinette did not follow her sister's example. She managed to escape the house without becoming pregnant. She went to college in Connecticut. She managed to marry into a wealthy family while there. Thankfully for Butchie, she stayed in Connecticut. He had no contact with her other than to field her yearly phone calls around Christmas. Disguised as a holiday greeting, it was really just an opportunity for Antoinette to berate Butchie for being a disappointment to the family.

It was easier for Butchie to just endure the diatribe than hang-up on her. If he did, Antoinette would just keep calling back until he picked up the phone. This would only serve to prolong his agony. He let Antoinette rail at him until she was satisfied. Then he would forget about her for another year.

Two years after the move from Bushwick, Nonna Zacardi died in her sleep. Carolina found herself alone, without a single ally in that house. Nardo had already turned the girls against her. Butchie returned from Vietnam, horrified at the hollow, lonely woman his mother had become. His subsequent visits with her revealed she was becoming more and more despondent. After Butchie and Monica had been married and his son Michael was on the way, Butchie shared his concern for his mother with Monica. She didn't even bat an eyelash.

"Go get her. She'll live here with us. Those Bucciogrossos can go to hell. We don't need them. Carolina belongs with people who love her. Bring her home, Butchie."

The next day Butchie and Eddie were at the house in Ridgewood. Butchie told his mother what he intended to do. She seemed bewildered, as if she didn't fully comprehend what was being proposed, but she didn't refuse either. He told his mother to pack her things.

"What about Nardo?" Carolina asked uneasily.

"When I get you settled in at our house, I'll go to the bakery to straighten that asshole out," Butchie assured her.

As the three of them were leaving the building, Nonna Bucciogrosso was on the stoop. She had heard everything Butchie and Carolina had discussed. She understood her son's wife was leaving, never to return. She didn't particularly care one way or another. She despised her daughter-in-law, and was pleased to see the last of her, but she felt like she needed to mark the occasion with a snide comment.

"Good riddance to bad baggage. She was of no use to anyone around here anyway. Even her own daughters hate her."

This got Carolina upset. When she started to sob softly, Butchie walked over to his putative grandmother. He got very close, so he could speak quietly enough that only she could hear him.

"Fuck you, Nonna," he said. "You old, nasty, desiccated *fica*. And it's not gravy, you fucking imbecile. It's called sauce, and it's nowhere near as good as you think it is. Your coward sons like it only because their taste is in their asses."

Nonna B shrieked and hobbled off screaming into the house and up the stairs. Eddie was laughing when Butchie got back to the car.

"What did *ye* tell the old bat to elicit *dat* kind of reaction?"

"I told her she couldn't cook."

"*Dat's* a big deal to the Italians, I take it?"

"Only the biggest," Butchie said.

After Monica got Carolina squared away in the house in Glendale, she kissed Butchie, and sent him back to Bushwick with specific instructions.

"Tell that animal Nardo, if he comes around this house looking for his wife, I'll cut his nuts off. I'm serious, Butchie. I don't want to hear about that coward ever again. And as for your sisters; if you want to see those selfish, miserable bitches, it can't ever be here. They mistreat your mother terribly. I will not allow them in my house."

"I wouldn't have believed it was possible," Butchie laughed. "But I think you resent those three more than I do. No worries, Baby. We've seen the last of them."

***

When Butchie and Eddie got to the bakery, there was a handful of customers waiting to be served. Francesco was behind the counter, along with his fat, bitter, wife Angelina. Butchie disregarded the customers and addressed his hated uncle.

"Go get Nardo, Frankie—now. If I have to ask a second time I'll put your head through the display case."

Knowing that his nephew didn't make idle threats, Francesco waddled briskly into the back. He came back with Nardo, who seemed confused.

"*Che cos'e questo*?" Nardo asked.

"Mama is with me now. She's come to her senses and left you—finally."

"I won't give her a divorce," Nardo declared. "She won't get a dime from me."

"Nobody wants your money, you miscreant. Keep it. And as far as giving her a divorce; if I want you to, you will. Or, I could make a widow of her. When the time comes, you'll have a decision to make. Whichever you choose, I'm prepared to accommodate you."

Nardo could see from the dead-eyed look Butchie was giving him he was entering dangerous territory. He knew Butchie hated him so much, he was just looking for a reason to cause him intense pain and serious injury. He wisely put up his hands in supplication.

"One other thing, Nardo," Butchie added. "If you come to my house, I'll splatter your miserable ass in the street. *Capisce*?

"*Capisco*," Nardo said.

Having rescued his mother, and distancing himself from his sisters, Butchie still couldn't get around the fact that they were still family. Not much of a family, but related by blood nonetheless. As such, he couldn't divorce himself from the notion he still owed the girls a measure of loyalty. He harbored a protective instinct when it came to his sisters. It was with this in mind he went over to the *telephone switchboard* to return Rosemarie's call.

CHAPTER TWENTY-FOUR

August 14, 1979
Bushwick

When Butchie called Rosemarie at her and Carmelo's home in Ridgewood, Carmelo picked up the phone.

"Hi, Butchie. How are you?"

Carmelo sounded frazzled. Knowing his brother-in-law to be a frightened, vacillating man, Butchie knew he didn't really care how he was doing. He was just making nervous conversation—to avoid making meaningful conversation. Butchie also knew the mousey Carmelo was in no position to be making any decisions, not with the dynamic of the relationship between him and Rosemarie. He was fortunate to even have a speaking part in that household. Knowing Carmelo wouldn't dare to overstep his bounds and actually provide anything useful, Butchie asked him anyway, just to make him more uncomfortable.

"What's the trouble there, Carm?"

"Ah…I better put Rosemarie on the phone," he said.

Butchie could hear Carmelo calling Rosemarie to the phone in the background. She started yelling at Carmelo for even picking it up in the first place. When she came on the phone, she was already cross.

"It's about fucking time, Butchie. My daughter could be dead already for all you care. What took you so fucking long?"

"I was working, Rosemarie. I just got the message. What's wrong with Lucia now?" Butchie asked.

"Working, yeah right!" she scoffed. "And don't give me any of your attitude. If you were doing your job, she wouldn't be missing again."

Lucia Casabello was the Princess born to the Queen, at least for a while. Rosemarie bestowed her outrageous sense of entitlement on her daughter. Lucia took it a step further, and grew into adolescence with respect for no one—not even her over-indulgent parents. She discovered heroin when she was just twelve. Before she was thirteen, she was running away from home and walking the hooker stroll outside the shooting gallery on Porter and Thames.

Butchie and Eddie discovered her out there a year earlier when they were on their way over to the *nine-oh* to get gas.

"Holy shit! That's my niece. Pull over Eddie."

When they pulled to the curb, Lucia staggered over to the unmarked on someone else's borrowed spiked heels. They were at least two sizes too big. They made her already unsteady gate almost cartoonish. She was wearing a halter top and a dirty pair of cutoff jeans. Butchie thought they looked ridiculous, riding as they were, up the crack of her butt. When she came over to the car, she was glassy eyed and slurring her speech. She was filthy and stunk of the unmistakable funk of a heroin junky. She obviously hadn't bathed in days. She mustn't have recognized her uncle, because she reached into the car with her right arm—pocked and speckled with the blood of too many needle tracks to count. She grabbed Butchie by the crotch and cooed in a way she must have thought was seductive.

"Hey, daddy, want a date?" she asked, leering crookedly at him.

Butchie was out of the car in a flash. He twisted his niece's arm up behind her back and snapped handcuffs on her. He threw her into the back seat of the un-marked before she knew what was happening.

"What the fuck is wrong with you, Lucia? How long have you been out here?" Butchie demanded.

Lucia focused long enough to realize who was talking to her. It never occurred to her she might be in trouble.

"Oh, wow! Uncle Butchie. What are you doing here?"

"Focus, Lucia. How long have you been out here?"

"I don't know; maybe a week or two. Hey, can you lend me ten bucks? I'll suck your dick."

"Shut the fuck up, you little tart!" Butchie ordered. "I'm taking you home to your mother."

"I don't live there anymore. I moved out."

"You're thirteen, Lucia. You don't get to move out. Now sit back and keep quiet."

Butchie directed Eddie to take them to Rosemarie and Carmelo's house on Gates Avenue, around the corner from Carmelo's real estate office on Fresh Pond Road. He had taken over his father's very lucrative business, and moved it to Queens at the behest of his domineering wife.

When they got there, Butchie had Eddie stay with Lucia in the car, while he went in to confront his sister. He let himself in to discover Rosemarie sitting on the couch watching soap operas, and painting her toes.

"Any idea where your daughter is, Roe?"

"She's at school. Why?" she said defensively.

"No. She's not at school. She hasn't been there for two weeks. She hasn't been here either. Want to guess where I found her?"

"I don't know where she goes when she leaves the house. What am I supposed to do, follow her?"

"Cut the shit Rosemarie. She hasn't been home for two weeks. I found her walking the stroll on Porter and Thames. She has been sucking cock for heroin. She's already an addict. How many dicks do you suppose she had to suck to get that way?"

"She doesn't listen to me. What am I supposed to do?"

"She's thirteen. It's called parenting, Rosemarie. I know you have no experience with it, but there are books on it. Read one and give it a try."

"Why is it any of your business, Butchie?"

Butchie grabbed his forehead in frustration. He couldn't believe the nature of the conversation he was having with his self-absorbed younger sister.

"Okay, Roe," Butchie said. "Let me see if I can break it down into small pieces for you. I am the fucking police. Your daughter is a child. You have abandoned her to the wild; to be a junky and a prostitute. When she dies of an overdose, you will be arrested for abandonment and neglect. I know you don't give a shit about Lucia, but do you want to go to prison? Because if things keep going the way they're going, it's an absolute fucking certainty."

Rosemarie finally looked properly concerned. Butchie had no doubt her concern was exclusively for herself, but at this point he would take what he could get.

"What should I do, Butchie?" Roe finally asked.

"First, call that limp dishrag of a husband of yours. Tell him to take a break from slum-lording for a while. The two of you are going to take Lucia to either Bellevue or Elmhurst. They have detox facilities. After she's admitted, you find an in-patient rehab, somewhere far the fuck away from New York. See your daughter gets the help she needs."

"Why can't you take her to the hospital?" Rosemarie asked.

"Oh, I'm sorry. Are you busy? Is this an episode of General Hospital you just can't afford to miss? Because I'm the police, remember? If I show up at the hospital with a junky, prostitute, thirteen-year-old, they're going to want to know how she got that way, and where her parents are. I will be forced to take appropriate police action. Guess who goes to jail if I have to do that?"

Rosemarie finally complied with Butchie's instructions. At least as far as getting Lucia into a detox, but he doubted she would follow through with the in-patient rehab. That would be time-consuming and expensive. He didn't think his sister cared enough about her daughter to spend much of either on her. Butchie turned out to be correct.

For this phone call, Butchie was forced to absorb his sister's abuse before she would get to the point. It was just like her to blame her own poor parenting on the police. By her theory, because the police hadn't eradicated the drug problem, irrespective of the enormous demand, it was somehow the cops' fault when people became addicted. This was the typical mantra of people who refused to take responsibility for their own actions. Butchie decided he had heard enough.

"Actually, Roe, if you had followed up on Lucia's treatment the last time I snatched her off the street, we wouldn't be having this conversation. By you not admitting her in a long-term, in-patient rehab after she detoxed, you practically guaranteed she would be doing this again. Now, I'm going to go find her, but this time you better have a follow-up plan in place."

Butchie hung up on Rosemarie before she could have the chance to respond. He just didn't want to hear it anymore. He told Eddie what they had to do. Eddie just nodded. On the way to the shooting gallery where they both knew Lucia would be, Eddie broached the subject of Rosemarie.

"*Ye* know *yer* sister doesn't appreciate a fucking *ting ye're* doing for her? She won't follow through. The girl is as good as dead if she stays in *dat* house. *Ye* do know that, right?"

"I'm not sure if I don't know it yet, or I'm just unwilling to accept it. Rosemarie has had the world laid at her feet since she was born. She has no understanding of responsibility and hard work. As it relates to Lucia, my sister has tried absolutely nothing, and she's all out of ideas. I'm chewing on a fallback plan for when Roe screws the pooch again."

They headed down to the stroll on Porter and Thames. When they got there, they didn't see Lucia on the street, but they did recognize one of the girls on the stroll. A few years earlier, Butchie and Eddie had arrested Caramel Rivera for trying to discard her new-born baby into a garbage can after giving birth to him between two parked cars. They saved the baby, and Caramel avoided prison by completing a drug diversion program. Fortunately, the court never saw fit to award her with visitation, because here she was. Shopping her strung-out body to anyone with ten bucks. Butchie pulled up next to her and Eddie said hello.

"Oh, hey! Hi Eddie," Caramel said.

"Caramel, where is Lucia?" Eddie asked casually.

"I haven't seen her tonight," she said.

"If I have to ask a second time, Caramel, *ye're* going to jail for the next three days. I don't imagine *ye'll* be getting *yer* fix in there."

"She's in the house taking care of a trick," Caramel offered immediately.

"Thank *ye*, love," Eddie said.

Eddie and Butchie knew that the house Caramel referred to was the first floor of 135 Thames Street. An abandoned three-story home, the junky prostitutes had commandeered the first level. They were squatting in there to shoot up and take care of their tricks on the dirty mattresses scattered about the floor. When they entered the building, they encountered Lucia on the staircase with her head buried in the lap of a bald, fat man with a cheap suit. He had his head thrown back and hadn't realized two plain-clothes police officers were about to spoil his party.

Butchie pulled Lucia off of the fat man's penis by her hair. He tossed the stoned girl over to Eddie, who slapped handcuffs on her. Butchie confronted the trick.

"Do you know how old she is?" Butchie asked.

"No," the man said.

"Would it bother you to know she was fourteen?"

"Lips are lips," the man said, shrugging.

Butchie put his lights out with one punch. Then he alerted the rest of the junkies on the first floor the well-dressed fat man with all the money had passed out, and they should make certain no one robbed him of his large wad of cash and very nice things. They were already descending upon him like vultures as Butchie and Eddie dragged Lucia out of the building.

At Gates Avenue, Butchie and Eddie brought Lucia directly into the living room. They uncuffed her, and she immediately nodded out on the carpet. The look on Rosemarie's face communicated a combination of disgust and irritation. Butchie suspected she was irritated because she found the situation with her sick daughter to be an inconvenience, and little more. He was prepared to be disappointed, but asked anyway.

"Have you made arrangements at Elmhurst for the detox?"

"No. How was I supposed to know you would find her?" Rosemarie asked, clearly perturbed he had.

"Because I told you I knew where she was. Did you make a reservation for her in a rehab facility yet?"

"Who is supposed to pay for that, Butchie?"

"You and Carmelo are, Roe. She's your child, and you two have nothing but money—what with Carmelo's little real estate empire. Do you not have a single parental instinct? If you don't get her into an in-patient rehab, we'll be doing this again in two months…if she doesn't overdose before that."

"This is bullshit, Butchie! If you and your thieving Irish partner over there had been doing your job instead shaking down mobsters, and taking pay-offs to let them sell drugs, none of this would have happened."

Eddie's head snapped around at that. He glared hard at the chubby, entitled, overgrown brat in front of him.

"Watch *dat*, missy," Eddie growled. "*Ye're* no *fookin* family of mine. If *ye* want to call me a thief, *ye* should understand *ye* might not get to draw another breath."

At the thinly veiled threat, Rosemarie looked to Butchie for help. He would never lift a finger to help her again. He was regarding his sister with a dead-eyed malignant stare. She well knew Butchie's hatred for the Mafia, and she knew the reasons. She knew he would never take a penny that was not his own, and certainly never from a group of people he regarded as virulent. She had cast that stone for no other reason than to break a window. Rosemarie finally realized she had gone too far.

"Don't ever call me again, Rosemarie—not for anything. I am changing my phone number. When Antoinette wants to know why she can't get in touch with me this Christmas, you can tell her she's dead to me, too."

Butchie and Eddie left without another word. They both silently fumed in the car for the rest of the tour. Neither trusted themselves to do any police work after absorbing Rosemarie's abuse. If they had tried, someone would likely have gotten hurt—probably badly—and for no real reason other than misdirected rage. Eddie broke the silence when they were changing in the locker room.

"Please tell me *ye* meant it when *ye* said those people were dead to *ye*," Eddie asked.

"That's it, Eddie. I'm done with the lot of them. The only Bucciogrossos I give a shit about anymore live under my roof in Glendale."

"I'm glad to know *ye* finally realize where *yer* bread is buttered, Boyo, but what about Lucia. I know you. *Ye* won't abandon *dat* girl—even if her mother already has. What are we going to do about her?"

"I'm going to remove my sister and Carmelo from the equation," Butchie said.

CHAPTER TWENTY-FIVE

August 15, 1979
Ridgewood

After Butchie's tour ended, at a little after midnight, he called Monica to let her know he would be late.

"I have to take care of Lucia again. It should only take an hour or two."

"Is she back on the drugs?"

"She never got off of them. My sister didn't follow up on her treatment. Eddie and I had to snatch her out of that flop-house in the *nine-oh* again. Roe doesn't want to pay for rehab. She doesn't think it's her responsibility. I have to save Lucia from my sister. I'll tell you all about it when I come home."

"Whatever you need to do, baby. Just be careful."

"The dangerous stuff is already done. I just have to make some reports and notifications. It will be in the laps of the 104 Squad and the Administration for Children's Services after this."

"I'm more worried about your heart breaking than I am about you getting shot. You've given them too much of yourself already. When this is over, and Lucia is safe, can we finally be done with those people?"

"Yeah, Monica. What happens to Lucia after this will be up to her."

"I love you, Butchie."

"That's what keeps me going."

At the 104 Precinct, Butchie approached the Desk officer. The lieutenant was just making his command log entries for the incoming late tour. Butchie waited for him to finish. He noticed the matching gaslight sconces on the back wall—long since dormant, behind the desk. He knew the pre-Civil War precinct house had once been lit exclusively by gaslight. Until the advent of electricity, the whole city had. He wondered if there had been a heroin problem back when those gaslights were burning.

Lieutenant Kirkowski looked up from the blotter and recognized Butchie. Kirkowski had been a Sergeant in the *eight three* before being promoted. He knew and respected the cop in front of his desk.

"What's up, Butchie? You need help with something?"

He told Ernie Kirkowski what he had, and the family dynamic involved. He offered to walk the complaint directly upstairs to the Detective Squad. Kirkowski handed him a blank UF61—the uniform complaint report, and the report of suspected child abuse/neglect, and directed Butchie to the staircase leading to the Squad.

Detective Sam Gribben knew Butchie by reputation. Gribben had been a detective in the *one-oh-four* for the last thirty years. He had shot his way into the Detective Bureau back in the early 50s when he intercepted an armored car robbery on his foot post on Myrtle Avenue. He shot all three bandits dead with one head shot a piece, from twenty five feet. Miraculously, he had avoided being shot himself despite the robbers firing more than thirty times at him.

That night in the precinct, a lieutenant from the Police Commissioner's office came to the one-oh-four and pinned a shiny new detective shield on him. Gribben had been working in the Squad from that day since. Because of the sudden and fortuitous promotion, he had never had to even consider compromising his integrity to make detective. If he had been forced to, the devout Catholic and war veteran would have likely stayed on his foot post and eschewed the promotion.

Gribben was well aware of Butchie's integrity. Many of Sam's fellow detectives thought Butchie's adamant refusal to bend was just obstinate stupidity. Gribben knew it took courage to face down that kind of peer pressure and admired the cop for it.

"Sorry about dropping this on you at the end of your tour, Detective, but I believe my niece's life is in peril, and my sister is complicit. She's just going to abandon her fourteen-year-old daughter to the wolves."

"Tell me the story, Officer Bucciogrosso. We'll see if we can't take care of *our* problem."

When Gribben emphasized the problem was "ours" even before he heard the appalling truth of it, Butchie was moved and relieved. He knew he had an ally for the awful task at hand. He had already reconciled himself to the fact that he was cutting his sisters loose—finally turning his back on the ungrateful pair. The last thing he would ever want was to throw them under the wheels of the bus, irrespective of their criminal and moral ambivalence, but Lucia's life was in the balance. Even still, Butchie probably wouldn't have been able to go through with it, if not for the support and understanding of the detective who would have to do it for him.

While Gribben would have preferred to go home on time, for Butchie, he would do whatever he could. He felt an obligation to help the obviously suffering cop. He knew Butchie was struggling mightily with his decision to give his sister up. But when he heard the story, they both understood it was the only chance Lucia had for survival. Gribben would never turn his back on that kind of moral commitment.

The Special Services for Children Agency was notified. When it was verified Lucia was admitted to the thirty-day detox program at Elmhurst Medical Center, Gribben went to the house on Gates Avenue to drag Rosemarie and Carmelo in for questioning. After separating them, a few minutes of conversation revealed Rosemarie's indifference to the plight of her daughter. as far as Sam Gribben was concerned, Carmelo was little more than a cash-cow and a pussy. He and the Special Services for Children investigator both recommended to the District Attorney that Rosemarie and Carmelo be charged with endangering the welfare of a child and criminal neglect in this case.

This drama which would play itself out over several years. Gribben would stay on top of the case and keep Butchie appraised of its progress. An order of protection was generated from Family Court. Carmelo and Rosemarie would be prevented from having any contact with the daughter they had proven to care so little about.

Lucia would be awarded a Family Court Guardian. She would be mandated to attend an in-patient, long term drug program. Under these circumstances, her recovery seemed to take hold. She would live and continue her education in a halfway house far away from New York City, at least until her eighteenth birthday. After which, she would choose to remain at the halfway house in Walton, New York, up near the Pennsylvania border.

When Butchie got home early that morning, Monica was waiting for him in her bathrobe at the door. She hugged him tightly and kissed him. When he tried to relate what he had to do over the last few hours, Monica quieted him.

"I know what you did, Butchie. You saved Lucia again. I don't need to know the details. Just come to bed with me. Even Superman needs to sleep sometimes."

CHAPTER TWENTY-SIX

August 28, 1979
Bushwick

Two weeks later, while awaiting the grand re-emergence of Sallie Gorgeous, Butchie and Eddie found themselves back in uniform for the day. Because of manpower shortages due to the cops taking summer vacations, they were forced to man a sector car for a tour. This did not represent the imposition for them it might have. Most cops who finally get the privilege to work in plain clothes, bitterly resent having to put *the bag* back on—even for a day. Butchie and Eddie actually enjoyed interacting with the community on radio runs. Uniform patrol was not as effective or focused a platform for doing the hard police work with which the two had become accustomed, but it was by no means unpleasant.

The inane nature of chasing the radio gave them the opportunity to discuss their changing environment. The two had intimated to each other they hoped to have a more profound effect on the cancer of narcotics killing Bushwick. They had figured out to do it, they would have to work their way into a narcotics investigation unit.

With this in mind, they conferred with Mick Doheny. Mickey had finally retired after thirty-five years on the job—all of it on his foot post on Knickerbocker Avenue. Even though he never aspired to more, Mick had become well-known and respected by the many cops he had helped and trained over the years—both on the job and in the gym. Many of those cops ascended the ranks to positions of power within the department.

One of those cops was Inspector Thomas Sheridan. Sheridan was now the commanding officer of Brooklyn Narcotics. There were rumors he was putting a taskforce together to attack the heroin problem at its root. Butchie and Eddie had heard those rumors. They wanted in. Mickey promised the boys he would talk to Sheridan on their behalf. First, he wanted to make sure they knew what they were getting themselves into.

"I spent my whole career on a foot post because I wanted to," Mickey began. "I could have been a detective. Hell, I was offered the shield outright a half-dozen times."

"Why did *ye* turn it down?" Eddie asked.

"You gotta remember, this was the fifties and the sixties. The job was dirtier then. Corruption was the rule, not the exception—like it is now. I wouldn't take money. You couldn't go into plain clothes or the Bureau unless you went on *the pad.* You had to take the money or no one would trust you. Well I wasn't doing that. I chose my foot post and existed in my own private universe. It wasn't a bad career. I got to help a lot of people, and I didn't have to do anything I'd later be ashamed of. I recognized early on what a monster the drugs were. I saw it change everyone it touched, how it turned some cops into greedy thieving animals without a conscience. They would sell out their own mother for a crooked sawbuck. I wanted no part of it. As a footman, I wasn't allowed to enforce the gambling and drug laws anyway. So no one tried to pay me to look the other way. But know this; if you want to take this on, it's going to be hard, and it's going to be messy. You two have families now. You can't go running off like Wyatt Earp—without a thought for them. Your primary goal going in had better be not letting your families get splattered—by the filth, or the blood. Make no mistake, it will be bloody. Narcotics is the Mafia's lifeblood. If you try to cut it off, you will not be immune to the violence. They are ruthless animals with limited imaginations. They think a bullet is the answer for every problem, and when they are faced with an existential crisis, everyone goes on the kill list. That includes your wives and children. Remember, the Mafia know where Glendale is. Some of them live there, too. Are you prepared for that?"

When Butchie and Eddie assured Mickey they were, he agreed to call Inspector Sheridan.

With the expected return of Sallie Gorgeous, their sense of urgency had increased exponentially. They decided they would pump Roman Sciula for an idea regarding who among the drug crews were vulnerable enough to flip as cooperators. They wouldn't further expose Roman. He was too valuable as a fly on the wall. The old mobsters talked freely in front of him. They thought he was mentally deficient. About that, they were mistaken. Roman heard and retained everything. Then he shared it with Butchie and Eddie. The old gangsters didn't know it, but they no longer had any secrets.

At around 1530 hours, Butchie, as the recorder in the radio car, picked up a shots fired job at 604 Hart Street. Eddie was the operator for this half of the tour. From the driver's seat he recalled something about the address.

"That scumbag Durr family lives in *dat* building," Eddie remembered. "This could get dicey. *Dey* are *nothin* but trouble."

"Yeah," Butchie agreed. "But they're starting to lose their steam. The old man is just a sick old junky. Other than welfare fraud, he can't cause much mayhem anymore. And the oldest son got a window put in his chest this spring when he tried to rob the wrong liquor store in Greenpoint. The old Polish owner put two 12-gauge slugs through him. He's deader than Elvis. The other two brothers are scumbags, but they just rob other junkies. The dope will take care of them soon enough."

"Isn't there a younger brother? He's a bruiser I *tink*, with long hair."

"His name is Paddy, but I hear he's a good kid."

"How is *dat* even possible, coming from such disaster?"

"My neighbor's son played football with the kid in Glendale. He said he's smart, polite and a great ball player. He was an All-City linebacker this year at Brooklyn Tech. He's supposed to be going to Columbia in the fall."

"It would be a miracle if he escaped *dat* calamity. Still, let's be on our guard."

As they got to the building, just off the corner of Irving Avenue, the cops could see the front door wide open. When Butchie looked a little further, he could see the super's apartment door on the first floor ajar. Butchie informed central they were *10-84*, present at the job, and they were entering the first-floor apartment.

When Eddie and Butchie went in to the apartment, they were struck by the sharp sulfurry smell of freshly expended gunpowder. They drew their revolvers and advanced into the living room. What Butchie saw in there was in equal parts heart-rending and surreal. The young Durr kid was standing by the edge of the couch. He had a bewildered and wounded look on his face. His pants were around his ankles, his hands above his head, and incongruously, he had a great big swinging erection.

Slumped naked over the arm of the couch was the superintendent's notoriously sexy wife, Inez. She was obviously dead, a large spreading pool of blood forming under her body, soaking the sofa.

Laying on the rug in front of his dead wife and her stunned young lover, was the superintendent, Hector Vasconcellos. Butchie and Eddie knew Hector well. He was the super for this building and three others on DeKalb Avenue. He had been a confidential informant for the two cops for the last few years. Hector was also quite dead. He still had the .38 revolver clutched in his right hand. The majority of the top of his head was gone, and his blood and brain matter were dripping on him from the blades of the ceiling fan, slowly spinning above him. The faint wisp of gun smoke wafting out of his open mouth was unnerving to Butchie. He knew in a glance exactly what he was looking at, but he still had to ask.

"What the fuck Happened here?"

Paddy told the tale of his almost four-year affair with Inez, which began when he was just thirteen—all with his hands above his head, and his pants below his knees. He finally pulled his pants up when Butchie suggested he *put the howitzer away*, before he hurt someone else with it.

Butchie could see an inflamed, red, circular burn on Paddy's forehead. Butchie thought he knew what it was.

"How'd that happen?" he asked, pointing at Paddy's head.

"After Hector shot Inez, he pressed the gun to my head. Then he put the gun in his mouth and fired it."

"Why didn't he shoot *you*?"

Paddy had a confused look, as if the thought hadn't occurred to him.

"I don't know," he said.

After they dropped the kid off at the detective squad and were relieved at the crime scene, the two partners went *end of tour*. As they were changing in the locker room, Eddie was deeply saddened from the human wreckage they had found the young man mired within. He knew the Durr kid would be emotionally shattered. The crushed look on Paddy's face, and Eddie's own experience told him that much. The boy probably didn't know it yet, but he likely loved Inez, and he would blame himself for her death for the rest of his life. Just as Eddie still blamed himself for the death of Caitlin McGurk.

If Eddie was deeply saddened, Butchie was very nearly distraught. His heart was breaking for the kid. He never imagined he would meet anyone with a more lonely and miserable childhood than his own. Now Butchie had the misfortune of conceding he had. Paddy Durr, he knew, was totally and fundamentally alone in this world, and Butchie blamed Bushwick's heroin trade for it.

"This kind of misery could not exist but for the dope running through these streets. That's a good kid upstairs. Now he's broken. His whole family are junkies. Who's going to help him through this?"

"I don't mean to disappoint *ye*, Butchie, but some *tings* are so bad, no amount of help will get *ye* through them. Some *tings ye* just have to carry. But on the subject of the dope, *ye* are correct. It's killing the whole neighborhood, and everyone in it."

"Enough is enough, Eddie. Till now, all we've done is shovel shit against the tide. It just keeps coming back and washing over us. I'm sick of it. We've gotta do something about the source of this misery. It's La Cosa Nostra. We have to crush them. It's the only way we can give a kid like that a fighting chance. As it stands, he doesn't have a fucking prayer."

Eddie got a wistful look about him. He loved Butchie like a brother. He loved his earnestness, his absolute devotion to the people of Bushwick. He even loved his naiveté. Eddie recognized it as such. He had a little more experience with the darker side of human nature than Butchie. He knew you could change circumstances, but you weren't changing human beings. If they were meant to suck, then by God, they would suck.

Eddie knew misery would be their constant companion. In fact, as cops it was their reason to be. But he had to admit he liked it when the wicked got their chance to suffer. He also liked sleeping at night. Consistently doing the right thing let him sleep like a baby. Eddie conceded Butchie had always been his best opportunity to do so, and he never asked him to do anything that ever gave his conscience a minute of concern. So even though he knew

Butchie would never achieve the results he desired, Eddie would at least give him the chance to try.

"Okay, *boyo*. If *ye* want to, we'll do this *ting*."

CHAPTER TWENTY-SEVEN

August 28, 1979
Glendale

When Eddie got home that evening, his wife, Bernadette, was just preparing to serve the family supper. Her timing for this was always uncanny. Her years as a waitress at Donovan's had lent her an expertise she practiced regularly, what with Eddie's unpredictable schedule. All she required was an hour's warning, and she would have a sumptuous dinner just awaiting Eddie's arrival. She noticed her husband's pensive mood immediately.

They had been married shortly after Eddie returned from Vietnam and became a police officer. As children of the strife in Northern Ireland, they would have been forgiven for being jaded pessimists, but they were not. By necessity and conditioning they were realists. They understood that bad things happened sometimes to good people, and they happened randomly. All you could do was try not to bring misery on another and hope they would do the same for you. Despite this, their outlook on life was none-the-less optimistic. Their shared point of view was reflected in the names of their daughters; Constance, Faith, and Hope.

Eddie was delighted as always to see his girls, but he seemed reserved and somewhat sad to Bernadette. He was pleasant during dinner, remarking how much he loved Bernadette's Irish country meatloaf, but he was not his usual buoyant self. When dinner was done, Bernadette had the girls clear the table. While they were in the kitchen, doing the dishes, Bernadette came over to sit next to him. She reached across the table, and took Eddie's calloused and scarred hands in her own.

"What has you so troubled, my love?"

"I'm not troubled," Eddie lied. "Didn't I tell *ye* how much I loved *yer* Irish country meatloaf?"

"You're deflecting again, Eddie. You can put as many adjectives in front of it as you want. It's just meatloaf and mashed potatoes. Now stop with the bullshit and tell me what's wrong."

"Is it that obvious?"

"Come now, Eddie. You are as subtle as a punch in the face. I know my man. Tell me what has you so vexed," Bernadette prodded gently.

"We had just a God-awful day today," Eddie began. "We were back in uniform for the day. A little after noon, we had to handle a murder-suicide job. We knew the victims."

"Oh, Eddie, that's horrible."

"It's worse than *dat*. The husband was our informant. He is…was the superintendent for a bunch of buildings on Hart and DeKalb. He came home to find his much younger wife, Inez, getting shagged by the seventeen-year-old neighbor from upstairs. The poor man must have lost his mind with grief, because I don't *tink* he would have hurt a soul otherwise."

"What did he do?"

"He shot his wife in the chest three times—right in front of the boy. Then he blew his own brains out. When we got there, Hector and Inez were already dead. The kid was just standing in the middle of the carnage—in shock. He had his hands up, and his wanker bobbing in the breeze—as if it didn't know fuck-all what to do with itself."

"Why are you so concerned for him? It seems he brought this upon himself."

"Ordinarily, I might agree. But, we know him, too. He's the youngest from that awful Durr family I told *ye* about."

"Trouble and heartache seem to be that family's business," Bernadette observed.

"Not this one, love. He's the only redeemable thing in that whole *fookin* house. He's a student and an athlete. As shattered as he was, I got the impression he loved Inez. It might not have been right, but it looked real.

He's supposed to be going to Columbia in the fall, if he can get past this. I have my doubts. The boy is alone."

"Does he have no one at home?"

"No one of any use to him."

"That is truly sad."

"Not as sad as Butchie is right now. I *tink* he identifies with the boy. He's angry and he hurts for him. Butchie rightly blames the drugs. He says it's the final straw. He wants to take on the Mafia, *tinking* that taking down the Bonannos will change things somehow. I know better, but I'm going to help him."

"So, you'll hold his hand on his way to disillusionment, is that the plan?"

"He's my little brother, Bernadette. When he discovers what perfect monsters humankind can be, I need to be there for him."

"First of all, he's a grown man. You would think by now, Butchie would know as much. Life hasn't exactly been kind and gentle to that one. He's not the only one who can relate to what that young boy is going through, is he?"

"Whatever do *ye* mean?"

"Oh, Eddie, you're back in Belfast again. I've been watching you go there from time to time ever since you told me what happened to you. It's okay. But I just wish you could put the guilt down for once. You did all you could. For you—perfectionist that you are—it will never be enough. You're still beating yourself up about it. You should give yourself a break and be done with it finally. But, you won't. I know you loved Caitlin—no less than you love the girls and me. You would have given anything to protect her—even your own life—just like you would for us, and even though I know you can never forgive yourself for what happened to her, I forgive you. I forgive you, Eddie—for not being able to forgive yourself. I can't make you put it behind you, but I can make you understand that much. You are the finest, most honorable man I've ever known. There's no better husband, no better father, and no truer friend anywhere in the world. I'm here for you, Eamon Curran, no matter what you feel you have to do."

"What would I do without *ye*?" Eddie asked.

"Not very well, I should think."

"No truer words...," Eddie left the rest unsaid, as he pulled his beautiful, devoted wife onto his lap.

Bernadette kissed him and stroked the back of his thick neck, silently thanking God for sending her such a man to love.

CHAPTER TWENTY-EIGHT

September 2, 1979
Bushwick

Butchie and Eddie agreed to come to work a little early. They got approval from their Platoon Commander, Lieutenant Ederle, to start their tour at noon, rather than the customary four to twelve they usually did. Their purpose was to kick over some rocks to see what slimy things crawled out. They were committed to making the Bonannos miserable. To do it, they would need to conduct an in-depth narcotics investigation. They realized they had a rudimentary understanding of the heroin business in Bushwick, but they had no real hard intelligence.

Because of corruption concerns, the NYPD generally frowned upon uniform police officers enforcing drug and gambling offenses. As anti-crime cops, Eddie and Butchie occupied a sort of grey area. Their primary responsibility since getting into plain clothes was to focus on robberies and guns. They did that very well. As a result, they knew little about the day-to-day operation of the Bonanno drug spots. If they were going to bust that operation up, it was incumbent upon them to find out. They figured the best way to do it would be to set up an observation post on Troutman Street, between Knickerbocker and Irving Avenues. This was the busiest heroin block in the city.

Butchie and Eddie entered 212 Troutman Street from Wilson Avenue unseen. They hopped over the rooftops until they reached the roof of the six-story apartment building on Knickerbocker Avenue. This building had a panoramic view of their target drug set. They settled in to learn what they could by observing the block through binoculars.

Even at noon, the block was a hive of activity. The junkies were lined up on the sidewalk as if they were on a government cheese line. There was one, thin hyperkinetic male of obvious Italian ethnicity, barking out orders and directions—admitting one person at a time into the drug spot. The man was wearing what the cops called a Mafia tuxedo; beige velour sweatsuit over a white wife-beater tee-shirt, a thick rope chain necklace and white Capezio shoes. They recognized who he was even without the binoculars. His hideous mismatched hairpiece sat on his head like a dead squirrel.

"That's *Cockeye* Morabito running the show down there," Butchie said.

"Oh, I know him," Eddie said. "He's an asshole. His eyes are so crossed that when he cries, the tears roll down his back."

"The eyes are unsettling enough, but I can't get past the toupee. It's so obviously a rug, I swear I saw a tag sticking out from under it that said Monsanto. Plus, it doesn't match his natural hair color. The thing looks like it was soaked in black ink. Doesn't he know his hair is brown?"

"With those eyes, who the fuck knows what he's looking at when he's in front of the mirror. He could be looking out the window for all we know."

"What more do we know about him?" Butchie asked.

"Apart from the fact that he has the cheesiest mustache in the history of mustaches, he's an arrogant moron," Eddie said. "I once pulled him over for running a red light. He got all huffy and told me I would never find the drugs. I was just going to warn and admonish the imbecile. When he dared me to search the car, I took it as an invitation. He had all kinds of extra buttons on his dashboard. I rightly surmised he had a trap in there. The jerk challenged me to find the right combination to open it. I used a crowbar instead. I found a pistol and a half ounce of smack behind the radio. A liberal judge threw the evidence out. He said the search was unreasonable. Probably was. But it was worth it just to see the expression on the Cockeye's face when I tore the radio out."

"Is he still driving the same car?" Butchie asked.

"No, but I'll give *ye* one guess which car on the block *is* his."

"I'm guessing the babyshit-brown Riviera with the chrome spokes."

"Very good, Butchie. What gave it away?"

"It's the only car on the block not propped on cinder-blocks."

"There's no putting one past *ye*, Boyo."

The cops sat up there for several hours. It was all more of the same. The people on the cheese lines waited for their chance to go into the hallway to buy. The lines never seemed to get shorter. Cockeye Morabito continued to be an animated and annoying presence on the street—until 2200 hours.

Morabito looked at his watch. Then he ran into the drug spot. When a red Cadillac pulled in front of the building, Morabito came out to it with a large white paper bag, which appeared to be heavy. He gave it to the man in the passenger seat of the Caddy. Eddie recognized him to be Gaspar Ignacio, one of Lilo Gigante's former head zips. He supposed Gaspar belonged to Sallie Gorgeous now. Eddie didn't know who was driving, so he read the plate off to Butchie, who copied it down on his note pad. Eddie saw Gaspar hand Morabito a smaller white paper bag. This, Cockeye took over to his car where he locked it in the trunk. At this point Morabito went over to the line and seemed to be chasing everyone away. The junkies appeared disappointed and started shambling off the block dejectedly. After the crowd had been dispersed, Morabito got in his Riviera and drove off the block.

Butchie ran the plate of the Caddy for a registered owner. Central reported the car was registered to a Donato Amoroso. They both knew that name. Donato Amoroso was known to be the head zip in charge of the heroin racket for the Bonannos.

"What may we surmise from all of *dat*?" Eddie fulminated.

"I'm guessing the big bag the zips drove off with was probably the proceeds from the spot for the day. The smaller bag was most likely the dope Morabito will need to open the spot tomorrow. Seems like closing time is 2200 hours. I think we're going to have to be on the corner of Troutman and Irving at that time tomorrow to grab Morabito and find out for sure."

"Now we're getting somewhere," Eddie said.

CHAPTER TWENTY-NINE

September 3, 1979
Bushwick

At 2203 hours the next day, Butchie and Eddie were camped out in their unmarked car on the corner of Troutman and Irving. They observed Donato Amoroso and Gaspar Ignacio drive off Troutman Street, past them and up toward Wyckoff. Two minutes later, they saw Cockeye Morabito's light-brown Riviera pull away from the curb in front of the drug spot. Butchie and Eddie hit their lights and siren and came down Troutman Street the wrong way. They blocked Morabito's progress by pulling diagonally across the street. The cops got out of their car and approached Morabito with their shields around their necks and their guns out. Butchie took the driver's side while Eddie covered the passenger's door.

"Turn the car off and step out with your hands where I can see them," Butchie ordered.

Morabito rolled his window down a crack and wanted to discuss things.

"I didn't do nothing. Why are you bothering me?"

"Bothering you?" Butchie said. "Aren't you Sonny Bono? I just want to meet Cher and get your autograph."

With that, Butchie shattered the side window with the butt of his revolver. He reached in to grab Morabito by his thick rope chain, and yanked him through the broken window, driving him down onto the pavement, where he handcuffed him.

"Uh, Butchie," Eddie alerted him. "The bag isn't in the trunk tonight. It's sitting on the passenger seat."

"Well if that isn't a lungeable area, I don't know what is," Butchie said. "Thanks, Cockeye. You saved me the trouble of getting a search warrant for your trunk."

Butchie picked up Cockeye and sat him down with his back against the car. Eddie went into the car and peered into the bag.

"There's gotta be eight ounces of dope, and a *burner* in the bag," Eddie informed Butchie.

"Hey!" Morabito shouted. "You're not supposed to touch that! I know my rights. This is a bad search. You did this to me the last time, Curran. I'm going to have your job. You are so fucked! Wait till my lawyer…"

Butchie shut the weasely mobster up abruptly by grabbing him by the throat and hoisting him to his feet.

"Who the fuck are you even talking to, Cockeye?" Butchie asked. "You're looking in every direction but forward. How do you not crash into things? Nobody cares about your encyclopedic knowledge of the laws of search and seizure. You're under arrest."

"This won't stick," Morabito taunted. "You didn't read me my rights."

"You're a regular F. Lee Bailey. Aren't you, Cockeye?" Butchie said. "You want your rights? Here they are; you have the right to shut your fucking mouth, or I will knock those horse teeth down your throat, and out your ass. Any of that unclear?"

Morabito realized Butchie and Eddie had no intention of convening a Mapp Hearing on Troutman Street. Like it or not, he was going to jail. He still thought his lawyer would get him out of the charge. That was because Cockeye had no understanding of the automobile exception for warrantless searches. He was also unfamiliar with the codicil regarding weapons, lungeable areas, and plain sight observations. By the time he finally found out about those things, he realized he was already totally fucked.

In the meantime, Eddie and Butchie thought they might like to take a crack at interrogating him. They brought Morabito up to the Anti-Crime office. This time they formally read him the Miranda warnings.

"I ain't telling you cops shit," Cockeye seemed to be telling someone to the right and somewhere behind Butchie.

Despite threatening to clam up, Morabito spent the next two hours boasting about what a big man he was in the Bonanno crime family. He claimed to be the only one they trusted to run the very lucrative operation on Troutman Street. Cockeye described himself as indispensable. In the course of not telling the cops anything, Morabito told them everything. He bragged about getting the product from the big bosses. He even dropped their names. He boasted his spot was generating ten grand a day. He taunted the cops they couldn't charge him with the gun, as it was the gun for the kid he paid a hundred bucks a day to run the spot. He gave the spot worker the gun to protect himself in case one of the buyers got an idea about robbing him. Cockeye said he collected the gun every night, only to hand it off to whomever was running the spot the next day.

"But you'll never prove that," Morabito said. "I use a different Puerto Rican kid every week."

Despite refusing to tell the cops shit, Morabito provided Eddie and Butchie with a clear picture of the drug operation and a wealth of information regarding the power structure of the narcotics end of the Bonanno family. They sent Morabito to Central Booking, charged with Criminal Possession of a Controlled Substance in the 1st degree, as well as Criminal Possession of a Weapon in the 2nd degree, for the loaded firearm. Cockeye Morabito would be cooling his heels on Rikers Island until his case could wind through the labyrinth of the criminal justice system.

"That was exhausting," Butchie observed.

"Yeah, but now we know what we need to know."

"It would have been nice to flip Morabito."

"We're not ready to start flipping witnesses. We haven't even met our ultimate target yet. When we're ready, we'll know where to find Cockeye. After he does a little bit of hard time, I'm sure he'll be more amenable to helping us," Eddie predicted.

CHAPTER THIRTY

September 21, 1979
Bushwick

Butchie and Eddie were out in the street early for their four to twelve Anti-Crime tour. They were cruising the neighborhood in their unmarked car, just getting a feel for the vibe in the street. Near the corner of Himrod Street and Wyckoff Avenue, the cops encountered a peculiar traffic snarl. There were cars double and triple parked for hundreds of feet in every direction. The focal point of this conclave was the coffee shop on the corner there.

Il Trombone Arrugginito was known to be the hangout and headquarters of Donato Amoroso, the head Sicilian drug man in the Bonanno organization. Roman Sciula had already informed the cops Amoroso was regarded as the *Head Zip.* According to Roman, Amoroso sold out Gigante, and sanctioned the hit at the behest of the new, and soon to be returning "Boss of All Bosses," Sallie Gorgeous.

What was occurring on the corner was like nothing Eddie or Butchie had ever seen. The cars gathered there told their own story. The ones nearest the coffee shop and parked right in front were all elaborate Cadillacs and Lincoln Continentals. These were immediately recognizable to the two cops as *Mafia staff cars*, belonging to the higher echelon of bosses in La Cosa Nostra. As the assembled vehicles emanated away from the epicenter, the size and the luxury of the cars decreased, until you were a block or more away. Then they became Buick Regals and Oldsmobile 98s, or the sporty Rivieras. Butchie and Eddie understood these lesser cars belonged to the younger *associates* and *wanna-bes*. These aspiring *button men* remained near their cars, dressed in their usual velour sweatsuits, adorned with the thick gaudy rope chain necklaces and bracelets they usually wore. Whatever was going on in the coffee shop, they were mandated to be present, even if they weren't permitted to enter. Stretching from the front of the coffee shop and all the way up the block on Himrod Street was a reception line of older, well-dressed Mafiosi, waiting to be escorted inside one or two at a time, by Donato Amoroso.

Amoroso was resplendent in what looked like a three-thousand dollar, light-gray silk suit. When the fading sunlight hit the garment, it looked like it had been made from spun silver. Amoroso was being politely greeted by the other mobsters in front of the shop. They were all deferential to him, kissing his ring before being escorted inside.

Butchie recognized this as a bit of a coronation in itself. Previous to this, Butchie and Eddie knew the mobsters of American descent resented Amoroso and the other zips. It was only because they feared them that an all-out civil war between the factions hadn't already occurred. Now the cops got to watch the old guard paying Amoroso homage, waiting their turn to swear fealty to the big boss inside.

"Amoroso isn't the Pope," Eddie observed. "But he's clearly the head Cardinal in charge. I'll give *ye* one guess who the new *Il Papa* is."

"Dear old Dad," Butchie said acidly.

"Why's he hiding in the coffee shop, do *ye* suppose?"

"My guess would be, meeting known members of organized crime would be a violation of his parole. He's receiving them one and two at a time, out of the eye of law enforcement. He probably came in through the back, and he'll leave the same way. But I'm not curious about what Sallie Gorgeous' *modus operandi* is at the moment. What I want to know is, why the fuck is that fat, crooked imbecile Ernie Walton directing traffic on the corner?"

"Maybe we should ask him," Eddie suggested.

As Butchie and Eddie approached Walton, who was sweating profusely waving cars on in the intersection, they spotted his new, and equally corrupt partner, Joe Kemp, on the corner of Harman Street, moving the pedestrians across Wyckoff Avenue, preventing them from walking in front of Il Trombone Arrugginito. Butchie looked at Eddie with wonder. The audacity of the corruption was unfathomable. Eddie just shrugged, not surprised by anything anymore. As they were in plain clothes, Walton didn't sense their approach until they were right on top of him.

"You scared me, Butchie. What are you guys doing here? Me and Joe don't need no help."

"You've got it all on lockdown, do you, Whale?"

"Well, it's just a traffic condition. We can handle it."

"I'm calling bullshit," Eddie said. "What *yer* actually doing is keeping the traffic moving to thwart any possible vehicle surveillance. And *dat* fuckstick Kemp is diverting foot traffic away from the coffee shop, where something unholy is occurring inside. Tell me I'm wrong."

"How much are they paying you, Walton?" Butchie demanded.

"What, do you want a piece now?" Walton asked stupidly.

Butchie left Walton in a crumpled sweaty heap in the middle of the street, after punching him squarely in his diaphragm, knocking all of the wind out of him. Joe Kemp started to scuttle over, when Eddie waved him off with a glare.

That's all it took. Kemp wanted no part of Eddie Curran. Three years ago, they got stuck working together for a tour. Curran had shattered Kemp's nose when he tried to steal the diamond earrings right out of the lobes of an elderly woman who had died of natural causes in her home. Kemp was reminded of the low regard with which Eddie Curran held him every time he shaved in the morning. He elected now to remain at the corner on Harman Street.

Butchie and Eddie made a beeline directly over to Donato Amoroso, who was being kissed on both cheeks by one of the old Mafiosi. When this mobster and the others on line realized Eddie and Butchie were the police—and not the friendly kind on the pad—the receiving line rapidly evaporated. They scattered in all directions like cockroaches when the light in a dirty kitchen goes on.

Amoroso was furious when the cops grabbed him.

"You no come a here! This a private property!" Amoroso raged at Butchie in his fractured English. Butchie further incensed the new underboss when he laughed at him.

"You might want to confer with Trinchera and Meloro to get a better idea of how I deal with the concept of private property. It's a figment of your fucking imagination. Now, let's go, grease ball, in the coffee shop we go."

When Amoroso dug in his heels and refused to move, Eddie could only wince and shake his head. He knew what came next. Butchie grabbed the recalcitrant mobster by the throat and the groin. He picked him up and took three running steps toward the glass door of the coffee shop. When Butchie got two feet from the door, he launched Amoroso backwards through the old-fashioned etched glass.

From inside the coffee shop the assembled mobsters and their bodyguards were surprised when the new underboss came flying ass-first through the door and the wood-slat blinds, tumbling in a bewildered pile in front of Sallie Gorgeous, who was at the head of his own table receiving a pledge of undying loyalty from Fat Sam Indelicato.

Indelicato was already nervous about his own safety. He had been loyal to Lilo Gigante. That he was being kept in place under the new regime was a surprise to him. He suspected it might be a trick—that Sallie would have him clipped eventually at his own convenience. When Fat Sam heard the glass crashing behind him, he thought the convenience had presented itself. Until he heard the voice of that lunatic cop, Bucciogrosso. Sam was relieved he wasn't getting whacked by Sallie, but he was agitated, nonetheless. He had no desire to have further dealings with Butchie.

"We are the police, scumbags. I'm coming through this door for a conversation only. If any of you assholes has a gun pointed at me when I do, you'll die where you stand. So, if you value your life even a little, put your fucking guns away."

Butchie came through the shattered door, followed directly by Eddie. When the two cops were satisfied they were the only people in the room with guns in their hands, they holstered theirs. Butchie walked right up to the table, to loom over Sallie Gorgeous. He was glaring at the new Godfather when he spoke dismissively to Fat Sam.

"Disappear, scumbag. I'm here to talk to your boss."

Fat Sam wordlessly slinked to the back of the room, nearer the door. Sam noticed with chagrin that Sallie Gorgeous was scowling ferociously at him. He realized his assent without protest to Butchie's order to leave might well have sealed his fate. Sallie Gorgeous' face at this moment was murder personified.

Sal diverted his gaze now in the direction of Butchie and Eddie. He was focused on the shields dangling around their necks. His face went from rage to sour distaste. It was Sallie Gorgeous' experience plainclothes cops only came around for a payoff. At least that's how it was back in the early fifties, when Sallie first went upstate. He wasn't aware of the fact, nor did anyone tell him, the police culture had changed in his absence. Not every cop was for sale anymore. Sallie was too vain to put on his glasses, so he didn't focus on the face of the cop glowering at him from across the table.

"Pay these *sciatti* and show them the door," Sallie ordered his bodyguard.

"I'm not interested in your money, old man," Butchie informed him.

"Then what the fuck do you want?" Sallie demanded.

"Nothing less than your destruction."

"What? What the fuck are you talking about?"

"You should probably put your glasses on and take a good look at me. This is the face that's going to disassemble your entire life—piece by piece. I am going to take away everything you ever held dear. I will make you do things you never thought you could, and you're going to hate yourself for doing them. Until finally, you are broken beyond repair. You will loathe yourself so completely, you won't be able to live another minute in your own skin. That's what I'm talking about, you miserable, parasitic, scumbag rapist."

Sallie did put on his glasses, and he stared hard into the face of Butchie. There was a flash of recognition in the gangster's eyes. Sallie felt like he was looking into the mirror thirty years ago. When he remembered how this was possible, he laughed cruelly.

"You're the runt I made with that slut from the bakery! And you became a cop—un-fucking-believable! Have you felt neglected all these years? Do you want to sit on Daddy's lap now?"

Butchie smiled obsequiously at the leering gangster. He knew he was but a step and a lunge away from being able to tear out Sallie Gorgeous' throat. That solution would have been too abrupt and altogether unsatisfying for Butchie. Sallie's sins were too great, and too many to be expunged so quickly. He intended to make Sallie regret his entire life. Butchie would not be satisfied until the degenerate gangster rued his very existence. So he didn't step, and he didn't lunge. He grinned.

"You don't know it yet, Sal, but the end of you has already begun. I hope when it's over you appreciate the irony. You made the instrument of your own destruction in the back of a bakery."

Butchie turned and nodded at Eddie. As they stepped to the shattered front door, Butchie took care to stare menacingly into each and every face in the room. He wanted to be certain every mobster in Sallie's inner constellation understood they were targets as well. Just as Butchie was stepping through the door, Sallie felt the need to bellow at him.

"You'll never get within one hundred yards of me again, Copper! You just signed your own death warrant. You can't touch me. I'm invulnerable!"

"You evidently don't understand the meaning of that word," Butchie said as he paused briefly at the door. "I could have killed you and every other tough-guy pretender in the room today, but that would have been too easy. You're not invulnerable. I'm going to touch you roughly, Sal, in places you don't even know you have yet. I'm going to make you hurt for all you've done. Your death will eventually come. It will be by your own hand, and you will welcome it. But, first I'm going to make you suffer."

As the cops drove away in their un-marked car, Butchie was still silently fuming. Eddie waited a minute for his partner to cool down before addressing him.

"Do *ye* imagine *dat* was wise, Butchie?"

"I just threw down the gauntlet."

"This isn't a dual, Boyo. What *ye* did was warn the bastard we mean to destroy, that we mean to destroy him. And we're not in a position yet to do it. *Ye've* surrendered whatever surprise and initiative we might have had."

"I couldn't let him just sit there like a king on his throne—receiving his minions and their imaginary loyalty. I had to fuck with that."

"In so doing, you showed him how personal this is for *ye*. Now he knows where *yer* exposed. He doesn't have a family to protect. You do. Remember *dat* the next time *ye* feel like showing Sallie how big *yer* dick is."

"Alright, Eddie," Butchie said laughing. "I get your point. I'll keep it in my pants."

"I know you'll do *yer* best, Boyo, but *ye've* never been much of a defensive fighter. With that in mind, we better hope Inspector Sheridan calls soon. We can't beat Sallie Gorgeous from an Anti-Crime car. We need to get inside his narcotics operation. Let's let this lie for a day or two. Then we'll go find Roman to see if anything shook loose from your little meet and greet."

CHAPTER THIRTY-ONE

September 23, 1979
Bushwick

Two days later, something did shake loose from Butchie's psychodrama at the coffee shop. It wasn't from the Mafia, though. Butchie and Eddie were ordered to report to Inspector Sheridan's office, in the Internal Affairs building on Poplar Street in downtown Brooklyn. The notification specified they were to be in business attire. Given the address, and the fact that typically when cops were to be suspended or arrested, they were ordered to appear out of uniform, the partners were curious as to the nature of this invitation. There was no other information on the notification to give them a clue. So, they did what every cop does when confronted with the unknown—they speculated.

"What do you think, Eddie? Are we getting promoted, or arrested?"

"That it's Sheridan who wants to see us suggests we're getting the bump we were looking for. The fact he wants to see us at Poplar Street suggests the other *ting*."

"I guess we'll just have to go down there to find out."

"They didn't say anything about being armed", Eddie noted. "If Internal Affairs was going to lock us up, presumably they would have told us to come unarmed. I'm betting it's a job interview."

***

When they got to Poplar Street, they entered the building and spoke with a uniformed detective seated at a high, antique-looking wooden desk behind an ornate brass railing. He eyed the two cops suspiciously. In a tone dripping with condescension, he informed them they had wandered into a police facility. Eddie flashed his badge and answered the wormy detective.

"Yeah, I know. We have an appointment with Inspector Sheridan, but I'm willing to wager, police facility or not, we're the only two *real* cops in the building."

"You're talking to a detective," the uniform sneered.

"Just because they gave you a shiny gold badge doesn't make you a detective," Butchie told him. "You don't look like you've done a day of police work in your life. You don't make a pimple on a real detective's ass. You're a receptionist. So receive us. Or we'll just wander around the building until we find the inspector."

This got the functionary on the phone. He informed whomever was on the line, two cops were here claiming to have an appointment with Inspector Sheridan. He complained they had been rude to him. He evidently didn't like the response, because he held the phone away from his face and winced. Eddie and Butchie could hear a voice thundering over the wire, "Did you bother to ask them their names, you numb-nuts?"

Butchie was laughing at the detective as he told him their names and command. The bellowing voice ordered him to send the two cops up. He answered with a timid, "Yes, sir."

"Inspector Sheridan is in the left corner office on the fourth floor. The sign on the door says *Taskforce,*" the detective told Butchie. Then he added snidely, "Don't take any detours or wander around. There are confidential investigations taking place in this building to which you're not supposed to be privy."

"Fuck you, Little Lord Fauntleroy." Butchie told him, as he let himself and Eddie through the gate and headed for the stairwell.

"Who do you think put the bug in that loser's ass?" Butchie asked loudly enough for the detective to hear.

"That would be a moot question," Eddie answered just as loudly. "There are two types of people in Internal Affairs. There are the delusional true-believers who volunteered, and then there are the thieves who got caught and turned on their partners. Neither were worth the effort and mess to make them."

Butchie cackled, sensing the chagrined detective cringing from the abuse he was powerless and far too cowardly to do anything about. Having failed to get the desired response by telling on them, he was all out of ideas.

Inspector Sheridan told them to come right in when they knocked on his door. The snide and mousey receptionist had been correct about the sign. Except it wasn't really a sign. It was a paper plate crudely taped to the frosted glass door. In pencil, the word *Taskforce* was scrawled. When they came into the office the cops got the feeling they were walking into a Collier's Mansion. There were boxes and boxes of aging police reports, stacked upon each other as high as eight feet tall. From out of this maze walked Inspector Tom Sheridan. He introduced himself and nearly crushed Eddie and Butchie's hands when he shook them.

The inspector was a squat five foot seven, with thick shoulders and arms, and a brusque aggressive manner. One look at his face revealed the connection between him and Mick Doheny. Sheridan had the flattened nose of a pugilist. A glance at the wall behind the inspector's cluttered desk showed a framed fight poster from the early sixties. It advertised a boxing exposition at the Ridgewood Grove. In the middle of the poster was the much younger, but unmistakable image of Tom Sheridan. His combative pose and defiant glare made it look like he was intent on kicking someone's ass. The framed photo next to it was an NYPD promotion ceremony. A beaming Sergeant Tom Sheridan was being congratulated by a paternal looking Patrolman Mick Doheny. The possibility they were in trouble started to recede from Butchie and Eddie's concern.

"I heard you met Rex the Wonder-cop on your way in," Sheridan began.

"All due respect, Inspector, but that was no cop," Eddie offered.

"You got that right. That guy is dangerous—mostly to himself. He couldn't police his way out of a paper bag. That's why we stick him in uniform on the reception desk. His phone doesn't even get an outside wire. He can't even be trusted with that."

"What's he doing here?" Butchie asked.

"His father is a newspaper publisher with political juice. Junior was raised in opulence on Sutton Place, until he went to Dartmouth to learn how to really look down on the working class. He came on the job with the express intention of hurting cops. Now granted, there was and still is plenty of corruption around to fight—if that's your thing. But *he's* never going to find any. It would involve going out in the street, and that's something he'll never do. He couldn't find corruption if it was in his own ass, and we gave him an icepick and flashlight with explicit directions. So, we leave him on that desk, where he can do no real harm."

"*Dat's* comforting," Eddie observed.

"Enough about him, let's get down to business," the inspector said waving them around the boxes to a corner of the room.

An eight-millimeter projector was set up on a card table facing a portable movie screen on a collapsible tripod. Sheridan directed Butchie to cut the lights, before flipping on the projector.

When the film started rolling, they could see a clear image of the corner of Himrod Street and a view of the north side of Wyckoff Avenue, stretching east to Harman Street. Ernie Walton could be seen on the screen, waving traffic on frantically.

In the next few frames, Butchie and Eddie can be seen approaching Walton in the street. After a brief conversation, Butchie abruptly punched Walton and stepped over his crumpled body on the way over to the coffee shop.

"This is my favorite part," Sheridan said, smiling.

Butchie was arguing with the animated and silver-suited Donato Amoroso. In the next frame, Butchie can be seen grabbing him by the throat and the crotch, taking three running steps, and hoisting the head-zip like a shotput through the glass door of the coffee shop. Eddie and Butchie paused briefly outside the door, before stepping through the broken entryway.

The plain clothes cops were in there for only a minute or two before returning to their un-marked car and driving away. Sheridan cut the projector off and had Butchie turn the lights back on. He was chuckling and shaking his head.

"I have a few questions," Sheridan said. "Why did you throw Amoroso through the door?"

"Language barrier," Butchie said.

"That's impressive bullshit, but I happen to know you're fluent in Italian. You were looking to make an impression. Did you know who was inside?"

"We had surmised as much," Eddie offered.

"And who was that?"

"Sallie Gorgeous Ruttigliano," Butchie said.

"This is what we figured, but Sallie came and went without ever being seen by us. He's slippery like that. It's for that reason you two are here. You seem to be able to get into places and see things no one else can. The other reason you're here is because if I leave you to your own devices, you'll get your heads blown off. Mick Doheny would never forgive me if I let any harm come to his bright little altar boys. But this assignment will not be without its difficulties. This is a joint federal narcotics Taskforce. This means we will be working with the FBI and the DEA. I don't know if you've ever worked with the FBI, but they are a humorless bunch of assholes who are more or less clueless and incompetent. So much so, they wanted to lock you two up for yesterday's stunt. I had to patiently explain to them and the US Attorney you were not corrupt, just insane."

"If they're incompetent, why are we working with *dem*?" Eddie asked, reasonably.

"Because they have unlimited financial resources, and *all* of the toys. Partnering with them gives us the opportunity to buy information and gives us tools for electronic surveillance not ordinarily available to the NYPD. I'm talking about things like tracking devices for vehicles, body wires for informants, and Title III wire taps. Our targets are secretive. We need those things if we're going to bring them down. For the privilege of spending their money and playing with their toys, we have to endure their company and let them pretend they're cops."

"What about the DEA?" Butchie asked. "What are they all about?"

"They're high-strung as hell," Sheridan said. "They also have an inferiority complex when it comes to the FBI. It's a Justice Department thing, so we don't get involved. But when the shit hits the fan, the DEA are the police. They'll get behind their guns and stay there. They know whom to shoot, and when. They are also the absolute professionals when it comes to narcotics. They're all expert chemists, and nobody runs a drug-buy operation or works an informant like the DEA can. You are going to like working with them."

"What's our role in all of this?" Eddie asked.

"You two are the case detectives. You are going to run the human intelligence for this case. You are going to find out what's what, and who's who, and who we need to flip, and who we need to burn. As far as the department is concerned, it's your case. You run it."

"Inspector," Eddie interrupted. "How are we supposed to do that? We're just a couple of white shield Anti-Crime cops."

"Not after today. The Police Commissioner has two shiny new gold shields he can't wait to pin on you."

"That's exciting news, but why are we having this meeting on the fourth floor of Internal Affairs?" Butchie asked.

"This is the last time you two are coming here. As you should have surmised from the boxes of files, I'm moving. I'm just waiting for the paint to dry in my new office. Our headquarters will be a non- descript warehouse on 11th Avenue in Manhattan. It has an underground garage the feds have taken to calling the Bat Cave. That's where we're running the case from, but you guys for the most part will be running your end from the trunk of your car. You come to the command only to debrief informants and cooperators, or to pick up equipment and money. And of course, to meet with me."

"*Dat* still doesn't explain what we're doing in Internal Affairs," Eddie pointed out.

"Oh, that," Sheridan said. "Since the Knapp Commission, the job has gotten much better; cleaner, less corruption. But there is still a cadre of dirty cops around—the old-timer scumbags who haven't gotten the memo. They're a dying breed, but they're not dying fast enough. I've been putting this Taskforce together for the last two years. If my office had been in a real police facility, one of the dirty cops would have sold us out by now. We exist in secret only because I put this thing together in a building where there were *no* cops—dirty or otherwise. IAD was a perfect cover. Where we're going, it will be the three of us, a handful of supervisors and detectives—personally vetted by me—and two teams of heavy hitters from Emergency Service to help with the big takedowns and search warrants. We few and the Police Commissioner will be the only NYPD personnel who know we even exist."

"Now *dat* makes sense," Eddie said.

"Yes, it does," Sheridan agreed. "What doesn't make any sense at all, however, is how you two managed not to get shot inside the coffee shop. How in the world were you able to accomplish that?"

"I told them we were the police and we were coming in. If anyone had a gun in their hand, I assured them we would kill everyone in the room," Butchie explained.

"Amazing," the inspector remarked.

"Not really," Eddie said. "The Bonannos know us well enough by now. They know we wouldn't lie about a *ting* like that."

CHAPTER THIRTY-TWO

September 23, 1979
Brooklyn

The first thing Eddie and Butchie did after being promoted to detective by the Police Commissioner was head to the police auto pound to pick out a car. Inspector Sheridan had prepared the paperwork for the conversion. The partners were told to pick out anything they thought suitable. Sheridan had called the commanding officer of the pound to let him know the detectives were coming with the authority of the Police Commissioner himself, and they were to be given whatever they wanted.

The impound lot for the NYPD was at the Brooklyn Navy Yard. Police Officer Klemper of the Property Clerk Section had Butchie and Eddie touring row after row of rusted out clunkers in the most remote parking lots on the property, far away from the big warehouse where the offices were located. Butchie had to straighten Klemper out.

"Why are you showing us this shit? Did you not read the conversion order? Do you think the police commissioner signed that paper because he wants you to put us in a 1963 Rambler?"

"My boss told me to show you anything you want on the lot. This is the lot," Klemper said.

Eddie eyed the pudgy, balding little cop, sizing him up. He could see in a glance, Klemper was soft. Eddie figured correctly that he had been a used car salesman masquerading as a cop for much of his career.

"Do *ye* like it here, Klemper?" Eddie asked, smiling.

"Yeah, it's a good detail. Better than being in the street," he admitted.

"Well if *ye* want to keep it, *ye'll* show us what's in the big building. If we have to drive one of these rust buckets outta here, *ye* will spend the rest of *yer* career in the two-eight precinct on a foot post. Is it *yer* ambition to finish *yer* career in Harlem?"

"But my boss...," Klemper protested.

"*Yer* boss will be walking the adjoining foot post unless we are accommodated," Eddie interrupted. "Look at the order, and who signed it. We're *yer* boss today, and *yer* bosses' boss, too."

Twenty-five minutes later Eddie and Butchie left the Navy Yard behind the wheel of a tricked out 1967 Ford Fairlane 500 R code. Black, with dark tinted windows, this was as fine an example of American muscle as Detroit had ever produced. It had 425 horsepower, yet somehow was understated. This was a car that would be sturdy enough for narcotics work, and fast enough to chase down anything on the road. The vehicle had been seized by the Auto Crime Division when they took down a chop shop in Canarsie. The identification numbers had been altered or removed. Auto manufacturers hadn't started using confidential VIN numbers yet in 1967. The Auto Crime detectives never found the rightful owner. It had been sitting under a tarp in the warehouse for the last year. The cops in the auto pound would periodically pull the tarp off it to cruise around the Navy Yard. As a result, it was all limbered up and ready to go when Butchie and Eddie snagged it.

Their next stop was Vehicle Maintenance on 58th Street in Woodside Queens. There, they had a grill light package and full siren box installed. The car was now ready for service. Eddie and Butchie arrived at a plan as to how they would keep the car when they took it home each night. They lived a block apart in Glendale, buying Dutch colonials only a short walk from Mickey and Bunny's house. These houses each had a driveway and a detached two-car garage behind them. Whomever drove each day would store the car overnight in their garage. They would alternate days.

The first thing Butchie and Eddie did with their new exotic toy, was to look for Roman Sciula. They found him on the corner of Suydam Street and Knickerbocker Avenue. When they jumped out to pretend to arrest Roman, he was too fascinated with the car to argue over his arrest. Eddie had to overtighten the handcuffs to refocus Roman's attention.

"Ow, that fucking hurts!" Roman said.

"Not as bad as it'll hurt if these scumbags get the idea *ye* don't mind being hassled by us. Kick up a little protest," Eddie whispered.

The light went off over Roman's head and he started whining that the cops were always picking on him. He kept up this racket until they had pulled into the Cemetery of the Evergreens.

"Enough already, Roman!" Butchie said. "It's just us here."

"This is a nice fucking car, Butchie."

"Never mind the wheels," Eddie said. "Tell us what's going on in Sallie Gorgeous' world since we spoiled his coronation party."

"Oh boy, you guys kicked over a hornet's nest with that one," Roman laughed. "Amoroso was so pissed off, he offered a fifty-grand contract on each of your heads, until Sallie Gorgeous made him rescind it. Sallie is pissed, but he doesn't believe you can hurt him too much. He promised Amoroso he can clip you when the time is right, so I don't think he's quite forgiven you either. But, nothing is going to happen right away. I would know. They'll probably give that contract to me."

"Well, *tank* God for Sal's equanimity," Eddie said. "Is there anyone substantially more inclined to flipping since yesterday?"

"Fat Sam would be a good target. He is absolutely certain Sallie is going to punch his card, and he's right. Last night Sallie called me in and told me to get a fix on Indelicato's movements. He told me to figure out how to make that scumbag disappear. So if you don't flip him, they're going to make me kill him."

"How much time do we have?" Butchie asked.

"Maybe a week or two," Roman estimated. "But if you guys don't snatch him up before Sallie gives me the nod, I'm gonna have to push his button. I'd really like it if I didn't have to kill Sam. He never gave me no bother."

"Could *ye* get away with wearing a wire in front of Sallie?" Eddie asked.

"Not a chance," Roman said. "Sallie is very affectionate with everybody. Lots of hugs and kisses, like we're all family. Really, he's just rubbing everybody for weapons and wires. He trusts no one."

"Could we fake Sam's death?" Eddie asked.

"Sallie is going to want proof. Something physical, like a piece of him. How are we going to fake that?"

"It's not beyond the realm of possibility, but it's disturbing and probably illegal," Eddie informed them. "Does Sam still wear that big gaudy ring he likes everybody to kiss?"

"Yeah. He's never without it."

"Would Sallie accept a finger with the ring on it as proof?" Eddie asked.

"Yeah, but I don't think Fat Sam wants to part with the ring—or his finger."

"It won't be Sam's finger, and I *tink* he'll be happy to trade the ring to keep his head," Eddie surmised.

"You have dead fingers lying around? That's just sick. I thought you were the good guys," Roman said, incredulously.

"We are, Roman," Eddie assured him. "And we're not taking anyone's finger who will miss it. *Ye* said *ye* like Sam. Borrowing a finger from someone already dead to save another life isn't so much to ask. Is it?"

"I suppose not. How are you going to snatch Sam without raising up the neighborhood?"

"You tell us," Butchie said. "You're the one who's been following him around. Does he leave the neighborhood on the regular?"

"Yeah. Sam has a *goom* in Maspeth. She owns the beauty shop on Grand Avenue, next to that restaurant, Cono the Fisherman. She has an apartment upstairs. Sam is there like clockwork at eight P.M. every Monday, Wednesday and Friday. He's out and on his way home by ten. It's nice and quiet over there at that time. You should be able to nab him then."

"*Dat's* good, but we'll need a signal when Sallie puts out the contract," Eddie said.

"I got an idea," Butchie said. "When Sallie gives you the nod, hang a sheet out your front window, like you're airing it out. We'll go by every day to look for it. Then, you just have to stall Sallie long enough for us to nab Sam. After we do, we'll come find you in the street. We'll rub you like always, but this time we won't find your gambling slips. We'll just slip the finger and the ring into your pocket. After we cut you lose, the rest is up to you."

CHAPTER THIRTY-THREE

September 26, 1979
Maspeth

Three nights later Butchie and Eddie were scrunched down low in the front seat of their car on the corner of 72nd Street and Grand Avenue. They were watching the side door leading up to the apartment above Rosalie's Beauty Shop. It was a warm Monday night. Around 2145 hours, they observed a seemingly well-satisfied Fat Sam Indelicato come out the side door. When Butchie and Eddie pulled up quickly in the street in front of him, Fat Sam—believing his end had come—collapsed to the sidewalk and urinated on himself.

Sam was relieved to feel the handcuffs going on his wrists, and looked up into Butchie's face, recognizing him finally. His relief turned to panic when Eddie slipped the black felt hood over his head. Sam started hyperventilating as Butchie and Eddie shoved him into the backseat of the car and sped off.

"Oh, Jesus Christ," Sam moaned pathetically. "I didn't think you guys were on the take. That fucking Sallie Gorgeous owns everybody!"

"Relax, *ye* fat imbecile," Eddie told him. "We're not killing *ye*. We're saving *yer fookin* life."

"Then why the black hood?"

"We're taking you somewhere secret. You can't know where it is," Butchie explained.

"Am I under arrest?"

"No. We're going to offer *ye* the deal of a lifetime," Eddie said.

"What if I don't want the deal?"

"Then we'll bring you back to Bushwick where you can wait for Roman Sciula to blow your brains out or beat you to death. I forget which one he prefers," Butchie said.

"No, that's okay. I think I want to hear your deal," Fat Sam decided.

When they got to the Taskforce and locked Fat Sam in the interview room, Butchie and Eddie were summoned into Special Agent Warren Agnew's office for a quick conference. After which, they Joined Fat Sam in the interview room. Eddie took off the hood. Sam had to squint to adjust his eyes to the light. The black-out hood had done its job. He had been disoriented and in total darkness for the entire ride from Queens. Butchie took the handcuffs off of Sam and handed him a paper cup of water. He drank it in one swallow.

"What the hell do you guys want from me?" Sam demanded.

"We want you to listen to something," Butchie told him.

Unbeknownst to Butchie and Eddie, the FBI had figured a way to snake a wire through the plumbing ventilation pipes from the roof above Il Trombone Arrugginito. The parabolic receiver on the end of the cable had no problem picking up and discerning the conversation within the coffee shop. The cast iron ventilation pipe actually served to amplify the sound, rather than mute it. As a result, the FBI had a recording of Sallie Gorgeous discussing the hit on Fat Sam with Roman Sciula. Two days ago, they recorded Sallie ordering the hit. They shared this information with Butchie and Eddie tonight only because they saw them bringing in the subject of the hit order.

"What is Sam Indelicato here for?" Special Agent Warren Agnew asked Butchie in his office.

"We're going to flip him," Butchie told him matter-of-factly.

"What kind of leverage do you have on him?"

"Sallie Gorgeous ordered his murder two days ago. We are officially his only friends now."

"How do *you* know about that?"

"We're detectives. We know things."

"You have an informant inside," Agnew surmised.

"That was very intuitive, Warren. Are you sure you're not a cop?"

"Can your informant testify to hearing the order?" Agnew asked, ignoring Butchie's sarcasm.

"Yes, but we can't afford to burn him yet. He's too valuable in place. We can expose him after the takedown when we can get him into witness protection," Eddie said, realizing Agnew wanted to share something pertinent with them.

"I have something you and your partner need to hear," the agent said.

Warren had a reel-to-reel tape player on his desk. After Eddie closed the door, Warren cued up the tape, and pressed play.

The first voice they recognized belonged to Sallie Gorgeous. He was telling someone named Roman to sit down. They heard Sallie say he wanted Roman to monitor Indelicato's movements.

"Find out where he goes every day. Then you can figure out how to make that scumbag disappear. I don't want it messy, and I don't need to know the details. When I give you the okay, I just want him gone. Capisce?"

The next voice they heard belonged to Roman Sciula. They acknowledged to Agnew they knew him, but weren't ready yet to divulge the true nature of their relationship. In his typical fashion, Roman could be heard to say, *"Sure thing, Boss."*

Then Special Agent Agnew advanced the tape. When he hit play again, Sallie Gorgeous could be heard ordering someone to take out Fat Sam.

"Make him gone, quiet and clean. Just bring me some proof. Can you do that, Roman?"

"I can do that, Boss," Roman Sciula could be heard to say.

After Agnew turned off the tape, he looked at Butchie and Eddie as if he was trying to decide something. Finally, he just went for it.

"The Bureau warns us strenuously before these taskforces are formed. They tell us the NYPD is corrupt, and rotten to the core. They order us not to trust any of you—with anything. They even threaten us. They tell us if we share information with you, and it gets filtered down to the mob, we will be fired and prosecuted right alongside you. So understand; what you just heard, and what I'm going to share with you now is tantamount to me putting my professional life in your hands. I love my job. I really want to get these sons-of-bitches. I get a sense you guys are different from the cops I've known. I don't believe you're corrupt. I think you want to get these bastards as much, or more than I do. So I'm going to take a chance, and trust you. Please don't fuck me."

Butchie and Eddie looked at each other wordlessly for a minute. Butchie shrugged at Eddie, and he nodded.

"Okay J. Edgar," Eddie began. "If *ye're* willing to show us *yers*, I guess we can trust *ye* enough to show *ye* ours, but this little circle has to remain just the three of us. *Ye* can't share what we know or how we know it with *yer* other agents, except on a need to know basis, and even then, in very limited amounts."

"You don't trust the FBI?"

"Fuck no," Butchie said.

"We're not corrupt, Butchie."

"No, but the average FBI agent is stupid when it comes to life on the streets. Typically, he's a wheat-sucking hick from *Bumfuck*, Iowa, who doesn't know shit about dick and can't keep it to himself when he finds something out. They tell their wives. They tell their in-laws. They tell everybody around the Thanksgiving table how in the know they are. They just can't keep their fucking mouths shut. The problem is, we're swimming in the same water with these sharks. The minute they get an idea of how badly we mean to hurt them, we're the fucking chum. So if you want to know what we know, you have to be the filter."

"I can do that," Warren Agnew agreed.

When Butchie and Eddie played the tape for Sam Indelicato, he went pale and started sweating profusely. When he started hyperventilating again, Eddie got him a paper bag to breath into, which was fortunate. A few seconds later, Indelicato threw up into the bag.

Between the urine drying in Fat Sam*'s* pants, and now the vomit, the interview room started to smell like an outhouse. It was fortunate Sam agreed to cooperate as quickly as he did. It would be the FBI's responsibility to baby sit him until he was fully debriefed and hidden away in witness protection.

He wasn't too thrilled about giving up his ring. When it was pointed out the ring belonged to someone who was already dead, he got the point and surrendered it. Interestingly enough, Fat Sam did not want his wife and children to join him in Witsec. He preferred they thought of him as dead. After all, they were already dead to *him*. He inquired if Rosalie could be brought with him, but he didn't argue the point too strenuously when he was told no. It became clear to everyone; Fat Sam Indelicato only cared about gulping air on the top-side of the grass.

CHAPTER THIRTY-FOUR

September 26, 1979
Manhattan

After handing Sam Indelicato over to the FBI, who were not at all happy to have him—what with him smelling like a housing project elevator—Butchie and Eddie went into Inspector Sheridan's office at the Taskforce to brief him on the new developments. They brought him up to speed, informing him of their agreement to share information with Warren Agnew.

"You're going to want to be careful about putting your hopes and dreams in the care of the FBI. They'll break your fucking heart every time," Sheridan warned them.

"Agnew seems different," Butchie said.

"Agnew is different," the inspector allowed. "He's the son of an NYPD detective. He's not your usual dip-shit, clueless college boy from the right side of the tracks the rest of that bunch usually are. He grew up in Astoria. He graduated from NYU and went to law school at Columbia. He gets it. In his heart of hearts, he's a cop. In fact, when he was in the Bank Robbery Taskforce as a young agent, he smoked three mutts. But, he'll never tell you about his background. He can't afford to. The rest of the Bureau regards him with a little suspicion because of it."

"So why can't we trust him?" Eddie asked.

"You can trust Agnew. But you need to understand, come the end of the day, even though he is the Agent in Charge on this case, it's not his show. The Justice Department has the final say on who gets fucked, and they are the purest political animals you will ever encounter. The problem is every US Attorney thinks their next promotion will put them in the Governor's Mansion. Every decision they make is geared toward making that a reality. You two aren't even firewood in that scenario. You're the kindling. While Warren may agree with you, while he may be inclined to protect you, he will not be consulted when that decision is made, and he doesn't have the power to do it even if he wants to."

"So, we cut him off?" Eddie asked. "Then we don't get to see his movies and hear the wire taps. We need *dat* stuff."

"No," Sheridan clarified. "We continue to trust Agnew. We just have to keep in mind there are things we can't tell him. They are the things he doesn't even want to know. If he's not told, he's not obligated to report it to the US Attorney. With that in mind, let's talk about what you lunatics have been up to."

"We've told Agnew we have an informant inside, but we haven't told him its Roman Sciula yet," Butchie told him.

"He's okay with not knowing for now, and he promised to keep his existence between us *tree* until we have to bring Roman in from the cold," Eddie added.

"Does he know anything about Indelicato's ring? Does he know why you have it?" Sheridan asked.

"No," Butchie said.

"Why not?"

"Because we have to scare up a dead finger to put it on, so Sallie Gorgeous believes Fat Sam is dead," Eddie said pleasantly.

"Holy Fuck! You know what? Don't tell me. I don't want to know, and trust me on this, neither does Agnew. Don't tell him. And whatever the fuck you do, don't put it on paper."

"Yeah, we already figured *dat* out for ourselves," Eddie said.

"Well, that's a relief. At least your instincts are good. If you're not sure in the future what you should tell Warren, as opposed to what will get you maniacs locked up in Leavenworth, check with me first," Sheridan said.

"Aye, aye, Skipper," Butchie said.

CHAPTER THIRTY-FIVE

September 27, 1979
Manhattan

The next afternoon Eddie told Butchie they were going to get a finger. Butchie was curious, but he trusted Eddie absolutely, so he didn't ask. He just went along for the ride. Truth to be told, he was intrigued by the mystery of it all. When they parked in front of the Chief Medical Examiner's Office on First Avenue and 31st Street, Butchie's curiosity got the better of him.

"Is the Medical Examiner running a fire-sale on body parts?" Butchie asked.

"No. We're only here for a finger, and we're going to have to negotiate for it. But, don't worry, Butchie. I've got the edge for this deal. I have something in the glove box. Would *ye* grab it for me?"

The detectives left their car on First Avenue, and went around the corner to the loading dock entrance on 31st Street. The door was answered by a nervous little man who got even more nervous when the two visitors identified themselves as detectives.

"*Ye* can calm down," Eddie told him. "We don't even know who *ye* are, and we're here to speak with Mordecai Friese."

"Is he in trouble?"

"Maybe not, but we won't know until we speak with him, will we?" Eddie said pleasantly.

The nervous morgue attendant led the detectives into the basement storage area. However, the only things stored down here were dead bodies, and those on a very temporary basis. There were wall-to-wall refrigerated lockers everywhere. Despite the fact that no corpses were visible, there was a furious sensory war being waged between the caustic disinfectant deodorant used copiously here, and the rancid smell of decomposing flesh. It was a near thing, but decomposition was winning.

They were led to a small office near the freight elevators, by which were stacked two dozen or so six-by-three-foot rectangular pine boxes—with six-digit identification numbers stenciled on the side of each. These were the bodies waiting to be transported to Hart Island; New York's potter's field. Since the explosion of the heroin epidemic, there was no shortage of indigent, unidentified addicts who had succumbed to their deadly habit. The bodies were transported on Wednesdays. The twenty-six pine coffins represented not quite one week's worth of the afflicted—just for the island of Manhattan. Similar numbers were being generated in the other four boroughs as well.

The little attendant led them to the office and said, "Mordy is in there." Then he sprinted down the hall and disappeared into the stairwell.

"He wanted no part of us. What do you suppose he did?" Butchie asked.

"Whatever it was, I'm sure it pales in comparison to what my friend Mordy is into."

"I can't wait to hear this story."

"*Ye* might not want to after *ye* meet him. He is the original creep."

Eddie knocked and opened the door without waiting for an answer. When they stepped into the office, the man seated behind the desk saw Eddie, and looked like he was about to have a heart attack.

"Oh fuck, no!" he moaned pathetically.

"Relax, Mordecai," Eddie told him. "I'm here for *dat* favor I told *ye* I would one day need. Grant it to me, and I will be out of *yer* life again. *Yer* wife won't need to hear from me."

Mordecai seemed to calm down, but Butchie found the sight of him no less disturbing. He stood up from his desk when he saw Eddie. At first glance he thought he was looking at an anorexic, until Butchie's eyes got down to his waist. From there and down, the morgue attendant looked like he was two hundred pounds overweight. Most of his body fat was located in his rear end, and his thick soft legs. They were so fat, when he walked, they rubbed together noisily—even in the loose fitting Medical Examiner's jumpsuit. His bony head and face would have been comical, but it produced a disquieting aura that pushed the needle on Butchie's creepiness meter hard to the right.

The Coke-bottle-thick, black-framed glasses magnified Mordecai's severely crossed eyes, which projected a vacant, soulless quality that was positively reptilian. His huge bony nose was crooked, and complimented his weak chin, hollow cheeks and thin lips. He had yellow teeth, leaning toward brown, and scattershot with remnants of what he had eaten most recently. At this particular time, it looked like it was something with spinach in it. His enormous forehead was exacerbated by the fact his hairline began at the center of his knobby misshapen skull. The hair was long, bushy and wiry. Butchie found him unspeakably awful to look at and hoped he wouldn't have to for much longer.

"What do you want from me, Detective Curran?" Mordecai asked.

"Very simple," Eddie told him. "Give me the ID number to one of those boxes out there by the elevator *dat* contains a male white, approximately forty to fifty years old. Overweight if possible, but it's not critical. I also need a pry bar and a hammer, and for *ye* to remain in this office. We'll be out of *yer* life in fifteen minutes."

After Friese had checked his manifest and given them the items requested, Butchie and Eddie found the coffin they were looking for. Eddie pried the cover off, revealing a bloated discolored man of indeterminate age. Because of the absence of blood in his extremities, his thick, hairy knuckled fingers were not discolored. Butchie thought they looked very much like Fat Sam*'s* sausage fingers.

"Hand me the pinking shears," Eddie said.

Butchie reached into his back pocket and handed over the shears he had gotten from the glove box. Eddie carefully snipped off the dead man's left ring finger at the third knuckle. He removed Sam's ring from his pocket and slipped it onto the bloodless severed finger. Eddie handed the thing to Butchie, who wrapped it in the butcher paper they had brought with them. Before they replaced the coffin lid, Eddie felt the need to address the donor directly.

"Apologies for the indignity, Brother. I don't know if *ye* ever did a good *ting* in *yer* life, but with this small sacrifice, *ye've* probably saved at least one person. I'm sure the *Big Feller* will give *ye* credit for *dat* when *ye* get there."

The detectives carefully replaced the coffin lid, and Butchie hammered in the nails. They left the building without having to lay eyes on Mordecai Friese again, which Butchie counted as a blessing.

***

When they got back to the car, Butchie couldn't wait any longer. He had to know.

"What the fuck is the deal with Mordecai Friese?"

"Mordecai is an interesting specimen," Eddie began. "He was born into the Satmar sect of Hasidim in Williamsburg. He is what we used to call a *dicky waver*. He kept getting caught masturbating near schoolyards and playgrounds. The Hasidim are very insular. They don't call the police. When Mordy failed to mend his ways after several beatings by the Shomrim patrols, they tried him in front of the Rabbinical Court, where they sentenced him to banishment from the community and the neighborhood—as he was decidedly not a *mensch*. Because the Hassid kept all of this to themselves, we never found out about it," Eddie said, shrugging, before continuing.

"Because the dicky waver thing never came up, he was able to get a job with the Medical Examiner. Before he was reassigned here, he worked on the *meat wagon* in Brooklyn. *Dat's* where I had the misfortune to meet him. I got stuck on a DOA on Troutman Street. The victim was a lovely seventeen-year-old girl who had overdosed. I stepped out of the room while Mordy put her in the body bag. I really didn't want to look at her anymore. Her death was so senseless. Right around then, Bernadette and I just had Connie. I don't know why, but I couldn't stop thinking what it would do to me if I found *me* own daughter like *dat*. It was ridiculous I know, but sometimes I'm a bit daft in *dat* way," he nodded for his partner's agreement.

"Yeah, you're a sentimental jackass sometimes," Butchie concurred.

"In any event, Mordy was taking longer than he should have. When I walked back into the room, he had her blouse open, fondling her breasts. His pants were down, and the freak was jerking off. I couldn't believe what I was seeing," Eddie said, wide-eyed. "I gave him a good beating, but I was so repulsed, I just wanted him out of my sight. I warned him if I ever heard anything like *dat* occurring again, I would kill him. He didn't care about *dat*. All he was concerned with was his wife finding out."

"Are you serious?" Butchie was flabbergasted.

"I know!" Eddie agreed. "Fucking ludicrous, right? But it seems Mordy had found a nice Puerto Rican girl to marry him. She was an Evangelical Pentecostal who believed sex was only for procreation, and never, ever to be had with dead people. She had caught him masturbating one day while he was watching Mr. Roger's Neighborhood on the TV. She told him if she ever caught him doing *dat* again she would cut his cock clean off. Evidently, she was good with a knife, because he believed her absolutely. More than anything in the world, the one *ting* Mordecai fears above all else, is a Puerto Rican, Pentecostal *bris*. When he told me *dat*, I told him I might prevail upon him for a favor one day. I assured him he would accommodate me, or I would tell his wife what I had observed."

"You anticipated needing a body part from this cretin?"

"Oh, fuck no! I just like collecting owed favors is all."

CHAPTER THIRTY-SIX

September 28, 1979
Bushwick

Butchie and Eddie found Roman, as always, on the corner of Suydam Street and Knickerbocker late that morning. He was standing by himself out in front of the coffee shop like he was looking for someone. When he saw the detectives drive up, he looked relieved. Butchie put Roman against the wall and pretended to search him. Meanwhile he slipped the wrapped finger and ring into Roman's pants pocket. Roman took the opportunity to whisper to him.

"You need to arrest me. Things are happening."

Hearing this, Eddie put handcuffs on Roman and the three of them left in the Ford. When they were safely inside the cemetery, Roman was let out of handcuffs. He couldn't wait to start talking.

"Sallie Gorgeous has set off a war. I knew when he started sharing the drug profits with the old-line gangsters it wouldn't last. Now he wants me to thin the herd."

"What are you talking about, Roman?" Butchie asked.

"There is too much greed for the money. Sallie bought room to maneuver when he brought the old guard into the heroin racket. Once they backed his play against Gigante and installed Sallie as the boss, they fulfilled their usefulness. Besides, there's no way the zips were going to share with guys like Vito Meloro and Dominick Trinchera—not for long anyway. Not when the Sicilians were doing all the work, and taking all the risk. The only thing Trinchera and Meloro bring to the table is an open hand. Other than being Fat Sam*'s* torpedoes, they never did *anything*. Sallie wants me to take them out."

"Ah, *feck*!" Eddie exclaimed.

"Tell me about it," Roman said. "Sallie is picking and choosing who lives and dies. The zips are safe. They run the dope, so they're too valuable. The gamblers are protected for the same reason. But everybody else is on the chopping block. If you ain't a big earner or do *wet work*, you're disposable. Nobody is sure what category they're in. So they're forming secret alliances in case they have to take Sallie out to survive. But those greedy fucks can't even trust each other. They're waiting to see if Sallie makes them an offer."

"Something is missing in all of this," Eddie concluded. "Why are the zips still loyal to Sallie? They don't seem to be getting any more than they had under Gigante. What am I missing?"

"There is another stream of revenue coming in," Roman said, "and it's supposed to be huge. Sallie bought the zips' loyalty when he cut them in on it while he was upstate."

"What could it be?" Butchie wondered.

"I don't know," Roman said. "But it's big. It's also controversial. People are all worked up about it. It's centered out of Ossining, where Sallie finished his bit. He sent *Sonny Black* up there to run it for him. Sonny came back two weeks later to tell Sallie he just couldn't do it. Everybody told him he was punching his own ticket by refusing him. He said he didn't care. He was more worried about losing his soul than his head. He's been hiding out since, but it's just a matter of time. I hope Sallie don't give me that contract. Sonny's got eleven kids."

"What the hell could it be?" Eddie wondered. "Sonny Black is not the worst guy ever, but he's no Mother Theresa either. What could have put him so off?"

"I've heard it called two things," Roman said. "Everybody usually refers to it as *that thing upstate*, but I've also heard it called the *fantasy camp*. I don't know what it means, but everybody who talks about it seems to get a bad taste in their mouths."

"If that's all you know, we're going to have to go get Sonny Black," Butchie said.

"He won't be hard to find," Roman said. "His idea of hiding out is staying in that big marble thing with the columns in Middle Village—the one on Penelope Avenue. It looks like a mausoleum, but Sonny loves that house. I don't think he'll talk to you though. He's old school. He takes that *omerta* shit seriously. I hope you can convince him. He really is a good family man."

"We'll do what we can," Butchie said. "But he's a grown man. He'll have to make his own decisions. We don't have any leverage on him. For now, you have other things to worry about. You got the finger and the ring in your pocket. You're going to want to give that to Sallie before it starts to stink. By tonight should be okay."

"What do I tell Sallie if he wants to know where the rest of Fat Sam went?"

"Tell him *ye* cut him into *wee* pieces and dumped the packages in the Hell Gate under the Triboro Bridge. He'll like *dat*, I *tink*," Eddie said.

CHAPTER THIRTY-SEVEN

September 28, 1979
Manhattan

That evening Butchie and Eddie met with Warren Agnew in his office at the Taskforce. They needed to bring Warren up to speed with what they had discovered. They also needed to know what might have been gathered on the FBI's electronic surveillance. The three lawmen were being as open and candid with each other as they could. But it was understood certain details—on both sides—needed to remain secret. This was for everyone's protection.

For instance, under no circumstances would Special Agent in Charge Warren Agnew want to know about the severed finger allegedly belonging to Fat Sam. Another example was the identity of Butchie and Eddie's informant. Warren would need to know eventually, but for now it was safer if as few people knew as possible. As long as the detectives kept Warren apprised of what the informant was telling them, his identity for now was immaterial.

It worked the other way as well. While still unknown to the detectives, the FBI had their own informant. He was an accountant for the Bonannos, specializing in scrubbing the enormous amount of dirty money made from the narcotics trade. As such, he knew explicitly what legitimate businesses were being used to do it. Half of the FBI consisted of lawyers. The other half were accountants. When they got a look at the balance sheets, they noticed immediately the preponderance of pizzerias and Italian bakeries being used to filter the money. They could discern by the vast area covered by these businesses, they seemed to line up perfectly with the distribution territory of the Bonanno drug empire; in other words, the entire Eastern seaboard—from Montreal in Canada, down through Florida.

The income reported by these seemingly mom-and-pop businesses was mind-boggling, and beyond all probability. It became clear from the revenue they were declaring, they were not just launderers, but were instrumental in the importation and distribution of the drugs.

The existence of three Bonanno-controlled shipping firms, one in Montreal, another in Elizabeth, New Jersey and the last in the Port of New Orleans, cemented the conclusion. Montreal was the entry point to North America for imported items from Italy and Turkey. Everything from everywhere came and went through the Port of Elizabeth. New Orleans was a short boat ride across the Gulf of Mexico from Juarez. That all of these pizzerias and bakeries were getting their olive oil, cheese, tomatoes, flower and yeast exclusively through these ports bent the realm of believability all out of kilter. In drug trafficking investigations, there really are no coincidences.

The link was so pronounced, the Justice Department had officially given the investigation the code name *The Pizza Connection*.

Butchie and Eddie didn't need to know any of this just yet. Eventually they would, but for now, the FBI, the DEA and Customs Enforcement could solidify those leads. The detectives would concentrate on getting corroboration on the dirty streets of Brooklyn.

Warren was all ears as Butchie, and Eddie briefed him. He was impressed with the thoroughness of the information.

"Your informant is highly placed. He is not only credible; he corroborates what we're getting off the wire. We picked this up this afternoon from the mic in Sallie's coffee shop. Listen to this," Warren said.

He pressed play on the reel to reel on his desk. The detectives heard Sallie Gorgeous ask someone, "Did you lance that boil for me?" Then they clearly heard Roman Sciula say, "Here is what's left of him."

Sallie replied, "I hated that fucking ring. It was as big as his fat little fist. Who did he think he was, Julius Caesar? You can get rid of that for me."

Warren turned off the tape. He considered what he had to say next. Finally, he just asked.

"I don't mean to pry, but Roman Sciula just acknowledged murdering Sam Indelicato. If the tape is to be believed, he handed over Sam's gaudy ring as proof. Now, we know Sam Indelicato is very much alive and cooling his heels at the Courtesy Motel in Fort Lee. As recently as two nights ago, that ring was on Sam's finger in this very building. I'm afraid some of your cards are showing. Want to make it official?"

"Can we keep it between just the three of us for a while longer?" Eddie asked.

"Yeah, we can do that. But I need to know if Roman is your guy so I can protect him. If he comes up on the DEA's radar and they want to make him a subject, I have to know—so I can prevent that."

"Roman Sciula is our informant. We gave him the ring," Butchie admitted.

"That is impressive. Roman Sciula's reputation is frightening. He's talked about in the street like he's some kind of remorseless killing machine. How did you turn him?"

"We were nice to him, and we told him the truth. No one has ever done *dat* for him before," Eddie admitted.

"That couldn't have been all there was to it," Warren said.

"It kinda was," Butchie said. "Roman is dangerous, but he's not a monster. He is a lonely man-child desperate for some friends. I think he's sick of this life. All it's ever brought him was heartache. When he told us about Sonny Black, it was more because he wanted to protect Sonny rather than give him up. He was concerned because Sonny has eleven kids. Except for Sonny, Roman has been treated like shit by the Bonannos. They've exploited him, using him to do the wet work when they need to hurt someone. Then they turn around and call him an idiot to his face. We got him to realize his so-called friends would sell him down the river at the drop of a hat, and we never would. We'll bring him in from the cold if it gets too dicey. He deserves to be saved."

"That's fine," Warren said. "But we can't sanction any violence while he's providing us with information. Whatever he's done in the past, we can immunize him for. But we can't have anything new. If he gets assigned a contract he cannot stall, he has to have a way to call us. So we can rescue him, so to speak."

"Should we give him our home phone numbers?" Eddie asked.

"You know you both have offices here?" Warren informed them. "Each of you has a phone on your desk. Those phones have answering machines. You can access the messages from a payphone. Why don't you learn the numbers, so you can give them to Roman? You can check your messages every four hours or so. That way we won't get blindsided."

"We'll do that," Butchie said. "What about Sonny Black? Have you got anything else on him?"

"Sonny is a gambler. He runs wire rooms, and he's a good business manager. He did two short stints in prison over the years for running book. We got nothing else on him. We're hearing a lot of chatter on the wire. Everyone is expecting him to get clipped, but we haven't intercepted anything even remotely like a kill order. The danger isn't imminent enough to authorize a material witness order, and we don't have anything we can charge him with. So you guys are just going to have to sweet talk him."

"Oh, is *dat* what we're calling it now, sweet talk? I like *dat*," Eddie laughed.

"What about the other thing?" Butchie asked. "Anything come up about the thing upstate, or the fantasy camp?

"We've heard those phrases, but nothing specific. Now that we know it's important, we can ask the accountant if he knows anything about it. In the meantime, see if Sonny Black wants to tell you about them."

"What accountant?" Eddie asked.

"Shit," Warren remarked. "I wasn't supposed to let that slip yet."

"We told you about Roman," Butchie reminded him. "You might as well bring us in on your accountant."

"The IRS did this guy for tax evasion. When he started talking about the Mob, they called us. This guy is the Bonanno's money launderer. He's deathly afraid of prison. He's giving up every business they're cleaning their money through. They're mostly bakeries and pizzerias. We're following a huge trail of money all over the country."

"That's good stuff. What do you need us to do?" Butchie asked.

"Get Sonny Black to tell us about the thing upstate," Warren suggested.

"We'll ask him, but don't expect any miracles. He's an old-time gangster," Eddie said.

"I believe in you, Eddie. I think you could talk the balls off a brass monkey," Warren said.

CHAPTER THIRTY-EIGHT

September 29, 1979
Brooklyn

Butchie and Eddie checked their messages the following morning from the pay phone on Knickerbocker and Myrtle. There was a message from Warren Agnew to contact him soonest. So, Butchie dropped another dime in the phone and only had to wait a half ring.

"Special Agent Agnew, how may I help you?"

"You tell us," Butchie said. "You wanted to talk."

"I need you two to meet with Special Agent Acosta, from the DEA. We picked something up on the wire you need to confer with him about."

"Sure, Warren, but we're supposed to be trying to get Sonny Black to come in. He's already on a contract from Sallie Gorgeous. Can't the drug bullshit wait a day?"

"No," Warren said. "This is all related. Take care of this today and you can catch up to Sonny in a day or two."

"If he's even alive in a day or two."

"Just go meet Agent Acosta," Warren said, sounding annoyed.

He gave Butchie the address for the temporary field office for the DEA.

"Why doesn't the DEA have an office there at the Bat Cave?" Butchie asked.

Warren could be heard sighing in the background. Butchie realized he had touched on something the FBI agent would have preferred he hadn't.

"The DEA has a whole floor of offices here. They just haven't gotten around to moving in yet," Warren offered weakly.

"Oh, I'm sure that's what it is," Butchie smirked.

When he got back in the car, he briefed Eddie on the new development, as well as the peculiar situation with the DEA.

"Something stinks about this," Eddie said. "Warren's holding out on us."

"I'm sure he is," Butchie agreed. "But we'll never get it out of *him.* Let's go see this Agent Acosta. He doesn't seem to like the FBI any better than we do. Maybe he'll tell us what's up."

***

The temporary headquarters of the DEA was ensconced in the top floor of what appeared to Butchie and Eddie to be little more than a three story shack on the pier of the old Brooklyn Army Terminal. They were led up to the third floor by an agent in a navy blue DEA windbreaker. He pointed into the corner of the office at the only other living thing on the floor.

"Cormac," he said. "Your cowboy cops are here to see you."

The man rose from his desk and waved them over. He wore torn faded jeans, flip flops and a ratty but comfortable looking hemp hooded sweatshirt. Except for his unsettling blue eyes, Butchie thought he looked like Che Guevara.

"Bucciogrosso and Curran, I presume," he grinned.

"Are you Special Agent Acosta?" Eddie asked. "Or is the government running an operation to free Cuba from the shores of Brooklyn?"

Acosta laughed, scratching his beard and looking out the window as if he was trying to remember something.

"Funny thing about undercover work; once you get a taste, you don't want to stop. I prefer dressing down anyway. I would hate to be mistaken for an FBI Agent."

"Who would ever want that?" Butchie nodded.

Acosta gestured to two hardbacked wooden chairs in front of his desk. Eddie noticed the one behind his desk was of the same spartan design. Clearly, Acosta was no slave to creature comforts. The hard wooden chairs were in stark contrast to the FBI practice of awarding the most elaborate and comfortable throne to the biggest boss. Eddie knew Acosta was the biggest boss in the New York DEA office, and he chose to sit on old wood. He was already starting to like this agent.

After they sat, Acosta offered them coffee and prepared it himself.

"We just got these this week," he said, carefully putting down two large mugs of steaming coffee in front of them. The mugs had the DEA logo embossed on them. "I don't usually go in for all the bullshit ceremony the FBI is so in love with, but they sent these over. Once I was sure they weren't bugged, I broke them out. You gotta admit; these are some nice fucking mugs."

"*Dey* are at *dat*."

"So when are you moving your HQ to the Bat Cave?" Butchie asked.

"I wouldn't hold my breath on that one, Detective," Acosta said.

"Yeah," Butchie nodded. "That's what we thought."

Acosta made eye contact with them and held it. An understanding seemed to have been reached.

"So," Acosta said. "I was told you were coming, but I wasn't told why."

Butchie and Eddie looked at each other, convinced now that Warren was screwing with them.

"Warren Agnew told us you had to confer with us about something that came up on the wire," Butchie said. "Something about another narcotics crew in league with the Bonannos."

"I heard about that too." He laughed. "But for some reason Agnew wouldn't play the tape for me. I had to take his word for it."

"Well, who are they?" Butchie asked.

"They're no one. They're a fucking red herring."

"Well what the *fook* are we *chasin* it *fer*?"

"Because someone in the FBI or the Justice Department wants us to," Acosta answered.

"*Dey're writin* the checks, so we have to dance to their tune, I suppose," Eddie observed.

"Well, what's it all about?" Butchie asked.

"You guys know anything about the Savage Skulls?"

"Yeah," Eddie answered. "*Dey're* a dirt-bag biker gang from Hart Street."

"They also run all the weed, speed and angel dust in Bushwick," Acosta informed them.

"We know *that* much," Butchie said. "But I hardly think the Bonannos are doing business with a scumbag biker crew."

"Right again," Acosta nodded. "But the Bonannos are not above taking a cut of their action for permission to operate in Bushwick. The Skulls are paying thirty percent a week."

"Why is *dat* so critical to our case?" Eddie asked.

"It isn't," Acosta allowed. "It's just one more count on the criminal conspiracy. And I already got that on lockdown. The club president, Pepino Cuevas, is my confidential informant."

"Then why are we wasting time on this?"

"Because the powers that be want to slow your roll a little."

"What the *fook* for?"

"Because you're getting too close too fast. There are people the Justice Department don't want touched; big people."

"Like who?" Butchie asked.

"Like senators and congressmen on the mob's payroll," Acosta said. "These are people who also write the budget checks for the Justice Department and the FBI. Their continued political support gives them a license to take bribes. Right now you're getting close to exposing that."

"*Dat's fookin* disgusting. Is Warren in on it?"

"No. The orders are coming above his pay-grade. But he won't buck them. He likes being a special agent of the FBI. He also won't protect you when they fuck the case up and look to scapegoat you too for it."

"Why did they bring us into this case in the first place if they didn't want us to investigate it?" Butchie asked.

"Oh, they want you to investigate," Acosta assured them. "They just want you to do it at a speed they can keep up with, so they can protect *their* politicians. They won't admit it, but they need you."

"Why is *dat*?"

"Because, come the end of the day, somebody has to catch the bad guy. That won't be the FBI. And when the case stalls because of their sabotage, you have to be left holding the bag. How does it feel to be a patsy?"

"*Dere's* no *fookin* way *dat's* happening."

"Now that you know, probably not. But you have to be careful, and you have to be thorough. Leave them no political cover to *not* act."

"How do we do that?"

"Cultivate a trust-worthy source in the media. I know, it's like trying to find a fucking unicorn, but find one. Then leak what the Feds are trying to suppress. If you can leak it anonymously, that would be better."

"I tink I know a guy," Eddie said. "He's a drunk and a boob, but he'll write any *ting* we tell him."

"Maybe let Butchie call him," Cormac suggested. "That brogue of yours is a dead giveaway."

"I was thinking my wife would do it," Butchie said.

"Why fook with us like this?" Eddie asked. "Why not just shut us down when the time comes? Why do we have to be scapegoated?"

"Because they're afraid you'll find out something they don't want you to know. They have to discredit you, just in case. You have to know you scare the shit out of them. You're an unfamiliar animal to them. You get a lead and you pound it into the ground. You follow the case where it goes, and you don't ask permission to take the next step. You just jump. Can you imagine how frightening that kind of decisiveness is to the lawyers and bureaucrats in the justice department? They have no sense of urgency. So, they have no understanding of the speed with which you do things."

"It seems like we're getting more interference from the feds than we are from La Cosa Nostra," Butchie said. "Does anything in this world make sense?"

"Yeah, but you gotta read the playbook," Acosta said. "The people who run these cases are the big bosses in the FBI and the justice department. They're lawyers, which makes them cautious. But they're also politicians, which makes them scared shitless to make a mistake. They also can't afford to have their budgets cut. Then you guys come into their orderly little world and start overturning the furniture. You attack this case like you were shot out of a cannon. I love it, but I'm not in charge. They want everything vetted and corroborated before they move on to the next thing—afraid their bright shining futures might go up in smoke. You could fight them on it, but that's not going to help. You just have to understand that their caution and treachery are additional obstacles."

"So, what do we do?" Butchie asked.

"Give them what they pretend to want. Then go do what needs to be done. When you get that wrapped up, drop it in their laps like a hand grenade." He laughed. "Let's see how patient they want to be with a live frag sitting on their nuts."

"Can you be more specific?" Butchie asked, grinning.

"Go sit on the Skulls for a few hours. No one from the Bonannos is showing up. My CI drops the money off every Wednesday at Il Trombone Arrugginito. It's funny actually. I got it all on video. They won't let Pepino wear his colors there. He looks like he's got his son's communion suit on."

"*Den* what?"

"Then file a *no contact* report. By tonight you can get back to what you were doing," Acosta said.

"What else can we do for your drug case?" Butchie asked.

"Not a fucking thing. I'm already bought in to the Bonannos for more than a kilo of heroin. The chemical analysis proves that the dope all comes from the same processing lab in Sardinia, owned by Donato Amoroso. Thanks to your arrest of Cockeye Morabito, I got a cooperator who can give me six years of history on the ongoing conspiracy. The only thing I don't have is where and when the drugs are being moved out of Bushwick, and I've been prevented by the FBI from trying to find out."

"Just to slow us down?" Eddie asked.

"Yeah, they want to keep the information compartmentalized in this case. Warren claims that they're going to get that from the wire, but he's lying," Acosta said. "You guys are gonna get that from your informant."

"How do you know we have one?" Butchie narrowed his eyes.

"Because you couldn't be making the Bonannos and the FBI so fucking nuts if you weren't already inside. You guys are going to break this case. You'll let me know once you find out where the heroin is coming out of. We'll work backward and find out where it comes *into* Brooklyn and connect it to Sardinia. Put a fucking bow on it."

"So, you need nothing from us?" Butchie asked.

"No," Cormac admitted. "You could join us though for our next and last buy. We're going to personally take delivery of two kilos of heroin from Donato Amoroso."

"How'd *ye* manage *dat*?"

"I've got an amazing undercover. He's been buying up for weeks. Now we're at the promised land."

"That's some work in a few short weeks. Where did you find this guy?"

"I didn't," Cormac admitted. "Sheridan dropped him in my lap. Turns out he's one of yours."

"Isn't that a little dangerous?" Eddie asked. "If he's a cop, what's to stop one of the turncoats from diming him out to the Bonannos?"

"Because they don't know he's a cop," Acosta smiled. "Sheridan scooped him up the day before he was to go into the police academy. I trained him, but the kid is a natural. He could bullshit the wings off an angel. Sheridan is the only one in your department who has even met him."

"*Dat's* tight," Eddie marveled. "How did he buy up to Amoroso so quickly?"

"I gave him an airtight legend," Acosta said. "I nailed a mobster from Provincetown, named Lucca DeSimone. He was bringing heroin into south Boston from the Bronx. I got him buried in a supermax with no visitation. Ostensibly, because he's an escape risk, but really, I need him tucked out of sight until this buy-op is over."

"Why is this Lucca a problem?"

"He's not. He's my open door. When we put him away, he left his nephew Genaro in charge. My undercover is pretending to be him, trying to better-deal the Puerto Ricans in the Bronx with Bonanno heroin."

"How is *dat* safe?" Eddie asked. "Anyone vetting your guy just needs to go to Provincetown to find out there are two of *dem. Den yer fooked.*"

"Except, the real Genaro DeSimone is on a slab in the morgue in Boston. He od'd on his own product. I got the medical examiner keeping him on ice as a John Doe until I say different."

"How do you know your ME won't turn on you?" Butchie asked. "Doctors can be bought."

"Doctors can also be drug addicts," Cormac pointed out. "Let's just say, I got him leveraged to the tits. He does what I say, or he loses his job and license to practice medicine."

"*Dat's fookin* brilliant."

"Thank you, Eddie," Cormac said, smiling. "So will you be joining us tomorrow for the buy?"

"Absolutely," Butchie said.

"Great. We're *tacking-up* at a warehouse on Traffic Avenue in Ridgewood at 19:00 hours. Here's the address," Cormac said, handing Eddie a slip of paper.

"We'll see you there," Butchie said.

"I can't wait for you to meet Angelo," Cormac said. "You're going to love him."

"Who the fuck is Angelo?" Butchie asked.

"Our undercover."

"*Tanks* for your candor, and good advice," Eddie said. "It's nice to be working with the real police for a change. Before we go, I've got one more question. Cormac Acosta; what the *fook* is *dat* all about? Except for the bright blue eyes of Saint Sebastian himself, you look like a Latin American revolutionary. What gives?"

"I'm from the South Bronx," Cormac said smiling. "My father was Puerto Rican, and my mother from County Kerry."

"Well, it produced a fine man, as far as I can see," Eddie said.

"You know what else it makes me?"

"What's that?" Butchie asked.

"A drunk knife fighter," he said with a wink.

CHAPTER THIRTY-NINE

September 29, 1979
Bushwick

Later that afternoon, Butchie and Eddie were on Hart Street, just off the corner of Knickerbocker Avenue. They were looking through binoculars at the clubhouse of the Savage Skulls. Butchie could see that the bikers had cordoned off the sidewalk in front of their club. Pedestrians were forced to cross the street rather than walk in front of the biker club. Their motorcycles were parked in a row at the curb, gleaming in the sun. Butchie could see the club president, who they now knew was Cormac Acosta's informant, seated out front. On the sidewalk enforcing the "no pedestrians edict" was his top henchman, Hector *Gordo* Melendez.

"Ah, fuck!" Butchie said. "Here comes trouble. Paddy Durr just came onto the block. He's headed right for Gordo and he looks pissed."

"He's looked like *dat* since Inez was killed," Eddie reminded him. "I don't *tink* anything else is particularly bothering him. Let's just keep an eye on *tings*."

They watched as Durr walked purposely down the block. He ducked under the rope blocking the sidewalk, tied from the bus stop sign to the wall. For an enormous man, Gordo Melendez moved quickly toward him. When he grabbed the kid by the throat, bedlam broke out in an instant.

"Holy fuck!" Butchie exclaimed, when he saw Paddy grab the hand at his throat and hold it there. His left forearm came up with such force, it shattered Melendez' elbow, forcing the broken bones through the skin and wrenching his shoulder from its socket. As the big man screamed, Paddy lifted his right foot and crashed it down on the side of Melendez' knee. Butchie and Eddie could hear the sounds of the bones snapping from down the block.

Melendez let out a continuous wail of agony that sounded to Eddie like a cat got itself caught in a meat grinder, until Paddy went to work with his fists. He hit Melendez with a dozen or more thunderous blows to the head, finally driving him face-first onto the pavement—a silent broken mass.

They watched as Paddy flipped Gordo onto his back, grabbing the fallen giant by his groin and the back of his fat neck and hoisting him from the ground.

"Are *ye fookin* seeing this?" Eddie exclaimed. "*Dat* fookin man is at least *tree-hundred* pounds. He lifted him up like he weighed *nuthin* at all."

Butchie was struck mute, as he watched Paddy lift Melendez as high as his neck. He then dropped Gordo over his bent knee, allowing more than three hundred pounds of mass to join with terminal velocity to smash Melendez' lower back to pieces.

Eddie and Butchie could only wince as Melendez was flipped onto his prodigious belly again. Grabbing Gordo by his belt and braided ponytail, Paddy began swinging him back and forth like a pendulum, walking toward the front of the clubhouse. When he got there, he used Melendez' own momentum to sling him through the Savage Skulls logo etched on the glass of the storefront. When Durr climbed through the shattered plate glass window, Butchie and Eddie finally moved.

They tore from their hide, lights and sirens blaring, screeching to a halt in front of the clubhouse. As they got out of their unmarked Ford, they could see the kid inside, strangling Melendez with his own wallet chain. They had to pull Paddy off him. That finally broke through his murderous rage, eyes slowly focusing on Butchie and Eddie, though his breath was still coming in ragged exhalations—sounding more like a growl than anything like breathing.

"Get the fuck out of here, Paddy," Butchie ordered.

Paddy stared briefly at Butchie, before he turned and stomped out through the shattered window. He marched over to Cuevas, still seated in shock out front, and grabbed him by the beard to lift him out of his chair. He leaned in and growled at him.

"If any of you ink-stained motherfuckers get in my way, or try to put your hands on me again, I'll kill every last one of you."

Dropping Cuevas back into his seat, Durr went over to the curb and pushed The Skulls' bikes down like they were dominoes, before storming off the block.

After making sure the broken Gordo wasn't going to die, Butchie and Eddie came outside to confront Cuevas. They had to smack him a few times to break the spell of his fear and get him to focus on their words. They dragged him inside the clubhouse so none of the other bikers could hear their conversation.

"Tell *dat* fat fuck over *der dat* he fell off his bike," Eddie commanded.

"And make sure he tells that to the doctors when you drag him to Kraut Town," Butchie added. "If we hear anything else, we're coming back here to finish what Durr started."

"Another *ting*," Eddie added. "*Dat* kid is protected. You don't *fookin* touch him. If you do, all of our power and might will be dedicated to the proposition of ending you. And the fact that you're a DEA informant will provide you with no cover at all. Is *dat* clear?"

Cuevas eyes went wide with the revelation of his treachery. He believed his informing was a secret only he and Agent Acosta knew. He had brokered the deal when the youth of Bushwick started dying from the poisoned angel dust the Savage Skulls had begun making and selling. Not gifted chemists, Cuevas knew it was just a matter of time before they killed a few more kids, and the law would roll up the motorcycle club once and for all. The deal with Acosta was his insurance policy. He had no idea how these cops knew what they did and was not interested in finding out. He took them at their word. He knew one thing for certain; Paddy Durr and these two cops were the last people on Earth with whom Cuevas wanted further problems.

"That kid is *Diablo Gringo,"* he said. "He won't have no problems with the Savage Skulls. Just tell him to leave us alone. We won't bother him."

"I don't think you appreciate the gravity of your situation," Butchie told him. "If anything happens to that kid, an accident, an act of God—anything at all—*you* will be held accountable. So, keep him safe. Your life depends on it."

They left Cuevas in his wrecked clubhouse, standing over his shattered friend, with much to digest and very few options. He had no desire to be involved at all with that lunatic kid. Now it seemed he was destined to be his guardian angel. Pepino Cuevas wasn't sure how his world got turned so sideways. All he knew was that if he failed to protect Paddy Durr, Bucciogrosso and Curran would turn it upside-down.

CHAPTER FORTY

September 29, 1979
Middle Village

After sundown, Butchie and Eddie were parked across the street from Santino Ippolito's enormous Italianate mansion in Queens. Sonny Black had gotten his nickname to differentiate him from his cousin who had red hair. The cousin, also named Santino Ippolito, was known as Sonny Red. Sometimes mob names were just that simple.

Around 2100 hours, Sonny Black came out of the wrought iron gate between his house and his detached three-car garage. He was carrying two garbage cans which appeared to be full. Still thick and sturdy in his early seventies, Sonny was wearing gray sweatpants, slippers and a white sleeveless tee-shirt, commonly called a *wife-beater*. When Sonny got to the end of the driveway, to put his cans on the curb for collection in the morning, Butchie and Eddie got out of the Ford to approach him.

"Mr. Ippolito, we need you to come with us," Butchie told him.

"Are you guys the police, or are you here to kill me?" Sonny asked matter-of-factly.

"Mr. Ippolito," Butchie said with annoyance. "It's me, Joey Bucciogrosso."

"Oh, I'm sorry, Butchie. I can't see shit without my glasses anymore. Is the Irish kid with you?"

"Yes sir, Mr. Ippolito," Eddie acknowledged.

"Hello, Eddie. What can I do for you boys?"

"We need to have a conversation," Butchie said.

"Okay, I'll take a ride with you. But don't take it personally when I tell you to go fuck yourselves. I'm not cut out to be a rat."

They drove into the heart of Saint John's Cemetery, on 80th Street and Metropolitan Avenue. The irony wasn't lost on any of them. They knew there were more dead Mafiosi buried in this cemetery than were breathing in Brooklyn. They didn't bother to get out. They idled and spoke in the car.

"Mr. Ippolito," Eddie began. "We're hearing everywhere *dat* Sallie Gorgeous is about to have *ye* clipped. We were hoping *ye* could tell us why."

"First of all, call me Sonny. You keep calling me Mr. Ippolito, I start looking for my father. It's disconcerting. He's been dead for fifty years and I never liked the son-of-a-bitch. My problem with Sallie Gorgeous is my business. But if you know I'm on the hit parade, then you're already talking to someone on the inside. So you know he wants to kill me because he asked me to run something, and I turned it down."

"Can *ye* tell us what it was? Did it have anything to do with the *ting* upstate? What is the fantasy camp?" Eddie asked.

"They're the same thing. I shouldn't be telling you this, but I'm going to; because it's the sickest, most depraved thing anyone has ever made money from. It's awful, and it has to stop. That fucking Sallie Gorgeous is the vilest prick who ever walked the earth, and he needs to be excised from this world like the malignant tumor he is."

Sonny went on to tell them all about his business trip to Ossining.

"When Sallie went upstate back in 1950, he thought he was going in for the rest of his life. He was always sex-crazed. It seemed like he could never get enough. I suppose it's why he started out as a pimp. We got our *buttons* together, so I got to see his act up close. I realized it wasn't the sex he was getting off on. It was the abuse. He was a rapist."

"That's not exactly new information, Sonny," Butchie reminded him.

"I'm sorry, Butchie. Sallie has been so bad, for so long I forgot about what he did to your mother. I understand why you hate him."

"I *tink* we've come to the point where we can all hate him. Please go on, Sonny," Eddie said.

"All Sallie cared about was dominating people until they broke—feeding on their fear. The more his victims fought and protested, the better he liked it. When he went up state, he figured he had seen the last of women. He was already a feared man in jail. He had influence and power in there because he had the mob's backing. They bought off everybody, up to and including the wardens, and Sallie started selling contraband to the inmates and the guards. To amuse himself, he would have the guards bring him the youngest, most vulnerable inmates. He would rape and brutalize them. One of the guards asked if he could pay him for a turn. Sallie figured out he had a new business."

"Sallie Gorgeous is gay?" Butchie asked.

"Not exactly. It's not about the sex at all for him. It's all about terrifying and dehumanizing people. Strictly speaking, he doesn't have a sexual preference. He's a monster without prejudice."

"How did he make a business of such a *ting*?"

"He had already co-opted all of the guards. He controlled all the drugs in there. So he had all the money. When he found a couple of guards as depraved as him, he convinced them to put the word out among their perverted social circle. There was now an inexhaustible source of victims for their sick compulsion—for a hefty price, of course."

Sonny lit a cigarette and blew a heavy stream of smoke disgustedly out the rolled down back window before continuing.

"After a while, he was able to move it out to the Juvenile Detention centers—boys and girls. He started pimping out kids as young as thirteen. With all the guards he bought, he was able to expand his operation into every facility in the state. On weekends after midnight, there now is a caravan of perverts trying to get *into* jail. I saw those kids through the fence. They were afraid of me. They knew what I represented. They had this hopeless, beaten look in their eyes. I decided I couldn't do it. Then I found out it was even worse."

"I already want to throw up. What could be worse?" Butchie asked, horrified.

"They're making pornographic movies with these kids. Sallie is selling this shit all over the world now. The ones who are willing are permitted to participate in the movies. The ones who aren't willing get raped on film anyway. The ones who are unwilling and won't be missed by anyone are being murdered. They're making snuff films, Butchie. You can't even imagine the horror. How anyone could even think of such a thing is revolting enough, but its big business now. Those movies are going for a million bucks a piece in Europe. And there is no shortage of buyers."

"If *ye'll* testify, we can protect *yer* family, and *ye* can all go into witness protection," Eddie told him.

"I got eleven kids. Some of them already have their own families. You guys can accommodate all of them?"

"Yeah," Butchie said. "We've already been authorized to offer it to you."

"Thank you, boys, but I can't turn rat—not even for this. You know what you need to know. As for me, just drop me off at home. I made arrangements for this years ago. Everything is in my wife's name already, and I got plenty of life insurance. I'll wait for Roman Sciula to come blow my head off."

"Roman won't be killing *ye*, Sonny. He asked us to help *ye*."

"Roman is working with you? Good for him! Those bastards always treated him like shit. I hope he takes them all down. But if you are talking to him, tell him if he gets the contract to whack me—it's alright. Tell him to fulfill it. I won't have any hard feelings. Just ask him to leave my body where it'll be found. I don't want my wife to have to wait a year to collect the insurance money."

CHAPTER FORTY-ONE

September 30, 1979
Ridgewood

At 19:00 hours, Butchie and Eddie pulled into the gated lot next to 6555 Traffic Avenue. After being buzzed into the building, they were escorted by a DEA agent into a large partitioned conference room recently erected in the corner of the warehouse. Seated at the table were Cormac Acosta, the agent they met at the Army terminal, and a young, stylishly dressed Italian kid who looked like he was fourteen-years-old. He had a mop of bushy brown hair, a baby-face with the slightest hint of a peach-fuzz mustache, faded designer jeans, a tight flower-print Huckapoo shirt, and white leather Capezios. The silver-gray Members Only jacket completed his mod-squad look. All energy; he looked like he was squirming in his seat waiting for his chance to talk.

"Detectives, glad you could make it," Cormac said. "This is Police Officer Angelo Florio, but we've gone to great pains and expense to make him Genaro DeSimone from Provincetown Massachusetts. Angelo, say hello to Detectives Bucciogrosso and Curran, and don't forget to drop your Rs."

Angelo bounded out of his seat and set upon the detectives, vigorously shaking their hands and clapping them on their backs.

"I'm so glad to meet you guys!" he said. "You got these Bonannos shitting in their pants. All these months buying into them, you're all they talk about. It's like you're the boogie man to these assholes. I overheard them talking about a contract Amoroso put out on *youse*. No one will touch it. They're afraid of you."

Butchie and Eddie assured him they were already aware of the contract. They informed him that Sallie Gorgeous had temporarily suspended it. So for the time being, he could relax. They weren't anymore under the gun than usual.

"We have a wrinkle," Cormac announced.

"What's that?" Butchie asked.

"Warren wants us to call off the buy-op. He said it's premature. That's bullshit, of course."

"So, we cave?" Eddie asked.

"Fuck no," Cormac said. "I foresaw this, so I gave it a separate DEA case number. I told him I would cancel *his* buy-op. This one is mine. We'll marry it to the RICO later."

"*Yer* diabolical, Agent Acosta. I like that about you," Eddie said, laughing.

Cormac took everybody through the buy-op. Angelo would be meeting personally with Amoroso in apartment 3D, of 281 Wyckoff Avenue, just off the corner of Grove Street. In the last week, he had sat down with him twice at Ill Trombone Arrugginito to discuss price and delivery. Really, it was an opportunity for Amoroso to ask questions about his prospective customer and make time for his background to check out. They agreed to a price of $25,000 a Kilo, or kilogram of the uncut heroin. While this was a few thousand dollars more per key than the bottom dollar price, Angelo was able to negotiate twenty thousand per key for future transactions. His long term planning helped convince Amoroso he was a legitimate partner.

"Angelo will be wearing a Nagra recorder and a Kell transmitter," Cormac informed them. "So theoretically, we should hear everything he and Amoroso say. While he's upstairs, me, Agent Burgeous, and Detectives Bucciogrosso and Curran will be across the street in the van. Your trouble code for this op is, *take it easy*. If the shit hits the fan and you have to say those words, grab a piece of the floor, Angelo, cause we're coming in hot, shooting everything still standing. Got it?"

Angelo nodded.

"He'll be carrying the fifty grand of pre-recorded buy money in two envelopes in this Pan Am flight bag," Cormac said sliding the satchel with the money across the table. "The heroin will be coming out in the same bag. So, it should be noticeably heavier. You going in armed, Ang?"

"Got my pea-shooter right here," Angelo said, displaying his .22 magnum two-shot Derringer. "I'll have it in my jacket pocket, but, God help me if I need it."

The nervous smile on Angelo's face left Butchie conflicted. He wasn't sure if he wanted to hug the kid or slap him. He appreciated his fearlessness but wanted him to focus. Having been shot, Butchie understood it was nothing to joke about, and he hoped Angelo might never find out.

The tac-plan ended, leaving them with more than an hour to kill before Angelo's meeting with Amoroso at nine o'clock. This gave Angelo the opportunity to tell his life story to Butchie and Eddie, which he did in great detail.

Just twenty-two-years-old, he was born and raised in Red Hook, still living with his mother on Columbia Street. He graduated from Erasmus Hall High School where he played football and baseball. His father had been a longshoreman, until he was killed in a wild shootout on President Street in 1970. Just a bystander, he was gunned down accidentally when Joey Gallo and his brothers shot it out with hired gunmen from the Colombo family. No one on either side ever expressed remorse or made a financial gesture to the widow and her only child. Only a detective from the precinct showed them any kindness. He assured young Angelo and his mother that everyone involved in the shootout would get what was coming to them. Checking in on them periodically, he dispensed advice for Angelo and the little money he could afford to part with as an honest cop.

He was true to his word. By 1975, everyone from the gunfight was either dead or dying. The Gallos had been gunned down. Joe Colombo was comatose in the hospital, never to regain consciousness. Meanwhile, the Colombo Crime Family were picking themselves apart in the internecine gang-war that followed. Because of this one kind detective, Angelo decided to become a cop. He had developed an intense hatred for the Mafia, experiencing firsthand their treachery and hypocrisy. He was delighted for the opportunity to take a piece out of the mob, even if they weren't Colombos. He figured the Bonannos would do in a pinch.

Butchie realized they were kindred souls. Angelo had been living under the thumb of the Mafia all his life. He wanted only to take care of his mother and elicit a little payback from the scumbags who took his father from him. Butchie's motivations were similar enough for him to feel like he was having a conversation with himself. Acosta was right. He loved the kid. For that he kicked himself. Now he had to worry about him. That worry was compounded a few minutes later.

"Warren Agnew just sent this over," Cormac said, a crease of concern on his face, waving a tape reel. "They picked this up on the wire at Il Trombone a week ago. After making this appointment, Amoroso was still unsure about Angelo. He put somebody on the case to follow him."

Acosta cued up the tape. Everyone heard a phone conversation between Amoroso and an unknown male.

"This kid from Provincetown, he checks out so far, but I'm still not sure," Amoroso said. "He's staying on Hancock Street. Come get his picture. I have his license plate. Follow him around. See where he goes."

"Sure, we can do that," a gruff male voice said. "Anything extra for the effort?"

"I'll put an extra thousand in your envelope this month," Amoroso said, the disdain clear in his voice. Then the call clicked off.

"Agnew said there were no further calls to or from this number, which turns out to be a payphone on Flushing Avenue. Last night Amoroso called Angel's answering machine to confirm the sale tonight. He didn't sound raised up. Anybody know this second voice?"

"I know it," Butchie said. "That's Patrolman Ernie Walton from the eight-three."

"Him and his partner, Joe Kemp, are two of the dirtiest cops ever to wear a shield," Eddie added. "They've been on the Bonanno payroll since the fifties."

"These are the uniform *jamokes* you guys slapped around outside the coffee shop?" Acosta asked.

"*Dat's dem*," Eddie confirmed.

"That shouldn't be a problem," Acosta said. "It's not like they're detectives, and Amoroso confirmed the buy. Angelo's legend is solid."

"Except, they won't be checking his story in Provincetown," Butchie pointed out. "They'll be following him around Brooklyn."

"I *tink* we gotta call it off," Eddie said.

Angelo was looking concerned from across the table. He respected the detectives opinions, but he had put too much work into this to be frightened now. He didn't think they were burned.

"I would 'a made a tail," Angelo said. "Nobody followed me."

"All due respect, Angelo," Butchie said. "But you've been doing this all of six months. On top of which, you would have been looking for a Cadillac or a Buick in your rear-view. These guys are a couple of broken-down valises. Cheap-ass corrupt cops; they would've been following you in a rusted out Dodge Dart. They're the furthest thing from a Mafioso. They would be invisible to you."

"I don't think so," Angelo said, shaking his head.

Eddie attacked the issue from a different direction.

"Is the Hancock Street apartment legit?"

"Yeah," Cormac confirmed. "Other than meeting Amoroso at the Trombone, that apartment and the Army Terminal are the only places he's been."

"What if they followed him to the Terminal?" Butchie asked.

"They can't get in," Cormac said. "There are armed guards at the gate, and you need clearance to enter. No offense, but a patrolman's shield ain't cutting it. Even if they inquired, there would be a record of it. With that in mind, I'll send my guys to check the book right now to be sure. Let's all standby."

Everyone cooled their heels while Cormac called the DEA Office. A few minutes later he returned.

"I had them check the log for the last two weeks. There were no suspicious attempts at entry. I think we're good," Cormac said.

"I *tink* we're burned," Eddie disagreed. "It's not worth the risk to Angelo. Between his Nagra tapes and the FBI's wiretap, we've got Amoroso cold on conspiracy. Let's cut our losses, get a search warrant for the buy apartment, and hopefully hit pay dirt if Amoroso and the dope are there."

"I tend to agree," Acosta said. "The FBI and the US Attorney won't, but it's just our assess on the line, and we're expendable in their world. I'm inclined to call it off, but this is Angelo's case as much as anyone's. He's been out there on his own dealing with these scumbags. He knows them better than any of us. I'm in charge of the op, so whatever happens is on me, but I'm gonna let Angelo make the call. What do you think, Ang, are we burned?"

Angelo had been slumped in his seat, waiting for the others to torpedo his buy-op. He sat up, quickly brightening when Cormac left the decision with him.

"I don't think we are," Angelo said. "Like I told you, I would have made a tail. I wanna do this. If I get a bad feeling, I'll pull the plug. You guys will have me on the Kell. I'll be safe."

"Then we go at 20:30 hours," Acosta decided.

Butchie didn't agree. Not with the decision or Angelo's assessment of his safety. He had argued his point, but was consigned to obey the group's consensus. But he didn't like it. He had a terrible premonition of doom. Before they headed out, he grabbed Angelo and pulled him to the side.

"If you get any inkling that something isn't right," Butchie said. "You bail. Don't concern yourself with the case. It's just drugs. We already have enough on Amoroso."

"Thanks for your concern, Butchie, but I gotta see this through. Everything I've done so far has been to set this buy up. Now that we're at the end, I gotta finish it."

Butchie left it unsaid that he feared it was destined to finish badly.

***

Two weeks previously, Ernie Walton and Joe Kemp checked in with Donato Amoroso. As was the usual case, the crooked cops called in with the heroin merchant to give him up-dates on what the cops were doing and to receive instructions about anything else Amoroso needed. The partners had been pocketing an extra two grand a week for their double dealing. Walton loved when Amoroso needed something extra. It gave him the opportunity to shake the Bonanno underboss down for a little something more.

When Walton got back in the patrol car, he brought Kemp up to speed on what their Mafiosi masters needed from them.

"After we go end of tour, we gotta pick up some info and a picture at the Trombone."

"What's up?" Kemp asked.

"There's a guy in from outta-town to buy some smack. His story checks out okay, but Amoroso wants him followed, to see who he's with down here."

"What's our end?" Kemp asked.

"An extra grand in the envelope."

"I'll follow him to hell for that!" Kemp laughed.

The two partners had been *on the pad* since they were rookies in the eight-three. Back in the fifties, many uniform patrolman took small bribes from the gamblers to look the other way. It was regarded as fairly harmless. Even when arrested, the bookies paid a small fine and were usually back on their corners before the cops were even out of court. This type of graft, well publicized during the Knapp Commission, was referred to as *grass eating*. As narcotics became the primary revenue source for the mob, a more proactive dirty cop was needed. There were fewer willing to actively engage in committing crimes to abet the gangsters, but the payoff was so much more substantial, the mob had little trouble finding a couple. This type of graft was called *meat eating*. Joe Kemp and Ernie Walton were decidedly carnivorous.

Though not detectives, they hung around with them. Cops drank and decompressed in the same bars, irrespective of rank. The combination of alcohol loosening tongues and inhibitions allowed the two empty suits, Walton and Kemp, to ascertain a lot of information to which they ordinarily shouldn't have been privy. For the price of a round of drinks and a few open ended questions, they discovered a plethora of useful and lucrative things.

Cops love to talk. They know things other people don't. When they're drunk, they want to tell everyone their secrets. Ernie and Joe had a steady group of drinking buddies they met with at Nettles, the cop bar on Myrtle Avenue across from Forest Park. Every cop from Brooklyn North and Queens congregated there. Sometimes the information poured out so thick, Joe Kemp felt he should be writing it down. But, that would have drawn suspicion. So he started carrying a voice recorder in his pocket. His favorite drinking buddy had become a Detective Nesbit from Brooklyn North Narcotics. Nesbit was in the Debriefing Team. So, he knew who all the snitches were. It never occurred to him that his conversations with Joe Kemp had anything to do with the slew of informants recently ending up as murder victims. His alcoholism had advanced to the point where he wasn't thinking about anything beyond his next Cutty Sark. When he had one in hand, he would regale Patrolman Kemp for hours.

Kemp and Walton had been tipping off the Bonannos about on-going investigations, wire taps, search warrants and every other police activity that might negatively affect their illicit business. They even went so far as to identify informants and undercover cops, imperiling their lives. The first time they did this, Walton asked Kemp if it wasn't going too far.

"Fuck him!" Kemp said, consigning the informant to death. "They shouldn't have tried to upset *my* apple cart."

This contented Walton, who wasn't really concerned anyway. He was just looking for his partner to validate what he already intended to do.

***

After picking up the packet from Donato Amoroso, Kemp and Walton headed over to 1066 Hancock Street, where Genaro DeSimone, from Provincetown Massachusetts was purportedly staying. They saw his purple Buick with Massachusetts tags parked out front. Walton pulled over across the street and down the block to wait for DeSimone to come out.

"This kid looks familiar," Kemp said, studying his picture. "I feel like I've seen him before."

"He's just another wop; New York, Boston--what's the fucking difference—one guinea hood, more or less."

"No, seriously Ernie, I've seen this kid somewhere. He ain't from outta-town."

"It doesn't matter, Joe. We're just doing a tail on him. We follow him, tell Amoroso where he went, spend the extra grand. Easy-peasy."

"I'll think about it," Kemp said. "I'll figure out where I've seen him before."

When DeSimone surfaced a half hour later, Kemps memory came flooding back.

"I know that fucking guy!" he exclaimed. "And he ain't from Provincetown."

"What the fuck are you talking about, Joe?"

"That kid right there is from Red Hook," Kemp said, pointing. "He's my neighbor. He lives on Columbia Street with his mother."

"How do you know this?"

"You know it too, Ernie. Remember that longshoreman who got greased on President Street?"

"You mean the idiot that walked into a gunfight between the Gallo brothers and Joe Colombo?"

"Yeah, that one," Kemp said. "That's his son."

"Is he a cop?"

"Not as far as I know, but he ain't no fucking Mafioso from Provincetown either. Something stinks here."

"Let's just follow him and see where he goes," Walton said.

They followed him out of Bushwick and down Flushing Avenue to the Brooklyn Queens Expressway, where he got on heading south. Kemp was convinced he was heading to Red Hook.

"When he gets to his mother's house, we can brace him there."

It was an easy tail. The garish purple Riviera allowed Walton to let two cars fall in between them, with little risk of losing sight of the ugly little coupe. Kemp was flummoxed when DeSimone blew right past the Red Hook exit.

"Where the fuck is he going?"

"We'll just have to wait and see," Walton said.

They followed him to the last exit and through the streets until DeSimone pulled up to the gate at the Brooklyn Army Terminal, flashed some sort of identification at the federal security guards and disappeared into the grounds.

"Was that a shield he flashed?" Kemp asked, from across the street where they were forced to park. They both knew they weren't getting on the federal property. Even if they flashed their patrolman shields, they would be as good as blown; no doubt being reported to Internal Affairs for even trying to enter the restricted property without a viable reason. Neither of them could think of one.

"We are so fucked," Walton said. "Where the fuck could he be going in there?"

"Calm down, Ernie. Let's use our heads for a minute. This is a federal facility. I can think of three places—all of them bad—where that kid could be going."

"Want to share them with me?"

"Who runs their secret bullshit investigations from a place like this?"

"How the fuck should I know? I'm just a fucking white-shield cop with two divorces to pay for."

Kemp rolled his eyes at his partner's density—in body and mind. He thought the next clear thought that came out of Walton's booze addled brain might be the first. He waited patiently for Ernie to start listening again.

"So, who is in there?" the Whale asked.

"The FBI is one possibility. The DEA is another. Here's a wrinkle I'm sure you never thought of; The Waterfront Commission."

"Why would the Waterfront Commission give a shit about Donato Amoroso?"

"Oh, I don't know. Maybe the tons and tons of heroin he's bringing in on ships from Sardinia? It doesn't matter who he's with, this guy is the law. We gotta tell Amoroso to call off that sale."

"He's gonna be pissed, Joe."

"Better than being shot dead when the DEA crashes in his door."

***

When Walton and Kemp went back to the Trombone, they were confronted with the most peculiar thing. Amoroso either didn't believe them, or he didn't care.

"I would have heard if the feds were up on me," Donato said. "I've got an FBI Agent on payroll. We own the cops, the DA's, the judges; I pay them to warn me about things like this. Besides, Senator McKibben's man has sworn to keep us protected. I have no worries. You two are wrong. I'm doing this deal."

They were incredulous when they left. It was as if his ego and greed had made Amoroso believe he was invincible. The prospect of branching out into New England had made him reckless.

"We gotta kill this deal before Amoroso can shit the bed." Kemp said. "If he goes through with it and gets taken down, he's gonna blame us. I'm not giving that psycho a reason to whack me."

"We're cops. You really think he'd kill us?"

"If he gets nabbed selling two kilos, he's done. He'll have our heads in a vice before nightfall."

"How are we gonna pooch the deal?" Walton asked.

"I got a guy," Kemp said.

CHAPTER FORTY-TWO

September 30, 1979
Bushwick

At 20:45 hours, Acosta, Bourges, Butchie and Eddie arrived in the surveillance van opposite 281 Wyckoff Avenue. They took up position in the rear to monitor the front of the building and listen to Angelo's Kell transmissions.

At 21:00 hours they observed Angelo park in front of the building in his undercover car. He got out and proceeded into the building with the Pan Am flight bag slung over his right shoulder. At the door, he stopped to preface the Nagra recording.

"This is Police Officer Angelo Florio. The time is 21:00 hours, Friday, September 30th, 1979. I am in front of 281 Wyckoff Avenue, Brooklyn. I am scheduled to meet Donato Amoroso in apartment 3D on the third floor."

Angelo entered the lobby and headed for the dual staircases in the rear of the hallway. As he ascended onto the third floor landing, he felt a stab of terror tremble through his limbs and fall like a pit of ice in his stomach. For a second, he remembered Butchie's plea; *If you get any inkling that anything isn't right, you bail.* This wasn't just an inkling. His superstitious mother would have said he presaged his own death. Then she would have blessed herself twice and shoved him down the stairs. He took a deep breath and composed himself, willing his fear away. It wasn't gone but held at bay. He stepped out of the stairwell to make his way to the sale apartment.

***

When that scumbag cop Joe Kemp approached Louis Eppolito in front of his house on Stockholm Street, Eppolito didn't think his life could get any worse. With Kemp coming his way, he figured it just did. Kemp is the one who dimed him out to the Bonannos that he was getting high off his own supply. Prior to that, he ran all three spots on Stockholm Street for Amoroso. He thought he had it made, until Cockeye Morabito and three burly zips beat the living shit out of him in the street with baseball bats. That's how the Mafia fired you; they beat you within an inch of your life and left you bleeding and broken in the street. If you died, it was your problem. Since healing, he was left to provide for himself. With no help from the Bonannos—they weren't known for their generous severance packages—he had been relegated to home burglaries and gun point stick-ups. His heroin habit only increased after getting out of the hospital. So much so, he was at the tipping point. He couldn't steal enough to support his growing habit. Before Kemp came on the block, Eppolito was giving some serious thought into throwing himself under the L train.

"Louie, my boy!" Kemp said. "How you doing?"

"How's it look, scumbag?" he snarled, no longer afraid of the dirty cop—no longer afraid of anything.

"Oh, don't be like that, Louie. I maybe got something for you," Kemp said, tossing the strung out junkie a whole bundle of *Bad Boy* heroin, unironically, the very same stamp Louie used to sell on Stockholm when he was riding high.

"Make it fast, Kemp. I got a train to catch. And the last time you *maybe had something* for me, you robbed me, dimed me out to Amoroso, sent my life into the toilet, and I got a permanent limp. So forgive me if I don't seem happy to see you."

"What I got here is gonna make you right. We'll let bygones be bygones and all that happy horseshit."

Kemp gave him the photo of Angelo and told him a story. He identified Angelo by his legend. Genaro DeSimone was here to rip-off two keys from Louie's old boss. Not only that, but it was going to be a hit. Kemp said it was some Sicilian bullshit from the other side. But, if he hit Amoroso, it would knock the whole operation into chaos. Then nobody gets paid, not even dirty cops. He gave Louie the time and the place the rip was to go down. He handed the strung out thug an old Dan Wesson single-action six shooter; the gun that won the west. The thing weighed nearly seven pounds and was a foot long from stocks to barrel. He had it wrapped in a towel because it was too big to hide. Kemp handed him the gun and sweetened the deal some more.

"He's gonna have fifty large with him. The money is yours. You just gotta kill him."

"Kemp, you know I never killed anyone. Why come to me with this?"

"Because nobody needs it more. You are the most desperate man in Brooklyn right now. You do this you'll make fifty grand and save Amoroso's life. You'll be back in his good graces and back on top."

Eppolito didn't think to ask Kemp what he was getting out of the deal. The enticement was too strong, and he stopped being suspicious too soon.

***

"Did he go for it?" Walton asked when Kemp got back in the car.

"Yeah, like a junkie to smack. He's probably highballing that bundle right now."

"You ain't worried he'll OD?"

"Nah, I cut it in half with baby laxative. He'll be high as a kite and shitting his brains out for two days—just long enough to realize he needs us."

"Then we gotta carry him after it's over? I don't want to babysit a junkie for the rest of his life."

"Relax," Kemp said. "We just gotta be outside that building when he comes out. I got a nine millimeter with a silencer. We punch his ticket, take his fifty grand, and disappear into the night."

"Do we really have to kill him?"

"You said yourself you didn't want to babysit him."

***

As Angelo stepped out of the stairwell and toward apartment 3D, his heart started pounding like a hammer in his chest. He willed himself to keep walking. His legs became rubbery and the hair was standing up all over his body, like static electricity during a lightning storm. His flesh felt like it was crawling as it tightened into goose bumps. Still he walked.

Midway down the corridor, he thought his mind was playing tricks on him when he saw black shoes sticking out of an alcove on the left. *Fucking Butchie!* He thought, blaming his irrational fear on the detective's concern for him. His hands were a sodden mess, as he palmed the nylon air bag and pulled it closer to his body. He was willfully looking past the alcove and down the hall when Louie Eppolito stepped out of the alcove and thrust that enormous gun into Angelo's face. Angelo closed his eyes and waited for the bullet to crash through his skull. He heard a loud metallic click.

Eppolito realized in an instant, he forgot to cock the old western gun. It wouldn't work otherwise. He expected to see Angelo's brains cascaded on the wall behind him. The .357 Magnum rounds should have practically taken his head clean off. Instead he was left to hear that sickening click echoing off the walls.

Angelo was briefly in shock as he watched Louie curse and bring the gun up again. Then he remembered his protocol—often practiced—hopefully never to be used. Angelo put his hands out in front of him in supplication.

"Okay, take it easy. Don't panic," Angelo said, his voice squeaking with fear, as he looked toward the staircase for the Cavalry. He couldn't understand why they weren't already there.

***

Outside in the van, Acosta cursed. They had just heard Angelo preface the tape over the Kell transmitter and watched him enter the building. A loud scratching hiss came over the Kell. They had lost radio contact with their undercover as soon as he stepped into the building.

"I fucking hate this equipment they make us work with," Acosta said. "The FBI has wireless transmitters that can broadcast from the bottom of the ocean. We get these antiquated pieces of shit that go deaf and mute under a coat of lead paint."

"Why don't we have what they have?" Butchie asked.

"Because they don't want us to have their newest toys," Agent Bourges explained. "They classified the new stuff so we can't play with it."

"*Dat's* some *fooking* bullshit!" Eddie exclaimed.

"We can't leave Angelo unprotected like this," Butchie said.

"Agreed," Cormac said. "I should have listened to you guys and aborted the op. If that kid gets hurt, I'll never forgive myself. You and Eddie get out there and ghost him from the sidewalk. John and I will try and get this shitty transmitter working."

Butchie and Eddie climbed out of the back of the van as nonchalantly as possible, which wasn't very. Right now the two of them felt like their hearts would explode from the anxiety, and the deafening blood pressure pulsating in their ears. They crossed Wyckoff Avenue toward the entrance to the building when they heard a thunderous gunshot, followed a few seconds later by another, and then a small pop. Their legs didn't seem able to carry them fast enough to the front door.

***

"Gimme the fucking money!" Eppolito yelled, pointing that howitzer in Angelo's face again. Angelo threw the airline bag on the floor between them, the two manila envelopes sticking out the open top.

"All of it!" Eppolito demanded.

"That's all there is."

At that point, it looked to Angelo like the perp—because that's how he thought of him now, a perp—was trying to decide what to do next. In reality, Eppolito was mustering the courage to pull the trigger again. He became angry with Angelo for making it so difficult. This guy didn't look like a Mafia hitman. He looked like a nice kid. He reminded Eppolito of himself, before he became a strung-out loser. The realization pissed him off.

"Way to go, Motherfucker!" Louie said, cocking back the big hammer and pointing the gun in Angelo's face.

Angelo again closed his eyes, waiting for his end to arrive. He heard a thunderous bang, but only for an instant. For the immediate future, all he would hear was a loud ringing in his ears. He felt the door frame, an inch to his right and behind him, explode into splinters of wood and plaster. He realized—impossibly—the perp had missed. From point blank range, he had missed. His mind reeling, Angelo was able to process this much; this guy was not a pro, but he had at least five more chances. At this distance, at some point he had to hit him. He couldn't keep missing. *Maybe, just maybe*, Angelo thought, *I can fight my way out of this*. He jumped on his assailant as he saw him cocking the huge revolver again.

As they struggled, the big revolver, pressed between them discharged. The force of the round exiting the barrel and entering Angelo's chest sent him flying across the floor. A pool of blood spread beneath his body, leaving him lying motionless on his left side.

Eppolito quickly collected the flight bag and slung it over his shoulder. He thought Angelo dead, until he heard the raspy breathing and the whistling from the sucking chest wound. He cocked his pistol again and walked over to his prone victim.

"Sorry about this kid, but for me to get paid, you gotta die. Nothing personal," he said, as he grabbed Angelo's shoulder to flip him onto his back to deliver the coup de grace between his eyes.

Angelo, being left handed, had reached into his rear waistband. Expecting to die, he at least wanted his gun in his hand when they found him. When Eppolito turned him on his back, Angelo had a fleeting second to stare into his vacant, soulless eyes. Without thinking, he thrust his little derringer out in front of him and fired, the bullet striking Eppolito in the left abdomen.

Louie Eppolito was a thief, a junkie, and a would-be killer, but by his own estimation he was not a tough guy. He certainly wasn't a gunfighter. So when the little .22 round perforated his kidney and exited his body, he had all the armed combat he could stand. He had the money. The hitman who had come to kill Amoroso was probably going to die anyway, even without the headshot. Eppolito elected to cut his losses and beat feat out of there. Still with his gun in his hand and the airline bag over his shoulder, he tore down the stairwell.

***

After hearing the gunshots, two thunderous ones, and a pop, Butchie yelled into his point-to-point radio, "Shots fired!"

Acosta and Bourges still couldn't hear Angelo's Kell, but they heard that. They bailed out of the van and sprinted for the building. They could see Butchie and Eddie just reaching the door as the armed Eppolito came barreling out.

"Drop the *fooking* gun!" Eddie screamed, drawing down on the bleeding perp.

"It wasn't me!" Eppolito screamed. "Kemp told me I had to kill that guy!"

"What fucking guy?" Butchie yelled.

Just then, Angelo, a bloody stumbling mess, came falling out of the lobby, landing at Eppolito's feet.

"That fucking guy," Eppolito said, pointing with his enormous gun at the fallen Angelo.

Before the detectives and DEA Agents could open fire, Butchie and Eddie heard four quick pops. The marines recognized the sound of a suppressed weapon. They saw in their peripheral vision the muzzle flashes, and Patrolman Joe Kemp holding the smoking nine millimeter they came from. Kemp paused briefly, realizing he was staring at the two cops he hated more than any others, and they were drawing down on him. He turned on his heels and fled up Stockholm Street toward Saint Nicholas Avenue.

"You take care of Angelo!" Eddie yelled. "I'll get that *fooker*, Kemp."

Then he was off after the new quarry, moving so fast he didn't even realize until later he had almost run over fat Ernie Walton, who took the momentary confusion to disappear like a cockroach when the lights went on.

Cormac Acosta got to Angelo first. Tears were streaming down his face as he cradled his undercover's head in his hands. Cormac cleared the blood out of Angelo's mouth and held him upright so he could breathe. The difficulty apparent with each raspy belabored breath, each exhalation accompanied by coughing, blood, and phlegm flowing out of his mouth.

"Take it easy, Angie baby," Cormac said softly, trying to comfort the young cop who felt like he was dying in his arms. "I'm here, Ang. Everything is gonna be alright," he said, feeling nothing of the sort.

"I didn't make the buy," Angelo rasped, disappointed.

"Who fucking cares? It's just drugs."

"Then why did you send me up there?" Angelo said, smiling through his blood stained teeth.

This caused them both to laugh, which got Angelo coughing up blood again. Cormac calmed him, getting his breathing under control.

"Now I know you're going to be okay," Cormac smiled. "You're too crazy-brave to be killed."

"Amoroso is still up in that apartment with the drugs," Angelo reminded him.

"Will you stop worrying about this case? We'll take it from here. Butchie and John can hit the warrant while we get you to Bellevue. You've done enough. We'll take it from here. Your only job now is to stay alive, and that's an order."

Angelo clutched Cormac's hand in his own. He looked up at Cormac and winked.

"You know," he said, before closing his eyes and smiling. "You're not the boss of me."

"So you NYPD pukes keep reminding me," Cormac said.

***

After Eddie had pursued Kemp around the block, Butchie first ran to Angelo, but Cormac was already at his side. So Butchie checked on the perp.

He was dead, struck four times—three in the chest and one between the eyes. Whatever had been going on in his head was now oozing out the back in a flow of blood and brain matter. Butchie got on the radio to slow down the other cops responding.

Cormac left for the trauma center at Bellevue in the ambulance with Angelo, Butchie and Agent Bourges coordinated with the responding precinct detectives and Emergency Service, quickly executing the search of apartment 3D. They needn't have hurried. Butchie later found out from witnesses that Amoroso and his three guys had gone out the window and down the fire escape with the two kilos immediately after the gunshots in the hallway. Arrested later at the café for conspiracy to sell the two kilos, Amoroso was indignant.

"You never caught me with the drugs," he told Cormac and Bourges. "I ditched them after we left the apartment."

Along with not understanding the law as it relates to conspiracy, Cormac realized Amoroso didn't grasp the concept of an incriminating statement either. He was furious when he was strip searched and outfitted with a jumpsuit at the federal jail. He couldn't wait to get to a phone.

Amoroso, by now had come to his senses and realized his dirty cops were correct. Something was not right with this deal. He was not invincible, and there were cops he couldn't buy. He didn't particularly care for or trust the ones he could buy either. Not liking loose ends, he realized that Kemp and Walton had become a liability. It was later picked up on the wire in the cafe that he had put a contract out on them. If they had known their lives were only worth a paltry five thousand bucks for the both of them, they would have been insulted. But their problems would become manifestly more odious than a mere insult.

Just as Butchie and the squad were wrapping things up on the third floor, he heard Eddie come over the radio.

"Narcotics Task force Portable to Central."

"Go, Portable," Central acknowledged.

"I'm on the roof of 420 Stockholm Street with a perp down, unknown condition at this time. Roll a bus, the patrol supervisor, Crime Scene, whomever has the detective duty…Oh hell, send everyone," Eddie said.

"10-05, unit?" Central said, asking him to repeat his message.

"Send everyone, Central," he said. "This is a big *fookin* deal. We're all going to need to get a little wet on this one. And if it's not too much trouble, darlin, perhaps you can get a call into Inspector Thomas Sheridan. I'm one of his, and he definitely needs to know."

Butchie and John Bourges were the first to arrive on the rooftop. Eddie wordlessly brought them over to the edge between the buildings. In the dark, if you weren't already aware, you could miss the fact there was an open air shaft at this spot. Butchie peered over the edge and saw a crumpled Joe Kemp in a vast lake of his own blood. His head had exploded upon impact with the cement six stories down. Butchie knew it was Kemp only from the blue plaid hunting shirt he had been wearing the last time he saw him alive. One of his Knapp patrol shoes had popped off his left foot which was bent in an unnatural direction. The silenced nine millimeter lay a few inches from his right hand, Kemp evidently clutching it till the bitter end.

"Want to run it by me before the hats and white shirts show up?" Butchie asked.

"Better I tell it once, boyo," Eddie said, smiling. "And not until Sheridan gets here. We owe him *dat* much."

"Need anything cleaned up before? Maybe rake the gravel over there?"

"No. The evidence will speak the truth. It'll all be in accordance," Eddie said, grasping Butchie's shoulder. He could tell his partner was still apprehensive.

"Butchie," he said, grabbing him firmly and making eye contact. "It's alright, brother."

They waited a short time until Inspector Sheridan arrived. Eddie gently but firmly explaining to the bosses of varying ranks that he would enlighten everyone once his commanding officer had arrived. His tone was so pleasant and earnest, no one pressed him further. Until the one-star duty chief showed up and decided he was in charge. Eddie quickly dispelled him of that notion.

"All due respect, Chief," Eddie said glaring at him. "But this is a confidential police investigation and *ye* don't have clearance to know. *Ye* can stand over in that *fookin* corner until the man in charge shows up. Whether or not *ye* stick *yer* thumb up *yer* ass in the meantime is entirely up to you."

The chief had turned beet red, shining even in the darkness. He was about to blow his top when the voice of Inspector Sheridan thundered across the rooftop.

"What the fuck do you think you're doing with my detective, Prescott?" Sheridan said to the chief, who got one look at the combative inspector and realized he wished he was anywhere else. From the look on his face, Butchie could tell these men had a history, and Chief Prescott was anxious that no one else knew the details of it.

"Oh, Tommy," the chief said nervously. "He's one of your guys."

"Don't fucking address me by my first name. We are *not* friends," Sheridan said, glaring. "The Chief of Detective's called you at the Boro and expressly ordered you not to respond. You blew the order off because it was just a lieutenant delivering the message. Did you think there was something here for you to steal, you rat piece of shit?"

"There's no need for that kind of talk, Inspector," he said, taking off his hat and wiping his sweating bald head with a soiled handkerchief.

"Chief Sullivan is responding. So is the Police Commissioner. They put me in charge until they get here. You can take it up with them when they do. But they ordered this be exclusively a detective operation. That means you and everyone who works for you needs to un-ass this crime scene forthwith. You've been ordered to cordon off the block. That's the extent of your involvement. Now hop, motherfucker."

After the chief stormed off, Inspector Sheridan addressed the uniforms still present.

"Is the patrol supervisor or the platoon commander here?"

A sergeant and lieutenant from the eight-three precinct stepped up.

"Your guys have done an excellent job tonight. We appreciate all your help and support, but the PC wants this thing compartmentalized. I can't say any more about it right now, but when I can, I'll bring you both up to speed—maybe over a beer. For now, I need your people to cordon off the block. We're gonna have a lot of Crime Scene, Emergency Service and Medical Examiner's people showing up. No one else gets on the block—*especially* the media. Keep those parasites outta here. Can you do that for me?"

They agreed. Sheridan thanked them and shook their hands.

"Consider this a favor I owe you."

As the supervisors grabbed their cops and headed downstairs, Butchie addressed the sergeant.

"That's a good man to have owing you a favor. He pays back in spades."

"He seems like a good guy," the sergeant said.

When it was just the detectives and the DEA left on the roof, Eddie asked the inspector what the deal was with Chief Prescott.

"He's a thief and a rat," Sheridan said. "When he was a platoon commander, he had the late tour in Midtown North. They had a commercial burglary thing going, big stuff; banks, antiques, pharmaceuticals, even some fur warehouses. When they started to get heat, Prescott flipped and cut a deal. He gave up every one of his cops. It's the only way he survived the Knapp Commission."

"How does a cancer like that still exist among us?" Eddie asked.

"A new day is upon us, Eddie," Sheridan said. "We're different than before. Say what you want about

Ben Ward; he's a drunk, inarticulate, he can be a fat embarrassment at times, but he's not stupid. He's not afraid to cut out the dead wood—or in this case, corrupt wood. Prescott's days are numbered. It's comforting being one of the good guys, knowing that with very few exceptions, the people you work with are good guys too. Until very recently, you couldn't say that. This is a good time to be a cop."

Sheridan called everyone together.

"You've got our undivided attention, Detective Curran. There's a dead cop laying at the bottom of an airshaft with a very peculiar weapon in his lungeable area. Please enlighten us how that happened."

"I'd be delighted," Eddie said. "It all began with a little plan to buy some drugs..."

He went on to give a dispassionate, account of the day's events and those leading up to them. When he was done, he could have been quoted verbatim for the Detective Unusual Occurrence Report, as well as the Chief of Detectives' and PC's press briefings. Even the new mayor, Ed Koch—never at a loss for words—would have trouble embellishing on Eddie's account.

In sum and substance, he related how they observed Patrolman Joe Kemp shoot and kill the man who shot and robbed undercover police officer, Angelo Florio, just as the perp was identifying Kemp as hiring him to kill the undercover.

"Say *dat* ten times fast," Eddie challenged.

What occurred after was something to which only Eddie could testify. He chased Kemp up Stockholm Street, with Kemp firing at him over his shoulder several times with his silenced semi-automatic. Eddie said he didn't shoot Kemp because he wanted to interrogate him, to substantiate he was in the employ of Donato Amoroso and the Bonanno Crime Family. He chased him into 420 Stockholm, gaining on him as they went up the stairs and crossed the roof. He said he was fifteen feet behind Kemp when he disappeared over the edge into the airshaft. He heard Kemp shriek on his short ride down, followed by the loud cracking of his skull and thud of his body on the cement. The metallic clanking of his firearm was accompanied by a brief low gurgling as the air escaped one final time from Kemp's lungs—then an eerie silence.

After Eddie and Butchie were alone, Butchie finally gave in to his need for the truth. Not so much because he needed to know. He trusted Eddie. He trusted his judgement. He would take to the grave whatever Eddie told him. But if there was a dark secret he had to carry, Butchie didn't want his brother carrying it alone.

"Where do you suppose Walton was in all of this?"

"I *tink* I might have run by him off the corner of Stockholm."

"Really?" Butchie marveled.

"Yeah, but it was just a blur. I was focused on Kemp. He was shooting at me, after all."

"We're gonna need to talk to that fat fuck, if internal affairs or Amoroso doesn't get him first."

"Sure, he's got a target on his back now."

Having stalled enough, Butchie could wait no longer. He addressed the elephant in the room.

"Did Kemp go off that roof on his own, or was he helped?"

"*Ye* know how sometimes there are questions *ye* just shouldn't ask?" Eddie said, a sad tinge in his voice.

Butchie nodded.

"Perhaps this is one of those questions."

"Fair enough," Butchie allowed. "But you know, I would have helped the motherfucker."

"I know *ye* would have, *boyo. Dat's* why I told *ye* to stay with Angelo. *Ye* have enough on *yer* plate already."

CHAPTER FORTY-THREE

October 1, 1979
Bushwick

Butchie and Eddie were waiting that morning for Paddy Durr to come out of his building on Hart Street. They were looking to intercept him on his way to school. When he emerged from the Durr house carrying his football equipment in a duffel bag over his shoulder, Butchie waved him over to the Ford.

"Get in," he said.

"You're not locking me up for those assholes yesterday, are you?" Paddy asked.

"Just get in the *fookin* car, *boyo.* We've a proposition *fer ye.*"

Paddy opened the back door and climbed in after throwing his duffel bag across the seat. He slammed the door shut and smiled at the two detectives in the front.

"You may proceed when ready, Jeeves," he said.

Butchie and Eddie both gave him dirty looks for that crack, but they had to laugh along when the kid startled cackling at his own joke.

"Thanks for yesterday," Paddy said. "What's this all about?"

"We want to get you out of Bushwick," Butchie said.

"I'm leaving in July when football starts at Columbia," Paddy reminded them.

"We're afraid *ye* won't make it *dat* far if we leave *tings* the way they are," Eddie said.

Paddy didn't like his chances either. He shrugged and held his hands out.

"I got nowhere else to go."

"That's the nature of our proposition," Butchie said. "We have somewhere for you to stay till then."

Unaccustomed as he was to having options, Paddy was dubious. He just stared mutely at the two detectives.

"Did you know Patrolman Doheny?" Eddie asked.

"No, but I heard of him. *Mick the Quick* is a legend in this neighborhood."

"He's retired now, still living in Glendale. He and his wife, Bunny, will take you in," Butchie said.

"Wow! A Durr living with a cop family? The Earth may slip off its axis," Paddy laughed.

"Relax, John Dillinger," Eddie admonished him. "*Yer* not the first troubled kid the Dohenys have saved. Butchie and I are here today only because of their intercession. So, what do *ye* say?"

"Oh, let's see," Paddy said, pretending to enumerate the pros and cons on his fingers. "I live in a shithole apartment with people who hate me. I have to sleep with one eye open for fear that one of them will slit my throat. If that weren't enough, every time I enter or leave that building, I am reminded that the only person who ever cared for me is dead, and her death was my fault. That's a tough one, guys. It's a lot to give up. What would you do?"

Butchie leaned into the back seat and glared at him.

"I like you, Paddy," he said. "But you can be one sarcastic son-of-a-bitch sometimes."

"It's kinda my thing," Paddy admitted.

"One last *ting*, *boyo*," Eddie said. "*Ye* have a tendency for stoicism. *Ye* project an unfeeling attitude sometimes. *Dat's* not gonna work with Bunny. She's going to love *ye*, whether you want her to or not. It's just what she does; she takes care of people, and she loves them. Do everyone a favor and just *fookin* let her."

CHAPTER FORTY-FOUR

October 1, 1979
Bushwick

That afternoon, Butchie and Eddie went to go see Angelo at Bellevue. Out in the hall they met Cormac Acosta. He looked guilt-stricken.

"Is he okay, *boyo*?" Addie asked.

"He's having the fucking time of his life," Cormac said.

"Then why the long face," asked Butchie.

"He's twenty-two years old. And I almost got him killed."

"I *tink yer* overestimating *yer* importance, Cormac. Angelo made the final call."

"He doesn't even qualify as a rookie, and I let him decide his own fate. That's bullshit on an otherworldly level. I was supposed to protect him. Instead I let him walk into an ambush."

"We all did, Cormac."

"I should have listened to you and Eddie."

"*Dat's* always a good policy," Eddie agreed.

"What I want to know," Butchie said. "Is how the hell Angelo survived getting shot with that hand-cannon. It should have made a window in his chest."

"The surgeon is chalking it up to a miracle," Cormac said. "Somehow, it missed everything vital. Broken ribs and a collapsed lung; he'll be back at work in two weeks."

"Jayzuz," Eddie whistled.

Just then, Inspector Sheridan arrived. He took one look at the ashen faces and thought Angelo had died.

"What the fuck is going on out here?" he demanded.

"We're fighting over who was responsible for getting Angelo shot," Butchie said.

"Save a piece of that for me. I'm the one who pulled him out of the academy to buy drugs," Sheridan said. "But I wouldn't dwell on it too much. Angelo isn't. The mayor and the police commissioner were here this morning. The kid lit up like a Christmas tree when the PC pinned his detective shield on him. He probably thinks getting shot was the best thing that ever happened to him."

"I don't think his mother agrees," Cormac said. "She's in there now. I came outside because she was giving me the *mal occhio*."

"We'll all go in together to apologize," Sheridan said. "But first, business. What's next to do?"

"We've gotta go find Walton to put the screws to that fat fuck," Butchie suggested.

"That's been taken care of," the Inspector said. "He tried to surrender to Internal Affairs last night with a lawyer. They didn't know what the fuck he was talking about, so they sent him home. This morning he was found dead in the trunk of his car behind the precinct. The only reason anyone looked was because he was in the C.O.'s spot and there was a note on the trunk that said, "Look in here."

"*Dat* was fast."

"Yeah," Sheridan agreed. "We caught Amoroso giving the order from Central Booking. He still doesn't realize we got a wire in the cafe. When they opened the trunk they found Walton shot a dozen times with a dead rat stuffed in his mouth. I don't think anyone is going to miss that guy."

"I would have liked to talk to him," Eddie said.

"No need," Sheridan said. "The FBI is talking to his attorney. He's telling us everything he and Kemp were up to. Turns out there were no other cops involved. I think we're getting cleaner by the minute. Now, let's go in and throw ourselves at the feet of Mrs. Florio."

Inspector Sheridan introduced everyone and apologized on behalf of them all. He informed Mrs. Florio about the case and Angelo's important contribution. Angelo beamed and puffed out his chest when Sheridan went into detail about his heroics. She took it all in and nodded, a stern look on her face. Then she waved the four of them into the hallway.

"I can see how much you love my son," she said. "You men are all he talks about. He wants to grow up to be just like you. I would very much like that. But it's not going to happen if you keep sending him in with these Mafiosi scumbags. He hates them. So, he'll never stop. So, you have to stop him. He's all I have in the world. If you let him get hurt again, I'm coming to see you. Am I understood?"

They nodded as one, sufficiently chagrined.

"I appreciate what you're doing to these Bonanno shit stains," Mrs. Florio said. "But when you're done with them, do you think you could take a piece out of those Columbo scumbags who killed my husband?"

"They're next on our list," Inspector Sheridan promised.

After leaving the room, Sheridan gathered his guys and Cormac in the hallway.

"Warren sent word that he wants to see Butchie and Eddie in his office, forthwith," Sheridan said. "He didn't want me to know. He told my PAA not to tell me. He was hot about something. Any ideas, Cormac?"

"He's probably pissed about the buy-op. He told me to cancel it."

"What the hell for?"

"Warren doesn't confide in me," Acosta admitted.

"But you ran the op anyway?"

"I don't answer to the FBI; equal pay-grade. Besides, I don't take direction from crooked politicians who have the Justice Department's budgetary nuts in a vice. DEA isn't in the Justice Department. We answer to the Secretary of the Interior. That's a holdover from when we were part of Customs. There's talk of absorbing us, but I hope not. The Chairman of the Senate Judiciary committee is Senator McKibben. He's been on the mob's payroll since the forties. He's also the Chairman of the Governmental Affairs Committee. They oversee the State Department. So he's collecting bribes from the Sicilian Mafia too. I can almost guarantee he's calling these shots."

"So, Warren is sabotaging the case?" Sheridan asked.

"Not Warren directly, but it probably came from the US Attorney, by way of the Attorney General, straight from the lips of McKibben. The order has probably already come down to prosecute you guys for something," he said to Butchie and Eddie. "But, make no mistake; Warren knows what's going on."

"What do we do about that?" Butchie asked.

"First of all," the Inspector ordered, "You don't talk to anyone at the FBI or the Justice Department without me present."

"That's not gonna be enough protection," Cormac said. "Before you go see Warren, come with me to the Army Terminal. I may have something that can help."

***

At Cormac's Office, he went back into the supply closet and returned with three boxes with pictures of some kind of handheld machine and Japanese characters on them. The logo said Sony.

"These are voice activated micro-recorders," Cormac explained. "They're battery operated and take mini-cassette tapes. They're not available yet to the public. In fact they're only available in Japan right now. One of my guys is a Marine. When he was in Tokyo visiting a girlfriend from when he was stationed there, he saw these and thought they might be useful. He brought back a dozen. I couldn't imagine what we were ever going to use them for, but I do now. Keep these cued up and in your pockets at all times. What you record might just save your ass."

***

Later that evening, Butchie, Eddie and Inspector Sheridan sat down with Warren Agnew. Warren looked perturbed to see Sheridan.

"I only wanted to see the detectives, Inspector. You don't have to be here."

"It's okay, Warren," Sheridan smiled. "I was getting bored sitting in my office. Say whatever you need to my detectives now."

"Uh…that's okay"

"No it isn't. You told my PAA not to tell me about this meeting. What bullshit is this? What are you hiding?"

"The US Attorney wanted that buy-op postponed," Warren allowed. "Now we're blown. We'll never get Amoroso dirty again."

"We already have him tied to everything," Butchie said. "Now we have the payment records from Walton and Kemp, straight from Amoroso—courtesy of Walton's attorney. We got Amoroso ordering hits on the wire at the café. How fucking dirty do we need him, Warren?"

"We still can't connect him to the drugs," Warren argued weakly.

"The *fook* we can't!" Eddie thundered. "He's delivering a nightly dissertation on his drug business on the phone you've got wired. What *fooking* game are you playing?"

"You're not even supposed to know about those wiretaps," Warren said. "They're federal."

"Don't play that shit with us, you dick," The Inspector seethed. "This is a joint NYPD/Federal investigation. They are my lead investigators, and they get to know what I want them to know. Which is every-fucking-thing."

"This is all coming from the US Attorney. He wants us to slow down. He's afraid we're getting ahead of ourselves," Agnew said.

"Well then, you go call him and tell him we want to meet," Sheridan said. "He can share his concerns with us, and we can reassure him."

Warren left to make the call in another room. Sheridan wanted to talk to his detectives without him there, so he didn't object to him making the call out of their presence. Eddie was the first to take advantage of his absence.

"What do we do, Boss?"

"Warren, the US Attorney, the Attorney General and who the fuck knows who else wants us to slow down, but no one can give us a credible reason why," Sheridan mused. "They're protecting someone, probably someone very dirty—and we're getting too close. So, we speed the fuck up, see what shakes loose."

"They're not going to share what's on the wire with us anymore," Eddie surmised. "At least, not what we need. They'll treat us like mushrooms; keep us in the dark and feed us shit."

"Funny thing about that," Sheridan smiled. "They're not the FBI's wiretaps. They belong to Cormac. As a courtesy, he's letting the FBI monitor them. We need to call him and see if he can get the raw tape. That way we'll know when Warren is holding out on us."

"I'll call him when we get done with Warren," Butchie said.

"Not from any phone in this building you won't," Sheridan ordered.

Warren came back a few minutes later. Butchie thought he seemed somehow relieved. As if a decision was made taking him off the hook for doing something devious.

"The US Attorney is very busy, but he agreed to meet with you later this week. We'll set it up when his schedule permits."

"That'll be fine," Sheridan said.

Warren wanted to go over what they had gleaned from Sonny Black. They were in a quandary. They had a direction to look, but no viable way to begin collecting the evidence to prove and dismantle the unholy business Sallie Gorgeous had begun in the state prison system. Warren agreed they couldn't just start questioning people at random. This would eventually make Sallie suspicious, and cause problems for the DEA with the ongoing drug investigation, compromising their wiretaps.

Thus far, the DEA were buying in to the Bonannos' for greater and greater amounts of heroin. But they weren't at a point yet where they could follow the money. They got Amoroso, but they still had no way to tie Sallie Gorgeous to him, or the money at the top of the pyramid.

Warren considered putting the phrases, "the thing upstate" and "fantasy camp" on the Federal *Dex-Tex* listings. These were records of any federal investigation into their subjects and subject matter. He decided against it for the same reason Butchie and Eddie didn't make it the subject of a *Be On the Look-Out for*, or BOLO message. The risk of alerting Sallie they were on to him was too great. If he got a whiff of heat, the wily mobster would insulate himself to the point where law enforcement might never get this close to him again.

What they needed was to speak with someone with information about the scheme. They needed to identify who among the correction officers and wardens was handling and paying Sallie the vast sums being generated. Warren was hopeful they would hear something on one of the wire taps. So far, they had not. Until something broke on the wires, or the three investigators could think of another way in, they were temporarily stuck in place. Butchie and Eddie decided to surveille Sallie Gorgeous to record who was meeting with him at the coffee shop.

As every cop eventually discovers, sometimes it's better to be lucky than good. All the smarts in the world can't make providence fall into your lap. Perhaps, as Eddie frequently mused, being in the right place at the right time is just the good luck that follows sound instinct. Butchie didn't care how or why good fortune decided to fall their way. He was just determined not to let the opportunity slip through their fingers.

The two detectives were parked on Himrod Street, with a view of Il Trombone Arrugginito. They had been at it since morning. Nothing new occurred. The usual suspects had been dropping in and out. They were looking for someone new, or at least someone unexpected. Just before lunch, Butchie, who had been manning the binoculars, saw someone who qualified.

"Do you recognize the kid loitering behind Sallie's car?" Butchie asked.

Eddie had his own binoculars. He looked through them and let out a low whistle.

"Hello there, Nestor," he said.

"I thought it was him," Butchie said. "Didn't we send him and his brother upstate for robbery?"

"*Dat* was five years ago already. *Dey* were just fifteen and got convicted as juvenile offenders. I guess Nestor maxed out. He must be twenty-one now," Eddie surmised.

Nestor and Antonio Aranda were identical twins from Stockholm Street. They did everything together. When they reached those awkward teenage years, the activity in which they most liked to participate was gunpoint robbery. Over the space of a year the twins committed more than thirty bodega robberies in Bushwick and Williamsburg.

Hector Vasconcellos, the super from Hart Street, tipped Eddie and Butchie off. The twins had tried to sell Hector a cash register they could not open. Hector bought the register for twenty bucks, and promptly called his two favorite cops. He knew Butchie and Eddie would know what to do with the cash register. He also knew they would reimburse him for the twenty.

Once Hector told the cops the story, they had little trouble connecting the dots. The robbery pattern had been so prolific, every cop in Brooklyn and Queens was aware of it. The brothers Aranda had gone unapprehended for as long as they did because they were fifteen. Because they looked older than their age, the victim's descriptions of the perpetrators of each robbery were uniform in estimating them to be in their twenties. There were no arrest photos for the boys available—they were juveniles. Butchie and Eddie decided to follow them until they struck again. It didn't take long.

The next day, the cops, in plain clothes, followed the Aranda twins until they walked into Peter's Deli on Wyckoff Avenue and Cooper Street. When the boys pulled out a shotgun and robbed the place, Butchie and Eddie were waiting for them out front. Nestor came out carrying the cash register. Antonio had a six-pack of Rheingold beer tucked under one arm and the shotgun under the other. As neighborhood toughs, the twins knew Butchie and Eddie. They were well-acquainted with the two cops' fearsome reputations. The Arandas almost tripped over each other trying to surrender.

The twins were subsequently identified in all of the robberies. They were tried as adults and convicted. They got the equivalent of adult sentences. As juvenile offenders, they did their time at the Juvey facility attached to *Sing Sing,* the very scary adult prison in Ossining, New York. This was coincidentally where Sallie Gorgeous was holding court while doing time for multiple murder.

Right now, Nestor was alone. This was the reason Butchie needed Eddie to confirm his identity. He had never seen him without his brother, Antonio. Antonio had not survived his incarceration.

"Why is he wearing a wool top coat, and what does he have under it?" Butchie asked.

"I'm guessing a shotgun, but I'm more curious as to why he's so interested in Sallie Gorgeous' car and coffee shop. *Ye* don't suppose he's crazy enough to *tink* he can stick-up the Mafia, do *ye*?"

A minute later, one of the wiseguys came out of the coffee shop and got into his car on the corner, driving away. When he did, the detectives watched Nestor quickly duck behind Sallie's huge Coupe de Ville. Clearly, Nestor was focusing on the doings in the coffee shop. This behavior was way too suspicious to leave uninvestigated.

When Butchie and Eddie pulled in front of the coffee shop, jumped out of the Ford with their guns drawn, and ordered Nestor not to move, he let out a mournful wail. They could see Nestor was crying—the tears streaming down his face. As he stood there, he looked like he was trying to make a difficult decision. A second later, he seemed disappointed in himself.

"Antonio would have drawn down on you. He would have ended this shit-show right here. He was always stronger than me," Nestor lamented, raising his hands over his head, letting the shotgun fall out from under his coat.

Eddie quickly handcuffed him, while Butchie grabbed the shotgun. They whisked him into the Ford and drove off before anyone in the coffee shop knew they were there. When they headed west on Wilson Avenue and drove right past the precinct on DeKalb without stopping, Nestor became curious.

"Where are you taking me, Officer Curran?"

"We're detectives now, Nestor. We have a lot of catching up to do, and important *tings* to talk about. We have a new headquarters in Manhattan. It's safe there, and no one will know we're talking to *ye*," Eddie assured him.

"I'm not under arrest?"

"That's negotiable," Butchie said. "We'll figure it all out over coffee at our new office."

When they got to the Bat Cave and took the freight elevator up to their offices on the fourth floor, Nestor grew more and more impressed. By the time they got him uncuffed in the interview room, he was practically awe-struck.

"This is the FBI. You guys are a big fucking deal now, huh?"

"Not so big a deal *dat* we can't have a conversation with an old friend," Eddie laughed.

"We were sorry to hear about Antonio," Butchie told him, handing Nestor a styrofoam cup of coffee.

"You should have left me be on Wyckoff Avenue. I was going to square things for Antonio. I had that fuck, Sallie Gorgeous, right where I wanted him," Nestor said.

"I don't understand, Butchie said. "We heard Antonio hung himself in jail. How is Sallie Gorgeous involved?"

"Antonio didn't kill himself. He was murdered. Sallie took my brother from me. I'm going to make him pay for it."

Nestor went on to detail what happened to him and his brother when they arrived at the *Boy's Town* in Ossining. The first weekend there, after lights out, they were led by a squad of correction officers into a room, which smelled of incense and semen. It was a bizarre mixture between a night club and an S&M sex dungeon. There was a bar in the corner, several couches and plush chairs, and a few large televisions mounted on the walls. In the far corner, there was a torture rack, a pommel horse, a large bed and a wheel big enough to strap a fully-grown man to. The wheel was capable of spinning 360 degrees. All of these things had hand and foot restraints attached.

In front of all of these was a sophisticated movie camera, a boom microphone and professional cinematic lighting. On a surgical cart, there were all manner of pliers, probes, ligatures and a blow-torch—along with a variety of sex toys that looked like they hadn't been cleaned—ever.

In the center of the room awaiting their arrival—almost as a guest of honor—was Sallie Gorgeous Ruttigliano and a dozen or so men who were all wearing visitor's tags. What happened to the brothers against their will that night was horrifying. Nestor was crying as he related it. All of the guards, Sallie Gorgeous, and the visitors participated in the abuse, which was filmed and simultaneously displayed on the mounted televisions around the room. Nestor broke down, fully ashamed at this point.

"I stopped fighting. I gave in and let them do whatever they wanted to me. My brother never did. He fought them every day. The night they killed him, they dragged him kicking and screaming down to the basement. When they brought him back, they had to carry him. He was put into solitary by three guards. He was silent and didn't even move. I knew then he was already dead. The next morning, they *discovered* him hanging from his bedsheets in there. Because that's where they fucking hung him. My brother *never* would have killed himself."

"We believe *ye*, Nestor," Eddie said. "But people kill *demselves* in jail all the time. *Dat* Antonio was murdered at this point is just speculation. We would need some proof to charge anyone with murder."

"Sallie Gorgeous was gloating about it," Nestor said.

"How is that?" Butchie asked.

"After I had stopped fighting, Sallie got mad at me. He and the warden were going to work on me in those sick leather masks they liked to wear. When I didn't resist anymore, they got angry. Sallie started taunting me. He told me Antonio fought to the last. He said I was a disgrace to his memory. Then he put a tape into the VCR and made me watch it."

"What was on it?" Eddie asked.

"They had my brother facing the camera. He was strapped naked over the pommel horse. The fat warden was standing off to the side, pulling on his own dick. Sallie was fucking Antonio from behind. My brother fought the whole way. He was grunting and trying to scream through the gag they had wedged in his mouth. Sallie had a piece of rope wrapped around Antonio's neck, choking him out. I had to watch Antonio's eyes bulge out and go bloodshot—until he stopped breathing. When Sallie climbed off of him, that sick fuck warden climbed on. They did this to him, and they made a movie of it. Find it. There's your proof."

"How do *ye* know the fat guy was the warden?" Eddie asked.

"Because the first night we were there in that room, he was wearing a suit, and didn't have a visitor's badge. Along with Sallie, he seemed like he was in charge. One of the other guys who had an ID tag said to him when it was over, 'Warden, that was the best ten grand I ever spent—worth every penny. I just hope the widows and orphans appreciate the donation.' The warden answered him, 'On behalf of the widows and orphans, I can assure you, we appreciate it. In fact, we hope to see you again next weekend.' Then they had a good laugh about it."

"Did you ever hear anyone use his name?" Butchie asked.

"Just Sallie Gorgeous. He called him Phillip—pretty much all the time."

"Ever hear his last name?" Eddie asked.

"No, but he signed my discharge papers when I was released. It's Phillip Kaine."

CHAPTER FORTY-FIVE

Early October 1979
New York State

After debriefing Nestor Aranda, he wasn't under arrest for possession of the shotgun anymore. He was interested in being a witness against Sallie Gorgeous. Inasmuch as his brother Antonio was the only family he cared about, going into witness protection was an easy choice. He thanked Butchie and Eddie for giving him the chance to avenge Antonio.

His information and testimony was enough to spur the US Attorney to convene a secret grand jury. They began hearing evidence of the narcotics and sex trade conspiracies.

Warren Agnew was able to expand the investigation to include Warden Phillip Kaine. His home and office phones were tapped. He was recorded conducting millions of dollars of business each week on behalf of something called *The Widows and Orphans Benevolent Fund of NYS Corrections*. A surreptitious check revealed no such organization existed which was affiliated with the state government, or its employees. It did exist as a registered tax-exempt charitable organization, however. There were only two executive officers. They were listed as Salvatore Ruttigliano and Phillip Kaine. The only other person authorized to handle the funds for the charity was a one-man accounting firm in Poughkeepsie, under the stewardship of an Edmund Clinton.

A secret search warrant for the banking records for the charity revealed since the early 1950s, more than one hundred million dollars of tax exempt donations had flowed through the charities' account. Presently, they had a balance of zero dollars. Every penny that came in subsequently was withdrawn. The funds, after expenses, were wired into a numbered account in the Cayman Islands, accessible only by a Salvatore Ruttigliano.

Edmund Clinton turned out to be a convicted pedophile, and a long-time client of the fantasy camp. He rolled immediately when the FBI questioned him. He testified in the grand jury and was able to fully implicate Sallie Gorgeous and Warden Kaine, both as operating and participating in every aspect of the sex conspiracy. But he drew a blank when asked about snuff films.

Evidently, Sallie hadn't brought Clinton *all the way* inside. He knew about a revenue stream from Europe. He had records on multiple donations from overseas, each in excess of seven figures. Clinton just assumed Sallie was selling the rape videos in Germany and Switzerland, where the wire transfers were being generated. He also had detailed records of everyone who ever paid into the fund or were paid by it. The subject list just kept growing like a malignant tumor that had metastasized.

At this point, other than finding proof of the snuff films, the only thing left to do was to ascertain how the narcotics were distributed, and how the money was dispersed and made its way to the top of the pyramid. This was all they needed to bring down Sallie Gorgeous and the Bonannos. But Butchie and Eddie would not be content until the murdered victims of the fantasy camp were spoken for. They needed Sallie to answer for those kids.

Thus far, all they had was Nestor Aranda's testimony to link Sallie and the warden to the snuff films. They had the financial records, but no empirical proof the films existed.

Butchie was the first to notice the sheet hanging from Roman's window on Jefferson Street. Eddie checked the answering machine on their desk from the payphone on the corner of Troutman Street. There was one message.

"You need to arrest me now," was all Roman said.

CHAPTER FORTY-SIX

October 12, 1979
Bushwick

When Eddie and Butchie grabbed Roman Sciula outside the coffee shop on Suydam Street, he was clearly perturbed. This was not the feigned insolence he had been practicing for these farces in the past. He was genuinely and deeply upset about something. He waited until they were out of the car in the cemetery to tell the detectives about it.

"That motherfucker, Sallie, murdered Sonny Black," Roman said.

"How do you know?" Butchie asked.

"Because I just buried Sonny's dead body in cement in the floor of Sallie's basement."

"The basement of the coffee shop?" Butchie asked.

"No. In his house on Summerfield Street."

"How did *dat* go down?" Eddie wanted to know.

"Let's be clear about something. I didn't kill Sonny. He was already dead in that basement when Sallie called me over there to hide the body for him. He wouldn't let me take Sonny out of the house. He thinks he's being watched. I had to rent all of the equipment, like the jackhammer and cement mixer to make the hole and bury him. It took a full yard of cement to do it."

"So how do you know Sallie killed Sonny?" Butchie asked.

"Sallie told me he did it. He said he called Sonny in for a sit-down. When he got there, Sallie got up to fix him a drink. When he came back up behind Sonny, he didn't have a scotch in his hand. He blew the back of his head out with that .45 he likes to carry."

"How do *ye* know this?" Eddie asked.

"Sallie was bragging to me. He laughed about it. He said Sonny knew it was coming. He called him a sheep, that he just sat there, passively waiting for it. He had been wearing his best suit, and he looked straight ahead when Sallie came up behind him."

"What else did Sallie say?" Butchie asked.

"He said it was like the lamb leading itself to the slaughter. But that isn't the half of it, Butchie."

"What's the rest?" Eddie prompted.

"Sallie left me there alone to work for two days. He's got an office down there, with a big TV and a VCR. There are bookshelves full of videotapes. They all have dates and what looks like first names on them, along with the name of a prison. The one I watched was from five years ago. The name on it was Jayson. The prison listed was Dannemora."

"Oh, *Jayzus*! What was on it?" Eddie asked.

"They had a kid tied down to a bed. He couldn't have been more than sixteen. There was a guy in a leather mask raping him from behind. It was Sallie Gorgeous."

"How do you know it was Sallie?" Butchie asked.

"From the tattoo on his chest that said, 'Sallie Gorgeous.' He choked the poor kid out with a rope. I'm pretty sure he killed him."

"What makes *ye tink dat*, Roman?" Eddie asked.

"Because the kid wasn't moving when the other fat fuck in the room took his turn. There are hundreds of these tapes down there. Did they kill all of these kids?"

"We won't know until we review all the tapes. We're going to have to swear out a search warrant. I think it's time to bring Sallie down before he can kill anyone else," Eddie said.

"Well, you better hurry. Sallie is clearing out all of his dead wood. The zips and the old guard are starting to realize there isn't enough money for both of them. Sallie has heard the grumbling. There's about to be a bloodbath," Roman said.

"We're going to have to bounce it off Warren first. He'll know where we are and who we can flip," Butchie said.

Roman reluctantly agreed to accompany Butchie and Eddie to the Bat Cave. Once ensconced in Warren Agnew's office, he relaxed enough to be introduced.

The detectives quickly brought Warren up to date with the new information. They were perturbed when Agnew didn't share their sense of urgency.

"We can't roll Sallie up yet," Warren said.

"Why the fuck not?" Butchie demanded.

"The DEA hasn't gotten inside enough to determine where the drugs are being centrally distributed from, and how the money eventually gets to Sallie Gorgeous," Warren explained, a little too dispassionately for Eddie's comfort.

"So we're going to leave *dat* animal out there to continue killing anyone he wishes? There are children being raped and murdered as we sit here and do nothing. Sallie and an army of miscreants are making a fortune off of their blood and misery. We now know all about it, and *ye* want to wait? Have *ye* no conscience, man?"

"I hate it as much as you do, but if we move on Sallie now, we can't connect him to the drugs. In federal court, that's what he's going to do his time for. The murders are just counts on the RICO. If we can't prove his connection to the conspiracy, we lose those as well," Warren said patiently.

The three lawmen continued to bicker pointlessly between themselves. Butchie and Eddie were yelling, demanding action and stamping their feet. Warren Agnew, responsible for the entire Task Force, was just as adamant about waiting. He needed to coordinate the DEA, the FBI's forensic accountants, the Treasury Department—who had been called in to help with Sallie's off-shore accounts—and the Justice Department, who would ultimately try the case. Warren's position, as distasteful as it was to him, was intractable. They needed the missing link the DEA hadn't yet provided.

Roman was fascinated watching this argument unfold. It reminded him of a squabble in the schoolyard between eleven-year-olds who could not agree on the rules of a game of *ringolevio*. As much as he enjoyed watching cops fight with each other, Roman felt compelled to interrupt.

"Are you fucking kidding me?" Roman asked incredulously. "All this time and you clowns don't know where the drugs are coming from, or the bank the money flows through? I thought you guys were smart."

That got their attention. All three of them fell silent and snapped their heads around.

"What do you know that you haven't told us, Roman?" Butchie asked directly.

"All of the dope is coming from the docks and being distributed through Garibaldi's Wholesale Bakery. The plant takes up the whole block on Fairview Avenue," Roman said.

"The one in Ridgewood?" Eddie clarified.

"Yeah. They supply every dirty Italian bakery on the eastern seaboard. They send the heroin inside loaves of bread. The shipments are baked inside unseeded semolina loaves. There's no such thing as unseeded semolina. That's how they know which loaves the drugs are in."

"That couldn't account for all the dope on the street. This is a nationwide distribution ring. How are they getting it out to the hinterlands?" Warren Asked.

"Garibaldi's is the number one supplier of pizza dough in the country. They send it out frozen. The dirty pizzerias involved know the tin of dough marked with red tape has the heroin in it," Roman explained as if everybody knew this.

"Is this something *ye* heard, or something *ye've* seen?" Eddie asked.

"Did you guys ever notice you can never find me on Thursdays and Fridays?" Roman laughed. "That's cause I'm there protecting the money coming in on Thursday, and the dope going out on Friday. Every single week, I get to look at that shit. I have to watch the money—and there are duffel bags of it—get put into the vault in the basement. Early Friday mornings, I watch the delivery trucks loaded with the bogus bread and pizza dough. They're moving two dozen kilos of smack out of there every week. You would know which trucks have the contraband from the shipping manifests. My initials are on everyone that had dope on it. I also have the honor of accepting a briefcase full of money to give to Sallie Gorgeous. Old man Garibaldi hands it to me himself. My last stop on Fridays is to Sallie's house, to deliver the briefcase. He puts it in the walk-in safe he keeps behind his desk."

"How much money is in the briefcase?" Warren asked.

“I don’t know. How much can you fit in a briefcase?” Roman replied.

“It didn’t occur to you *dat* this might be something *ye* should have told us before now, Roman?” Eddie asked.

“Why didn’t it occur to you to ask me?”

It dawned on Butchie then. Roman, though perfectly candid with them thus far, was only answering the questions which were specifically asked. He wondered what else Roman knew that he hadn’t shared.

“Is there anything else we should know?”

“I’m sure there is, but I won’t know unless you ask,” Roman said.

“Do you know who killed my wife’s father?” Butchie asked.

“You don’t know that?” Roman asked. “I thought everybody knew that.”

“I was getting my ass shot off in Vietnam when it happened. By the time I got home a year and a half later, no one would talk to me about it.”

“Your father-in-law refused to pay for protection. When Bruno told Fat Sam to go fuck himself, Sam sent Trinchera and Meloro over to straighten him out. The old man gave those two pretenders a beating. Lilo Gigante heard about it and was furious. He said he had to set an example. He put a contract out on Badlamenti. The farm team saw an opportunity to get in good with Lilo. They didn’t even tell me about it until it was over. I’m not sure if they cut me out of it because they didn’t want to split the ten grand four ways, or they thought I was their personal muscle—not worthy of a button.

“So, Gigante ordered it, and Mousey, Angelo and Carmine did the hit?” Eddie asked, incredulously.

“Yeah,” Roman said. “But, Gigante and Donofrio are dead, and I can’t see Angelo and Mousey surviving Sallie’s purge. So I guess justice also comes to those who wait.”

Butchie got a faraway look, as if he were distracted. Eddie and Warren Agnew had expected him to erupt with that famous temper of his. Instead, a calm seemed to wash over him.

“Sometimes justice won’t wait as long as you think it will,” Butchie said softly—almost to himself.

Eddie was the only one who understood what that statement portended. He could only grab his forehead in resignation. Basaluco and Mercante’s fates were now decided. Soon they would be etched in stone.

CHAPTER FORTY-SEVEN

October 15, 1979
Ridgewood

With the new information, Cormac and the DEA were able to set up a round-the-clock surveillance of Garibaldi's Bakery. On the next Tuesday, they followed a single refrigerated delivery truck all the way to the docks in the Port of Elizabeth in New Jersey. The agents watched the truck pull into the fenced lot of *Olive Branch Shipping*. This turned out to be an international shipping concern, wholly owned by Donato Amoroso. They saw four pallets of freight loaded onto the truck, before it headed back to Garibaldi's in Ridgewood.

The FBI asked the Waterfront Commission to pull the shipping manifests and articles of incorporation for Olive Branch Shipping. These revealed all shipments received by Olive Branch came from the same port in Sardinia. This port, and all of the ships sailing from it were owned by a consortium of figures revealed to be high ranking members of the Sicilian Mafia. A circumstantial connection and partnership was being developed. Interpol would have to be involved eventually. Right now, the risk of alerting their subjects was too great.

Continued surveillance of Garibaldi's revealed trucks coming in all day Thursday, dropping off heavily laden boxes and duffel bags. The agents watched as Roman Sciula accepted each delivery and escorted them into the plant. A search warrant was drawn up for the bakery, to be executed the next morning.

***

At a little after 0700 hours Friday morning, Roman Sciula came out to the loading dock behind Garibaldi's. He dramatically lit a cigarette and blew smoke rings into the air, which he swatted away with his left hand. This was a pre-arranged signal to Butchie and Eddie that the dope and the money were all present. The Bakery was descended upon by more than one hundred federal agents from the FBI and the DEA, and two NYPD Detectives along with their boss, Inspector Thomas Sheridan.

As Roman had predicted, two dozen kilos of un-cut heroin were recovered, evenly distributed between bread loaves and tins of pizza dough. Roman had purposely left the vault unlocked in the basement. An as yet uncounted sum of currency was recovered. The amount would turn out to be in excess of ten million dollars. After seizing all of the drugs, and the duffel bags and boxes of money, and arresting the foreman, along with Roman Sciula—who had to be arrested to protect his cover—the feds were preparing to wrap things up.

Old man Garibaldi came shuffling out of the back office with a briefcase. He walked right up to Butchie and handed it to him. The eighty-nine-year-old Garibaldi patriarch could barely lift the heavy satchel.

"What is this?" Butchie asked.

"It's okay," the old man said in his accented English. "That's for you. For all of you. Give me back my bread and pizza dough and leave. You can have a briefcase like this one every month. Just leave me alone to ship my goods."

Butchie laughed at him.

"That's two million dollars. It's yours. You can have another one just like it every month. Just leave me with my goods and go," the old man repeated, thinking Butchie dense.

Butchie realized Garibaldi wasn't joking, and he got angry about it. That the old gangster could dismiss his integrity so casually infuriated him. He was about to go off on him when Eddie stepped in.

"On behalf of *me* partner, *meself*, the City of New York and the United States of America, we dearly thank *ye* for *yer* generosity. Just to be clear; *ye* are willing to pay us two million dollars a month to let *ye* ship heroin. Is *dat* what *ye're* proposing, Mr. Garibaldi?" Eddie asked pleasantly.

"That's the deal," Garibaldi confirmed.

"Did we get all of *dat* on tape, Warren?" Eddie asked Special Agent Agnew.

"You know we did, Eddie," Warren said.

"Well *den*, Mr. Garibaldi," Eddie smiled obsequiously. "Please put *yer* hands behind *yer* back, *ye* corrupted, foul, canker-sore of a human being. *Ye* are under arrest for bribery, among all of *yer* other transgressions."

"I don't understand," Garibaldi complained as Eddie cuffed him. "You don't want the money?"

"Oh, we're taking the money," Eddie assured him. "We're going to stamp and voucher every dollar of it. This is the evidence we will use to fashion the rope with which to hang *ye*. *Ye* can't buy us. We're not for sale."

"That's ridiculous. Everyone has a price," the old man scoffed.

"No, some of us don't," Eddie corrected him. "The problem is perspective. *Ye* haven't got any. *Ye* know the value of a buck, but not much else. We on the other hand, are in possession of something far more precious. We have our souls. *Ye* have been destroying people for so long, and profiting from it, *ye* no longer do. *Yer* soul is black, and *ye'll* burn in hell for it, but first, I'm going to see *ye* die in prison, or on the slow boat back to Sicily when we revoke *yer* citizenship and expel *ye*."

"Don't strain your arms patting yourselves on the back," Garibaldi said wearily. "That money you were so quick to turn down belongs to Sallie Gorgeous. That's his product you stole from me. He's not going to buy your acquiescence. He's going to identify *you* as the problem. Sallie doesn't negotiate with problems. He removes them. I know you Bucciogrosso, and I know who you hold dear. Sallie knows just as much, and he will not think twice about hurting your family—even if they are *his* family. He is not a sentimental man, and the fact you're his son by blood offers you no protection at all. This little war you've started is coming to your door step."

CHAPTER FORTY-EIGHT

October 15, 1979
Manhattan

After the big takedown, Inspector Sheridan called Butchie and Eddie into his office. He said it was urgent.

"It's time to bring Roman in from the cold," Tom Sheridan told them.

"We're not sure he'll come in," Eddie said.

"Well if he doesn't get immunized fast, they're going to make a subject out of him. I like him too, but he's a fucking mass murderer. If we don't get him under the umbrella, he'll spend the rest of his life rotting in fed, right next to Sallie Gorgeous."

"So, what should we do?" Butchie asked.

"The *Feebs* are already posting his bail. Go down there and get him. Bring him back here. You gotta sell him a *Queen for a Day*."

Butchie and Eddie went and got Roman Sciula out of the federal bookings under the courthouse at Cadman Plaza. They brought him to their office at the bat cave. Over coffee they commended Roman on his contribution to the case so far. They needed to broach the subject of his cooperation, but they were wary of offending their big friend and risk shutting him down. Roman took them off the hook, easing their worries.

"You guys aren't usually this awkward," Roman observed. "You want to talk to me about my cooperation, but you're afraid to piss me off."

"The circumstances for you have changed since we started this thing," Butchie said. "We want you to know what's at stake."

"You need me to testify," Roman said.

"No, Roman," Eddie corrected him. "*Ye* need to testify. When we start proffering all the people we already took down, most of these scumbags will be looking to flip. The US Attorney won't care that *ye're* a good guy now when they find out how many people *ye've* killed. If *ye* don't have a cooperation agreement in place, they'll just make a subject out of *ye*. We need *ye* to be the first one who gets a Queen for a Day offer."

"What's a Queen for a Day?" Roman asked.

"That's where you sit down with the US Attorney. You admit to all of your criminal acts; every beating, every murder, every wrong thing you ever did," Butchie told him.

"If I do that, they'll dust off the electric chair just for me."

"Actually, *boyo*, they'll give *ye* blanket immunity for all of it," Eddie said.

"Blanket immunity for being a Mafia hitman? What's the catch?"

"You'll have to testify against everyone in open court—completely and honestly. You can't hold anything back," Butchie said.

"After everything is said and done," Eddie told him. "*Ye* get a new life in the Witness Protection Program. *Ye* leave Brooklyn, never to return. No more being a scary gangster; *ye* get a new name and a new job—a whole new identity."

"I figured we were going to get here from the beginning. I knew you guys weren't telling the truth when you told me I wouldn't have to testify. But that's alright. After Sallie made me bury Sonny Black, I was looking to jump in with both feet anyway. I want to do whatever I can to bury those motherfuckers. They never did anything but use me."

"If *ye* knew we were lying to *ye*, why did *ye* trust us?" Eddie asked.

"The truth is, when you offered me a way out of the life, I was already done with this shit. Besides, you weren't lying to me as much as trying to let me down easy. I always liked you guys. I know you two are doing this thing because you think it will help. You risked your lives for the people of this neighborhood. They don't appreciate it, but I do. Your hearts are in the right place. I wanted to help you. I'm not sorry I did."

"*Dat's* a comfort to know *ye* understand, Roman," Eddie said.

"When I get into witness protection, can I take my mother back to Sicily?" Roman asked.

"When you fulfill your cooperation agreement, you can go anywhere you want. But if you leave the country, you don't get protected anymore. You're on your own at that point," Butchie informed him.

"Look at me, Butchie," Roman said, laughing. "Do I look like I need protection? Besides, after we're done with the Bonannos, there won't be anybody left on the street who wants me dead."

"You know they got Mafia in Sicily?" Butchie reminded him.

"Yeah, but they hated the zips for leaving and coming to New York. The Sicilians won't take a contract from them, and even if they do, I've been living with eyes in the back of my head since I was fourteen. I don't think I'm going to be easy to kill, and I can guarantee, I will go down so hard, I won't be worth killing. But if it happens, it happens. I won't have any regrets."

Butchie and Eddie understood Roman's reasoning. They also knew there would be no dissuading him. He wasn't necessarily combative, just decisive. It was clear to them, on this matter, Roman had already decided.

"What do *ye* think *ye* might do in Italy?" Eddie asked.

"My family owns a leather manufacturing company in Castellamare del Golfo. The family has been at it for hundreds of years. My grandfather was the most sought-after shoe maker in Italy. Now they make all manner of leather goods; from coats and jackets to those designer Armando purses women are paying four hundred bucks for in Manhattan. They still make shoes. They still give them away to the poor kids in the village. I think I want to learn to make shoes. I want to do something nice for someone else for a change. I want to be an honorable man—like my grandfather."

"In our estimation, you've been that for quite a while, Roman. We couldn't save Bushwick without you," Butchie observed.

"I know that's what you think you're doing, Butchie," Roman said. "But, getting rid of the Bonannos won't fix this shithole. You'd need an airstrike to level it, so they can start over. But, I respect you for trying. Hell, I even love you for it. As righteous as getting the Bonannos is, I'm afraid when we're done with them, you're still going to be disappointed. I worry about that."

CHAPTER FORTY-NINE

October 16, 1979
Glendale

Eddie was washing the frying pan in the sink in his kitchen on 82nd Street in Glendale, after eating his breakfast. The girls were at school and Bernadette had gone to the library where she volunteered. He was to pick up Butchie to head into work in an hour. Eddie was trying to get his head around what the day would look like. He and Butchie had grown concerned about the less than exuberant response from the FBI and the US Attorney after the big takedown at the bakery. They seemed particularly concerned with the financial papers seized, anxious to get them to the forensic accountants of the FBI and out of the hands of the NYPD. They surmised that the identity of the saboteur of their case were connected in those ledgers and check stubs. They would have liked to look at the papers but knew the FBI would never let them. Eddie was wondering if there were another link to the man's identity when it rang his doorbell.

Eddie looked out the peephole of his front door and recognized the man there. His stomach filled with acid and a foul taste took hold of his mouth. In his silk suit and imported Italian loafers stood retired Detective Robert *Rocky* Phillips. Eddie despised this man. Once a famed detective, he was renowned for all the wrong reasons. He was a thief, extortionist and bagman for the old Chief Inspector's Confidential Squad. The forerunner to the

Internal Affairs Division, unlike IAD, whose stated mission was to root out corruption, this Squad identified dirty cops who were not kicking up their fair share of tribute to the bosses. Phillips' job was to go warn the offending cop, to set him straight. If he didn't fly right after that, Phillips and the Squad would go get him and frame him for something. The case would be referred to an equally corrupt district attorney who was also on the pad. The cop would be jailed, fined and ultimately fired, discrediting him so he would be ignored when he tried to snitch on the ongoing corruption.

Eddie had a previous experience with Rocky Phillips. When he had been a rookie he arrested a twenty-four- year-old junkie for a series of street robberies. They were particularly galling because the thief was snatching purses from elderly women. They put up no resistance, but he beat them and kicked them to the ground anyway. Mean as a snake and entitled as well, he was the nephew of Senator Lance McKibben. Phillips was still a detective in the Chief Inspector's Squad when he came to see Eddie. He asked him to change his testimony in the grand jury to throw the case. He offered him a bribe on behalf of the senator. Phillips got a black eye for his trouble.

What followed was a two year campaign of harassment on the part of Eddie's corrupt supervisors and the Chief Inspector's Squad. They got forty vacation days from him, but they couldn't break him. Phillips was forced to retire or become a target after the department created IAD in 1972, in the wake of the Knapp Commission investigation into police corruption. When he realized he couldn't extort tribute from crooked cops anymore, and would be arrested if he tried, Phillips retired and went looking for other work. His fame as a corrupt fixer came to the attention of Senator McKibben, who needed someone with Phillips slimy skillset and the depravity to use it. He had been his fixer ever since.

Eddie went to the credenza in the hallway and cued up his micro-recorder before slipping it into his pants pocket. Then he went back to the door.

"Who?" Eddie barked.

"Eddie, It's me, Rocky Phillips. I need to talk to you."

"About what?"

"C'mon, open up. It's not something you want shouted through a door."

Eddie checked the windows and the peephole again. When he was certain Phillip's was alone, he opened the door and stepped out on the porch.

"How did ye know where I live?" Eddie demanded.

"A fellow in an Italian coffee shop on Wyckoff Avenue gave it to me," Phillips smirked. "Butchie's around the corner too."

"A veiled threat; not very clever even for you. What do you want?" he asked.

"I came to talk to you instead of that hot-headed partner of yours," Phillips began. "You were always the smarts in that car. I figured you would at least listen to reason. Butchie would have just punched me in the face."

"And *yer* sure I won't?"

"Like I said; reasonable."

"Quit stalling and get to the *fookin* point."

"You guys are upsetting a lot of people's apple carts with your investigation. They just want to do business. They'd be happy to cut you in if you would let them."

"Okay, I know a carrot when I hear one. What's the stick?"

"My boss…"

"Senator McKibben," Eddie clarified for the tape.

"Yeah, McKibben. He sent me on behalf of some of his constituents."

"*Dat* would be the Bonanno Crime Family."

"Why do I gotta spell everything out? You know who I work for."

"I want *ye* to hear *yerself* say it. Just maybe it will cause *ye* some shame."

"I'm a little old to start worrying about my Catholic guilt," Phillips said.

"The stick, Rocky. What is it?"

"Sallie Gorgeous just wants to whack you guys. McKibben talked him down, telling him he'd take care of it. If you don't take the payoff and leave Ruttigliano alone, McKibben is going to untie Sallie's hands and sic the Justice Department on you. Even if you manage to get Sallie before he gets you, you won't get the FBI. They'll frame you and take everything you own."

"Oh, *yer* making me feel like Napoleon at the end; enemies everywhere," Eddie said. "Even if I were to accept the offer, how am I supposed to convince Butchie? He doesn't care about money, and he's not afraid of *anyting*."

"I'm counting on your famous powers of persuasion. They say you could talk Jesus off the cross. Talk some sense into your partner. Remind him you already got Amoroso. Hang your hat on that. Sallie is unrelenting. He'll take your whole fucking family and not bat an eye. Do it for them, Eddie."

Eddie laughed and shook his head at the nattily dressed former detective. He smiled widely at Phillips, with that mischievous sparkle in his eyes that everyone loved.

"*Ye* know, Rocky, you were right. Butchie *would* have punched you in the face."

Phillips nodded and smiled back. He never saw the gut punch and right uppercut combination; it was so fast. He was lifted from his feet and propelled backward, hitting the back of his skull on the cracked concrete of the sidewalk. Eddie stood over him, enjoying the sight of Phillips eyes rolling around in their sockets. Definitely concussed, Eddie could see the left pupil was as big as a dinner plate, the other a pinhole. He grabbed Phillips by his tie and slapped him until he got a response akin to awareness.

"You tell McKibben and Sallie Gorgeous, no deal. Tell the FBI, tell the Justice Department, tell *yer fookin* priest if *ye* must, but nobody is getting a pass. We're going to burn *ye* all to the *fookin* ground."

***

A half hour later, Eddie and Butchie were seated in a rear booth at the Glendale Diner with Mickey Doheny. Eddie related the confrontation with Rocky Phillips.

"Rocky; was he a fighter?" Butchie asked.

"He couldn't fight his way out of a paper bag," Mickey said. "He gave that name to himself, said he was the Irish Rocky Marciano. It galled me. He would fight as a middleweight in the Police Olympics every year. He paid-off his competition to throw every fight, just so he could say he was the champ. One year, I put on twenty pounds and wore weights in my pockets to qualify as a middleweight. He offered me a bribe to throw the finals and I threw the money back at him. It was the only time in my fighting career I ever went into the ring intent on hurting someone."

"Did *ye* hurt him?"

"Oh yeah. He took his meals for a month through a fucking straw and never fought again."

"Well, if it's a comfort to *ye*, he's probably dealing with a bit of a brain injury at the moment," Eddie said.

"Never mind that," Butchie said. "What do we make of the threat?"

"We have to take it seriously," Mickey said. "You've pissed off some powerful people."

"Why do *ye* suppose Phillips used Amoroso as an enticement? What does *dat* mean?"

"It's telling," Mickey said. "It means they've already written him off. Sallie has no doubt already consolidated the zips under his umbrella."

"I already know how to handle Sallie Gorgeous, if it comes to that," Butchie said. "But what do we do about the FBI and the Justice Department?"

"To begin with," Mickey said. "You need to make copies of those tapes you've been recording. The feds will search the homes and businesses of everyone you know if they find out they exist. We need to set up a 'dead-man switch'. I have a friend from the Marine Corps who is a big-time attorney in Manhattan. We can trust him to take the tapes to the media if the feds start fucking with you."

"Cormac suggested we start leaking some things to a reporter," Butchie said. "But who? I don't trust any of them."

"You don't trust reporters, Butchie," Mickey smiled. "You use them. I got that covered for you. You know Jack Brafman from the Daily News?"

"You mean *dat* drunk troublemaker who never met a bullshit story he could profit from *dat* he didn't like? What cop doesn't know him?"

"Well he owes me," Mickey said. "He'll write anything I tell him and keep the source anonymous."

"That *fooker* couldn't be your friend," Eddie noted. "What kind of leverage do *ye* have on him?"

"I caught him blowing transvestites on Flushing Avenue a few times."

"That would certainly fuck with his tough guy cred if it ever got out," Butchie laughed.

"Yeah, but it never will. At least not from me. What do I care how he gets his jollies; consenting adults and all."

***

When Rocky Phillips got out of St. John's Emergency room on Queens Boulevard, seven stitches in the rear of his head, a hairline fracture to his jaw and a severe concussion later, he had a driver bring him home. He called Senator McKibben to report his profound failure to get Butchie and Eddie to play ball.

"These guy are crusaders. True believers; they won't listen. Do what you gotta do," he said.

The senator in turn called Sallie Gorgeous directly at Il Trombone Arrugginito. This set off a whirlwind of activity that Butchie and Eddie needed to know about immediately but would have to wait to find out—if ever.

CHAPTER FIFTY

1970s
Glendale

Butchie and Monica had married in the spring of 1970. They had planned to wait to start a family, hoping to save money to buy a house in Glendale, and not have to carry too large a mortgage to do it. Once financially sound, they figured they could take their time filling the house with children. It was an excellent plan. The young couple failed epically in its execution. For one thing, they couldn't keep their hands off of each other. For another, they didn't bother to give the idea of birth control even a passing consideration. They were married in March, and the reindeer games began in earnest. They shouldn't have been surprised when Monica was pregnant by early May.

The young Bucciogrosso couple shifted to plan B. Butchie was able to get a mortgage on the G.I. Bill at an advantageous rate. He took a pension loan for the down payment. They were in the house on 83rd Street and 78th Avenue before their son Michael Joseph Bucciogrosso was born in December. Less than two years later, their daughter Caroline Marie came into the world.

Even before she was born, Caroline was problematic. Monica suffered horrendous morning sickness through her pregnancy. Then the delivery was complicated by the fact the baby girl was a breach. In the act of trying to turn the child around and free her from the umbilical cord, the doctor had perforated Monica's cervix. She almost died from the internal bleeding.

There would be no relief when the baby was born. For the first six months of her life, Caroline was colicky. The misery was interminable. Otherwise, the child was perfectly healthy. But the unending wailing, coupled with their worry over the close call from the difficult birth, helped Butchie and Monica agree—two healthy children were enough. Butchie volunteered to get a vasectomy.

When the colic lifted, Caroline was no less difficult. A sweet and extraordinarily beautiful girl, she could at times be as stubborn and obdurate as her father. She refused to eat anything except what she wanted, and she always seemed to want the one food they had just run out of. As bad as that was, it was nothing compared to bedtime. At the mention of going to bed, Caroline would throw herself on the floor, kick, scream, and hold her breath until she would almost pass out. Butchie and Monica learned to wait this out. Eventually she would exhaust herself and they could put her in without further complaint.

She did this nightly until she was six years old. For the last year, she was still disagreeable about going to bed, but at least she had stopped with the tantrums. Despite all of this, she was the perfect apple of her father's eye. As far as Butchie was concerned, she could do no wrong. After all, she looked just like Monica, and was named after his mother, Carolina. The fact she had Butchie and her grandmother's radiant green eyes did nothing to mute her father's adoration.

Caroline realized this and exploited it for all it was worth. She knew she had her father wrapped around her little finger, but she worshiped him for it. Whenever Butchie came home from work, Caroline would leap on him in the doorway and shower him with kisses and hugs and stories about her day. Monica and Michael would have to wait patiently for their turn to converse with him. Because of this mutual devotion, Caroline would do whatever her father wanted her to—without argument. It's how they finally got her to stop throwing tantrums at bedtime. Butchie just had to ask her nicely. She trusted her father absolutely, instinctively knowing as children do, their parents will protect them from anything.

A year before Butchie and Monica were married, Eddie and Bernadette had beaten them down the aisle. Unlike their best friends, they had made no effort to pretend to be patient. Eddie had also availed himself of the G.I. Bill and got his own pension loan to buy a similar house on 84th Street. Eddie and Bernadette began filling the house immediately. They had three daughters in as many years, before Eddie got his own vasectomy—realizing he couldn't afford more children on an honest cop's salary.

Mickey and Bunny lived a block away from both families. Bunny was still working in nursing, but she had cut her schedule down to three days a week so she could spend more time with the kids she considered her grandchildren. She was a constant doting presence at both houses. The children came to call her "Gramma Bunny" and adored her. When Mickey retired from the NYPD, he split his time between playing grandpa and training fighters at Brewster's. So the Doheny's had become a great big extended family.

When he would get leave from the Marine Corps, Nelson, now a Gunnery Sergeant, would bring his wife, Irma, and his three boys to stay with Mickey and Bunny. Nelson was assigned to the Marine Barracks in Coronado, California. He was training Recon Marines in special weapons and tactics. His sons, Miguel, Jose and Eduardo were learning to surf and assimilating as native Californians. Even so, they relished their trips east every year to spend time with their family. Usually, the Cruzes were able to spend Christmas with the rest of the clan in Glendale. That was the plan for Christmas 1979.

Sallie Gorgeous, furious at the interruption of his narcotics network, was in conspiracy with the remaining members of the farm. They were making plans of their own, but Sallie had no intention of waiting for Christmas.

CHAPTER FIFTY-ONE

October 21, 1979
Glendale

Before Michael and Caroline had been born, Monica had been a third-grade teacher at Saint Brigid's. When the Bucciogrosso children were both in school full-time at Sacred Heart, Monica was hired there to teach. It was a perfect arrangement.

Caroline had befriended a girl in her second-grade class. Gabrielle Ianucci was the daughter of Isadore Ianucci, the director of the eponymously named funeral home on Onderdonk Avenue. Unbeknownst to Monica, Isadore was also a low-level associate of the Bonannos. Along with taking care of their funereal needs, he also fenced stolen property for them. Half of the funeral home's basement was for embalming. The other half was for storing *swag*. Their home in Glendale was an Italianate monstrosity. Originally a Dutch Colonial, Isadore had slapped on as many columns, wrought iron gates, and marble accoutrements as he possibly could. This included two massive stone lions on pedestals bracketing the stoop. The house looked ridiculous—what with the incongruent architectural influences and feigned opulence. Everyone in the neighborhood came to call it "the Mafia house."

When Monica told Butchie about Caroline's new friend, Butchie cautioned her about it.

"Her father Isadore is a wannabe with the Bonannos," Butchie said.

"I thought he was an undertaker."

"Yeah, he does some of that, but his real job is as a fence for the thieving mobsters. He buys all their stolen goods. He sells them to anyone who wants them. He's sold suits to every mobster in New York from the back of his funeral parlor. He sells them as burial suits to the families of his funeral clients. Isadore would sell gasoline and matches to a pyromaniac. These are people it would be prudent to stay away from."

"I wish you told me this sooner," Monica said. "Caroline has a play-date with his daughter next Friday."

Butchie rubbed his forehead as if to massage away the tension headache building there. Deciding his investigation's need for secrecy was trumped by his responsibility to keep his family safe, he decided to divulge some classified information to his wife.

"You can't tell this to anyone, Monica, but the Bonannos are in a civil war right now. Under no circumstances are you and Caroline allowed anywhere near that fucking house on 80th Street. I don't know if Isadore is on anybody's 'kill list' yet, but I don't want my family anywhere near him when someone with bad intentions pays a visit."

"Fortunately, Gabrielle is supposed to come over here."

"Well, I guess that's okay, but maybe we can find someone else for Caroline to have play-dates with."

***

Thursday, after the big takedown at the bakery, Roman Sciula was out on bail. His cover still in place, he reached out to Eddie and Butchie. He wanted to be arrested again. He said it was an emergency.

When they got him into the Cemetery of the Evergreens, he told the detectives Sallie Gorgeous had put a contract out on Butchie.

"He doesn't just want to hurt you. He wants to take out your whole family for the Garibaldi's thing."

"Did he give *ye* the contract?" Eddie asked.

"No. That's how I know he wants to hurt your family. He said I was too valuable. After he gets done slaughtering everyone in the house, he wants it burnt down. He said the heat for this is going to be so severe, the cops won't stop till they nail the killers. I heard him give the contract to Mousey

Basaluco and Angelo Mercante. He called Mousey yelling and screaming over the phone at the café. I know you remember them, Butchie."

"Sure, they're what's left of the Farm Team, and they murdered my father-in-law." Butchie said.

"They're still mad at you for giving us that beating on Suydam and Knickerbocker when we were fourteen. They jumped at the contract. What they don't know is, after they do it, Sallie wants me to kill them and leave the bodies in public—where the police can find them. He wanted me to whack them a month ago. Now, he figures he can use them to kill two birds with one stone."

"When is this supposed to happen?" Eddie asked.

"I don't know, but soon," Roman said.

When Butchie got home that night, he told Monica about the reported contract. Being from Bushwick, and a witness and victim of the ruthless violence the Mafia was capable of, she was neither perturbed nor surprised. She just wanted to know how they were going to deal with it. Butchie suggested she and the kids get out of town for a while. Monica vetoed that plan out of hand.

"Where are we supposed to go, Butchie? There's no one but us. My mother still lives on the same block as Roman. She's right in the heart of it. We certainly can't hide there."

"You could camp out at Eddie and Bernadette's for a while," Butchie suggested.

"They live right around the block. If they're watching us, they're watching them, too. So far, nobody has threatened the Currans. If we hide out there, we're just bringing the trouble to their doorstep. This is our problem. Besides, you know running from these people is pointless. They're relentless—and patient. The vendetta is in their blood, and you triggered Sally Gorgeous' vendetta impulse. We're going to have to deal with this—here and now."

Not having anywhere else to go made the decision to confront their fear necessary, but Monica wasn't interested in avoiding the danger. She knew this was just postponing the inevitable. She only wanted to know how they were going to defeat it. Realizing she would never run, Butchie swallowed his own fear and conceived of a plan.

"I'll get a couple of point-to-point radios from Cormac. I'll have one, the other you'll keep with you. We'll have our own dedicated channel. You will be call sign *Raven One*. I will be *Raven Actual*."

"Why Raven?" Monica asked.

"Because we both have dark hair, and it's all I could think of in a pinch."

"Okay, Raven Actual," Monica said, smiling.

"If they're going to do this the way Roman says, they'll be waiting for you and the kids to get home from school. If you see anything out of the ordinary, hit me on the radio. I can be here from Bushwick in two minutes."

***

Butchie and Eddie went to see Cormac Acosta at the DEA. He gave them three point to point radios with chargers and locked them on the same dedicated frequency. He would keep the fourth radio for himself, in the event he and his team were near enough to help when the distress signal went up

"Did *ye* manage to listen to the take yesterday from the wire at the Trombone?" Eddie asked.

"No, why?"

"Roman says he heard Sallie put a contract out on me and my family over the phone yesterday," Butchie said.

"About what time?" Cormac asked, already retrieving the tape and cuing it up on the player on his desk.

"Approximately eleven hundred hours," Eddie clarified.

Cormac advanced the tape. They heard Sallie thundering over the phone.

"I want that *sciati* Bucciogrosso dead! I want his whole fucking family dead! You and your imbecile partner need to do this yesterday!" Sallie shouted over the phone at Mousey.

"We're on it, boss," Mousey said.

"And make it fucking hurt, Mousey. I want that motherfucker broken when he dies."

"We'll burn the family and shoot Butchie and Eddie when they show up," Mousey said.

"Good," Sallie said, calming down. "Then take care of the Irishman's family. There's a button for you two if you get it done."

After the call ended, Cormac shut off the tape. He scratched his chin and looked troubled.

"We should have known about this yesterday," Cormac said. "The FBI is listening to the take so quickly their getting it almost in real time."

Cormac went to the phone on his desk. He shushed Butchie and Eddie and pressed one of the speed dial buttons. He put the phone on speaker and the metallic sound of the ringtone filled the office.

"FBI, Special Agent Agnew, how may I help you?"

"Warren, it's Cormac. Anything come up on the wire at the café yesterday from about eleven o'clock?"

Warren could be heard hesitating. He cleared his throat.

"No, why?" he asked, sounding unconvincing.

"We're getting some informant chatter about a big shipment coming in from Sicily," Cormac lied.

"We got nothing on it," Warren said, sounding like he wanted to end the conversation.

"You and I are going to have to sit down and talk soon," Cormac said.

"Yes, definitely. Give me a call. I'll set up a meeting," Warren said, hanging up.

Cormac looked up at Butchie and Eddie, fury in his eyes. His jaw so tight, you thought you might hear his teeth grinding.

"Those motherfuckers!" he spat. "The FBI and the justice Department know about the hit. They're letting Sallie whack you, greasing the skids to get it done. Now you know who your enemies are. I'll do all I can for you, but you have to be careful. Make sure those radios are charged and you have them—always."

***

The next day was Friday. Monica was outside school at dismissal. She saw Rosemarie Ianucci picking up Gabrielle. This was supposed to be the day of the kids' playdate. Rosemarie looked like she was in a hurry to leave with her daughter. Monica approached her.

"I thought the girls were coming to my house to play," Monica said.

"We can't," Rosemarie said, obviously nervous about something. "I forgot. Gabrielle has a dentist's appointment."

This smelled like bullshit to Monica. There was definitely something Rosemarie knew, but didn't want to share with her. Monica felt the bottom give way in the pit of her stomach. When Rosemarie looked at her with those pathetic eyes, as if she would never see her again, Monica's instinct for danger was on full alert.

"Please be careful," Rosemarie said.

"Careful of what? Is there something you're not telling me, Rosemarie?"

"No," Rosemarie said, looking away. "Just be careful is all."

As Monica and the children walked home from Sacred Heart, her head was on a swivel. When she got to the front of the house, she saw what she was looking for. Mousey Basaluco and Angelo Mercante were seated in a maroon Eldorado parked across the street and down the block. She hurried the kids in the door and locked it, before pulling out the DEA radio and peeking out the window.

"Raven One to Raven Actual, come in," Monica broadcast over the point-to-point.

Butchie and Eddie were doing surveillance outside Sally's clubhouse when they heard Monica's voice come from the DEA radio. Butchie recognized the panic in her voice immediately. It triggered his own. The blood in his veins felt like it had turned to ice, and he had to swallow hard to answer her.

"Raven Actual—go Raven One," Butchie croaked hoarsely.

"Butchie, Mousey Basaluco and Angelo Mercante are in a car across the street. They're looking at the house with binoculars."

"Can you get out the back?" Butchie asked.

Eddie had already begun racing up Myrtle Avenue when he heard the radio first squawk. The two cops were a third of the way there by the time Butchie could respond. So, despite his crushing fear, he started to believe he and Eddie would get there in time. Monica dashed that, turning his fear to desperation.

"No, it's too late! They're already walking toward the house. They've got gas cans in their hands. If we went out the back now, we'd be trapped back there. What should we do?" Monica cried, in a panic.

"Sit tight," Butchie told her, sounding much calmer than he was. "We're two minutes out."

The trip took less than a minute, even though it felt like hours. Butchie was forced to feel something he had never experienced. He was largely unacquainted with the sensation of fear. Despite spending his entire life with the ever-present danger of being hurt or even killed, he had never been truly afraid. They were just things that might or might not happen. His survival instinct made him cognizant of danger, but only with respect to avoiding being injured or killed. He made every effort, but he didn't really feel one way or another about them.

This ambivalence leant a clarity which had always allowed Butchie to take decisive action to protect himself. Now he was confronted with the imminent peril of those he loved. His sudden understanding of fear was reacting badly on his body. He started sweating—everywhere. His heart felt like it was trying to thunder right out of his chest. The dry mouth, shaking hands and throbbing at his temples were an artifact of the adrenaline coursing through his veins. Butchie understood the possibility of losing his family caused him to feel genuine fear for the first time. He never valued his own life enough to care about its demise. But he was afraid now.

When Butchie and Eddie arrived at the house, Butchie could see the front door was splintered at the lock. He gave Eddie the key and sent him around to the back door. This would give him access to the kitchen through the mudroom. He waited a half minute so Eddie could get in position.

Butchie pulled his Colt Detective Special and hid it behind his back, as he silently entered through the shattered front door. He could hear his son Michael and daughter Caroline whimpering. He crept quietly through the foyer until he could see into the living room and the kitchen beyond. The house already reeked of gasoline, the fumes' caustic vapors forcing a wave of nausea over him. He choked down the urge to vomit.

He saw Monica, his mother, and the kids seated on the couch. Angelo Mercante was just emptying the last of his gas can at their feet, soaking the carpet. Mousey Basaluco held them in place at gunpoint. Monica was glaring at Mousey. He didn't care for her defiance. He was hoping to see fear in those eyes. Instead he was treated to the infinite hatred with which Monica had for him and Mercante.

"Stop looking at me, you fucking cunt!" Mousey demanded, slapping her across the face with his gun—blood beginning to trickle from Monica's split lip.

The abrupt violence shook Butchie's mother from her terror. Carolina's protective instinct took over. She tried to insinuate herself between Mousey and her family.

"You know if you hurt this family, my son is going to kill you, Mousey. If you leave now, maybe he'll let you live."

"You don't know shit, Carolina. You're just Sallie Gorgeous' whore. He made a point of saying he wanted *you* to burn too."

Just then, Butchie saw Eddie briefly pop his head up outside the kitchen door. He advanced into the living room. The fear that had been paralyzing him had turned to controlled fury. Coupled with the adrenaline already present, Butchie had gone into the zone. For Mousey and Angelo, this was a very bad place for him to be.

"Is everything okay, Monica?" Butchie asked, his voice almost mechanical.

Mousey heard this and snatched little Caroline off the sofa by her hair. He pulled her in front of him and Angelo and put his nine-millimeter pistol to her head.

"Don't take another step, Butchie!" Mousey ordered.

"Easy, Mousey," Butchie said, trying to calm the hoodlum and buy Eddie some more time.

"Not one more step, or I'll blow your daughter's fucking brains out," he threatened.

"Let's just kill them all and get it over with," Angelo Mercante shrieked, pointing his big, nickel-plated .357 alternately at Monica, Carolina, and Michael.

Butchie realized Mousey was in charge here. So he ignored the unhinged Mercante and calmly addressed Basaluco.

"You don't want to do that, Mousey. Sallie Gorgeous will never let you live if you do. He's already got somebody lined up to whack you."

At this point, Eddie had crept through the kitchen and was pointing his revolver at the back of Angelo Mercante's head. He gestured with his left hand, pointing two fingers at his own forehead, and then at Mercante, letting Butchie know he had Angelo covered, and was ready to give Mercante a *double-tap* to the head. Butchie casually held his left fist up to his shoulder. Both cops, former Marine infantrymen, understood this meant to hold on Butchie's order.

The gangsters were not infantrymen and had no idea what the meaning of this gesture was. Mousey was mistakenly savoring his perceived power over Butchie, and instead wanted to argue.

"Shut the fuck up, Bucciogrosso! You don't know shit. Sallie is going to make *button men* out of us for killing you and your family."

Caroline heard this and understood perfectly. She was definitely her father's daughter—every bit as angry and defiant. She glared up at Basaluco.

"You're a doodie head, rat face!" Caroline yelled, and tried to stomp on Mousey's foot.

Butchie spoke quietly to his daughter.

"It's alright, baby. You don't have to do that. Daddy's got this," Butchie began. "Do you remember when you were little? Remember what you used to do at bedtime?"

"Yes, Daddy," Caroline said.

"Well, do that now."

When Caroline abruptly threw herself on the ground, she removed whatever cover Basaluco had. Butchie shot him two times in the chest and stomach—a good tight grouping at center mass. In the instant Butchie had brought his gun up, Eddie also fired twice, carving what looked like a canoe out of Mercante's head.

Caroline scrambled over to the sofa, jumping into the arms of her grandmother. Butchie walked over to where Mousey Basaluco sat propped against the wall. He was bleeding out slowly on the floor, but he begged for his life anyway.

"Please don't kill me, Butchie! I can be a witness for you. I can testify against Sallie Gorgeous!"

Butchie looked over at Monica and his mother. He gestured with his chin toward the door. The women understood what had to happen next. They grabbed the kids, running with them out into the street. When they had gone, Butchie squatted down to meet Mousey's eyes. What Basaluco saw staring back at him scared him half to death.

"I don't need any more fucking witnesses," Butchie said, as he shot Basaluco right through the face, splattering his brains against the back wall, taking Mousey the rest of the way. Butchie surveyed the carnage on his gasoline-soaked living room rug. He was satisfied another score had been settled.

"That was for you, Bruno," Butchie said quietly. "We got em' all now."

CHAPTER FIFTY-TWO

October 22, 1979
Ridgewood

After the conflagration at the Bucciogrosso home, any pretensions of an element of surprise were gone. Warren Agnew could no longer counsel patience. But he was still mandated by the Attorney General to keep Senator McKibben's name out of it. He was confident they could keep Sallie quiet with a nice plea agreement. Only Bucciogrosso and Curran would be problematic. They would have to be dealt with. He was considering what time of frame-up would be needed to shut these cops up. Right now, the taskforce needed to move on Sallie Gorgeous.

If they waited even a day longer to take down the case, Sallie would methodically destroy the evidence in his basement, thus removing the ability to tie him to the fantasy camp. So emergency search warrants were drawn up in Federal Court for the home of Sallie Gorgeous on Summerfield Street, and the home of Warden Phillip Kaine, in Windsor Terrace in upstate New York.

At 05:00 hours, Roman Sciula called the home phone of Sallie Gorgeous from the payphone on the corner of Summerfield Street and Seneca Avenue. When Sallie picked up on the third ring, Roman gave

Butchie a nod. More than fifty agents and detectives hit the house with guns drawn. They needn't have. Sallie Gorgeous was so convinced of his own invincibility, he had no bodyguards. His .45 semi-automatic was tucked away in his basement walk-in safe, along with five briefcases stuffed with two million dollars of cash in each.

When Sallie Gorgeous jumped out of bed naked to protest the invasion of his home, Butchie quieted him with a punch in the face. He was handcuffed—still naked—and dragged down to the basement at Butchie's insistence. Butchie wanted him to see the evidence recovered there. He needed Sallie to appreciate how royally fucked he was.

When Sallie refused to provide the combination of his safe, a representative was brought in from the Wilson Safe Company, who was also a contract employee of the FBI. Sallie watched with dismay as this man opened his vault with nothing more than his right hand and a stethoscope. Inside were the five briefcases of money, Sallie's beloved .45, and books and ledgers detailing payments and deposits for the heroin trade and the fantasy camp. There was another ledger with the information and identification of the European buyers for the rape porn and snuff films.

The most enjoyable aspect of the morning for Butchie was when he looked Sallie in the eyes, smiled, and rolled up the rug on the floor, revealing the fresh concrete patch under which Sonny Black was buried.

"That was here when I bought the house," Sallie offered.

"No," Butchie told him. "You had Roman Sciula dig the hole a few weeks ago to bury Sonny Black after you shot him in the head."

"You'll never prove it," Sallie challenged.

"I already have. You're under indictment for the murder. Roman Sciula already testified to it in the federal grand jury."

"Good luck with that," Sallie said. "You think you're going to take me down with that retard as your star witness? Even if he could hurt me, it won't matter. He'll never make it into court to testify. You just signed his death warrant for him."

"Who is going to execute it? Not *you*. Who will pay for it? Right now, every one of your so called loyal zips are being arrested. They're gonna eat each other like piranha trying to flip on you. Your entire distribution network is being rolled up all across the country. We've seized all of your cash and frozen all of your bank accounts—including those accounts in the Cayman Islands you thought nobody knew about. You are without friends, without money, and when I go through those videotapes on your shelves and match each one with the victims you so mercilessly brutalized, you will be without hope."

"I'll do fine in prison," Sallie boasted. "I have every facility in the state in my pocket."

"You still don't get it, you silly old fuck. Right now, every jail guard and every warden you ever bought is being arrested by the State Police. Phillip Kaine will be offered the opportunity to flip on you. He's just a pervert and a necrophile. You did the murders on those snuff films, so you get to pay for them. Besides, you're going into the federal system. You don't own anybody there. For however many years it takes to exhaust your appeals, you will be a daily rape victim. When word about you gets out—and rest assured, I will see it gets out—they will strap your giant canyon of a wrecked asshole into *Old Sparky* and send two thousand volts of electricity through your pathetic, wasted body. No blindfold or hood for you either, you're going to have to look right in my eyes the moment you finally escape the misery of this world, and you will know, I am the one who did this to you."

It finally dawned on Sallie Gorgeous just how thoroughly Butchie had beaten him. As he sat there naked on the floor, watching the Emergency Service cops with jackhammers slowly reveal the decaying corpse of Sonny Black, emerging from his shallow grave, the look on Sallie's face was one of abject terror. The sensation for Butchie was pure ecstasy.

CHAPTER FIFTY-THREE

October 25, 1979
Manhattan

Butchie was home when he got the call from Inspector Sheridan, who was alternately furious and confused. Butchie and Eddie had just been suspended from the taskforce and subpoena'd to appear at the US Attorney's Office the next day.

"What the fuck is going on, Butchie?"

"The feds are probably going to try and frame us for something to keep us quiet about Senator McKibben," Butchie said, matter-of-factly.

"What do you have on McKibben?"

"Just some hearsay testimony on his involvement with the Bonannos. The feds have all the phone records and financials and they've already buried them. McKibben has already been scrubbed."

"What are they worried about then?"

"They're not. This is just what they do. Everyone who isn't Justice Department is a loose end, so, they cut them off."

"What are we going to do?" Sheridan asked.

"You are going to stay out of it."

"Hell, I will!"

"Yes, you will," Butchie assured him. "Eddie and I already have something in place. We kept you in the dark for your own protection. We're going to need you to put us in the eight three squad when this is all over."

"I'm supposed to be protecting you. Are you sure you got this?"

"We got it covered. Check the front cover of the Daily News tomorrow," Butchie said.

After hanging up with Sheridan, Butchie called a number on a business card that read, "Hidden Agenda." A deep voice answered after two rings.

"Yes?"

"Send the first one," Butchie said.

"Done."

***

The following morning, the front cover of the New York Daily News featured a story by famed columnist and muck-raker, Paul Brafman. Anonymous law enforcement sources were reporting that the Justice Department and certain elected federal politicians were in collusion with an as yet unnamed Mafia Family for the purposes of distributing narcotics. Coming hard on the heels of the big take-down of the Bonannos, it was inferred it might be them.

When Butchie and Eddie got to the sixteenth floor of the US Attorney's Office of the Eastern District, they were led by a marshal into a large corner conference room. Arrayed around the top end of the table in front of the impressive seal on the wall was an embarrassed looking Warren Agnew. Next to him, they recognized the US Attorney, Myron Simmerman. The seat of honor was occupied by a third man they never saw before. They understood from his pinched, imperious face and his forbidding attitude he was probably from the Justice Department in Washington. The fact that he was underdressed—still wearing a light summer suit in the cooler New York climate of late October, signaled that he was out of place—or, at least outside of his comfort zone. Eddie thought he was going to become increasingly uncomfortable in the very near future.

The detectives were left to stand at their end of the table, not invited to sit. The US Attorney began introducing himself when he was silenced by the sound of Butchie and Eddie scraping the two nearest chairs away from the table and plopping loudly into them. When they both looked up at him and grinned, Myron Simmerman continued.

"As I was saying before being so rudely interrupted, I am Myron Simmerman, the US Attorney for the…"

"We know who *ye* are," Eddie said. "*Yer* not as fat as in *yer* pictures—the camera lens and ten pounds and all of that."

"And we know who that treacherous asshole is too," Butchie said, thrusting his chin at Warren Agnew, who looked away.

"But we don't know who the pinched-faced man is, shivering in his seersucker suit. It's fall in New York, man. Put on a *fookin* coat. I can hardly hear *meself tink* over *yer* chattering teeth."

"This is Deputy Attorney General Bosley Quait, from the Justice Department," Simmerman sneered, as if his name and title were objects of fear.

Butchie and Eddie laughed, causing Quait further consternation, glaring at them from across the table.

"If that name isn't typecasting for an elitist, soulless, bureaucrat, nothing ever was," Butchie said.

"You'll be laughing out of the other sides of your faces when this day is done," Quait seethed. "All of the power and prestige of the United States government is about to fall on your heads."

"Though the heavens may fall," Eddie replied, quoting the motto on the mantle of the federal courthouse. "Let justice be done."

Quait was taken aback. These ruffian detectives apparently had no appreciation for the trouble they were in. Their bravado seemed genuine. They evinced no fear. They didn't appear stupid, which gave Quait pause.

"You'll be indicted by this afternoon for leaking classified information, violating a host of federal laws, including the top count of obstruction of justice," Quait said. "Before you say anything else to incriminate yourselves, you should hire an attorney."

"We've already got one retained," Butchie informed him. "And we're going to talk for a while. You need to listen."

"The piece in the paper today was not planted by us, but it was planted *for* us," Eddie said. "Unless a document is drafted in this room in the next few minutes granting us immunity from prosecution for *anyting*, there'll be another one tomorrow, but this time with documentary evidence and full citation."

"You're bluffing!" Simmerman said. "What documentary evidence?"

"Financials linking payments from Sallie Gorgeous Ruttigliano to Senator Lance McKibben," Butchie said.

Simmerman looked over at Warren Agnew, as if to ask, *Can they possibly have them?* Warren shook his head, but he seemed unsure.

"Then there is this," Butchie said bringing a micro recorder out of his jacket pocket, while the one in his left pocket kept recording.

He placed it on the table.

"What the hell is that?" Quait said, looking as if someone had put a dead rat in front of him.

"Insurance," Butchie said, pressing play.

The federal triumvirate were treated to the recording of Senator McKibben giving Sallie Gorgeous the greenlight to do what he wanted with Butchie and Eddie. Then they heard the recording of Sallie giving the hit order to Mousey Basaluco. Finally, they heard Warren denying having heard these calls to Cormac Acosta.

"You've overplayed your hand, Detectives," Quait said. "You're not leaving the building with that."

"Did *ye tink* we had only one?" Eddie laughed. "*Yer* a bigger imbecile than *ye* look. We have dozens."

"And every conversation with the FBI as well," Butchie clarified.

"It doesn't matter," Quait waved them off. "We'll find them soon enough with search warrants, and you'll be releasing nothing from federal custody, which you are in, you no doubt realize."

"No, we are not," Butchie assured him.

"Do *ye* know what a dead-man switch is?" Eddie asked. "Of course not, because *ye* were hiding behind *yer* daddy's influence while *fellas* like us were fighting two wars for this country in Asia. It's a military term usually referring to ordinance or explosives, but it works well as a metaphor in this instance as well. Tell the coward, Butchie."

"In plain terms, if we don't give an all clear phone call to a particular person in the next forty-five minutes, then he calls someone else who automatically releases the second story with all of the evidence to Paul Brafman. By tomorrow, this will make The Watergate Conspiracy look like a church choir practice. It's called a dead-man switch because you can't stop it even if you kill us, which you've already shown a willingness to do. Isn't that right, Warren?"

Agnew looked like he was going to throw up. The other two just looked confused. Eddie brought them back on point.

"*Ye* need to get cracking with those immunity documents. The clock is ticking, and we're not leaving without *dem*."

"I need time to clear it with Washington," Quait stammered.

"That's time *ye* don't have. Keep in mind, this is on automatic. One man's wristwatch is another man's detonator."

***

After Butchie called Mickey Doheny, aborting the dead-man switch, he and Eddie met him at the Glendale Diner. Butchie handed over the official looking documents with the seal of the Justice Department of the United States embossed on the letterhead and the Attorney General's signature at the bottom.

"These need to go to your attorney friend for safekeeping," Butchie said.

"So, we've beaten the Justice Department?" Mickey asked.

"For now," Eddie said. "With Jimmy Carter fucking *tings* up as he has, it won't be long before we have a new president and a different tribe of bureaucrats to deal with."

"Won't matter anyway. After this, I'm through with federal law enforcement," Butchie said. "I think I'm ready for the Detective Squad."

CHAPTER FIFTY-FOUR

Late October 1979
Brooklyn

As the month wound down, the follow-up arrests and indictments kept building. When all was said and done, over four hundred people were under indictment for either the Pizza Connection narcotics conspiracy or The Fantasy Camp Sex Trade, as it was now officially called. Warren Agnew and the US Attorney made the ultimate decision over who would get consideration as cooperators, and who would face the full-fraught vengeance of the law. With respect to that, Butchie and Eddie only cared that Sallie Gorgeous wasn't in line for any consideration, and that the feds were committed to leaving none of the zips with the liberty to maintain the drug trade in Bushwick.

Their wishes were accommodated. With the exception of the old guard wise guys not involved in the heroin trade, no Bonannos were left in Bushwick. All of the zips, and all of the pizzeria and bakery owners who participated in the trafficking were looking down the barrel of ten years in prison, even after their cooperation deals.

Nobody was offering Sallie Gorgeous anything. The investigation following the seizure of the snuff films found twenty-four verifiable murders and a dozen more which had yet to be corroborated. The evidence was so formidable, Sallie Gorgeous tried to plead guilty to the top counts on the indictment. He was prevented from doing so when it was revealed the government was seeking his execution.

While he was waiting for his trial to start, Sallie Gorgeous was sent to general population in the Metropolitan Detention Center in Brooklyn. The brutalization and forcible rapes began immediately. Butchie had put the word out about Sallie to the federal correction officers. They dutifully reported it to the inmates, some of whom had been victims of the fantasy camp themselves, back when they were young and vulnerable. Now they were fully grown, angry and vengeful.

In short order, Salvatore Sallie Gorgeous Ruttigliano became known as *Sweet Sallie.* Having no friends, no money, and no power or influence, the inmates started trading him for cigarettes. As a victim, Sallie came to appreciate the horror of the crime of rape. He absolutely hated it from this perspective. And he got to hate it every day.

Butchie was infuriated when Sallie offered to trade his cooperation as a witness and informant for the ensuing Sicilian Mafia case, born out of the Pizza Connection. The State Department put pressure on Justice to allow this to occur. All Sallie wanted in return was a life sentence in protective custody. Butchie and Eddie nearly lost their minds when they heard this was happening. Finally, Eddie saw a possible advantage to this scenario.

"This might not be such a bad *ting*," Eddie observed.

Butchie looked at him as if he went daft.

"Remember, *ye* promised him *ye* would make him do things he never thought possible," Eddie reminded Butchie.

"Yeah, so?" Butchie said, still furious.

"Do *ye tink* he ever envisioned being a rat? Now he is one. I *tink* we should go see him in the MDC and tell him and everyone else about it. I'll wager he won't make it through the weekend."

***

The next day, Butchie and Eddie visited the MDC. They had Sallie Gorgeous brought to an interview room, already informing the correction officers Sallie had become a cooperating witness. In less than an hour, everyone in the MDC would know as well.

When Sallie was led into the room, he looked emaciated and haggard, and much older than his seventy years. His face was bruised and swollen. He was hunched over and shuffled as if in pain. Butchie was pleased to see the blood stain seeping through the wad of gauze wedged in his rectum, soaking through the seat of his orange jumpsuit. When Sallie realized who was there to see him, he slumped even lower and affected a look of absolute defeat.

"What more do you want from me, Butchie?" he asked pathetically.

"Don't you remember what I told you the day I threw Amoroso through your window? I'll settle for nothing less than your absolute destruction. You're not there yet."

"What else can you do to me?" Sallie asked.

"We told everyone in here you turned rat. If you think it was bad before, what do you think it will be like now that you're a snitch?"

Sallie fell to his knees and began to weep. He prostrated himself at Butchie's feet, begging him not to do this. Butchie kicked him in the face to get his attention.

"I told you that day I would make you become what you never thought possible. You are now a weak old man, despised by everyone. You are the girlfriend of anyone in here who has five cigarettes to trade, and you're powerless to do anything about it. You hate what you have become so much, you've agreed to violate your sacred oath of *omerta* and snitch for the government—just to make the torment stop. My only question is; how do you look in the mirror to shave in the morning without cutting your own throat?"

They left Sallie there, defeated and crying on the floor. Butchie was revolted to have even been in the same room with the man, but he knew Sallie was at his end. He found this satisfying.

That night, after lights out, Sallie Gorgeous would have liked to have slit his own throat, but he didn't have a razor. What he had were bed sheets. He fashioned a noose from these, and used it to take his own life, as Butchie had told him he would. When Cormac Acosta Called Butchie at home the next day to tell him the news, he was not at all surprised.

CHAPTER FIFTY-FIVE

Christmas, 1979
Glendale

The Doheny house was stuffed full of Mickey and Bunny's extended family. The boys they thought of as their own, their wives and their children, and Nonna Bucciogrosso and Nonna Badlamenti all sat down for a Christmas feast. Even Paddy Durr was there. After desert, the boys joined Mickey out on the back porch for scotch, cigars and conversation.

Nelson wanted to hear all about the demise of Sallie Gorgeous. He was fascinated with the story, told alternately by Mickey and Eddie. Paddy, being new to this group, quietly soaked up what he thought was a treasure trove of information. These four men were the epitome of moral authority to him. Even though each of them had been war heroes, they were not content to merely sit on their laurels. They spoke of a need to do more, disappointed even with what they had so far accomplished. Paddy could see the devotion to do the right thing burned deeply in these men. He yearned to be part of that, so he listened carefully to ascertain the secret of their moral certainty. Mostly, they poked fun at themselves for never quite achieving that which they had intended; doing good for sure, but never completely eradicating the darkness and chaos as they had hoped. Except for Butchie; he was in no mood for joking, sitting there sullenly brooding. Finally, Nelson had to ask him what was eating at him.

"What gives, Butchie? You nearly did the impossible. You took down the Bonannos. You've hated those people forever. What are you so dour about?"

"It feels like a pyrrhic victory, Nelson."

"How so?" Mickey wanted to know.

"We did all of this work. We risked our lives—hell, we risked our families' lives, and for what?" Butchie asked.

"Well, we did take out Sallie Gorgeous. We chased the Bonannos out of Bushwick, and we ended *dat* abomination in the jails and youth pens. Surely *dat's* gotta count for *something,"* Eddie said.

"My point exactly," Butchie nodded. "We ended the rape porn and snuff films, but the demand for it isn't gone. Someone else is already filling that sick market. And yeah, the Bonannos are out of the drug business, but the heroin is still flowing. The Puerto Rican gangs have moved in without missing a beat. Except, they're worse—if that's even possible. They're shooting it out in the streets with each other, trying to take over each block. Innocents are dying by the dozen. It's just like shoveling shit against the tide; it keeps coming back and washing over us. What the hell was it all for?"

Nelson noticed Paddy staring with wonder at Butchie. He wasn't sure what the kid was made of yet, but his brothers, and now Mickey and Bunny had seen something worthy in him. Nelson wanted to know his mind.

"What do you think, *FNG*?"

"What's an FNG?" Paddy asked.

"A *Fucking New Guy*," Mickey laughed. "Carry that name with pride. It means you're one of us. But, you're still the new guy, and you'll be one until the next FNG shows up."

"I like that," Paddy smiled.

"Good for you, kid," Nelson prodded. "Now answer the fucking question."

Paddy thought about his answer for a minute. Until he thought he knew what he wanted to say.

"I'm only seventeen," he reminded them. "Nothing has *ever* gotten better from my perspective. It only gets worse. But you seem to believe it can, so you keep doing the right thing. It can't be for the money; they don't pay you shit. Maybe you do it for the love, but these people you help won't love you back. So there has to be something deeper driving you. Something that won't let you do anything else. People suck. You know this, and they're not gonna stop. Things are gonna be fucked up for as long as they do. If you're lucky, you can keep their bullshit at bay."

"*Dat's* a grim assessment from a kid," Eddie remarked.

"I guess it is," Paddy went on. "But on the bright side, you do get to help people. Sometimes they deserve it. Sometimes they don't. You don't pick and choose. You just do it. Along the way you get to crush some sick people who need fucking up. That should be enough. It would be enough for me."

Eddie became thoughtful. Paddy's words had struck at the heart of what he already understood. There was no other way to look at it but philosophically. He knew when they started this crusade Butchie wouldn't quit until he had gotten Sallie Gorgeous and all the Bonannos, but he also recognized it wouldn't have the effect he had hoped for. He anticipated they would get to this point eventually. Butchie was teetering on the edge of disillusionment, so Eddie chose his words carefully.

"Have *ye* kept the faith, *boyo*, working as hard as *ye* could for others?" Eddie asked him.

"You know we did," Butchie said.

"Aye, but do *ye* know it, Butchie?"

"Yeah, I know it."

"Have *ye* done anything to trouble *yer* conscience?" Eddie asked.

"No. I never hurt anyone who didn't have it coming. We only made bad people suffer."

"And if *ye* had to do it again—knowing what *ye* know now—would *ye* have done *anyting* different?"

"Not one fucking thing," Butchie admitted.

"Well then," Eddie said. "Maybe *dat's* all we get in *dis* life, *boyo*—maybe all we get."

AFTERWARD

On January 1, 1981, the Republican Party reclaimed the executive branch, the senate and the house of representatives after the disastrous and inept one-term presidency of Jimmy Carter. Senator Lance McKibben had his chairmanship of the Justice and the Ways and Means Committees snatched out from under him, along with his protection. Unbeknownst to him, he had already come to the interest of the Official Corruption Unit of the FBI.

Originating on Long Island, the case which would come to be known as The ABSCAM Investigation, had Lance McKibben on film and wiretap negotiating the sale of ostensibly stolen art from foreign agents to the Mafia. The foreign agents were actually employed by the FBI, and the objects of art were forgeries made on the behest of the government. McKibben facilitated the sale to members of his constituency—the Gambino and Luchese Crime families of New York. When Edwin Meese became Attorney General, Lance's days were numbered few.

In an effort to ascertain just how bald faced corrupt McKibben could be, the FBI had a man purporting to be a member of the KGB, working for the Soviet State Department try to buy classified plans for a new military jet prototype being developed by the Grumman Corporation, in Bethpage New York. For a cool million dollars, Lance McKibben used his still substantial influence to demand the plans from the CEO of Grumman, who was one of his biggest donors. The CEO, being a patriot, dutifully informed the FBI, extricating himself as a subject of the investigation. The FBI slipped him dummy plans which he gave to McKibben. McKibben promptly handed them over to who he thought was our nation's enemy for a suitcase full of hundred dollar bills that were as fake as the plans he sold.

For effect, the FBI arrested McKibben the next day, dragging him kicking and screaming out of the full senate chamber. He was subsequently convicted in federal court of Official Corruption and Treason. He was sentenced to three thousand, six hundred months in federal penitentiary—ostensibly to die in a Super-Max in Colorado.

The government's best witness against him—other than the undercover FBI Agents—was Detective Rocky Phillips, NYPD retired. After receiving immunity and testifying against his old boss, Rocky was left without employment opportunities. No one wants to hire a fixer with a snitch jacket. His disreputable lifestyle and degenerate gambling soon had him, as they say, *on the balls of his ass*. He had to go to work as a late-night short-order cook at the Clinton Diner on Rust Street in Maspeth—a miserable and desolate industrial area not far from the Long Island Expressway. He tries to regale the truck drivers with stories of when he was a big-shot detective in The Chief Inspector's Confidential Squad. They seldom are interested and usually tell him to shut up and let them eat.

Young Paddy Durr went on to Columbia University, with Butchie and Eddie keeping tabs on him, providing a strong incentive to keep him on the straight and narrow. He's a brilliant student and an all-conference football player. But Ivy League or no, he has a sneaking suspicion he wants to be a cop.

Roman Sciula and his mother returned to her home village in Castellamare del Golfo. Roman is a shoe maker. The Sicilian Mafia is aware, but they couldn't care less.

ACKNOWLEDGEMENTS

A very gracious thank you to all my beta readers from the Farmingdale Creative Writers Group, the Long Island Literary Guild, Mystery Writers of America, The International Thriller Writers, and the Future Best-Selling Novelists of Long Island (phew! That was a mouthful.) Their attention to detail, advice, and feedback were essential in crafting this novel.

Inestimable credit goes to my lovely wife, Janet. She is my first and primary reader. No one gets to see my work unless Janet has given it her seal of approval. She has been instrumental in suggesting plot threads and character developments that are always on point, and invariably end up in my novels. So, they are as much her's as mine. Ever my muse, I doubt I would be writing without her firm and unwavering support. Yeah, she inspires me like that.

Thanks to my children Ryan and Kelly. They tolerate me monopolizing the kitchen table to write, and endure my voice when I read aloud. Ryan also serves as an ego check, occasionally whispering in my ear, "Remember Caesar, you are mortal," when he suspects my head is getting too big. Kelly is my primary helper at my launches and author events, setting up my table and selling my books. I know she won't cheat me, and she knows I won't skimp with the profit-sharing.

I need to give special thanks to my friend and one of my first professional mentors, Sam Gribben was my training detective when I was a rookie in Midtown. He was the one who convinced me to transfer uptown to follow him back to the 34th Precinct. It was a wild bumpy ride. I was fortunate to have his counsel when I was running around *The Heights* trying to get myself shot. He was a great support to me when it looked like it was all going bad and I was on the verge of being indicted for murder. He and many others back then helped me weather the storm. Despite the ordeal, it was worth it. I wouldn't change a thing. Sam was also instrumental in providing background and a first-person account of what *The job* was like in the 70's. I was gratified when he let me name a character in this novel after him.

Also appearing under his own name, albeit in the guise of a Navy Commander and surgeon, is my dear friend Kevin Spellman. Kevin is a retired Fugitives Apprehension Detective from the NYPD's HIDTA Taskforce. At the time of his retirement, he was regarded as one of the best in the business. He has always been a loyal friend and inspiration. For that reason, you can expect to see a certain Detective *Spike* Spellman making future appearances in my forthcoming Paddy Durr novels.

I was honored to be able to portray my dear friend, Angelo Florio as himself in the novel. A retired NYPD Detective, in 1973 Angelo was shot and almost killed during an undercover drug buy in Brooklyn. He took the time to share his story with me, providing documents, photos and even the Kell tape recording of the event. Needless to say, it was harrowing. That story appears almost exactly as he related in the book. I am so grateful he trusted me to portray it.

A big thank you goes out to my friend and neighbor, Patty Buckheit, who assists me with my cover designs. She brings a professionalism and expertise to my wild ass creativity that wouldn't be there without her.

Most importantly, I need to thank my editor, my mentor, and my dear friend, Judy Turek. Known professionally as J R Turek, she is a celebrated award-winning poet who has written at least a poem a day for 15 years. I trust her editing and advice absolutely. None of my writing will see the light of day until it is well marked up by her purple pen—yes, purple. And she has never steered me wrong.

Lastly, to my readers; thank you for continuing to appreciate my work. These books are for you. I hope you like reading them as much as I enjoyed writing them.

Want more Michael O'Keefe?

Check him out @ WWW.MichaelOkeefeAuthor.com.

Sign up for the newsletter and get free stuff, as well as where to purchase his other books!

Previous books by Michael O'Keefe

Shot to Pieces, a Paddy Durr novel—2016

Not Buried Deep Enough—2017

13 Stories-Fractured, Twisted & Put Away Wet—2018

Available on Amazon.com

CPSIA information can be obtained
at www.ICGtesting.com
Printed in the USA
LVHW040728231219
641444LV00002B/185